A Gig Too Far

C. Oliver

Bright Pen

A Bright Pen Book

British Library Cataloguing Publication Data.
A catalogue record for this book is available from the British Library

ISBN 978-0-7552-1519-5

Authors OnLine Ltd
19 The Cinques
Gamlingay, Sandy
Bedfordshire SG19 3NU
England

This book is also available in e-book format, details of which are available at www.authorsonline.co.uk

About the Author

The author was born in Hereford, to parents of European extraction. She travelled abroad with her family from an early age, always on a low budget and with many humorous adventures. She spent some time living in the Middle East, where she encountered colourful characters and bizarre situations. She now lives in Bristol with her husband and daughter and works in an accountancy firm. In her spare time she learns foreign languages and reads holiday brochures.

CHAPTER 1

Tom frowned and glanced at his watch. They were cutting it a bit fine. The New York gig had been arranged as a King Biscuit special, but they would barely have time to do the sound check. They should have been on a direct flight from Paris, but French air traffic control had decided to take the weekend off. The band had been shunted on to a Heathrow connection.

"They ever gonna fly this kite?" Pete complained, as he drummed his fingers on the armrest.

In the adjacent seat, Jim flicked through the in-flight magazine. "Stop bleating. We're lucky we got on here at all."

"So how come you know that girl on the BA desk?"

Jim shifted in his seat. "We came through here a couple of years ago."

"And she still remembers? Whoo!"

Joe had been staring out of the window. He suddenly turned to Tom, and said in an anxious tone, "Do you think we'll get there in time to do a run-through?"

"Maybe, maybe not. Anyway, we've been doing this stuff enough years. One rehearsal ain't gonna matter."

"But we don't know the venue. It bothers me."

Tom twisted around to talk to the others. "Are you guys happy to skip the sound check?"

Pete shrugged. "Does the Pope shit in the woods?"

Tom turned back to reassure Joe. "See, there's nothing to worry about."

"Mr. Banks?"

Tom looked up and smiled at the stewardess who was standing beside him.

"Yeah, that's me. What can I do for you?"

"I'm sorry to inconvenience you, but there seems to have been a mistake by our ground staff. These seats should not have been allocated to your party. I'm afraid I'll have to ask you to vacate."

1

"All right," said Tom. "Where do you want us to sit?"

"It's regrettable, sir, but I'm afraid you'll have to get off the plane. There are no other seats available."

Tom glared at the unfortunate girl. "Listen up, sweetheart. The only way I'm getting off this plane is if a stretcher case gets on!"

Jim leaned across from his window seat and chipped in, "Show us these guys who want our seats and we can make them into stretcher cases. That ain't a problem."

The stewardess persevered. "I can't apologise enough, sirs, but these seats were pre-booked by Diamond Card holders."

This was the red rag to Tom, who had once been persuaded by his ex-wife to take a Diamond Card. He had been paying off her debts on it ever since. Tom fixed the stewardess with a hard stare.

"These Diamond Card holders, how are they at hand to hand combat?"

The stewardess tightened her lips, then she turned and walked briskly back down the aisle.

Joe bent forwards, putting his worried face close to Tom's. "If we get bounced off this flight, we won't make the gig. You should have told her that."

"She wouldn't have cared," Tom replied. "We stand a better chance by causing trouble."

The stewardess did not return, and twenty minutes later they were airborne.

"She must have bounced some poor bastards in economy," Tom muttered, before he nodded off to sleep.

* * *

On the upper deck there was a bar and a few horseshoe seats with tables. Susan was sipping her cure for flying nerves and doing some work. She didn't look up when the rest of her seating area was occupied by a group of men. They started a card game, and whilst she was immersed in her own numbers a mellow voice beside her said, "We've kinda hemmed you in here. Can I get you another drink? My name's Jim."

Susan looked up. The man had film-star good looks, and his blue eyes studied her with disconcerting appraisal. She smiled back at him, and said earnestly, "Hello Jim. My name is Susan. Is Jesus your friend?"

"Excuse me?"

Susan pulled a Jehovah's Witness pamphlet from out of her briefcase. "Jesus is always our friend, even in our darkest moments."

Jim grimaced, and turned his attention back to his hand of cards.

It always works, thought Susan. Having been raised as a Roman Catholic, she had no compunction about using religion as an offensive weapon. Her concentration was broken, so she gazed absent-mindedly at the card players. The men looked to be in their thirties, maybe even a little older. Jeans and sweatshirts gave them a youthful air, but there was no plump flesh in any of their faces, and Jim's blond streaks had a tinge of grey at the roots. Definitely not business men, she decided, who always wore grim dark suits as an international uniform. Susan was pondering their occupations when Jim spoke again.

"Joe, strange as this may seem, you'll probably have better luck if you hold your cards so Pete can't see them."

The small, tousle-haired man on Susan's right gave the swarthy man next to him a hurt glance, and tilted himself sideways.

Jim turned back towards Susan. A bemused frown flickered across his brow.

"I don't remember seeing you in RB lounge."

"RB lounge?"

Joe cut in, "He means upper class lounge, back in Paris."

"No, I mean rich bastard lounge."

"Oh, right. I was in economy," Susan explained, "But I went to the loo just after take-off, and when I got back to my seat, some kid had thrown up in it. There isn't a spare seat on the plane, so the stewardess said I could sit up here. I'm getting off at Heathrow, so she wasn't bothered."

"I'm surprised she didn't make you sit in the bathroom."

"You're kidding. There's always a queue for the toilets in economy. They only let you have three minutes, then the door opens automatically."

The three men chuckled, then turned their attention back to their cards, and Susan bent her head back down to the set of figures that she was working on. She had been working steadily for half an hour, when she suddenly heard another voice at the table.

"Shove round a tad."

Susan glanced up and caught the eye of a slim man who slid on to the seat beside Jim. He nodded politely at her.

"Sorry about the crush."

Susan was instantly mesmerised by the depth of his dark eyes. Her lips parted as she tried to remember how to smile.

The bar attendant picked that moment to come to their table. She surveyed the assortment of glasses, then said to Susan, "Can I get you another dry Martini?"

Jim gave Susan a puzzled look. "I thought the JH brigade were teetotal?"

Susan cursed inwardly. Admit to being a liar? Not in front of a man with the earnest eyes of a poet. She raised her eyebrows. "Oh, was it Martini? I thought it was Perrier."

"Sorry," the stewardess murmured. "I must have put too much ice in it." She turned to the new arrival. "Can I get you anything, sir?"

"Do you have any Jack Daniels?"

Joe leaned across the table, and tried to whisper above the engine noise.

"Tom, it's kinda early in the day. Have a beer, huh?"

"Do I pay you alimony?"

Joe shook his head.

"Then quit being my ex wife."

As the stewardess moved towards the bar, Joe spoke again, in a hesitant tone.

"Uh, me and Pete were wondering if you'd decided on the running list, yet?"

His swarthy companion sniffed. "Yeah, it would be useful to know what songs we're gonna play tonight."

Tom shrugged. "We'll play the same set as last night, just in case we don't get time for a run-through."

"So, you're musicians? Where are you playing tonight?" Susan gave Tom her sweetest smile.

He flushed slightly. "New York."

"What sort of music do you play?"

"Southern rock, with a little bit of jazz thrown in."

Jim sniffed. "The audience usually throws the jazz back at us."

"They've taken to throwing the southern rock, too," Tom added, with a weary sigh. "I guess we're a little out of fashion." His charcoal eyes clouded, and Susan wanted to put her arm around his broad shoulders.

"Fashions come and go," she ventured. "I'm sure you'll be all the rage again, soon."

He raised an eyebrow doubtfully, and gave her a sideways look which made her feel a little foolish, so she said nothing more.

As Tom lowered his head to study his hand of cards, Susan let her gaze travel over him. He had long dark eyelashes which seemed almost to brush against his cheekbones. The skin curved tautly into the hollows of his cheeks, and his lips were curved and full. She watched him as he flicked deftly through his playing cards. His long, fine-boned fingers were supple as a Spanish ladies fan. Susan was imagining his gentle fingers on her skin, when Jim rudely interrupted her daydream.

"Are you one of these religious types who go around making a nuisance of themselves by constantly knocking on folks' doors? I can't see the point of all that. If you're gonna go around pestering people in their homes, you might as well be a debt-collector, and turn a profit."

"Turn a prophet into what?" Joe asked, in a baffled tone.

"They don't come round our way no more," Pete muttered. "Couple of them got mugged for their leather satchels. Good quality leather is at a premium these days."

"I don't mind them coming to the door," Joe said, "But I don't think the Mormons are right with their attitude to women. You should only have one wife."

Jim grunted. "It's even better if you don't have one at all."

"That's a bit rich, coming from you," Joe observed. "You've had a few wives."

"Yeah, mostly other people's," Pete muttered.

The plane suddenly lurched sideways, and the stewardess lost control of a tray of tumblers. Tom darted over to help her, and as he stooped to gather the fallen glasses, another stewardess approached Susan.

"We've managed to clean up your seat, and as we're beginning the approach to Heathrow, maybe you'd like to resume your place."

Susan responded with a tight smile, then gathered up her papers and calculator. Jim peered over her work.

"So, you're a bookkeeper, huh?"

She nodded.

"You can slip between my balance sheets, anytime," he told her, with a wink.

Susan resisted the temptation to smack him with her handbag. As she left the lounge, she glanced over her shoulder. Tom was smiling down at the grateful stewardess. Typical, she thought. The first half-way decent bloke I've met all year, and we'll be on different continents by tonight. Susan sighed, and squeezed her way back to economy.

Jim collected up the cards and slipped them back into their pack. As he totaled up the points, Joe scolded him.

"How could you make such a crude remark to a Jehovah's Witness? You should have more respect."

Jim snorted in derision. "She's no more a Witness than I am! Didn't you see the way she was looking at Tom? Like a hungry dog looks at the last bone in the store. She's probably Italian Catholic, with those big brown eyes. Convent schools always make them horny."

* * *

Just before midnight, Tom flopped on to his bed in the hotel room. They had played worse gigs, that much was true. There was that time in Nevada when the second keyboard player had been too stoned to play with both hands. Tom was trying to console himself with the third large tumbler of scotch. They had definitely cut it too fine. Maybe it would have been all right if the promoter had arranged to have the piano tuned. You would expect people to do that sort of thing without having to be reminded. Tom wished he had been playing back in the sixties, when the audience had made more noise than the band. He clutched the glass close to his chest, and stared at the wall. A sudden panic gripped him. Suppose the piano had been in tune? Maybe he had been hitting the wrong keys! He tried to calm himself down. It was just a bad gig, not the end of the world. He sighed heavily, feeling sorry for himself. Things hadn't always been this way. Things had started to go downhill after his wife ran off with his bodyguard. And his Ferrari. And his yacht.

Tom chuckled bitterly. It would probably have been better if they had been bounced off the plane. Then he remembered the enchanting little brunette on the flight. Sitting opposite her, it was hard not to get lost in the view. He cursed himself for his shyness. What he wouldn't give to have Jim's self-confidence. He put himself into a happier mood, thinking about her. She had a face that could inspire all the angels in heaven to strum on their golden harpstrings.

That damned piano! He couldn't push it out of his mind! Maybe he was getting past it. Maybe he couldn't trust his fingers on the keys any more. He would ask Joe in the morning. Joe always told the truth. Tom wondered if the rest of the band would be speaking to him by morning. The empty tumbler fell to the floor as he dozed off.

* * *

They had taken a suite of rooms for their overnight stay after the gig. When Tom walked into the lounge area the following morning, the others were sitting around drinking coffee. Tom said "Hi" and the others "Hi'd" back with varying degrees of enthusiasm, except for Roger, who remained silent. Roger looks as if he's in a real mean mood, thought Tom.

Roger was not a regular member of the band, but he had played several gigs with them, including the previous night's. Roger was essentially a session musician, but not to be looked down upon. His rhythm guitar was reckoned to be one of the finest.

"How are you today, Roger?" asked Tom, anticipating trouble.

"I'll tell you exactly how I am, Banks. I am never in my life gonna play with you again, and I am going to leave this hotel with a paper bag over my head, so that nobody will recognise me!"

Tom thought about making some remark about how Roger's wife would probably appreciate the improvement, but he thought better of it when he noticed how Roger's fists were clenched.

"Well, it's your loss, if you don't want to play with us again."

"My loss!" spluttered Roger. "How can it be my loss if I don't want to appear with a guy who plays an out-of-tune piano and is too jet-lagged to remember the words of his songs!"

"Oh, I don't think anyone noticed that," Joe murmured.

Roger swung around and snarled, "Is that supposed to make us look good?" As Joe flinched, Roger turned his attention back to Tom.

"I don't care how many Grammys you've won, Banks. You may think that you're a star, but in my book you're a fallen one! I don't know why this lot put up with you. Well, I know why Jim puts up with you. The poor bastard has no choice, what with three ex-wives and seven kids to support."

Jim nodded mournfully in agreement.

"No-one but your friends would play a gig with you, Banks, and from what I hear, they are diminishing in number on a daily basis!" and with this parting shot Roger slammed out.

Tom aimed a kick at the coffee table. "Screw him. Who needs pissy guitar players, anyway. No offence, guys," he hastily added, as Pete and Joe exchanged glances.

"You should have stuck to the running order," Jim said. "Not everyone can follow your intros. These session guys like to have it all laid out in black and white."

"I had to change the set, the piano was up shit creek! What a fucking

7

mess. Maybe I'll go back to playing accordion at Italian weddings. Anyway, Roger will be back. When he's desperate and broke."

"Yeah, just like the rest of us," muttered Pete.

* * *

"Get out of my chair, you little oik."

"Susan! You're back, then. I thought you might be stranded in Paris. I was just checking your E mails, see if I needed to do anything." Simon eased himself out of her swivel chair.

"If you've stuck chewing gum under my desk again, I'll swing for you," Susan threatened, as she settled in front of her computer screen.

"How was Paris?"

"Pissing down. The bloke I was supposed to see wasn't there. They cancelled the little prop plane back to Bristol, so I had three hours of hanging about in that concrete polo mint waiting for a flight to London. What a waste of bloody time."

Simon shook his head in sympathy. "You don't have much luck on your business trips. I don't know why the boss keeps sending you."

Susan gave him a withering glare. "Are you being facetious, or have you got your village idiot head on today? You know he sends me on these trips in the desperate hope that my plane will crash."

Simon gave a nervous giggle. "You're paranoid."

"Just because I'm paranoid, it doesn't mean he's not out to get me. Anyway, has anything happened while I was gone?"

"Not really. HR want to organise a commando-style bonding weekend for all the staff."

"Ugh! Paint balls and all that stuff? Is this instead of a summer picnic? I can hardly wait. What will pest control think of next ."

"You're not supposed to call them that. The boss sent an E mail round."

"Can't call them human remains, can't call them pest control - Is this a TV production company or Gestapo HQ?"

Simon shrugged. "Gestapo HQ probably pay better."

As Susan tapped in her computer password her thoughts drifted back to the crowded plane and the slim musician. He hadn't said more than six words to her, but she felt as if she could read his mind. Chances are she would never see him again. She gazed out at the drizzling sky, and tried to picture him, an ocean away.

Simon cut into her daydream. "Some bloke called Costa phoned for you on Friday. He said he wants his cheque book back?"

Susan detected the curiosity in her assistants voice, and tried to throw him off the scent.

"Red Nose day has a lot to answer for. It seemed a good idea, picking pockets on the bus. But not everyone wants to give to charity."

CHAPTER 2

The telephone started ringing. Tom ignored it, and gulped another mouthful of scotch. He had been back home for a month, and every time he picked up the receiver there was someone on the line demanding money. He let the answering machine cut in, and a few seconds later he heard a hard New York voice.

"Tom, pick up. I know you're there. Don't make me get on a plane for a face to face meeting."

Tom snatched up the phone. It was Judith, his agent. She was even worse than the debt-collectors. She never let up.

"Uh, hi Judith. How are you?"

"Don't waste my time with small talk," she snapped. "Have you made up your mind about the Latvia tour?"

Tom hesitated. He knew that he should take it. Roger had broadcast his low opinion of Tom to all the right people, and Tom's diary was full of blank spaces where the bookings should have been. He was relieved that the rest of the band had been able to slip into session work. They'd all been together for a long time, and he felt responsible for their recent poor fortune. But the only booking that Judith had offered was a six week solo tour of Latvia.

"I don't really fancy Latvia. It's cold up there."

"You people south of the mash and biscuit line are too damn dense to know how to blow on your hands," she retorted.

Tom gritted his teeth. He couldn't stand these brusque Yankees. He had thought about getting one of those bumper stickers that read, "The Civil War? It ain't over yet!" But he was afraid that the newspapers would pick up on it, and he couldn't afford to lose any Northern fans. He knew he had to get something real soon. He owed a lot of money locally, and he felt bad about that.

"Isn't there anything else?" he asked.

"I've been approached by a television production company in England," Judith replied. "They only want one show, but I might be able to stretch it for you."

"In London?"

"No, in Bristol, wherever that is. Shall I let them know that you're interested?"

"Yeah, but check first to see if the rest of the guys are available."

When Judith phoned back later in the day to confirm the booking, Tom was halfway down the bottle of scotch. I guess I'd better tidy myself up a little, he mused, and he emptied the tumbler into the sink. They were paying a pittance, but he felt obliged to show willing. He had a suspicion that Judith had purposefully negotiated the low fee in order to teach him a lesson. Tom sighed. He always had trouble with women.

* * *

In Bristol, a south-westerly wind was blowing drizzle in from the sea. Hugh pushed open the door of the car showroom and shook the rain from his face. An assortment of sleek coupes rested on raised podiums. Plush carpeting absorbed the sound of his footsteps as he moved reverently between the expensive cars. The smell of aftershave wafted towards him as a sharp-dressed salesman approached.

Hugh beamed at him. "I've come to collect my Porsche."

When the paperwork had been signed, Hugh was taken to the back garage. He saw the car being buffed to a glistening shine by two mechanics in dirty overalls.

"Purple, the colour of emperors," Hugh murmured.

After Hugh had driven away, one of the mechanics remarked, "It bain't purple. It be violet. Says so on the log book."

His companion gave a disparaging sniff and tossed the waxy cloth into a corner. "Bloody poofy colour. I wouldn't 'ave one of they was givin 'em away."

"Ar well, there be no accounting fer taste. Anyways, we can bugger off home now. I wants a baf before I goes off ter see the match."

* * *

The following day, it was still raining in Bristol. In the offices of a television production company, three men sat around a table.

11

"Will Susan be joining us for this meeting?" Hugh asked.

The boss sighed, and nodded his head.

Hugh smiled. "Oh good. She's been frightfully helpful since I got here. Is she, er, unattached?"

"Yes," replied Simon. "She's footloose and forty three."

"Why isn't she here yet?" the boss grumbled. "Is she getting the coffee?"

"I hope not," Simon muttered. "Susan only offers to fetch coffee when she wants to poison someone."

The boss glared at him, and turned towards Hugh. "Are you settled in your flat now? I daresay it's a bit different from what you're used to. I hope it's not too much of a come-down from Chelsea."

"Oh, I don't know. It is rather quaint around here. And the flat in Clifton is super. I can see the harbour from my bedroom window. I can even walk to work, if I want. Mind you, I don't suppose I'll want to, now that I have the Porsche. It was a splendid gesture, on your part."

"Least we could do," the boss replied. "Glad to have you on board. Things have been a bit wobbly round here, that's why they sent me down to sort things out. Can't stand the place, myself. No decent golf within fifty miles."

The door opened and Susan stepped into the room. She glanced around and chose a chair that was furthest from the boss. She had decided that it was safest to keep a distance between them, in case the urge to stab him with her propelling pencil got the better of her. The detestable little oik had been sent from their parent company in London after the previous financial controller had disappeared. Susan got the impression that he thought she had been involved in some way. He had brought in Hugh ostensibly to improve their cash flow, but she was certain that he was there to dig up some dirt and ease her out.

"Hello Hugh," she said, forcing a smile. "Have you been through my programme costings yet?"

He shook his head. "Not had time. I've got a new project lined up which takes priority over all the other stuff."

The boss chipped in with a tone of triumph, "Hugh has made quite a coup. Got us a big name for rock bottom."

Susan arched an eyebrow. "I thought the Village People had split up."

Hugh gave her a confused look. "It's not the Village People. We've signed Tom Banks."

"Who's he?"

Hugh pulled a photo from his folder and passed it to her. Susan's eyes widened. It was a picture of the dark-eyed man on the New York flight. She felt her cheeks colour, and she murmured, "Tom Banks? That's quite a small name."

Hugh was indignant. "Not at all! Lots of people say wonderful things about him. He's a terrific pianist, and his rock band is very popular."

She frowned. "Then how come he's available at a rock bottom price?"

"According to his agent, he has some financial problems. Anyway, she's offered us a very good deal. We've decided to open the strand with one show featuring Tom and his band, and then use them as backing group to a variety of major names, from jazz through to country music. The aim is to cover as wide a musical area as possible, in order to maximise network interest. If we play our cards right, it will be quite a little moneyspinner."

"Mmm, terrific idea." Susan drifted out of the conversation as she recalled his intense dark eyes. She couldn't define his face as handsome, but he had a pensive air that made him instantly appealing. A memory niggled at the back of her mind, something he had said about being out of fashion. She was startled out of her reverie by the brusque tones of the boss.

"Susan, will you do all the necessary paperwork? Hugh needs to get started on this right away, so don't drag your feet."

Susan's propelling pencil fell to the floor. The boss had left the room by the time she reappeared from under the table.

Hugh glanced at his watch, and tidied up his papers.

"I must dash out and put some more money in the meter. I don't want to find a ticket on my new Porsche."

"That's a useful town car," Susan remarked. "Have you got as far as third gear, yet?"

* * *

Two weeks later, it was still raining in Bristol. Tom slouched in his chair and stared vacantly at a spot on the wall. He idly swirled the contents of his coffee cup. The murmur of voices around him in the conference room did not penetrate his thoughts. The woman from the New York flight had been on his mind ever since their brief encounter.

Tom couldn't put his finger on why he found her so fascinating. He pictured her in his mind, struggling to recall every detail of her face, but the harder he tried to remember, the more elusive her image became. Tom closed his eyes to deepen his concentration. He pictured her dark hair, falling softly around her shoulders, and the arching eyebrows that tapered finely towards her cheekbones. Her skin was smooth and tighter than a bongo drum. And such immense eyes, dark as a forest at twilight.

She was definitely British. The few words that she had spoken had revealed that much. But she didn't look English. There was nothing "peaches and cream" about her. More like "olives and red wine".

"Hugh has a purple Porsche! That's pretty impressive, huh Tom?" Jim's voice broke into his reverie.

Tom nodded abstractedly. "I have a nice porch, too. It has a double hammock and lots of flower tubs."

Tom drifted off into a daydream. He was in his double hammock, with the little angel from the plane. No. Hammocks were always a mistake. They tipped you out at the most crucial moment. You needed to be an Olympic gymnast to keep two bodies balanced in a hammock. He took her by the hand and led her through to the bedroom. Her moist lips were close to his mouth.

"You used to be a speed freak, didn't you Tom?" Jim elbowed him sharply to get his attention.

"I don't do drugs, you know that!"

"I was talking about your Ferrari."

"Oh."

"I love travelling at speed," Hugh cut in. "Surfing is something that I've always wanted to do."

Jim smirked. "You should visit Florida if you want the worlds greatest surfing."

"Really? I thought that all the best surfing was done in California?"

"No. The most exciting surfing is done in Florida. I was born and raised there, so I know."

The door opened at that moment, and their attention was diverted. Tom's eyes widened in surprise, and his lips parted as he drew a breath.

Hugh spoke. "Susan. Let me introduce you to Tom Banks and his band."

Tom scrambled to his feet, and swiftly extended his hand to Susan. "I'm Tom Banks. We've met before, but you probably don't remember."

"On the plane to New York. Yes, I remember," Susan replied, smiling as she clasped his hand.

Tom felt his cheeks flame. Her smile could rival sunrise over Chesapeake Bay. His lips moved, but no words emerged from his mouth.

Jim's voice cut in. "You're supposed to let go of her hand after ten seconds, otherwise it's classed as a misdemeanor."

Tom realised that he was still grasping Susan's fingers. He dropped her hand as if it had suddenly become red hot, and sank back into his chair.

Hugh began to talk about the programme schedules, but Tom concentrated his eyes on Susan. She was flicking through a sheaf of papers, ticking items as she went. The top buttons of her short sleeved blouse were undone, revealing a triangle of tanned skin. Tom peered more closely, and wished that she would lean further forwards.

Susan suddenly flicked at something on her arm. It was a very small spider that had attached itself to her. Her aim was accurate. The little spider flew into the air, described a perfect arc, and landed neatly in Tom's coffee cup.

Tom grinned. "Eight point five."

Jim had also been gazing at Susan. "It's legs weren't straight when it dived in. I only give it eight point two."

Tom fished the spider out of his cup, and shook it off his finger.

Jim tilted back in his chair. "I think that Susan should give it the kiss of life."

She gave him an icy stare. "If I wanted to kiss arachnids, I'd be dating Spiderman."

"That's just typical of women," Jim told the spider. "She wants you to learn how to swim, but she won't give you any help."

Susan gritted her teeth, then she smiled at Tom and said, "Can I get you another cup of coffee?"

A look of alarm flashed across Hugh's face.

Tom beamed back at her. "No, it's all right. I've drunk worse things than this. Jim's home-brew usually has dead mice in it."

"They're alive when they go in," Jim muttered.

"Not that I drink a whole lot," Tom continued. "Only on high days and holidays."

Jim sniffed contemptuously. "Yeah, and when there's an "R" in the month. And a "U". And a "Y"- eeeh!" he broke off, as Tom kicked him on the ankle.

"Sorry Hugh," Tom said. "You must think us very rude."

"Not at all. It's a great pleasure to have you and your band here. I've heard that you have quite a cult following in the States."

"Oh yeah," Jim agreed. "He's often been called a cult. Especially by his ex."

"Ex wife?" Susan murmured. "Do you have any ex children, too?"

"Nope. We only ever had dogs. Big ugly bastards. They cost me a fortune in dog food."

Pete grunted. "Dog food. What a waste of money. Find out where your nearest liposuction clinic is, and hang around back on trash can day."

Susan shuddered.

Jim noticed, and smiled wickedly as he said, "Tattoo removal clinics are good, too. Lots of waste flesh gets chucked out. They don't care none if some of the black bags disappear."

Susan felt the colour drain from her face. She looked at her watch and stood up. "I've got another meeting now. Hugh can fill you in with the expense budgets." She turned and walked swiftly out of the room, her hand over her mouth.

Tom's eyes followed her shapely figure as she swayed out of the room.

"I'll run through the rehearsal schedule with you tomorrow," said Hugh. "I've tried to keep it pretty tight. We should be able to complete the shows within six weeks."

"Who's picking up the tab for the hotel rooms?" Pete asked.

"I believe we are," Hugh murmured.

"Then it don't matter too much if we over-run."

Hugh stiffened. "Uhm, we want a quality product, of course. But I expect you've all got families waiting for you back home. We wouldn't dream of keeping you here longer than absolutely necessary." He turned towards Tom. "I daresay you have lots of important things to do when you get back to the States."

Tom shook his head. "Nope."

"Er, right. Anyway, I must dash out for a moment. Put some more money in the meter."

Hugh scurried out of the room, pulling coins from his pocket.

"What a nice man," Joe remarked. "Not many people these days care about family life." Then he frowned at Jim. "Why did you tell him that Florida is a good place for surfing? You know that the only time you can surf in Florida is just before a hurricane blows in."

Jim smacked the side of his head. "Damn! I knew there was something I forgot to say!"

* * *

"Can I get you a drink?" Tom asked, later that evening.

"I'll have a dry vermouth with ice," Susan answered.

Tom poured a generous measure from the bottle. He watched Susan as she walked across to the window. Her slim hips swayed gently as she moved. He spooned heaps of ice into her glass, then took it over to her.

Susan looked at the glass and clicked her tongue. "You could sink the Titanic with this!"

"Sorry. I got lost in the view. Shall I fish some of it out?"

"No, don't worry. This room does have a lovely view of the floating harbour." Susan was gazing out of the large window. Tom's room was at the back of the hotel, with a vista over the water to the hills in the distance.

"Kind of a strange name for a harbour," Tom remarked. "Is there such a thing as a sinking harbour?"

Susan gave him a sardonic smile. "Venice?"

Tom grinned, showing a dazzling set of even teeth. "You're too smart for me. Is this a high-power job, what you do at the television company?"

"No. I do everybody else's work for them, and the money is terrible."

"Why settle for it, then?"

"It's not so easy to find work, these days. The job used to pay more, but we had a bit of trouble, and the staff received an ultimatum. Take a pay cut, or face redundancy."

"A smart, good-looking girl like you should be able to get another job, no problem," Tom remarked, as he edged closed to her.

"References," she told him, setting her mouth in a taut line. "The present boss has only been there for a few months. I don't think he's likely to say anything nice about me."

"What have you done to piss him off?"

"I'm guilty by association. The previous boss disappeared, and emptied the company deposit account at the same time. I worked closely with him, on the financial side."

"Didn't you have a clue what he was up to?"

"He always had a plausible reason for whatever he did. I thought he was a genuine nice guy. He was always sweet to me. But I suppose he figured that if I owed him a favour, I wouldn't ask too many questions." She sighed heavily, and took a large sip of her drink.

"What favour did he do?" Tom asked, with a concerned frown.

"When I applied for a mortgage to buy my flat, he told me to inflate my salary. Then he signed the papers to verify my earnings to the mortgage company."

"Is that legal?"

"Everyone does it."

"Does your current boss know this stuff?"

Susan gulped her martini. "Of course not! So keep your mouth shut. Trouble is, since I've had to take a pay cut, I can't afford the mortgage repayments, so I have to do extra work on the side. If he finds out about that, he can boot me out. It's a breach of my contract."

"Why don't you sell the flat and get something cheaper?"

Susan grimaced. "Do the words negative equity mean anything to you?"

Tom shook his head.

"House prices have fallen, lately. If I sell, I'll get less money than I borrowed."

"So you're in deep shit?"

She drained her glass. "I can see that you need some lessons in financial terminology."

"I'm willing to do night classes."

"Shall we start tonight?"

"Mm. Let's pull the drapes first, though."

CHAPTER 3

Simon looked at his watch. It was nearly six. He switched off his computer. As he put on his jacket, he said to Susan, "Are you seeing Tom tonight?"

"Mmm. We're going away for the weekend. I need to finish off a few things before I go."

"See you on Monday, then."

Susan merely nodded, her concentration fixed on the computer screen in front of her. She didn't want to admit to Simon that she was behind with her work. During the past month, she and Tom had spent every night together, but they didn't get much sleep. She could hardly keep her eyes open in the office. And she was confused by the fact Simon seemed to be turning into a pervert. Every morning, he would ask if she had seen Tom the previous night. Susan knew that he wasn't jealous. It was a standing joke within the company that Simon was deeply smitten with Sophie in Stills. She shook her head to regain her concentration. She had to get everything up to date before she went on holiday. Tom was taking her to Florida, for two weeks of glorious sunshine. He had even promised that they would visit Disneyworld. She had always wanted to go there.

Susan was tapping at her keyboard, and dreaming of a tropical sandy beach, when Hugh suddenly appeared in the doorway.

"Er, Susan, could I have a few moments of your time?"

"Mm," Susan replied, scrunching her toes in imaginary white sand.

Hugh shuffled into the office, his shoulders drooping.

"It's about the Tom Banks production. We seem to have a slight problem."

Susan had traversed the beach, and was now paddling through a sparkling blue sea. "What sort of problem?"

Hugh glanced over his shoulder uneasily, then said quietly, "I don't think we're going to make much profit on it, after all."

Susan was startled back into reality. "What do you mean?"

"I seem to have over-estimated our revenue from the programme sales in the US. Several networks have decided not to take it. It appears that Tom Banks isn't as sought-after as his agent led me to believe. Apparently, his last concert was a major disaster." Hugh lowered his voice, and added, "We really need to reduce our production costs."

"We can't do that. The production is nearly finished. There's no scope for cut-backs."

Hugh sighed. "Oh dear. The boss is going to give us a roasting over this."

"What do you mean, "us"?" Susan snapped at him. "This is your fault, not mine."

"The boss will blame you as well. He'll say that you should have double-checked my estimates. You did say that you were going to."

Susan cursed inwardly. Hugh was right. She should have checked the figures at the start.

"Show me your revised revenue figures," she demanded.

Hugh handed her a sheet of paper. As Susan studied the numbers, her eyes widened in horror. "We'll barely break even!"

Hugh nodded gloomily. "Umm. That's why I suggested reducing our costs. I was hoping that you could do some creative accounting and push some of the costs on to other projects."

Susan frowned. "The boss will have forty fits if he catches me doing that."

"He's going to have forty fits anyway when he sees our net profit on this. What have we got to lose?"

Our jobs, either way, Susan thought, glumly. She gave a resigned sigh. "Let's get the files out and see what we can arrange. Go and get some coffee. We'll be here for a while."

As Hugh went out, Susan rang Tom's hotel. When he answered the phone, she said briefly, "I probably won't be able to make it tonight. I'm working late. Something's come up."

"Anyone I know?" he quipped.

"You wouldn't be laughing if you were here," she said curtly, and hung up.

* * *

Tom replaced the receiver and pursed his lips. He didn't like being at a loose end. He walked out of his room, down the hotel corridor, and into

Jim's room. Jim never locked his door, ever since that time in Las Vegas when a girl had mistaken his room for hers, and was half-undressed before she realised her mistake.

Jim, Pete and Joe were sitting around the table, engrossed in a card game.

"Hello stranger," said Jim, without looking up from his hand of cards. "I guess you've been stood up."

"Nope," said Tom. "I just fancied a night in with the boys, instead of a night out with the girls."

Pete grunted. "Yeah, he's definitely been stood up."

"Deal me in the game?" Tom asked, hopefully.

"Well," said Jim slowly, "We'd like to, but you know how it is. We've been running this game for three days now, and if we were to deal you in and you were to win the pot, it wouldn't go down too well. You know how it is."

"Yeah, sure, I know how it is," said Tom sourly, and he left the card players to their game. He paused briefly in the corridor, then turned and strode to the lift. There was a wide-screen TV in the hotel bar. The guy behind the bar might scan the satellite channels for a basketball game, if he slipped a couple of notes across.

On the ground floor, Tom made his way through the wide lounge and towards the restaurant, the entrance to which was flanked by leafy indoor plants. To one side of the vegetation, three steps led down to a sunken bar. Pale cane furniture was spaced well apart, and the noise from a huge television screen echoed around the room. Tom was about to sit at the bar, when he caught a waft of barbecued meat. A waiter was carrying a burger platter to a guest at one of the wicker tables. The large plate of fries, salad and juicy burger was instantly appealing to Tom. He ordered at the bar, then sat down at an empty table. He gazed sulkily at the game that was showing on the TV. The barman had refused his bribe. Tom groaned inwardly. He didn't expect to come to England and have to endure ice hockey.

He had forgotten how dull it could be, with just his own company. Susan had been with him almost all of the time since he had arrived in Bristol. Things were never dull when she was around.

Jim had made some sarcastic remark that afternoon about her being "sharper than a serpent's tongue." One of the sound engineers had messed up a recording, and Susan had chewed him out so bad that he looked as if he might burst into tears. Tom shook his head. Some of these Brits could be real sloppy with their work. The guy hadn't been doing his job properly, so he deserved to get yelled at. Susan didn't take any shit from anyone. That was one of the things he liked best about her. It was probably her Mediterranean roots that made her that way. Tom was a little confused about her family history, but he deduced that there was Latin blood somewhere along the line. He was disappointed that Susan wouldn't be with him tonight, because he wanted to talk about the vacation in Florida. He had thought about getting one-way tickets, but the travel clerk said it had to be done as a return package. Anyway, he didn't want to railroad Susan into staying in the States. It had to be her decision.

Tom's thoughts were interrupted by the arrival of his food. As he munched, he gazed around absent-mindedly, and he was surprised to see a woman waving at him from across the room. He instinctively waved back, and she smiled, then disappeared into the adjacent dining room. Tom pondered briefly, then remembered who she was. It was the girl who had done the stills shoot, a few days before. Sophie. Yeah, that was her name. She was real cute. Tom sipped his beer, and resigned himself to the hockey game.

By ten thirty, Tom was feeling slightly tipsy. It's funny how you always drink more when you're on your own, he mulled. He was about to stagger back to his room when a voice close by suddenly spoke to him.

"Hello Tom. Are you on your own?"

He looked up and saw Sophie standing opposite. She was wearing a cream-coloured blouse that buttoned tightly across her bosom, and a black skirt that was slit up one side.

"Uh, yeah," he muttered in reply, blinking rapidly and trying not to stare at the front of her blouse.

"Do you mind if I sit down? I'm so excited, I'm just bursting to talk to someone."

Tom quickly stood up and pulled out a chair for her. "Sure. I'd enjoy some company."

Sophie sat down, crossing her legs so that the slit skirt revealed an expanse of slender leg. She glanced across at the television screen, and asked, "Am I in the way? You're probably watching this."

"This is the third hockey game I've seen this evening," Tom grumbled. "I'd much sooner look at you."

He realised how crass the words sounded as soon as he had uttered them, but Sophie didn't seem to take offence. She sipped at her tomato juice, then said in a confidential tone, "I'm here for a job interview."

As Tom raised his eyebrows, she added, "It does sound a bit odd, doesn't it? These people are here for the weekend. My brother knows one of them, so he got me an in. They're from LA. They're here to see the plasticine man."

Tom nodded slowly, wondering what exactly was in Sophie's tomato juice.

"Anyway, the main man won't be here till eleven. Catching the train from London. So I have to hang about to see him. I'm not getting my hopes up, though. Camera crew are two a penny these days. They may not offer me anything."

Tom wrinkled his nose.

"Sophie, you kinda lost me some place back."

"Sorry, I'm a bit wound up. They're looking for female camera men. Women, that is. I don't just do stills, you know. I trained at the beeb, back when they did their own filming. Female directors out in LA just love to have girls behind the cameras. Empathy, you know."

Sophie took a slurp from her glass, then shrieked.

"Oh shit! How did I manage that!" A large red splodge dripped down the front of her white blouse. "I can't possibly meet him, looking like this!"

"Don't panic, Sophie. I've got some Mr. Clean in my room. Should take the stain right out. C'mon, I'll get you tidied up."

They made their way upstairs to Tom's room, and he went into the bathroom to find the stain remover. As Sophie stood there, the phone started to ring.

* * *

Simon had just finished eating his take-away when he remembered the dental appointment. The last mouthful of spare ribs had wedged itself into his cracked filling. He had made the appointment weeks ago, and had forgotten all about it. He hunted for the small appointment card, then groaned as he read it. Monday 9.30. He decided to phone Susan and let her know that he'd be late for work on Monday.

He looked up her home phone number in his address book, and dialed. No reply. He tried three times, then concluded that she was probably with Tom. She seemed to spend most of her time with him. Simon was hopeful that when Tom went back to America, Susan would go with him. He had tried to sound her out, but she hadn't given much away. Simon was confident that he would get Susan's job if she left. The boss had even hinted at it on a few occasions.

Simon drifted into his favourite daydream : He was the chief accountant, dynamic and powerful - and the lovely Sophie was at his side, gazing adoringly at him. He knew that she would fall for him. It was only a matter of time. And the large salary would definitely help. All this happiness was now possible. Tom Banks had made it possible, thought Simon, gratefully. He was such a nice man, too. Always gave you the time of day. Unusual, for a rock star. Most of them were born-again gits. Especially if they were married to models. Lucky bastards. If only he'd persevered with the guitar lessons. His mum had been right. It was the only way to make money. More than he'd ever make being assistant accountant. Simon suddenly remembered that he was trying to find Susan.

He dialed the number of Tom's hotel and waited while the switchboard put the call through. After several seconds a familiar female voice said, "Hello, can I help you?"

"Is that you, Susan?" asked Simon, suddenly flustered.

"No, this is Sophie. Do you want to speak to Tom? He's just gone into the bathroom."

Simon was too astonished to speak. He hung up without replying. No, he thought, there must have been some mistake. He rang the hotel again.

"Tom Banks, please," said Simon, in his clearest and most precise voice. Get the right room this time, he thought impatiently.

"Hello, Banks here," said Tom.

"Oh, hello Tom, could I speak to Susan please. This is Simon from the office."

"Susan's not here," replied Tom. "She's working late tonight."

"Oh, er, I thought I heard a girl's voice there," said Simon, hesitantly.

"Yeah, that's Sophie. You probably know her. She works in your building. I gotta hang up now. Sophie's getting impatient."

"Oh, right," Simon said, despondently. He was totally confused and somewhat shaken. "Sorry to have bothered you."

Simon hung up the phone and slumped into his armchair.

* * *

"Wonder what he wanted," Tom mused, as he handed the stain remover to Sophie. "Here's the Mr. Clean. All you have to do is wet the garment, then rub the stick over it, and rinse."

"Tom, you're a life saver."

Sophie disappeared into the bathroom, and Tom stretched out on his bed, with the remote in his right hand. If he was lucky, maybe he could find a re-run of Miami Vice.

* * *

"I'm not doing any more," Susan said, wearily. "The numbers are swimming around in front of my eyes."

"How much have we re-allocated?" asked Hugh.

"Enough to give us a reasonable profit. We'll be lucky if we get away with it, though. Someone is bound to notice the increased costs on these other projects."

Hugh shrugged. "It's worth the gamble. At least we've bought ourselves a bit more time. And I might be able to sell Tom to a few more networks. I'm still working on it."

"Let's call it a day then. I'll have to ring for a taxi," Susan said, with a yawn.

Hugh's eyes lit up. "I'll give you a lift home. We could have a drink in that quaint little pub by the harbour. I'm parked down that way."

"All right. Only one drink, though. I've got to be up early in the morning."

They left the office and walked the short distance to the quayside pub. When they entered the lounge bar, they were hit by a blast of "Life in the Fast Lane."

"Wicked," murmured Susan. "It must be Eagles tribute night."

She peered through the fog of cigarette smoke and saw three guitar players huddled in a small alcove towards the back of the bar. A small drum kit was squeezed behind them, blocking the way between the gents toilet and the door to the beer garden.

Hugh shouted at her above the din. "Shall we sit outside?"

Susan shook her head. "I always get eaten alive by bugs if I go outside at night. Anyway, this lot sound pretty good."

It was nearly closing time when they left the pub. Susan had insisted on staying until she was sure that the band had finished playing for the night. It was a moonless night, and a light drizzle was falling, so they hurried along the narrow street that ran alongside the harbour.

"Why do you park here?" Susan asked. "It's a bit creepy around here at night. Aren't you worried about your car being stolen?"

Hugh gave a nonchalant shrug. "My car has got an incredibly complex alarm system. The man in the showroom said that not even Albert Einstein could crack the security code on the car alarm mechanism. Each device is individually programmed to be completely fail-safe."

A high-pitched wailing sound suddenly assaulted their ears. Susan halted, and gave Hugh a worried look. "That might be yours. What shall we do?"

Hugh started to sprint along the pavement, gasping over his shoulder, "Don't worry. They'll run off when they see me coming."

Susan jogged after him. They rounded a corner, then Hugh stopped abruptly. As Susan caught him up, she said breathlessly, "Why have you stopped? Do they look dangerous?" Then she peered down the street and saw that it was empty. "Where's that racket coming from?" she demanded.

Hugh took off again at a sprint, then halted when he was half way down the street. Susan trotted up behind him, and realised that the hideous din was coming from a small metal object that was lying in the gutter.

Hugh shrieked, "I don't believe it! They told me this could never happen!"

He gave the screeching car alarm a savage kick. It clattered across the road, bounced off a concrete bollard, and fell into the murky harbour with a loud plop.

"At least it's stopped wailing now," Susan muttered.

Hugh gave a broken sob. "How the hell did they get it out? It was computer designed to be tamper proof!"

Susan shook her head sagely. "There's a lot of unemployed electronic engineering graduates around, these days. Things have gone downhill since they closed the aircraft factory."

Hugh pulled a mobile phone from his coat pocket and punched three nines. When he had finished speaking to the police, he said to Susan, "Shall I get a mini-cab for you? I have to wait here for the police."

"No, don't worry. I'll walk around to the taxi rank. Mini cabs always take ages to turn up. Er, see you Monday."

Susan slipped away into the darkness, leaving Hugh to grieve alone. She retraced her steps along the dimly-lit street. Once past the pub, the road widened, and it curved around the harbour in a broad sweep. She walked briskly, feeling more secure when the lights of restaurants and chip shops came into view. Tom's hotel loomed up ahead, the lights at the windows sending twinkling reflections into the black harbour water. Susan decided not to get a taxi home. She trudged wearily into the hotel foyer, and made her way to the lift. Tom would probably be watching TV in his room. Susan sighed. It had been a long day. She was looking forward to putting her feet up and her head down. When the lift door pinged open, she shuffled out and took two paces to Tom's room. Before she had the chance to knock, the door was flung open and Sophie bowled into her, stepping heavily onto her aching feet.

"Sorry! Oh, Susan, it's you! Hi!" Sophie dashed along the corridor and leapt into the lift as the doors were closing.

Susan frowned, and hobbled into the room. The TV was blaring, but there was no sign of Tom. She made her way to the bathroom, and saw Tom kneeling on the floor, picking things up from beneath the washbasin.

"What was Sophie doing here?" she demanded, as she bent down to massage her injured toes.

Tom lurched upwards, and smacked his head on the basin.

"Ow! Shit! Jeez, Susan! You startled me!" He dropped all the items that he had been gathering, and Susan saw that they were condoms.

She frowned. "Why were you juggling with Durex?"

"That Sophie has got to be the world's clumsiest woman," Tom mumbled. "She was in here, cleaning up, and she managed to tip my wash bag on to the floor."

Susan glared at him.

"I don't believe your brass nerve! You go behind my back with another woman, and then you have the gall to complain about her being untidy! Your arrogance is breathtaking!"

"No, you don't understand." Tom was feverishly rubbing his head. "Gee, I can see two of you."

"No, the other one has just left. And this one is leaving too!"

As Susan stormed out of the bathroom, Tom staggered to his feet and stumbled after her.

"See you tomorrow?" he whimpered, to her departing back.

"Only if you're in traction, and I'm carrying grapes!"

CHAPTER 4

Simon sidled into the office, trying to look invisible. It was close to lunchtime.

"What time do you call this?" Susan demanded.

"Sorry I'm late," he mumbled from a numb mouth. "I had to go to the dentist."

"You should have phoned and told me."

"I tried, but I couldn't get hold of you on Friday night. And you were away for the weekend, so I didn't know where to reach you."

Susan pressed her lips together. "I was at home all weekend, but you weren't to know, I suppose."

"How come you didn't go away for the weekend?"

"Tom was too busy," Susan snapped. She stood up and opened a low filing cabinet drawer. She snatched at a file, then vigorously kicked the drawer shut.

Simon did not dare to ask any more questions. He had a feeling that Susan had found out about Sophie being in Tom's room. It had obviously put paid to their romance. Simon pressed the start button on his computer, then splayed his elbows on the desk and held his head in his hands. As the computer pinged into life, he stared vacantly at the screen, and fell into a silent depression.

* * *

Down in the basement studio, Tom sat scowling at his piano keyboard. The stupid object was playing all the wrong notes today. Pianos did that sometimes when they were in a bad mood. Well he was in a bad mood too, and he felt like giving the rest of the world a hard time.

He had phoned Susan numerous times over the weekend. The first few times she had picked up the phone, then hung up as soon as he spoke.

28

Then she had stopped picking up at all. She wouldn't even give him the chance to explain! She was totally unreasonable. Women! More trouble then they were goddam worth!

The piano started playing the wrong notes again.

"Which song is this?" Jim asked dryly. "Or is it a new one?"

Tom swore at him, and bent his head back down to the keys.

Susan had chosen that moment to enter the studio and distribute their expenses cheques. She stood listening for a moment, then commented to Jim, "He doesn't exactly tie himself down to a tune, does he?"

"They're my songs. I can re-invent them if I want," Tom muttered darkly.

"Re-invent? Is that American for "I can't remember the melody?""

Sniggers came from the guitar players across the room. Tom frowned at them.

"I don't forget nothing. I just like a bit of variety."

"You don't need to tell me that," Susan retorted, icily. "You made it more than apparent with Sophie." She turned on her heel flounced out of the studio.

Tom watched her go, then yelled at the rest of the band, "What are y'all waiting for? Let's do this stuff."

Joe slung his guitar across his chest, then whispered to Pete, "How come those two are sniping at each other? I thought that they were secret lovers."

Pete shrugged. "Maybe they were secretly married."

* * *

That evening, when Tom was alone in his hotel room, he answered a knock at the door and was surprised to see Hugh standing there.

"Hello Hugh, come on in," said Tom. "I was real sorry to hear about your car."

"Umm," groaned Hugh. "I don't suppose I'll ever see it again. The police think that it's probably half-way across Europe by now."

"Have a drink," offered Tom. "Drown your sorrows."

"Thanks." As Hugh sipped his drink he said gingerly, "There's something I need to discuss with you. Would you and your band be interested in doing a European tour?"

"We've just finished one," replied Tom. "I can't see any point in going back so soon. They weren't very keen to see us then."

"I'm talking about Eastern Europe," Hugh said eagerly. "Not many bands will tour over there, so they're willing to pay good money."

"I didn't think they had any money."

"The Germans have sunk pitfulls of cash into the rusty curtain countries, to make sure they don't turn red again. It's boom time out there."

"Is the show going to be screened out there?"

"That's the problem," Hugh admitted. "The networks are squeezing us to ship you out there. They may not take the show if you don't go."

"Surely that don't count for much. We have much bigger takers, right?"

Hugh gulped at his drink. "Well, every little helps."

Tom contemplated his tumbler of scotch for a long moment, then he stared at Hugh.

"Hugh, I've been in this game a long time. I know a pile of bullshit from a hole in the ground. So what is it that you're not telling me?"

"Susan and I have over-estimated our revenue on the show. Some of the major American networks have ducked out. The profit margin is diminishing rapidly. We could both lose our jobs over this."

"So if I agree to this tour, it will get you two out of the shit?"

Hugh gave an embarrassed smile.

"That's one way of putting it."

Tom gazed into his tumbler and swirled the ice cubes thoughtfully.

"The insurance premiums on the equipment will be sky-high, that's a certainty. But we only use a small amount of gear. One thing, though. This will probably sound kinda strange. Is there any chance that Susan could come on the tour with us?"

"Susan! Well, it's not really her line of work."

"Pity. I'd be more inclined to be enthusiastic if I knew she was coming along."

Hugh sat upright. "I'm sure she'd be happy to go, once she realises how important this is to you."

Tom frowned. "I think not. Could we use a little subterfuge, or would I be offending your British sense of fair play?"

Hugh beamed. "Tom, you're the main man. I can arrange whatever you want."

After Hugh had left, Tom grabbed a bottle of single malt and went along the corridor.

"How come you're not playing poker?" Tom asked, when he walked into Jim's room and found the guys watching television.

Jim grimaced. "Pete wiped us out."

"So, what are you all planning on doing at the end of this job?" said Tom, looking enquiringly at each of them.

"I guess this means that Judith has nothing for us, again," grumbled Pete. "Why do we pay her ten per cent?"

"What's ten per cent of nothing?" answered Tom. "She won't get rich on our earnings, that's for sure. Anyway, I've had an offer from Hugh."

Jim raised an eyebrow. "I didn't think he was your type. And he hasn't got his fancy car to take you out in any more."

Tom ignored this and continued, "He wants us to do a tour of Eastern Europe. He reckons we could get a decent payoff. What do you think?"

"Isn't that where the Communists live?" Joe protested.

Tom swiftly reassured him. "They don't live there any more. They all moved away."

Pete frowned. "Isn't there a good deal of shooting over there?"

"Hardly any at all," Tom replied. "Anyway, you live in DC. You should be used to it."

"What are the girls like?" demanded Jim. "Are they cute?"

"Sure," said Tom. "Just think of what you could do for East-West relations."

He poured them all a generous measure of scotch and toasted, "One for the road."

* * *

The following afternoon Hugh dashed into Susan's office and beamed broadly at her.

"You look very pleased, Hugh. Have they found your car?"

Hugh flinched. "No such luck. Anyway, I need to talk to you, in private." He gave Simon a hard stare.

Simon rose to his feet. "I'll go down to Photographics and see if Tom's stills are ready."

Hugh waited until Simon was well out of earshot, then announced, "I think I've saved us from disaster! I've persuaded several Eastern European networks to take the T.B. production. We should get a healthy profit on it now."

"T.B.?" echoed Susan. "You mean Tom?"

"Yes, of course."

"It seems appropriate. He is fairly damaging to one's health."

Hugh looked puzzled, but sailed on. "They want a tour to accompany the programme, and Tom has agreed to that, thank goodness. He's doing us a big favour."

"How very noble of him," she replied, sarcastically. "But I dare say he's getting paid for the tour."

"Yes, I'm negotiating with a sponsor, some Hungarian sports shoe manufacturer. They jumped at it." Hugh suddenly sighed. "Organising the tour is a logistic nightmare, though. I really need some help. Could you spare any time? I know you're always frightfully busy, but you're such a whizz at sorting things out."

Susan frowned, and was about to give Hugh an abrupt reply, but then a germ of an idea flashed through her mind.

"Of course I'll help. I used to work in a travel shop, so I know the ropes. What do you need me to do?"

"We have to book all the travel arrangements - flights, hotels, the tour bus. You'll have the phone more or less welded to your ear, I'm afraid. You can use the spare desk in my office, if you like. I've got my own fax machine, so you won't have to be trotting up and down the corridor all the time. I'm in meetings most of the time, so you'll have a bit of peace and quiet."

"Your own fax? Yes, that would be useful," she murmured, thinking of how she was going to get even with Tom for carrying on with Sophie. This would be a tour that he would never forget, she was going to make sure of that!

* * *

"How many times are you going to read through that contract?" Jim asked Tom. "You must have been through it a dozen times. It hasn't changed none since the last time you read it."

"I can't believe our luck. If this works out right, I should be able to pay off a lot of my debts. It seems too good to be true. That's why I keep reading it through. I want to make sure that there's no catch."

"What's the sponsor's name, again?"

"Z-B-L-A-T-O-V," Tom spelled out. "Pronounced "Splatoff", according to Hugh."

"If you have to mention their name at each gig, we should tell the front row to bring umbrellas, what with your Southern accent and all."

Tom pulled a face in reply, and carried on studying the contract.

"It says that they've got their own representative to act as tour manager

- some English guy who's been out there for a while, so he should know his way around. There doesn't seem to be anything that can go wrong," Tom concluded, and he reached for his pen to sign the contract.

* * *

Three weeks later, Susan was very pleased with her hard work. Everything was booked and confirmed. The itinerary was complete. She had encountered a slight problem at the start, though. When she told the girl at the travel agency that she wanted the cheapest possible hotel rooms, the agent had tried to talk her out of it.

"We always book our clients into four-star hotels as an absolute minimum. The standards out there can vary enormously. We would only consider booking economy accommodation for students, or people travelling on a limited budget, certainly not for business travellers."

"But they're not business travellers," Susan had swiftly countered. "They're a group of elderly musicians. On a very limited budget. They want to study the ethnic music of the eastern bloc, so they need to travel at grass roots level. They say that it's all part of assimilating the culture."

Susan was pleased with her impromptu speech, and it seemed to convince the travel agent.

Over the following days Susan received a host of faxes, confirming the one-star hotel bookings throughout Eastern Europe. Susan wished that she could have specified hotels without indoor toilets, but it would have made the booking process even more complicated.

She chuckled while she read the fax that confirmed the bus hire. All of the equipment was going out in a huge articulated truck, but the band would be flying to Warsaw and picking up a tour bus there. It had been easy to get a really cheap bus. There wasn't much else available at such short notice. The travel agent had been very apologetic when she had phoned about it.

"I'm terribly sorry," the girl had said, "But the only coach that we can arrange in Warsaw doesn't have toilet facilities on board. We can change the bus when they get to Prague, though. They have a purpose-built tour bus available."

"Don't worry," Susan assured her, as she stifled a giggle. "They can take the same bus all the way through the tour. They won't mind about the facilities."

Susan remembered what Tom had said about the rigours of touring, and about how it was only bearable because of the luxurious tour buses that they had in America. She was certain that he would be absolutely livid when he saw the one that he had to travel on for this tour.

Things couldn't have worked out better. Tom would have to spend nearly two months in total discomfort, hopefully with audiences chucking things at him. Revenge is sweet, thought Susan, smiling happily to herself.

* * *

That night, as Simon was eating his dinner, he was frowning over his beans on toast. He had spent a couple of weeks doing Susan's work, because she was busy organising Tom's tour, and he was puzzled by some of the things that he had come across in her files. There were some very strange numbers in the projects that she had been looking after. He felt sure that the costs on most of them were higher than they should have been, and when he checked more closely into the figures, he found that Susan had made some rather odd book-keeping entries. Especially on the Tom Banks project.

He sighed. Maybe he should just forget about it. After all, it was her work, not his. And no-one would thank him for pointing out the discrepancies. The dust had only just settled after the last lot of trouble. He continued munching and smiled as he mulled over what Tom had let slip to him that day, about how he was trying to get back together with Susan. And to top that, Sophie had confided that she hadn't got the job in California, after all. Simon slipped into a daydream. Sophie stood beside him, holding his hand, and the boss was handing him the keys to a Porsche.

* * *

The following morning, Susan was back in her own office, still gloating over the itinerary from hell that she had so recently completed, when Hugh strode in.

"Susan! I was just looking at your tour info. Brilliant job! You've got everything sewn up. The boss is very impressed. He's come up with a whizzer of an idea."

She eyed him suspiciously.

"What are you talking about?"

"He reckons that someone from this company should go out with Tom and the band, as liaison, you know. It's down to you or me. I'd jump at it, ordinarily. But I've got a holiday booked for the next three weeks. Florida. So he suggested that you should go along on the tour. Makes a nice change from work, eh?"

Susan glared at him.

"Hell will freeze over before I get on a plane with that idiot piano player. You'll have to make other arrangements."

Hugh grimaced. "Oh dear. I thought you'd leap at it. That puts us up the proverbial creek. I got a fax from Zblatov this morning. This bloke that they've got lined up as tour manager has disappeared. No trace of him anywhere. Tom will be cast adrift, as it were."

"With any luck, he might sink," Susan muttered.

"You should go. You need a break," Simon chipped in.

"What makes you think I need a break?"

Simon hesitated. "Well, you've been making a lot of mistakes, recently. Pressure of work, I expect."

She gave him a wary look. "What mistakes?"

"Some of the costings have been misallocated. Tom's project has lots of errors on it."

Hugh swiftly cut in. "I'm sure it's nothing to worry about. I daresay that the boss won't bother to check the figures. Not if we go along with his decision, that is."

Susan felt a cold cramp in the pit of her stomach. Had Hugh set her up? She forced a tight smile.

"I'll go wherever the company wants me to, but I haven't got a hotel room booked. There's no-where for me to stay."

Hugh gave a casual shrug. "The boss's secretary is working on it as we speak."

CHAPTER 5

Susan grumbled to herself as she shuffled into the airport, trailing her suitcase along on its rubber wheels. She couldn't believe her bad luck. The boss's secretary had worked overtime to get all the bookings done in time. She'd even managed to get Susan on the same flight to Warsaw as the band. The ticket had arrived just the day before, special delivery. Everyone was conspiring against her, even the Royal Mail. You could usually rely on them not to deliver on time. Susan hated the world, and everyone in it!

She said goodbye to her suitcase at the check-in desk, then mooched off to find the shops. She couldn't walk through an airport without feeling depressed. All because of a man. Susan sighed as she remembered. It was two years ago that she had flown to Paris to see Sylvan. That bastard! Five years of living together, then he skips off back to France. To find a house for the two of them, he had said. And when Susan flew to Paris to surprise him, she was the one who got a surprise. Bastard was shacked up with a Moroccan model!

They were all the same, men. Tell you any load of old crap just to get you between the sheets. She cursed her stupidity. Just as she had got her life nicely arranged, along comes Tom, and everything goes up shit creek again! Not only did she have to rub shoulders with him for the next six weeks, but she was obliged to stay in the rubbish hotels that she had booked for him!

And to cap it all, she would lose most of her private clients, being away from home for that long. If she wasn't at home when they rang her doorbell, they'd bugger off to some other book-keeper.

Susan found the pharmacy that she was looking for, and strode up to the counter.

"I want two packs of paracetamol, some travel sickness pills, and a packet of corn plasters," she told the woman at the cash register.

The sales assistant picked out the items and shouted to a hole in the wall, "Selling paracetamol."

Then she turned back to Susan and recited, "Don't use the corn plasters if you're a diabetic. Read the dosage instructions carefully for the paracetamol. We don't usually sell more than one pack per customer. Some people misuse the product. Are these items for your own personal use?"

"No. They're for my grandma. I want her house, so I'm going to make her swallow all the tablets with a bottle of gin, then I'm going to put her in her car and make her drive down the motorway. Then if I'm feeling suicidal, I'll stick all of the corn plasters on my foot at the same time."

The sales assistant fixed Susan with an astonished stare, and rang up the sale on the till without saying anything more.

Susan made her way into the departure lounge and trudged around looking for the band. As she rounded a potted palm, she heard someone call her name. She glanced across the lounge and saw a man in a scarlet tee shirt waving at her. As he stood up, she realized that it was Tom. She weaved her way through the seating area to where the band were sprawled across two benches, and slumped down next to Joe.

"Susan!" he cried. "What are you doing here?"

"I didn't see the stop sign, and took a turn for the worse," she replied, gazing with distaste at Tom's lurid tee shirt.

Tom beamed at her. "Where are you off to? Going on vacation?"

"I wish," she muttered. "I'm going with you lot. On this bloody tour."

"Really? What a nice surprise. I had no idea."

"Didn't Hugh tell you I was coming along?"

Tom shook his head. "He said there was a problem at the Zblatov end, and that he was trying to get us an escort. I assumed it would be some marketing guy."

Jim frowned at Susan. "How come you got the job? You don't know jack shit about this tour."

"Yes I do," she snapped back. "I did all the bookings."

Susan regretted the words the moment they were out of her mouth, and cursed herself for her stupidity. She had been planning to put all the blame for dodgy hotels on to Hugh. She was thankful now that she had been able to re-book the luxury bus in Prague.

Jim stood up. "I'll get the beers in. God alone knows what we'll be drinking on the other side."

"I'll have a dry Martini," Susan hastily told him. "And make it a large one."

* * *

On board the plane, Susan found herself wedged between Joe and Tom. Tom spread himself out, with his elbows and knees protruding into Susan's space. She wriggled about in her seat and tried to get comfortable, but Tom's feet managed to spread over on to her floor space. She felt squashed. She clicked her tongue in annoyance and grumbled to herself.

Tom rubbed his elbow against her, and said nostalgically, "Remember, the first time we met was on an airplane."

"Yes, and I've had bad luck ever since," she complained.

Tom stretched his arms and legs a bit further, then leaned his head back and closed his eyes.

Soon after take off, the stewardess came along and handed out menu cards, small bags of pretzels and drinks. Susan clutched her dry martini and studied the menu card. When the stewardess returned to take dinner orders, Susan said, "Have you got something that I could eat with a teaspoon?" giving Tom's intrusive elbow a severe jab.

"Give her the Lucrezia Borgia special," Tom muttered, without opening his eyes.

Susan sipped her drink and tried not to think about the hotel that awaited them. Maybe it would be best to get drunk on the plane, she thought morosely.

Joe suddenly nudged her and said, "Are you going to eat your little packet of pretzels?"

"No, probably not."

"Could I have them?" he asked. "I like to collect them and take them home for my wife."

Susan gave him a sideways look. "Don't you let her buy groceries while you're away?"

* * *

Several hours later they were pulling their bags and suitcases off the carousel, and arguing about money.

"I'm not changing any of my money into zloty," insisted Pete. "I've heard about the currency out here. It halves in value each day."

"But we have to pay the hotel bills in zloty," Susan explained. "I'm sure that's what Hugh said. He gave me a very hurried briefing, though. I can't remember for sure what he did say."

"I agree with Pete," announced Tom. "I can't handle all this conversion stuff. I vote that we wave a few dollars around when we want to pay for something."

Jim nodded. "Too right. I like to know what I'm paying in real money. That means dollars!"

Susan sighed and gave up. She click-clacked along the polished floors, hurrying along to keep pace with the men. As they made their way out of the empty baggage hall Tom said, "Keep your eyes open and see if there's anyone here to meet us. Someone from Zblatov may be here."

"I can't see anyone holding a placard with "Tom Banks" written on it," said Joe, screwing up his eyes and scanning the thin crowd in the arrivals hall.

"Looks like we're on our own then. We'll have to get a cab."

Joe frowned. "None of us speaks Polish. How are we going to manage?"

"Don't worry," Susan reassured him. "Everyone understands English. And if they pretend not to, just shout very loudly and wave a fifty dollar bill at them."

In the taxi queue Susan gave instructions. "We'll have to split up into two groups. I'll go with Joe and you three follow in the taxi behind." She handed Tom a piece of paper with the hotel name and address written on it.

"Show it to the driver and hope that he knows the way," she continued. "And don't pay more than twenty dollars for the ride."

Fifteen minutes later they were weaving through the streets of Warsaw. Joe was smiling as he looked out of the window.

"I didn't expect the regular hotels. There's the Marriott. And the Metropol. Which one are we staying in?"

Susan decided on distraction tactics.

"Look over there. What a ghastly building."

Joe followed her gaze and saw a monolith of brown stone looming skywards.

"Looks a bit like the Empire State. Must be a nice view from the top."

The taxi sped past another luxury hotel, then made a left turn and followed a wide road that skirted the river. As they travelled along the tree-lined carriageway, Joe stared at the bleak skyline across the river.

"Concrete tower blocks are so ugly, aren't they? And those chimneys must be belching out way over the safety levels. I guess that's the industrial zone. We'd best keep clear of that. I don't want to go home with half a lung."

At that moment the taxi turned right on to a bridge and headed across the river. The driver flung a quick remark in Polish over his shoulder.

"I presume we're nearly there," Susan remarked. "Get your gas mask out."

"Oh," Joe gasped. "But, there's a sign to a zoo. The air can't be that bad. It'll probably be fine," he ended, in a hopeful tone.

Susan gave him a tight-lipped smile, and rummaged in her bag for the itinerary.

A few moments later the taxi stopped outside a derelict-looking building with a faded sign hanging over the double doors of the entrance.

Susan climbed out of the taxi, and hurried into the foyer. She strode up to the desk.

"Reservation for Banks," she proclaimed.

The young man at the desk had sleeked back hair, a gold stud in one earlobe, and a tee-shirt with an Italian name embroidered close to his heart. He looked Susan up and down, then gave her a wide smile. Before Susan had a chance to say anything more, there was a commotion behind them. She looked around in time to see Tom, Jim and Pete coming through the doors, arguing with each other.

"Why did you give him a fifty?" demanded Tom. "I had a twenty."

Pete examined the notes in his hand. "And I had two tens."

"I thought he was going to give me change," seethed Jim. "I didn't know he was going to take off with the fifty! Thieving bastard!"

Tom turned his annoyance on to Susan.

"You call this a hotel?" he snapped. "It looks like a refuge for down and outs! Why the hell are we here?"

"All the good hotels were full," she lied. "There's a wurst convention in town."

Tom glared at her. "A what?"

"A German sausage-makers convention. They come here to sell their sausages to the Poles."

Tom gave her a hard stare, then turned to the desk clerk and said, "Do you have any nice rooms here?" He waved a twenty dollar bill in his hand whilst he was speaking.

The young man shook his head sadly and handed over three keys.

Tom held up the cash once more. "No, we want five keys."

The young man shook his head again, then looked at Susan and winked.

"Just take the keys and let's go upstairs," she said hurriedly to Tom.

As they heaved their bags up the stairs, Jim said, "Bags I share with Susan."

Susan gave him a scornful glare. "Dream on!"

Jim gave her a sly grin. "Well you'd better lock your door, or you'll probably be sharing with the desk clerk."

Susan snatched a key from Tom, and disappeared into one of the rooms, locking the door behind her. She gazed around the room. It was as bad as she had expected. There was an iron bedstead, a cracked washbasin in the corner, and a plywood wardrobe. She unzipped her suitcase, took out a roll of toilet paper, then went out into the corridor to find the loo. When she re-emerged from the toilet, she found Tom wandering along the corridor.

He frowned at the roll in her hand. "Why are you stealing the bathroom tissue."

"It's mine. I brought it with me. Lucky that I did. They don't seem to provide any here."

Tom grimaced. "This is some wonderful hotel that you've booked us into. There's not even a shower in my room."

"Mine neither," she complained, trying to sound surprised.

"I'll go and ask the guy at reception if there's a shower room somewhere."

He mooched off, muttering to himself.

Susan went back into her room and locked the door. She washed her hands and face, then stretched out on the bed, wondering how she could get her hands on a bottle of martini.

Ten minutes later there was a knock at the door.

"Who is it?"

"It's me," Tom replied. "Open up. This is urgent."

Susan opened the door and Tom darted in.

"Susan, sweetness, can I borrow some of your bathroom tissue?"

Susan wrinkled her nose. "What do you mean "borrow"? I certainly don't want it back after you've used it!"

"Don't play games, I'm desperate. Could I have a roll? Please please, pretty please?"

"No, I need it for myself."

Tom pressed his lips together. "I see. Well, you may like to know that I have the key to the shower room. I had to give the desk clerk ten dollars for it. Me and the boys will take a shower in turn, so that we don't have to pay him again. But if you don't give me some bathroom tissue, you won't get a turn. I'll give the key back to the desk clerk, and if you want to take a shower you'll have to go and ask him nicely for it."

Susan curled her lip. "All right."

She heaved her suitcase on to the bed, unzipped it and threw back the lid. Tom's eyes widened in surprise.

"Jeez! How many rolls of Andrex do you have in there?"

"Sixteen."

"Are you expecting to get dysentery?"

"I'll remind you of that after your first salad. Here, have this one. And don't waste it."

Tom gave her a bemused glance, then sprinted out of the room, clutching his paper roll.

* * *

In Tom's room, the following morning, Jim and Pete were counting their dollar bills, whilst Tom was shaving. There was a knock at the door, and Pete opened it to see the desk clerk standing there.

"Buz," he said, nodding his head sideways.

"What's he on about?" Jim murmured.

"I guess he means the tour bus is outside waiting for us," said Pete. "I'll go down and take a look."

An hour later, the door opened and Joe peered in.

"Can I hang around in here?" he asked. "It's a bit dull sitting in the room on my own."

Jim frowned. "Isn't Pete back yet?"

"Well, he came in and got something from his suitcase, then he said something about going shopping, and he went out again."

Tom was collecting his luggage together, and he said to Joe, "Go and knock on Susan's door, make sure she's ready to leave."

Jim chuckled. "Pretend that you're the desk clerk, and give her a fright."

When they went down to reception to pay their bills, Pete was leaning on the counter, waiting for them. Tom took several dollar bills from his wallet and waved them at the desk clerk saying, "How much?"

The desk clerk took a sheet of paper, wrote on it, and handed it to Tom.

"What's this mean?" asked Tom. "It says "Levi x 1". I thought the currency here was zloty, not Levi."

Pete glanced at the paper. "Tck. He's obviously been talking to Janek."

"Who's Janek?"

"The bus driver. I gave him a pair of Levis to help me get some shopping. I guess this guy wants a pair, too."

Pete laid his suitcase on the floor and opened it up.

Tom gasped. "How many pairs of jeans do you have in there?"

"Thirty," Pete told him, as he handed a pair of denim jeans to the desk clerk. "Everybody out here wants them. They're as good as hard currency. I'll make a killing."

The desk clerk examined the jeans, then nodded and shook Pete's hand.

"C'mon, lets go," said Pete. The band picked up their bags and trooped outside.

The street was deserted except for a dilapidated old bus, which was parked close to the hotel entrance. Tom stopped in his tracks, dropped his suitcase and bag on the pavement, then stood with his hands on his hips and stared at the tour bus. Susan tried to hide behind Jim, but he stepped sideways as Tom swung around to confront her.

"Have the wurst convention got all the best buses too?"

She scowled at him. "It was the best that they could do at such short notice."

Jim surveyed the bus, and remarked, "Looks as if it usually carries chickens."

"Oh, stop being so fussy," Susan snapped. "This is how the other half live, you know."

Joe nodded. "She's right. We should take this as an opportunity to re-assess our own superficial values and living standards. It could be an uplifting experience."

"We do have some uplifting spirits on the bus," Pete told them. "Janek helped me to get them."

As Susan climbed on to the bus she saw a sturdy young man stacking cardboard boxes between the seats. His sandy hair was almost shoulder-length, and it curled around his chubby face, giving him a slightly cherubic air. He fixed her with an amiable smile.

"Hello. I am Janek, buz driver."

"What's in the boxes?" she asked.

Pete pointed to each in turn. "Whiskey in this one, vodka over there, beer in those four, and vermouth in that one."

"I'm not sure that Susan deserves any vermouth," Tom said sourly. "We'll see what the next hotel is like before we give her any."

Susan pulled a face at him and sat down next to the box of martini.

"Let's get going to the venue," said Tom. "I want plenty of time to check on the sound equipment."

As the bus made the short journey across town, Jim said to Pete, "Where did you get all the jeans?"

"In England."

"I thought you were broke."

"I used my poker winnings," Pete explained. "And you all owe me for the hotel bills and the booze. I'll write out some invoices later."

* * *

Susan was waiting in the dressing room towards the end of the show, trying to find something to occupy herself with. She was beginning to wish that she had brought a suitcase full of books, instead of loo paper. Her back still ached from the lumpy mattress in the dingy hotel, and she had a numb bum from sitting on a moulded plastic seat for most of the day. If she was going to survive this trip, she would need a good supply of liquid comfort, that was for sure.

The rumble of drums above her peaked to a crashing crescendo. There was a second of silence, then a roar of applause broke overhead, pierced by whoops and shrill whistles. Susan stood up and gathered up the carrier bag that that the hall manager had given her. She had made a brief inspection of the paperwork, then shoved it smartly back inside the bag as the smell of stale cigarette smoke attacked her nostrils.

The door was suddenly pushed open, and Janek lurched in clutching a case of beer to his chest.

Susan frowned. "Are we having a party?"

He shrugged. "They tell me bring beer for finish." He dumped the beer on the floor, ripped open the cardboard and pulled out a small bottle.

"Don't even think about it," she said, sharply. "You've got to drive the bus."

Janek muttered something under his breath and clinked the bottle back into its slot. Then he pulled a cigarette case form his jacket pocket and flipped open the lid. As he extracted a black cigarette Susan gasped.

"What's that?"

Janek held out the case to her.

"My grandfather, he make. He very clever man."

"Idiot. I meant the black ciggie." Susan's eye was now caught by the blue and gold cigarette case, and she took it from Janek

She turned the enamelled case in her hand. The glazed blue finish was embellished with a gold sunburst effect, at the centre of which was a miniature portrait of a small child. Close to the edges of the box, tiny golden laurel leaves traced a path through the translucent azure.

"It's a bit fancy for a bloke," she remarked, handing it back to Janek.

Moments later there was a clattering of feet along the corridor, and the sound of jubilant male voices mingled with a few feminine giggles. The noisy rabble burst into the room.

"These Poles really enjoy their music, don't they!" exclaimed Tom. "It's nice to be appreciated again. Especially by pretty girls," he added, smiling at the young girl who was clutching his arm.

Susan glared at Tom.

"I always thought "press the flesh" meant shaking hands with the fans. I didn't realise it meant groping under-age females. I hope her dad doesn't turn up looking for her. He's probably younger than you. With bigger fists."

"Don't give me a hard time," he snapped. "I'll party if I want to."

"I don't think so. Janek, put the beer back on the bus."

Janek heaved the box off the floor and staggered out of the dressing room, with a procession of complaining people close on his heels.

As the room emptied, Tom turned angrily to Susan.

"Where do you get off, telling me and my band what to do? You're just a passenger here! I'm in charge."

Susan thrust the smelly carrier bag at him. "Right then, if you're in charge, you can sort out these ticket receipt schedules, and make sure that everything tallies."

She turned on her heel and strode out to the bus.

"Shit," muttered Tom.

He picked up his bag and followed her on to the bus, then he sat down beside her and smiled.

"C'mon. Let's not fight. I wasn't going to get up to anything with her, I swear."

"I don't care who you drool over. I'm just doing my job as minder."

"Are we friends again?"

Susan eyed him suspiciously. "What are you after?"

"You know I'm no good with numbers," Tom whispered, putting his mouth close to her ear.

She traced her finger gently along his thigh. "Let me have a bottle of martini, and I'll do all the paperwork."

Tom yawned. "Sure. Help yourself." He shoved the carrier bag into Susan's hands, then he stumbled to the back of the bus, stretched himself across the long seat and closed his eyes.

CHAPTER 6

Nine hours later, Susan woke up with a dry throat and a headache. The hard bus seat was uncomfortable to sleep in. The martini had sent her off to sleep, but had also given her the headache. The sight of Tom's scarlet tee shirt was too much for her eyes, so she closed them again.

Jim was stretching and yawning. "It would have been more comfortable to travel with my drums in the big rig," he complained.

He stood up and tripped over an empty vodka bottle, and cursed as he made his way to the front of the bus. He exchanged a few words with Janek, and shortly afterwards the bus came to a halt beside a small clump of bushes. Jim leapt out and disappeared behind the bushes, and returned soon afterwards in a happier mood.

"That's not very hygienic," Joe admonished him. "You could have waited until we found a public convenience."

Jim shrugged. "When you gotta go, you gotta go."

"I'm feeling the need myself," Joe admitted. "That meal I had last night has upset my stomach."

Jim was unsympathetic. "What did you expect, eating a plate-full of beans? You should have anticipated the consequences."

"It was the only vegetarian dish on the menu," Joe protested, "But I can see now that it was a mistake, stuck out on this road in the middle of nowhere."

"I'll ask Janek to keep a look-out for a rest room for you," offered Jim. "We might find one at a gas station."

Twenty minutes later Janek duly pulled the bus into a petrol station, and he pointed out the toilet to Joe. Joe hurried off the bus and sprinted away. A minute later he re-appeared, and climbed back on to the bus with a puzzled look on his face.

"You were quick," remarked Jim.

"I didn't go."

"Why not?"

Joe frowned. "Someone has stolen the toilet. There's a hole in the ground where it should be."

"What!"

Jim's shriek woke Pete and Tom.

Susan got out of her seat and made her way to the toilet. She peered inside, then went back to the bus and scolded Joe.

"Idiot. It's a squat loo."

"A what?"

"It's a toilet without a seat. You have to squat over the hole. They're quite common in Europe. There's a nail in the doorpost where you can hang your trousers. Hold the tissue paper in your mouth. You'll manage all right."

Joe returned to the toilet, clutching a supply of tissue paper. Ten minutes later he re-emerged and got back on to the bus.

"Feeling better now?" Jim asked.

"Yes and no," Joe answered, wrinkling his nose.

"What do you mean?"

"Well, I was doing ok, but then I lost my balance and my foot slipped down the hole."

"Oh man! Take your trainers off and hang them out of the window," Pete implored.

"And I thought the smell was chicken shit," Tom mumbled, as he drifted back to sleep.

* * *

It was lunchtime when they reached Krakow. They drove through the town and out into the countryside again. As they went along, Joe suddenly pointed to a road sign and said, "Look, this is the way to the zoo. It's just like Warsaw again."

Tom frowned and said darkly to Susan, "You'll be in big trouble if this hotel is like the last one!"

"This is a very popular town with tourists," she responded, dimly recalling something that the travel agent had said to her. "There are lots of medieval buildings here. The best hotels are usually fully booked."

Tom gave her a hard stare, but said nothing more.

The road climbed upward, and as they reached the summit of the hill, Joe gasped and pointed.

"Wow, look at that place! Looks like some sort of castle."

"It's probably the city jail," remarked Jim.

They were all taken aback when Janek stopped the bus outside the castle.

"We're not doing any sightseeing today, Janek," Jim shouted to him. "Just get us to the hotel, we're tired out."

"Yes, yes," nodded Janek. "This hotel. Nice, no?"

"Good grief," mumbled Susan. "It looks like something from "Prisoner of Zenda"."

"This is great," cried Joe. "We're staying in a genuine castle! My wife would love this. I wonder if they have four-poster beds?"

Pete was less enthusiastic. "I wonder if they have indoor plumbing."

"We'll probably find that our rooms are in the dungeons," Tom added.

As the reception desk clerk handed over three keys to them, Tom groaned and said, "How come we're sharing again?"

Susan tried to bluff her way through. "This is a very exclusive place, we were lucky to get rooms here at all. I thought you might enjoy the medieval surroundings."

She tried to sprint off down the corridor with one of the keys, but Tom quickly grabbed her arm.

"Hold up, if one of the rooms has got a shower, then it's mine."

Susan bristled with indignation. "Who do you expect me to share with?"

"Frankly my dear, I don't give a damn."

Tom darted in and out of each of the three rooms, and came to rest muttering, "They're all the same, no bathrooms. Susan, you can go and find the shower room for me. When you've done that, you can have the key to your room."

"What did your last slave die of?" she grumbled, as she walked back to the reception desk.

* * *

That evening they were having a meal in the hotel restaurant, admiring the view across the valley to Krakow.

"I see you've re-joined the world of meat-eaters," Pete commented, as he watched Joe eating chicken and fries.

Joe winced. "I didn't fancy beans again."

As Tom sipped his beer he said to Susan, "Are you coming to the show tonight?"

"No, I'll stay here and check the ticket receipts from Warsaw. I want an early night anyway. I feel like death on a stick after spending the night on that bus. I'll see you all at breakfast tomorrow. And don't pick up any girls just because I'm not there to keep an eye on you. The sponsors don't want any bad publicity."

Joe gave her a hurt look. "We're not all obsessed with girls. Some of us like to be faithful to our loved-ones at home."

"Don't you ever fancy a taste of something different?" Jim asked.

Joe gave a saintly smile. "Why should I go out for a hamburger when I can have steak at home."

As Pete stabbed at his fries he grumbled, "Some of us only have meatloaf at home."

Susan grimaced. "I bet you really hate it when he sings in the shower."

* * *

The next morning, when Susan went down to have breakfast, she scanned the dining room for the band. Joe was sitting on his own, with his shoulders slumped and his head bent over his plate. She sat down next to him and said, "How was the show? Are the others still in bed?"

Joe shifted nervously in his seat. "The show was great. We did three encores. Then we met loads of people backstage, and things got a bit confused."

He stared down into his cup of coffee.

"What do you mean, "confused"?" Susan asked sharply.

Joe hesitated, then said, "We've lost Jim."

"I don't believe it! I can't trust you lot for five minutes! Where did you last see him?"

"In the dressing room. He was having a beer and talking to a couple of girls, and the next thing we knew, he'd gone. He's probably at someone's apartment, sleeping it off. Anyway, Janek and Pete have gone looking for him."

"So where's Tom?"

Joe chewed his lip. "I'm not quite sure. He definitely came back to the hotel with us after the show, but he seems to have vanished now, as well."

Susan sighed. "You lot need a gaoler, not an escort. Well I'm going to have breakfast and do some sightseeing later on. Those two are big enough to find their own way home. You and I can have a peaceful day of cultural activities."

Joe smiled and nodded in agreement.

* * *

An hour later, Susan was in her room rinsing out some underwear in the washbasin, when there was a knock at the door. She opened the door and stared in astonishment. Jim was standing there, wearing a long black skirt, and clutching a plastic bag in his hand. He dashed into her room.

"Are you on your way to a fancy-dress party, or just returning from one?" she asked.

"I'm looking for Tom. I can't get into our room. He has the key. Do you know where he is?"

"Your guess is as good as mine. Maybe he's at the party that you've been to."

"This ain't funny," Jim said testily. "I've been robbed!"

"Oh no, don't tell me you've lost your passport!"

"No, I have my passport and wallet in here," Jim replied, shaking the plastic bag.

"What did they steal, then?"

"My jeans."

Susan stifled a giggle, and tried not to stare at Jim's hairy ankles.

Jim opened the door a crack and peered into the corridor.

"Where are they all?" he said impatiently. "There's no-one in Joe's room either."

"Pete and Janek are out looking for you, and Joe has gone for a walk."

She frowned pensively, and remarked, "I don't think black is really your colour. Though maybe a pencil skirt would look better on you than this pleated one. Couldn't you find a handbag to match? The plastic bag isn't very chic."

Jim scowled at her, then turned back to peering through the doorway.

"At last!" he exclaimed.

Susan edged around him and saw Tom and Joe striding down the hallway towards them. As Tom approached his door, Jim leapt out of hiding.

Tom stared at Jim for a long moment, looked him up and down, then raised an eyebrow. "Jim, I know that you like high heels and black stockings, but it's usually more fun if the girl puts them on."

"Whatever happened?" Joe asked.

"Well, I went to an apartment with those two girls, and we had a nice time," Jim recounted, with a fleeting smile. "But when I woke up this morning the girls were gone, and so were my jeans. My billfold was on the floor, along with my shoes, but my jeans had vanished. I found this skirt in a closet, so I put it on and managed to get a cab back here."

As he finished his explanation, Pete rounded a corner of the corridor. He paused briefly as he saw Jim, and shook his head as he approached.

"I don't know why I wasted my energy looking for you," Pete muttered with resignation. "You've obviously been having a great time."

"I'll take you along next time, I promise. Could I have a pair of jeans from outta your suitcase? Lucky for me you have so many."

Pete nodded. "Sure. Fifty dollars."

"What! You want me to pay for them?"

"Of course. Business is business."

"But you bought them with my money," Jim complained. "The money that you won off me!"

Susan sniggered and said to Tom, "You can come and sit in my room if you want. Jim needs a little privacy, so that he can shave his legs."

* * *

They spent the following day traveling to Wroclaw. Around mid-day they pulled into a lay-by that was bounded by a small copse. They clambered off the bus to stretch their legs, and Janek got out a small gas camping stove, which he placed on the bottom step of the bus. He set a pot of coffee to brew, then pulled his cigarette case from his pocket and lit up one of his black cheroots. The sun glinted on the case as he closed it.

Susan held out her hand. "Can I look at that again?"

Janek passed the case to her with a curious smile. "The ladies, they all like this one."

Susan caught her breath as she examined the intricate detail on the enamel case, seeing it in daylight for the first time. Tiny sparkles danced over its gold and blue surface. She turned it gently around in her hand, mesmerized by the opulent colours.

"It's not real gold though, is it? And they're not real diamonds?"

Janek shrugged, and said nothing.

Susan examined the tiny portrait set in the center of the case. The girlish face was framed with bouncing curls, and crowned by a fur hat.

"Is this your sister?"

Janek shook his head.

"Little girl who live next door to grandfather. She has right kind of face."

"Hey, Janek! Is that coffee ready yet?" Tom called from the gate that he was leaning on, a short distance away.

Janek turned his attention back to the stove, and Susan wandered off towards Tom. She stood beside him and gazed at the landscape. The field sloped away downhill, and at the bottom end she could see a couple of goats grazing. She turned to Tom, sniffed noisily and plucked at his scarlet tee shirt.

"You've been wearing this for a couple of days. It's a bit whiffy. Why don't you hang it over the gate while we're having our coffee. Give it a bit of an airing."

"Gee, I'm sorry. I didn't realize. I'll get a fresh one to put on."

Tom swiftly pulled the shirt over his head, and handed it to Susan. As he walked back to the bus, Susan climbed on to the gate and shook the tee shirt vigorously. Then she draped it over the adjacent hedge so that most of the shirt was hanging on the other side.

As they stood drinking their coffee, Susan said to Tom in a matter-of-fact tone, "I don't recall seeing that red tee shirt before. Did you have a wash-day disaster?"

He shook his head. "I got it just before we left Bristol," he replied, "At a market stall. They were real cheap."

"I'm surprised they weren't giving them away," she murmured.

They rested there for an hour, then they shook out their cups and Janek packed the stove away.

"I gotta take a leak. Don't forget my shirt," Tom called to Susan, as he sprinted towards the trees.

"Oh, lucky you reminded me," she replied, smiling sweetly at him.

She walked back to the hedge and pulled at the shirt. There was a bleating noise from the other side of the hedge, and an annoyed goat looked up at her, with half the shirt protruding from its mouth.

"Oh no!" she cried. "Tom, this awful goat has eaten your nice shirt!"

Tom strode to the hedge and looked down at the munching goat.

"Tck! Never mind. I've got another two."

Susan had a sudden sinking feeling. "You've got more than two tee shirts, surely."

"Yeah, of course I have. And don't call me Shirley. What I meant was, I have another two in that colour. They were doing three for the price of two."

"I didn't realize you were such an astute bargain hunter," she muttered from between clenched teeth.

CHAPTER 7

As they drove into Wroclaw that afternoon, Janek started pointing out of the bus windows and talking excitedly in his broken English.

"What's he on about?" Tom murmured.

"I think he's pointing out the medieval architecture to us," said Joe, "Showing us the interesting places to visit."

"Sort of," said Jim. "He lives in Wroclaw. I asked him to point out the best beer halls to us. He reckons that the beer here is the finest in Poland."

Janek brought the bus to a halt outside a Victorian-style edifice, with wrought-iron balconies overlooking the street.

Susan checked her itinerary. "This must be the hotel. I presume Janek knows where he is."

Joe stretched his neck to view the buildings around them. "What marvellous architecture the Europeans have."

Tom gave a disparaging grunt. "I guess all the plumbers emigrated to the States and left the architects here."

As the clerk at reception handed over the usual three keys, Tom gave a loud groan and said, "Sharing again, what a surprise."

Janek had brought in their bags, and was carrying them up the stairs, talking in an animated fashion to Joe, who was gazing about him with an expression of awe.

They made a quick inspection of the rooms, then Tom sent Janek off to search for the shower room.

Joe said, "Why don't you take this room? It has a bath."

"I don't like baths," growled Tom. "I want a shower."

"This is such an interesting hotel," Joe said eagerly. "Janek was telling me that Adolf Hitler used to stay here."

"Really?" said Pete, as he emerged from the bathroom. "I wonder if he brought his own bath plug."

Joe breezed on. "Apparently, Hitler would stand out on the balcony and address the crowds. It's awesome, being in such a historic place."

Tom waited for Joe to finish, then he pursed his lips in displeasure and turned to confront Susan.

"So, Susan, how come we have rooms without private facilities again? No, don't tell me, let me guess. You thought that we'd appreciate the historical surroundings."

He eyed her suspiciously and continued, "It's kinda strange, you know. Considering what an efficient girl you are, you haven't done much of a job booking our hotels."

"I'm an accountant, not a travel agent!" she snapped at him. "I was doing it as a favour for Hugh, because he couldn't cope with all the work. I wish now that I hadn't bothered! If you think that I'm useless then I might as well fly back to England and get out of your way," she ended, with her nose in the air.

Tom smiled at her and said, "Nice try, but you're not getting out of it that easily. Where we go, you go."

Susan scowled. She had hoped that Tom would be glad to get rid of her. The thought of trekking through the East, staying in dire hotels, was beginning to depress her.

"At least we'll get a nice bus in Prague," she muttered.

"We'd better!" Tom said, curtly. "Or the box of vermouth will end its journey there!"

* * *

"We haven't got far to go to the gig tonight. It's just next door," said Joe, later that evening.

Jim grinned. "Yeah, Janek reckons we can do a good tour of the beer halls after the show."

"So, no hanging around backstage tonight," ordered Tom. "Girls and beer don't mix."

Susan sat silently, looking downcast, as they ate their dinner in the elegant hotel dining room.

Tom noticed her long face. "What's wrong with you, sourpuss?"

"What am I supposed to do while you're all out having fun?" she complained.

"Count the ticket receipts."

"Oh, that's not fair," protested Joe. "I think that Susan should come along, if she wants to."

Jim said swiftly, "She doesn't want to. Girls don't like going out on a binge."

Susan glared at him.

Tom wrinkled his brow. "Maybe we should let her come along. If we leave her here alone, we might come back to find her standing out on the balcony, telling people what to do."

Susan resisted the temptation to smack him in the face with a starched napkin. She gave him a tight smile and replied, "Thank you Tom, I'd love to come along,"

Jim smiled at his plate and said appreciatively, "The food here is really good."

"Yeah," agreed Tom. "I usually eat better when I'm on the road than when I'm at home. My cooking ain't up to much." Then he frowned pensively and said in a puzzled tone, "You know, it's really strange. Sometimes I get food out of the refrigerator, and when I look at the use-by date, I see that the stuff has expired. And I can't understand it, because I only bought it the previous week, and I usually get things that have a two-week shelf life. Then I begin to think that maybe I've been transported into outer space by aliens, and held in their spacecraft for a week or so, and they erased my memory of it when they returned me to Earth."

"Huh!" scoffed Susan. "Your memory loss is more likely due to being transported by half a bottle of scotch every night!"

Tom chewed his lip. "Umm, that is an alternative explanation."

* * *

At eleven-thirty that night, they were sitting in a subterranean bar, with loud rock music being blasted at them. Janek was lurching back and forth in front of three girls, whilst Susan and the others watched.

"Is he dancing, or is it some sort of mating ritual?" pondered Jim.

Susan shrugged. "Comes down to the same thing, really."

"I thought they were following us out of the concert hall. I didn't realise it was Janek they were interested in," said Jim, glumly. "What's he got that we haven't?"

"A full head of hair and a waistline," Susan retorted.

Tom raised his tankard aloft and said, "The beer's good, anyhow. The rednecks at home would love this brew." He turned to Susan and said, "I don't suppose you know what a redneck is."

"Yes I do," she replied. "A redneck is someone who's been to too many hoe-downs."

Tom frowned. "What on earth are you talking about?"

"When you put your hoe down, you have to be careful where you step," she explained, "Because if you tread on the head, the handle whips up and whacks you on the side of the neck."

Jim raised his eyebrows. "What is she drinking?"

"What ever it is, take it away from her," Pete advised.

* * *

"What time is it?" asked Joe, trying to keep his eyes open.

Jim glanced at his watch. "About two."

Joe peered at the jazz band on the small stage. "Is that Tom up there?"

"Yeah," Jim replied. "He can't resist an invitation to a jam session."

Pete was sitting with his elbows resting on the table, his head in his hands, studying his drink. "I think he likes pianos more than he likes girls," he said, solemnly.

Jim slowly swirled his drink, and remarked, "Pianos are less trouble."

Susan giggled. "They take up more space in bed, though."

"But at least they don't steal all the blankets," Jim argued.

"Do you think that pizza place is still open?" mused Joe. "I really fancy a pizza. My wife makes wonderful pizza. I wish I was at home."

"It's wunnerful being away from home," slurred Susan. "I don't have to do any housework. I hate housework. Especially dusting. I really hate dusting. Someone should invent self-dusting furniture," she mumbled, as she groped across the table.

Jim clicked his tongue. "You talk such rubbish."

"It's not rubbish. We've got self-cleaning ovens, so why not self-dusting furniture? It's a logical step forward," she insisted, still searching the table for her glass. "Why are these clubs always so dark?" she complained, as she knocked a glass sideways.

"So that you spill half your drink and have to buy another one," Pete replied sagely, as he gazed intently into his beer.

Susan held her glass in front of her eyes and squinted through the cigarette fog. "That bloke playing the piano up there looks just like Tom."

Jim sighed. "It is Tom."

Susan started to sway in time to the music, and she mumbled, "I know this tune. It's that old blues song, "I got my moped working"."

Jim rolled his eyes and said loudly, "Mojo."

"More what?" asked Joe, looking confused.

Jim became exasperated. "No, no. Mojo!"

Susan elbowed Pete sharply. "What's he on about?"

"Dunno. He's probably drunk," muttered Pete, as he slid sideways off his chair.

* * *

On Friday morning, they assembled at reception just before noon, subdued and bleary-eyed. The girl behind the desk handed over their bills, and gave a telex to Tom. Tom managed to focus his eyes, and gasped in surprise as he read the message.

"Wonders will never cease."

"What is it?" asked Jim.

"It's from the man from Zblatov. His name's Tyreman. He says that he'll meet us in Prague at his hotel, the Grand."

Tom turned to Susan. "Are we staying in that hotel?"

She rummaged in her bag, found the itinerary and held it under her nose.

"No," she said eventually, when the words had stopped moving in front of her eyes.

"Well maybe we'll get some proper organisation on this tour when we meet this guy," Tom said scathingly, as he started counting out his zloty notes.

Susan paid her bill and waited for the others. As they were slowly counting out their notes she said sarcastically, "Having trouble with your arithmetic this morning, boys?"

Tom eyed her darkly and replied, "What ever you were drinking last night, it cost us a small fortune. We haven't got enough cash to pay our bills. You can buy your own drinks in future. Hand over all the zloty that you have left."

Susan emptied her wallet, and after another recount Tom said to the clerk, "Can we pay in dollars?"

She shook her head and said helpfully, "Exchange office just down street. I will make map for you to follow."

Tom clicked his tongue in annoyance and said, "Where's Janek? He could sort this out for us. Is he outside on the bus?"

Jim sprinted outside and returned shaking his head. "Guess he's still sleeping it off somewhere."

Tom pushed a bundle of dollars at Jim. "Here. Take fifty bucks and go down to the exchange place."

"Why me?" grumbled Jim, as he pushed the money into his pocket. "It's three blocks away." He walked off, muttering to himself.

Ten minutes later, Janek hurried into the hotel. He started to apologise for being late, but was interrupted by the sudden reappearance of Jim.

"You were quick," Tom remarked. "Did you run all the way?"

"I didn't go to the exchange office," Jim replied. "There were a couple of guys hanging around by the underpass, and they offered to change the money for me. They gave me a good rate, too."

Janek looked alarmed, and he snatched the bundle of notes from Jim's hand. He quickly flicked through the cash, uttering groans and exclamations as he went.

"What's up?" demanded Tom.

"Money no good!" wailed Janek. "No good!"

He waved the notes at the desk clerk, whilst talking excitedly and gesticulating wildly. She nodded sympathetically and shrugged her shoulders.

Tom picked up the bundle of notes and looked through it. Below the top five zloty notes there was a wad of newspaper, cut down to bank-note size.

Tom cursed, then said sardonically, "Well done, Jim. You paid fifty dollars for some newsprint."

Susan rolled her eyes. "If we sent him out for a newspaper, I wonder what he'd come back with?"

Janek emptied his pockets on to the counter, and handed over a few bank notes to the clerk.

"What about these?" asked Susan, offering the five notes above the newsprint.

"Old money. No good," explained Janek.

The desk clerk counted up all their notes once more, and spoke to Janek, nodding her head.

"She say we can go. She like show last night. No matter about money," Janek translated.

As they boarded the bus, Tom said, "Susan, sweetheart, can I have some of your aspirin. I have a slight headache."

"Are the chickens riding with us all the way to Prague?" Jim asked Janek, nodding at the two cages of clucking hens on the back seat of the bus.

"No," said Janek, shaking his head. "Chickens get off at Gora and get taxi."

Jim laughed. "You're a real funny guy."

"I could do without the smell off of them, that's for sure," grumbled Pete.

Joe protested, "You can't blame the chickens."

"Too right!" Susan butted in. "Most of the odour is due to the large quantity of black beer that you lot consumed last night." She moved to the back of the bus, to sit near the hens.

"You've obviously travelled with chickens before," Jim remarked.

"Yes, as a matter of fact I have," she replied. "I was visiting relatives in Italy one time, and we travelled around in my cousin's little Fiat Fivehundred - five of us and a hen."

Tom frowned. "Why where you traveling with a hen?"

"There wasn't room for the cow."

A couple of hours later, they stopped outside a cafe in a small town up in the hills. Two men emerged from the cafe and exchanged vigorous handshakes with Janek. The chickens were taken off the bus and deposited in the back seat of a battered old taxi that was parked nearby. Several wads of notes changed hands, and one of the men got into the taxi and drove off down the road at a reckless speed.

Jim called down the bus to Susan. "Did your friends promise to write?"

Janek climbed back on to the bus with the other man, saying to them, "This my brother, Karol. He take bus back to Warsaw."

The bus lurched away, as the two brothers talked and laughed, whilst giving each other friendly punches across the steering wheel.

* * *

Shortly afterwards they arrived at the Czech border. A couple of bored-looking youths in uniform gazed at the bus as it pulled to a halt. One of them walked over to the bus, and Janek obligingly opened up the door. The guard climbed inside the bus, then wrinkled his nose in distaste and quickly leapt out again. He beckoned to Janek, who quickly collected all the passports and took them out to the guard. The guard glanced briefly at the covers, then waved them away.

As they drove off, Jim looked out at the incomprehensible Czech signposts, and remarked to no-one in particular, "Is it illegal to use vowels in this part of Europe?"

* * *

"Susan, do you have directions to the hotel on your itinerary?" asked Jim. "Janek doesn't know this side of Prague too well."

It was a dark, rainy evening, and Janek had slowed down to study the motorway exit signs. Susan went to the front of the bus and showed the hotel name and address to Karol. His face lit up with recognition and he quickly spoke to Janek.

"Does Karol know the way?" Jim asked.

"Yes," Janek called back. "Camp near zoo."

Groans emanated from Pete and Tom, and Susan crept back to her seat as the bus swung off the motorway to follow the elephant signposts.

"What does he mean, "camp"? Are we sleeping under canvas tonight?" demanded Tom, as Susan slipped past.

"No, it's a hotel, I'm sure it is," she replied, fervently hoping that she was right.

A few miles later, Janek stopped outside a restaurant, and Karol gestured that they had arrived. They clambered off with their bags, and Janek pulled off again to find a parking space.

Karol led them through to the back of the restaurant, then on to a hotel reception desk. After picking up the usual three keys, Tom sighed and said, "Well, we can take a guess at what the rooms are going to be like. I vote that we have a meal and a few drinks before we crash out."

CHAPTER 8

"Jim! Jim! Are you awake?" Tom hissed, after he had opened his eyes and looked around him, next morning.

"Ugh, I am now," mumbled Jim, raising his head from the pillow. "You don't usually wake me up so cruelly. What's the matter?"

"I think we've died and gone to heaven," whispered Tom. "We're sleeping inside a beer keg!"

Jim opened his eyes and gazed about him. "It sure looks like a beer keg. But is it heaven or is it hell? It's a beer keg with no beer in it."

Tom said thoughtfully, "Hmm. Maybe "Hell" is being trapped inside an empty beer keg for eternity."

A loud snore interrupted their theological discussion.

Tom frowned. "What's that?"

Jim hoisted himself on one elbow, and peered around the room. He squinted at the heaving mound on the floor near his bed. "It's Janek in his sleeping bag."

Tom groaned as he sat up. "Did someone hit me on the back of the head with a baseball bat last night?"

"Not that I recall," said Jim. "But last night is a bit of a blur. I don't even remember coming in here."

A rapid knocking at the door startled them both, and woke up Janek.

Jim stumbled to the door, and found Joe standing outside. He bounded into the room, and said, "Isn't this amazing! Susan has done a wonderful job, finding all these unusual hotels. I have photos of all of them so far. Get dressed and Karol will take a photo of us all outside the keg."

From his prone position on the floor, Janek grinned at them and said, "Hope you not mind, I sleep here. I carry you here last night, from bar."

"Yeah, sure. Thanks Janek," Tom murmured, as he yawned and searched for his clothes.

* * *

"We'll split into two groups," said Tom. "We don't all need to go to meet this guy, Tyreman. Me, Jim and Susan will go, and Joe and Pete can go with Janek, to check out the venue for tonight's show. We'll meet you there."

They were discussing the plan of action over breakfast.

Tom turned to Susan. "Where are we staying after the show tonight?"

She consulted her itinerary. "Uh, it's Saturday today, isn't it? No hotel tonight. Off stage and on to bus."

Joe clicked his tongue. "But I wanted to see Prague. I've already bought a guide-book. There's lots of places that I want to visit."

"This is work, not a vacation," Tom replied.

Joe hung his head and fell silent.

"After tonight, the next show isn't until Tuesday," Susan said, studying the itinerary. "We could stay a couple of days, if we can find hotel rooms."

Joe pleaded. "Could we stay here? It's such a quaint place."

Tom nodded. "I guess so. Go and check with reception."

Joe rushed off, but returned several minutes later, disconsolate.

"They can't extend our stay. She said they're full. She said that Prague hotels are always full."

* * *

Inside the Grand hotel, Jim went to up the front desk to ask for Mr. Tyreman's room number. Susan and Tom wandered about, admiring the sumptuous decor. As Tom gazed at the chandeliers and ornate drapes, he remarked, "It reminds me of a place I used to know in New Orleans. A house of ill repute."

Susan raised an eyebrow.

Tom explained, "I used to work there."

As Susan raised both eyebrows, Tom hastily added, "Playing the piano."

When Jim rejoined them, he said, "It's a pity we can't get rooms here. It's real plush. Though it might be dangerous for Susan. Short people can vanish without trace in deep-pile carpet."

Susan was lost in thought. "I wonder if Mr. Tyreman could use a companion," she murmured. "He obviously likes to travel in style."

"You mean you'd dump us just to get a room in a luxury hotel?" said Jim. "Think how much Tom would miss you!"

Susan gave him an icy glare.

They found Mr. Tyreman's room, and Tom knocked briskly at the door. The door was opened by a slender man who beamed enthusiastically when he saw them.

"Hello, I'm Terry Tyreman. Nice to meet you at last. I'm terribly sorry that I wasn't in Warsaw to meet you. I had to go to Germany on urgent business."

Terry ushered them into the spacious room, and sat them around an ornate coffee table. Susan sat beside him, and caught a whiff of perfumed French soap. His face was baby-smooth, as if he had just shaved, and his clear skin was sprinkled with a handful of pale freckles.

"How's the tour going?" Terry asked. "Is everything running smoothly?"

Tom responded curtly. "Not exactly. We've had a bit of trouble with our accommodation." He shot a sideways glare at Susan.

"Oh, I can sort that out for you, don't worry luv," Terry answered, running a hand over his well-groomed sandy hair. "Just tell me what you need. I've got friends all over the place."

Before Tom could speak, Susan cut in, "We'd be very grateful if we could get hotel rooms in Prague for a couple of days." She smiled sweetly at Terry and fluttered her eyelashes wildly.

"Yeah, and I'd like you to look over our itinerary for the rest of the tour," Tom added. "See what you think of the hotels that have been booked."

Terry pouted. "Mmm. I do have a copy of your route, and I must say that I was a bit surprised by your reservations."

"Things got a bit mixed up," Susan muttered.

Terry flashed a dazzling smile at her. "Don't worry dear, I'll sort it out for you. I'll just get some coffee first."

He made a telephone call to room service, requesting coffee for five, then he dialed again and had a brief conversation in German.

"All sorted luvs," he said, after replacing the receiver. "I've got a good friend at the floating hotel. He's found rooms for you there. It's a super place." He wrinkled his nose in an expression of childish delight.

He wrote an address down on the back of a business card and handed it to Susan.

Just then the door opened and Terry exclaimed, "Well, it's about time! I was beginning to think that you'd run away from home."

The man who had stepped into the room replied, "There were a few problems, but it is all right now."

"This is Ahmed," Terry announced, waving his hand towards the new arrival.

Ahmed was a slim man with a swarthy complexion and a drooping moustache. He clutched a leather pouch which was attached to his wrist with a gold chain. A chunky gold watch adorned his other wrist, and around his neck a small gold crucifix was just visible above his open-necked shirt.

Coffee was brought in by room service, and as Terry poured, Susan noticed that his fingernails were beautifully manicured.

"I can't apologise enough for abandoning you in Warsaw," Terry was saying, "But I had to go to Germany to collect my new car. I've been waiting ages for delivery, so in the end I went to get it myself. You can't trust anyone out here," he added, in a confidential whisper.

Ahmed nodded sagely in agreement.

"Is it an expensive car?" asked Jim.

"Yes luv, it's a Porsche, so it needs looking after."

"So, will you be travelling with us for the rest of the tour?" Tom pressed.

Terry turned the corners of his mouth downwards and took a long sip of coffee before he replied.

"Umm, I don't think that will be possible. I've got a few things on the go, business deals, you know. I'm here, there and everywhere. Anyway, Susan seems to be doing a grand job. I'm just a phone call away if you should need me. And I'll sort out some good hotels for you for the rest of the tour. Things might not go too smoothly in Romania. They please themselves over there. But if you wave your money around, you should get what you want."

Terry emptied his coffee cup and glanced at his watch. He stood up, and gently put his hand on Susan's shoulder. She took the hint, and got up to leave.

"I'll be in touch," Terry assured them, as he shepherded them out of the room.

Back out in the corridor Tom grinned broadly at Susan and remarked, "So much for your plans of being his companion."

Jim smirked. "They might take you on as a maid, though. Those two are slicker than a mambo band."

Susan pulled a face and said nothing.

As they rounded a corner, there was a housekeeping trolley parked outside one of the rooms. The trolley was stacked with bed linen, towels and rolls of bathroom tissue.

"We could use some of those loo rolls," Susan commented. "I'm getting through my supply at an alarming rate."

They paused by the trolley and looked around. The maid was nowhere to be seen.

Tom nodded. "That's a good idea. But what can we carry them in?"

"There's some black plastic bags here," said Jim, rummaging in the bottom of the trolley. He pulled a bag out, opened it up, and began dropping rolls of paper into it.

"How many do we need?" he asked.

"Not too many," said Susan cautiously, "Or the reception desk will spot us carrying them out."

Jim looked at Susan's jacket and pursed his lips. "That's a fairly roomy jacket. You could carry the bag in there and make it look as if you're pregnant."

He tied the top of the bag. Susan pushed it inside her jacket and pulled up the zip.

"It won't stay up," she complained. "It keeps slipping down."

"Put your right arm underneath, in a sort of curve. Pregnant ladies do that sometimes when they're walking along," suggested Jim. "And hold on to Tom's arm as we go out."

"What! And have people think that he's the father? Not likely!"

"Oh darling, you shouldn't get upset in your condition," said Tom, solicitously. He grabbed her left arm and marched her along the corridor.

They went past reception without anyone giving them a second look, and at the hotel entrance Jim hailed a taxi.

The taxi driver glanced at Susan, then leapt out of his car when he noticed her bulge. He took hold of her right arm to help her into the car, and as he did so, the black bag dropped on to the pavement.

The taxi driver gasped in surprise, and Jim clasped his hands together, shrieking,

"Oh, the baby has come early! And he looks just like his daddy!"

Susan grabbed the bag and they quickly climbed into the back of the taxi. The driver pulled off at speed, shaking his head in bewilderment.

* * *

After the show that night, the dressing room was heaving with people. Tom was pinned against the wall by a reporter. Amidst the hubbub, Susan was introducing Terry to the other band members.

Terry grasped Joe's arm and asked, "How are you coping? I know that Americans can find it a bit strange, out here in the wild east."

"I love everything I've seen so far," Joe told him. "But the food is a bit limited. I'm usually a vegetarian."

"Usually a vegetarian? That's like saying that you're usually a virgin!"

Terry suddenly wrung his hands together and turned to Susan. "I forgot to say, this afternoon. The tour merchandise isn't ready yet. You can collect it when you get to Hungary."

Then he turned back to Joe. "Sorry if I snapped at you, dear. I don't like this crush of sweaty bodies." He wrinkled his nose in displeasure. "Smells like Canal number seven. Anyway luvs, is the boatel all right for you? Some people get seasick on it, but I think it's wonderfully romantic."

On the other side of the room, Ahmed was in conversation with Pete.

"Tell me," said Ahmed, "Is it true, all that we hear about sex, drugs and rock and roll?"

Pete sniffed. "Huh. I wish."

Ahmed smiled. "For which one?"

"I ain't fussy," Pete abruptly replied. "Would you excuse me, I want to check my strings." Then he hurried away.

Ahmed glided across the room and found Jim lurking in a corner, nursing a bottle of scotch.

"Why are there no girls here?" Ahmed asked. "I thought that musicians always have lots of girls following them?"

"Susan frightens them away," Jim said, sourly.

Ahmed smiled at Jim. "Never mind. We don't need girls to have a good time."

Jim edged backwards, and leant against the wall.

* * *

On Sunday morning, they had a late breakfast in the boatel restaurant.

"It's so cosy, sleeping in a cabin," said Joe. "The river rocked me to sleep last night."

"I kept having nightmares about Ahmed," groaned Pete. "I really hate it when guys try to chat me up."

Jim nodded. "I know what you mean."

"He was only being sociable," snapped Susan. "You lot are paranoid!"

Tom suddenly chuckled and said, "I remember when I was touring with a British band one time. We were rehearsing one afternoon and the bass guitarist suddenly sidled past the piano and whispered to me, "I have to slip out for a while. I'm desperate for a fag."

"I was so surprised that he just came right out and admitted it to me. Most people try to keep that kind of stuff a secret! Five minutes later he crept back in and said, "That's better. I really needed that!"

"And I thought, good heavens, how did he manage to find someone so quickly? He must really know his way around! And for the rest of the tour this guy would say to me, "Hey Tom, you want to come for a drink after the show?" And I'd always make my excuses, you know."

"It wasn't until ages afterwards that I found out, when the British say "fag" they mean "cigarette"."

* * *

As they pushed their way through the throngs of tourists in the old town square that afternoon, Susan complained, "Are we going to walk around the whole of Prague? I would have brought my hiking boots if I'd known!"

"The guide book says that if you want to see everything, it's a three-hour walk," Joe told her.

Susan grimaced. "You lot can go and see it all and tell me about it afterwards. I feel as if I've spent the afternoon in a rugby scrum."

The medieval clock tower struck the hour, and gothic clockwork figures glided out from behind the clock face. When the display had finished, the crowd dispersed, and Joe enthused, "You don't get anything like that back home!"

"Was it good?" asked Pete.

"Weren't you watching?" demanded Jim. "What kind of tourist are you?"

Pete mumbled, "I was watching the pick-pockets work the crowd."

Susan hastily checked the contents of her bag and hissed, "Why didn't you say something? We could have been robbed!"

Pete shrugged. "I didn't want to spoil the show."

Joe asked eagerly, "Are we all going to climb the tower?"

Susan looked at the crush of people around the foot of the tower. "I'd rather stick needles in my eyes!"

Jim shook his head. "I'm not climbing all those stairs. My knees ain't what they used to be."

"What did they used to be?" Susan said, sarcastically.

"Elbows," he retorted, and then he retreated to an outdoor cafe table.

Tom, Joe and Pete walked off to join the shoving crowd in the clock tower, and Susan joined Jim at the parasol table. Jim ordered two coffees and an English newspaper. When the paper arrived, he scanned the pages and exclaimed, "There's a bit in here about the gig last night."

Susan clutched her handbag on her lap and eyed the passers by with undisguised suspicion. "Tom was speaking to some reporter after the show," she recalled, vaguely.

Jim read the column and started to laugh. "He mentions the attractive young tour coordinator."

Susan snatched the paper from his hands and read the item.

"What a wonderful man," she gushed. "I must put him on my Christmas card list."

"Send him a pair of spectacles as a Christmas present," said Jim. "He obviously needs them."

* * *

Later in the evening, they were still plodding around Prague.

Pete complained, "How many medieval churches does this town have? I've been inside more churches today than in my entire adult life."

"It's a shame that they don't say the mass in Latin any more," Joe said, nostalgically.

Pete grunted. "I don't know why they used to say mass in Latin. No-one could understand it."

"It was a universal language," Joe explained.

"Yes," agreed Susan. "You could go to mass anywhere in the world, and not understand what the priest was saying."

The crowds pressed around them, and Susan gasped as they were carried forwards in a jostling human torrent.

"Are we going over a bridge?" puzzled Tom. "I'm sure I can smell water."

Joe consulted his guide book. "Yes, It's a bit too crowded to see it, though. If we go this way, we can visit the rest of the churches before it gets dark."

"Oh, great," said Pete, as they staggered uphill.

They squeezed through the crowded streets of medieval Prague and craned their necks through the throng of tourists to get a view of the cathedral.

Joe was enthralled. "It's amazing. Not the Nazi army nor the invading Russians managed to spoil this place."

Jim guffawed. "The tourists are doing a pretty good job though."

* * *

That night, they managed to find a restaurant which provided a menu in English. They sat studying it for a while, then Tom remarked, "Someone once said to me that getting married is a bit like choosing from a menu in a restaurant. You pick what you think you'd like, then when you get it, you decide that you prefer the look of someone else's."

"That explains why you're always picking bits off other peoples plates," Susan murmured, caustically. Her feet ached, and Tom was wearing another of his ghastly red shirts, the sight of which made her feel nauseous.

"I'll have to get another roll of film," Joe said, to no-one in particular. "I used nearly a whole film today. This is the most picturesque city that I've ever visited."

Tom nodded. "It's kinda strange - like stepping back two centuries in time. All those castles and things."

"I kept expecting Mickey Mouse and Goofy to come skipping along the sidewalk," muttered Pete.

"At least we didn't get robbed," Susan said, thinking about the pickpockets.

"That's what you think," Jim scoffed. "We got fleeced at the pavement cafe. They charged ten bucks for two coffees and a newspaper!"

CHAPTER 9

At breakfast the next morning they were all making different plans.

"I need to change up some travellers cheques," Tom insisted. "This town ain't cheap."

"Well I'm not doing any more walking," Susan announced. "I'm going to do my laundry. With any luck it should drip-dry before we leave tomorrow."

Joe pleaded, "I want to go back to that bridge we crossed yesterday. It might be less crowded today and I can get some better pictures."

"Could you possibly do my laundry as well?" Tom asked Susan, smiling sweetly at her.

"Oh, I suppose so," she sighed. "And for heaven's sake change that shirt. It's well grubby after all that trudging around, yesterday."

Tom looked down at his red shirt and nodded in agreement.

"I think that you should all take a stroll this morning," Susan declared. "We'll be on the bus again tomorrow, so you might as well stretch your legs today." She subjected each of them to a hard stare, so they all mumbled in agreement and beat a hasty retreat to their cabins.

Susan followed Tom back to his cabin to collect his dirty laundry. He took a plastic bag out of the wardrobe, and lobbed it to her. She glanced inside the bag, grimaced in distaste, and dropped the bag to the floor, saying to Tom, "Don't forget your shirt."

As Tom took off his shirt, Susan moved to the window and said, "You're lucky, having a cabin facing the river. Mine looks out on to the quayside wall. Open the window, I want to see the view along the river."

Tom passed his shirt to Susan and slid the window open. She leaned precariously out of the window to get a better view, and as Tom reached out to steady her, she pushed the shirt in his direction, saying, "Here, take this."

The red shirt fell out of her hand and dropped noiselessly into the river. It slowly floated away.

"Oh! How did you manage that?" she said accusingly to Tom.

"What!" he exclaimed. "It was you that dropped it!"

"I thought that you had hold of it."

Tom sighed. "Well, it's lucky that I have one left."

"Does that one need a wash?"

"No, I ain't worn it yet," Tom replied, and he eyed her suspiciously as she went out of the cabin carrying his dirty underwear and singing to herself.

* * *

Tom and the rest of the band were about two blocks from the boatel when Joe spotted a shop across the street with a "Fuji" sign in the window.

"Pete, would you come with me and keep hold of my camera case? I don't like to put it down in a shop here. I may never see it again."

Pete grunted an assent, and the two of them crossed the road. Tom and Jim leaned on a rail overlooking the river, and waited for them.

"Are you having any luck in thawing out Susan the snow queen?" Jim asked.

Tom shook his head. "She could get an Olympic medal in cold shoulder."

"It's her age. Once they get past forty, they turn into ball-breakers. You should find someone young and stupid."

"Been there, done that. It gets kinda tiresome having to tell them who JFK was."

They both turned around when they heard the screech of tyres behind them. A sleek sports car pulled across the road and halted beside them. Terry jumped out of the passenger seat and said breathlessly, "I was taking this to Susan at the boatel, but you can pass it on to her. We're in a bit of a rush. It's your revised itinerary." He pushed a sheet of paper into Tom's hand. "Sorry about Brno, there's a trade fair on. Anyway, we have some urgent business to attend to in Pest, so we'll see you again some time next week."

Jim was staring at the car, a frown on his brow.

"Hmm. A purple Porsche. They're not exactly two a penny, are they?"

"It's violet, luv, not purple," Terry flung over his shoulder as he clambered back into the low-slung car.

Ahmed deftly let up the clutch and swung the car around.

Jim watched as the Porsche sped into the distance. "That's odd."

"Uhh, what?" Tom muttered, as he studied the new itinerary.

"Terry said that they got the car in Germany, but the steering wheel is on the right-hand side."

"Oh, really?" Tom replied, only listening with half an ear. He continued to read his sheet of paper, then announced cheerfully, "These all look like five-star hotels. When Janek turns up with the new bus tomorrow, we should be in roses for the rest of the tour."

Joe and Pete rejoined them, and after a twenty-minute walk they came to the bridge that Joe wanted to see again. It was less crowded than the day before, and he managed to find a place to stand and snap the statues that edged the balustrades.

Pete was leaning on the parapet, gazing into the river, when he noticed a bright red object floating along in the water.

He shook his head. "Tck. People throw their junk anywhere these days." And he moved off to follow the others.

As Tom strode away, Jim asked, "Where are you going to get your dollars?"

"The Amex office."

Pete groaned. "That's a bit of a trek from here."

"Yeah, but it's the only place in town that doesn't rip you off for high commission. Anyway, I need to do some shopping as well. I'm out of razor blades and deodorant."

They found a large pharmacy, and Tom scoured the aisles, looking for his toiletries. He found the razor blades easily enough, but was having trouble with the deodorant.

"What's taking you so long?" grumbled Jim, who had followed Tom to the deodorant shelf.

"I can't find what I want."

Jim picked one off the shelf. "Here. Have this."

"No, I don't want a roll-on," Tom insisted. "They go on wet and stay wet. I want one of those dry stick ones. They don't seem to have any here. Let's try another shop."

They made their way into three more shops, hunting for the stick deodorant, but with no luck.

"Let's try in here," suggested Joe. "It looks like a seven-eleven. They have everything in these stores."

They ambled inside and went off in different directions to speed up the search. After a few moments Jim emerged from an aisle triumphantly waving a small plastic cylinder in his hand. He pulled off the top, and wound up the white stick inside.

"It's a bit small," Tom said critically, "But it has a nice neutral scent. I'll take it."

They carried on across town, to the exchange office.

While they were standing in the queue in American Express, Joe nudged Tom and said, "See that poster over there? I think it means that you can get a free fanny-pack if you have a Diamond card. It looks like denim, with an embroidered view of the old town on the front. Why not take one for Susan? She hasn't bought any souvenirs so far."

Jim grunted. "That girl has barbed wire around her wallet."

"These people don't give much away either," Tom remarked. "I'd take one even if I didn't want it," and he produced his card to claim the free gift.

* * *

When they assembled in the boatel bar that evening, Joe handed a package to Susan and said, "We've got something for you. You might find it useful. It's a fanny-pack."

"What!" spluttered Susan, nearly choking on her martini. She opened the package and smiled with relief, saying, "Oh, it's a bum-bag."

"Bum-bag?" Jim echoed. "Sounds like something a fag would use."

"No. A fag would use an eraser," she replied.

Joe frowned. "I don't understand," he murmured.

"Ignore her," Tom cut in. "But whenever you're in England, don't make any remarks to a girl about fanny-packs, or she'll smack you. And take your own rubbers, too. It's less trouble."

Joe shook his head and took a long drink of beer.

* * *

On Tuesday morning, they were standing on the pavement outside the boatel, waiting for Janek to turn up. As the bus appeared, Tom grinned with delight and exclaimed, "Yes! Comfort at last!"

They all clambered aboard the luxury coach. Tom scurried down the aisle, then back again, and halted with a frown on his brow.

"Where's the bunks?"

"Are they upstairs?" Joe ventured.

"No upstairs," Janek announced. "No bunks."

Tom gritted his teeth. "Holy shit! I thought this was gonna be a proper tour bus! Who fucked up this time?"

Janek shrugged. "Bayern Munich here to play this week. Maybe they get best bus."

"At least we have a bathroom, and tables," Joe said.

Tom threw his bag onto a seat. "Who are they anyway, German heavy metal?"

Janek gave him a puzzled look. "You mean, munitions factory team?"

"No, that's Arsenal," Susan chipped in. "I wonder if I could rig up some sort of washing line in here? My laundry isn't completely dry."

"Don't even think about it," Jim said, abruptly. "You're not gonna mess up our nice bus."

"Well what am I supposed to do with damp laundry?"

"You're supposed to wrap it in hotel towels," he replied.

"But I haven't got any hotel towels."

"Didn't they teach you anything at tourist school?" Jim said, scornfully. "I'll give you some of mine."

He laid his suitcase on a table and opened it up.

Susan gasped in amazement. "How many towels do you have in there?"

Jim swiftly counted his stock. "Fifteen from the Sparrow Royal in Bristol and six from the boatel. The Polish ones weren't worth taking."

"But when the laundry gets dry, the towel gets damp," pondered Susan. "How do you get the towel dry?"

"You don't," said Jim. "You leave the damp towel in the next hotel, and take away one of their dry ones. But the trouble is, the English towels are better quality than the ones out here, so I'm leaving behind nicer towels than I'm stealing."

"Just look upon it as a form of economic aid," suggested Susan.

The four men settled themselves around a table and Jim started to deal out a pack of cards.

"Can I play?" Susan asked.

"No," Jim replied, bluntly. "My daddy always said to me, "Son, never ever play cards with a book-keeper.""

"That's news to me," remarked Tom. "I didn't know that you had a daddy."

As the game started, Susan took the damp laundry from her bag and proceeded to wrap it in the towels that Jim had given her. She stacked it neatly on the seat opposite her.

"If you sit on the towels you can press your laundry quite nicely," Joe told her, helpfully.

"Most of this is Tom's washing," Susan grumbled. "He can sit on his own damp underwear. I'm certainly not doing it."

"I gave up pressing clothes long ago," Tom announced. "After my wife left, I did try to press my shirts, but I soon got bored with it. I decided to get a maid to do it for me, so I looked in the local paper under the "Services" section. There was an advert that said, "French maid services - personal attention." So I phoned the number and arranged for the maid to come round."

"She turned up the following evening, wearing the strangest outfit - black mini skirt with black stockings and a frilly white apron - but I thought it was probably just a business gimmick. I took her through to the utility room and showed her the ironing table and my stack of shirts - there were a good two dozen of them. I said to her, "Take your time, I'll pay for however long it takes you.""

"And she went berserk! Started calling me all sorts of rude names, telling me that she'd never been so insulted in her entire life, and what did I take her for. Turns out that the services that she was offering were of a sexual nature. So she left without doing anything, and cussing me up, down and sideways for wasting her time. She couldn't have been more offended if she'd been a real maid and I'd asked her to go to bed with me!"

* * *

The card game had only been going for half an hour when the bus pulled into a car park, and Janek shouted back to them, "Joe, you walk to castle from here."

Joe hastily dropped his cards and pulled his camera case from the rack.

"Why are we stopping here?" Tom demanded.

Joe smiled brightly and replied, "My guide book says that there's a wonderful castle here, and as it's on our way, I thought I could do a quick tour of it."

Tom frowned at Joe and said, "When a band goes on tour, it doesn't mean that they tour the sights. I think you've become a little confused."

"Oh leave him alone," said Susan. "We've got plenty of time to get to Plzen."

"Maybe we should teach Janek to play bass guitar, and let Joe go off back-packing," muttered Tom.

"Anyone else coming?" asked Joe, as he made his way off the bus.

"Has it got a church?" Pete said sarcastically. " I won't come unless it's got a church."

Joe hurried off with his camera, and Susan moved over into his seat. She picked up his hand of cards and said, "Get ready to lose your shirts, suckers."

"I've already lost two of mine," Tom grumbled.

* * *

Two hours later they pulled into Plzen. As they drove through the town Janek was shouting over his shoulder, "Pilsen! Pilsen!" whilst making drinking gestures with his right arm.

"I hope this isn't going to be like Wroclaw," Susan murmured.

"No, it isn't," Jim said. "This time you can stay at home. It's beer drinkers only after the show tonight."

"Where are we staying?" Pete asked.

Tom took his wallet from inside his jacket and unfolded the sheet of paper that Terry had given to him.

"The Continental."

Susan frowned at him. "I'm supposed to have the itinerary."

"I'll fight you for it," said Tom, smiling as he folded the sheet and put it back into his wallet.

When they presented themselves at the hotel reception desk, the clerk handed over five keys. Tom asked, "Do the rooms have a shower?"

When the clerk nodded an affirmative, Tom gave a whoop of joy. He skipped through the foyer singing, "Terry, I love you," and blowing kisses into the air as he went.

"What a lot of excitement over a shower," Susan remarked. "What would he be like if he won the lottery?"

* * *

The band were half-way through their breakfasts the following morning before Susan appeared, and joined them at the table.

"You look heavy-eyed," remarked Tom. "What were you up to last night?"

"While you lot were out boozing, I decided to go along to the casino and spread a little money on the table. I did quite nicely, too. But my Skoda jokes didn't go down very well."

"What's a Skoda joke?" asked Jim.

"Don't get me started," she replied, "Or I won't be able to stop."

"I've never been inside a gambling den," Joe said. "The very idea frightens me."

"You Americans are strange," mused Susan. "You can't go into a betting shop and put five dollars on a horse race, but you can go into a gun shop and buy an Uzi sub-machine gun for your kid's birthday."

Joe protested, "But in England you don't have an organisation that is dedicated to extracting vast sums of money out of people through threats, coercion and fear of reprisals."

"Yes we do," she retorted. "It's called the Inland Revenue."

* * *

Immediately after breakfast they boarded the bus and drove across the river to the brewery, where they loaded up with ten cases of beer before starting the long drive to Brno. As Tom carried the last box on to the bus he smiled and said, "This is work that I enjoy doing."

Susan sidled up to him and said coyly, "You're so cute when you're in a good mood." She slipped her arms inside his jacket and cuddled up to him.

"Ooh, this is nice," he whispered.

"Well don't get used to it," she replied curtly, disengaging herself from his body.

She sat down across the aisle and inspected the wallet that she had removed from his jacket. Susan took out the folded sheet of paper, then tossed the wallet back to Tom.

"I'm in charge of the itinerary," she told him sternly, "And don't you forget it!"

Jim raised an eyebrow at Tom. "Aren't you going to fight her for it?"

"Not likely," Tom replied. "I'd probably come off worst!"

As Susan studied the sheet of paper she frowned and said, "That's odd." She fished in her bag for the original itinerary. "I thought so," she mumbled, comparing both sheets of paper. "The Brno hotel is the same on both lists."

Tom suddenly groaned, "I remember now. Terry said something about a trade fair in Brno."

"Well, we can always sleep on the bus," Jim suggested. "Maybe Susan will volunteer to keep you warm."

Susan curled her lip at him.

"Maybe we should have brought Sexy Sophie with us on this trip," Jim continued. "She's hot enough to melt a Polar ice cap."

"Mm," agreed Pete. "Sophie's a real good-looker. She can stop traffic."

"Yes," hissed Susan. "The spots on her face glow red and orange!"

CHAPTER 10

It was late in the afternoon when they reached the outskirts of Brno. Susan had slept for most of the journey, and when she woke up, the card-players were reminiscing about the music heroes of their youth.

"When I was at college in Richmond," recalled Tom, "Me and some buddies got tickets for a Dylan concert, up in Pittsburgh. We set off after morning class had finished, and we tanked it up a little, to get there in time. We arrived about five-thirty, and it was too early to go to the hall, so we went around a few bars, had a few beers. I had done a lot of the driving, so I was a bit heavy-eyed. We didn't get anything to eat. You don't bother much with food at that age. If your mom doesn't put a plate in front of you, you kind of forget about it."

"So by the time we got into the concert I was a bit the worse for wear, with all the beer and no food, you know. And he didn't start playing right off. There was a warm-up act. And what with the crush of people around me, I dozed off to sleep. And the stupid bastards that I was with didn't wake me up when Dylan came on. I slept right through the whole damn show. So I never did get to hear him play."

"I like a story with a happy ending," Susan remarked.

Tom glared at her. "I take it you're not a Dylan fan."

"He's all right, as long as you don't have to listen to him. As a matter of interest, did he give singing lessons to Bruce Springsteen?"

"Don't try and be smart about music. I bet you don't even know what a metronome is."

Susan gave him a perplexed frown. "Is it a small bloke who travels on a Paris underground train?"

Tom groaned. "How long do I have to put up with your bad jokes?"

"For as long as I'm in control of the toilet paper supply."

Jim suddenly tapped his brow. "Damn! I forgot to liberate some rolls from the boatel."

"Things would be easier if Tom didn't use half a roll before each show," Susan complained. "Instead of having a star on the dressing room door, he should have the Kimberly-Clark logo."

Just then the bus came to a halt. They looked out of the window and saw a small motel.

Tom frowned as he peered outside. He shouted up to Janek, "We're in the middle of nowhere. This can't be right?"

"Yes," Janek called back. "This is auto-camp."

They carried their luggage inside. At the motel reception desk Tom glanced around at the comfortable surroundings and said, "Well, this isn't too bad. I don't know what Terry was apologising for."

The clerk handed Tom two keys. Then he ushered them to a back door, and waved towards a small copse in the distance.

"What's going on?" Tom demanded. "We don't usually get thrown out of the back door until we've had a few beers!"

"Cabin this way," Janek explained, and they followed as he trudged across a field. As they approached the copse they saw small wooden cabins scattered between the trees. Janek peered at the numbers painted on the doors, and directed them to their two huts.

Tom unlocked the door of the larger cabin, and the band followed him into a chilly room that contained four iron bunk beds with wafer-thin mattresses.

"I don't remember the trial," muttered Jim. "Did we get a life-sentence?"

Susan took the other key and unlocked the cabin next door.

"Mine's cosier," she announced. "I've got two beds and the spider from hell as a companion."

Jim peeped around her door, then he backed away. "You'd better let the spider have first choice of bunks. Still, look on the bright side, the spider will probably frighten away the bears."

"I fetch beer?" Janek asked.

Tom sighed and shook his head. "No, let's get down to the venue. We'll save the beer for later."

Jim nodded. "Well, at least we don't need to worry about a bottle-opener. We'll invite Susan's spider round, and he can open the bottles with his teeth."

* * *

At the concert hall Tom and the band were doing a run-through, and Susan was hanging about in the dressing room. She had refused to be left on her own in the desolate cabin. There was a knock at the door, and a plump little man trotted in and introduced himself as the manager of the hall. He spoke excellent English, and after a short conversation with Susan he left, rubbing his hands together with satisfaction.

Susan ambled up to the stage, and stood in the wings as the band finished their rehearsal.

"All right," called Tom. "Let's break for some dinner, then back here for seven."

"There's a very good restaurant in town," Susan said, as Tom and the band came off the stage. "The manager told me where it is. He was very helpful."

She hesitated, then continued, "Tonight's concert is sold out. He said that the demand for tickets was immense, what with all the people here for the trade fair. They could have sold three times as many tickets."

She paused again, then blurted, "I've agreed with him that you'll play two extra shows here."

"What!" gasped Tom.

"It's all extra cash for you," she coaxed. "The sponsor won't know about it."

"We're only on contract for one show here," he insisted. "It ain't worth my while to risk it."

Susan gave a persuasive pout. "The manager will give us fifty per cent of the ticket receipts. In dollars."

Tom bit his lower lip. "I don't know. I'd like to talk to Terry about it. Do we have his phone number? Is it on the itinerary that he gave me?"

Susan studied the sheet of paper. "No, there's no phone number." She hunted in her bag for the business card that Terry had given her in Prague.

"That's odd," she murmured. "There's no telephone number on this, either."

"Typical," commented Jim. "Don't call us, we'll call you."

"So, will you do the extra shows?" Susan pressed.

Tom shrugged. "I guess so."

"But the sponsor won't like it if they find out that we've been playing extra gigs," Joe protested. "We could get in trouble."

"Who's gonna tell them?" countered Jim. "Well done, Susan. You're getting the hang of this job."

* * *

After the show, the dressing room was full of people trying to shake Tom's hand. Susan escaped from the crush and went into the empty auditorium. She was walking up the aisles, counting the rows, when a man suddenly appeared from behind a fire-exit curtain. He had a sallow, pock-marked complexion, and a dramatic hook-nose. His hands were thrust deep into the pockets of a dark cashmere coat, and as he approached she was disconcerted by the unwavering stare from his coal black eyes.

"Excuse me please. I am looking for Terry Tyreman. He is here?"

His English was very precise, but with an accent that she couldn't quite place.

"No. I have no idea where he is. He may be in Budapest. Can I help? Is it to do with the tour?" she asked, worried that he might be a Zblatov employee.

"No," he replied brusquely, then he turned on his heel and pushed noiselessly out through the fire exit.

Damn, she thought, I've lost count now. And she went back to the front row to begin counting again.

* * *

Back at the cabins that night, Susan unlocked her door and leaned in to switch on the light. She stepped inside cautiously, but there was no sign of Arnie the spider. Next door, the band were clinking bottles and laughing in their usual juvenile fashion. She dimmed the light, crept into her bunk and closed her eyes.

The cabin next door went quiet, then a few seconds later, Susan was startled by a rapid scratching at the door, and a low growling noise.

"Goodnight Yogi," she called out.

There was some chuckling outside the door. As it subsided, Susan smiled and thought to herself, he won't be laughing tomorrow morning.

* * *

Susan was brushing her teeth in the communal shower block the following morning, when Tom emerged from one of the toilet stalls. He grunted a greeting, then disappeared into one of the shower cubicles.

Susan waited until she heard the cascade of water, then put her hands over her ears. Tom gave an anguished shriek, and came staggering out of the cubicle, wild-eyed and dripping wet.

"Cold," he muttered, shivering violently. "I'll try another one."

"Don't bother," she replied. "None of them have hot water. I met an Australian girl in here yesterday, and she told me."

He clutched at his towel and whimpered. "How am I gonna freshen up?"

"You'll have to wait till you get to the hall," she told him. "The dressing room toilet has a washbasin." And she hurried off back to her cabin before he could complain any further.

Tom was still miserable at breakfast, even though the motel restaurant provided strong coffee and good food.

"I hope the money we make from these two extra gigs is worth the discomfort that I'm suffering. I don't remember ever feeling so sticky. This Czech deodorant is useless," he grumbled.

"So, how do we know that the hall manager won't rip us off?" Pete demanded.

"I've counted the seats. I know exactly what his receipts will be for a full house," Susan assured him. She had decided not to mention the sinister man in the cashmere coat, in case it made Tom nervous about doing the shows.

"I told Janek to pick us up at ten," Susan continued. "There's no point hanging around here. We might as well go into Brno and hang around there."

The others nodded in agreement, and Joe said, "I'll take my camera."

* * *

In Brno, they were sitting on a park bench, enjoying the morning sunshine, while Joe was exploring the castle at the top of the hill. In the distance a church bell tower started to ring the hour. As the bells finished striking, Jim checked his watch and frowned.

"What time do you make it?" he asked Susan.

"Eleven," she replied, after glancing at her wrist.

"Strange," he muttered. "I could have sworn that I counted twelve."

She raised an eyebrow. "How do you manage to keep a beat if you can't count? Anyway, where did Pete disappear to?"

"He was talking to some guy after the show last night. Seems he has a stand in the trade fair arena. Pete's taken his suitcase of denims down there."

"Has he ever considered a career in retail?"

"Nah. He'd have to pay his own transport costs."

Tom was relaxing on a bench opposite Susan. He was wearing the last of his red tee shirts, and it glowed brightly in the sunshine.

Susan squinted at him and said, "I hope you're not going to wear that shirt at the show tonight, Tom. You'll give the audience radiation burns."

Tom scowled at her and replied, "I ain't worried. Just as long as there's no goats in the front row."

"Are we playing the same set as last night?" Jim asked.

Tom shook his head. "We'll change it around a little."

Jim took a small notebook from his pocket, and listed the songs as Tom told him what the running order would be. He then copied the list out twice more.

"How do you remember all that lot?" Susan asked, as she glanced down the long list.

"I don't. I tape it to my right-hand drum."

"You haven't done a list for Tom."

"There's no point. He never follows it."

Susan raised her eyebrows. "But how do you know what songs to play?"

"We give Tom a four-bar start, then play catch-up."

She shook her head, confused. "So why bother to write the list down?"

"It gives me something to read if I get bored."

* * *

That evening, before the show, the hall manager scuttled into the dressing room and pressed a large brown envelope into Susan's hand.

"Money for tonight," he murmured.

"What a nice man," she announced, after he had gone.

"Did you say something," Tom called from the toilet.

"The manager brought our money. It looks like a good deal of cash," she shouted back. "It'll take me a while to count it."

"Come and do my back first."

Susan pushed the envelope inside her blouse for safe-keeping, then squeezed into the tiny bathroom to help Tom.

"Is the water hot?"

"Barely," he replied, "But it's better than nothing."

As Susan sponged his back, he murmured, "Mm this is cosy. Reminds me of old times, you pressing up against me."

"Don't get excited. It's not me that you can feel, it's the cash."

"Why do you always have to disappoint me? You have a cruel streak." Susan rubbed his back vigorously with a small towel.

"Argh! Did you bring that towel from Poland?"

"Stop moaning. You're lucky I'm here at all. None of the others would do this."

"Joe probably would."

"He's too nice to be in your band."

"Yeah, I know. But don't tell him."

Susan draped the rough towel over Tom's shoulder. "I've finished drying you off. Can I go now?"

"What's the rush?"

"I've got to count this money."

"Why don't you want to be alone with me? You used to like my company well enough."

"Being crushed against a tall piano player in a Czech toilet isn't my idea of a good time, strange as it may seem."

"Susan, how long are you gonna be pissed with me?"

"Look, Tom. I'm here to do a job. I'm too old for all this soppy love-story stuff. And so are you."

"Do you have the copyright on bitter and twisted? Go on, take off. This bathroom ain't big enough for the both of us."

* * *

"Have you said goodbye to your room-mate?" Jim asked Susan, after breakfast on Friday morning.

"I haven't seen him since I sprayed the cabin with insect repellent," she replied.

Joe clicked his tongue. "It's not ecologically friendly to use pesticides. We didn't use any in our hut."

"Huh! You wouldn't need to, what with four pairs of trainers and Tom's armpits!"

They were at the reception desk, paying their bills.

"This place is very cheap," observed Tom. "We'll make a tidy profit on these two shows. Was the cash as much as you expected?" he asked Susan.

She nodded. "I should have negotiated a bonus for the long encore that you did."

"Well, it was more comfortable in the hall than in the cabin," said Tom, "So I figured we might as well carry on playing."

As they loaded their bags on to the bus, Tom gave an envelope to Janek and said, "Share this out with the crew. Tell them to keep quiet about these extra gigs."

They drove into town and tried to occupy themselves until the afternoon rehearsal. Pete went back to the trade fair with his suitcase of jeans, and the others mooched around the town.

"Lucky it's not raining," Susan remarked. "Life on the road is rather tedious, isn't it? All this hanging about."

"That's why we book into nice hotels," Tom said testily. "So that we can hang about in comfort."

"But it's great being able to visit all these medieval places," enthused Joe. "Much better than being in some plush hotel. Listen up, the cathedral bells are ringing for midday mass."

Jim glanced at his watch, then shook his wrist vigorously. "My Timex must be playing up. It says eleven."

"It's something they do here," Joe told him. "They had a siege back in old times, and they tricked the enemy by ringing twelve instead of eleven. The attackers went away because they thought it was midday."

"They obviously had a union agreement on lunch break times," Jim murmured.

They strolled along to an open-air market, and Susan caught sight of a stall selling tee shirts. She grabbed Tom's hand and tugged him across the street.

"You could do with a couple of new shirts to replace the ones you've lost," Susan insisted. She rummaged through the racks of clothing, then pulled a hanger from the rail. "This is a nice green. Subdued, but not insipid. Do you want large or extra large?"

Tom sighed. "Whatever. Take XL, in case it shrinks. How much will two cost me?"

"Best get three of them," Susan said, thoughtfully. "You seem to be rather careless with your clothes."

CHAPTER 11

After the show that night they clambered on board the bus for the journey south to Slovakia. They had been travelling for about two hours, and they were all asleep. Janek suddenly eased the bus to a standstill, and the hiss of the air brakes woke Susan. She looked out of the window, and as she peered through the darkness, she could just distinguish that they were at a border crossing. There was a small booth on each side of the road, with a couple of yawning guards inside.

Jim, who was sitting across the aisle from Susan, woke up and asked sleepily, "Where are we? Why have we stopped?"

"We're at the Slovak border," she told him. "They probably won't even ask for passports."

"European geography is too much for me," he muttered, and closed his eyes again.

Susan was surprised to see one of the guards come out of his booth and walk over to the bus. He motioned for Janek to open the door, and he climbed aboard. He stood looking at them, with his rifle slung over his shoulder, and then had a brief conversation with Janek.

Janek nodded his head, closed the bus door, and guided the bus through the checkpoint. The border guard sat down near Janek and continued to gaze intently at the occupants of the bus.

"Shit!" Susan gasped.

"Uh?" mumbled Jim, stirring himself again. "What's up?"

"The border guard has just got on," she said softly. "I think he told Janek to drive somewhere."

"Jeez! What have we done wrong?"

"You mean, apart from stealing towels and toilet rolls and playing unauthorised concerts and transporting huge quantities of booze across national borders?" she hissed, sarcastically.

"Mm. Right. I'd best wake up Tom." Jim crept out of his seat and stealthily nudged Tom.

"Argh!" Tom cried, as he awoke and saw Jim's face just a few inches from his own. "What are you playing at?"

"Ssh," whispered Jim. "There's a Slovakian border guard on the bus. Looks like we're in trouble."

Tom groaned. "Oh hell. We'd better wake the other two."

As Pete and Joe were shaken awake, the bus drove on through the darkness. After several miles the guard directed Janek off the main highway, and the bus bumped over the rough surface of a back road.

Tom chewed his lower lip. "Where are we going? This looks real bad!"

"I've got an idea," Susan murmured. "Why don't we try and bribe him. It might work. It's worth a try, anyway."

Tom nodded quickly in agreement, and pushed Jim out of his seat, saying, "Here, take fifty bucks and give it to him."

"Why me?" demanded Jim. "I think Susan should do it. It was her idea. And if she smiles sweetly at him, that would probably help."

"You're such a hero!" Susan muttered. She snatched the money from his hand and moved warily to the front of the bus. As she approached the guard, he tapped Janek on the shoulder, and motioned for him to stop the bus. They were near a small group of houses. The blackness of the night was pierced by a yellow light shining in the window of one of the houses. The guard stood up and took the rifle from his shoulder.

Susan hastily stepped up to him and gave her most disarming smile. She held the bundle of cash out to him and said, "For you. A gift."

The guard looked surprised. He took the cash, nodded at her, then got off the bus and disappeared into the darkness.

"Quick!" she exclaimed to Janek. "Get us out of here!"

Janek did a neat three point turn and headed back towards the main road. Susan sat down and said, "Oh, my legs are shaking."

Jim came up to the front of the bus. "Nice work, Susan. You did real well."

As they turned back on to the smooth highway, Janek put the bus into top gear, then he turned to Susan and said in a puzzled voice, "Why you give him money?"

"So that he wouldn't arrest us, of course."

Janek looked confused and asked, "Why he arrest us?"

Susan gave an exasperated sigh. "How should I know! What did he say when he got on the bus?"

Janek shrugged his shoulders. "He say he finish his shift and want lift home. His car not working."

Susan cursed softly and slunk back to her seat, with Jim chuckling quietly behind her.

* * *

It was close to dawn on Saturday morning when they pulled into Bratislava. They followed a road alongside the river, and came to a halt outside a concrete tower block with a glass and stainless steel entrance lobby. Tom studied the outside of the hotel and nodded in approval. "This looks comfortable."

"It looks a bit dull," Joe complained, as he picked up his bags.

Tom clicked his tongue. "I suppose you'd prefer Tom Sawyer's cabin again."

"Well, at least it had character," Joe responded. "I won't bother taking a photo of this one."

They checked into the hotel and disappeared into their rooms to get some more sleep. As Susan pulled her curtains together, the sky glowed softly with the first pink streaks of dawn. The mighty Danube flowed in majestic black silence, her bridges deserted and quiet in the calm before sunrise.

As Susan gazed out on the picturesque scene, she thought to herself, I wonder if Tom will want his fifty dollars back.

* * *

They met up in the hotel bar at midday.

"That was wonderful," enthused Tom. "I spent twenty minutes in the shower. It was bliss."

"Is it all right if I take off for a couple of hours?" Joe asked him.

"Please yourself," Tom replied. "What do you have planned?"

"One castle, four churches and five museums," Pete told him, looking glum.

"One of the churches has the skeleton of a saint on display," Joe informed them.

Susan sniffed. "It was probably some Gothic piano player who was over-zealous in the shower."

Tom gave her a hard stare and said, "I'll have my fifty dollars back as soon as it's convenient."

"It's not fair," she complained. "Why should I lose fifty dollars?"

"Because it was your idea to bribe the guard."

"Well you didn't have any ideas at all! If you had two brain cells to rub together, you'd probably set your head alight."

"Why do you always try to piss me off!" Tom exploded.

"Shall we get some lunch?" Joe cut in. "The restaurant has a fabulous view over the river." He clutched Susan's elbow and steered her towards the door.

Jim watched them go with a wry smile on his face.

"She really gets to you, don't she?"

Tom thrust his hands into his pockets. "I don't care about her being rude, but she's always so fucking right!"

Jim shrugged. "Yeah. So she's clever. But you're still the one with the dick."

"You're so deep sometimes, Jim. You should have been a shrink."

* * *

"I don't like this," Susan wailed.

Jim, Pete and Joe were grouped closely around her.

"Ouch," complained Pete, as Susan gripped his arm.

Jim said gleefully, "They have a ride just like this in Disneyworld. They put you in an elevator at the top of a tower, then they drop the car and let it free-fall for a hundred feet."

They were in a lift, scaling the side of a bridge pylon that soared up above the Danube.

Joe craned his neck. "It's a breath-taking view."

"I can't see anything," sobbed Susan. "Apart from my impending death!"

At the top of the pylon there was a cafe with panoramic windows.

Joe said, "Shall we get some coffee?"

"Get me a large brandy!" Susan muttered. "And a blindfold!"

Jim smiled. "You're not very happy with heights, are you, Susan?"

"You should have stayed on the ground," Joe said, sympathetically. "Why did you come up with us?"

"I didn't fancy hanging around on my own."

"Don't go to the rest-room," Pete advised her, as he joined them at the table. "It's like taking a leak at the top of a telegraph pole."

Susan shuddered and stared at the floor.

91

"Tom will be sorry he missed this," Joe remarked. "Who does he have an interview with this afternoon?"

"Some press reporter," Jim replied. He sipped his coffee, then said with a smirk, "Don't worry, Susan. It will probably be a hell of a lot quicker going down than it was coming up."

He moved deftly out of the way as Susan tried to kick him under the table.

After their descent from the aerial cafe, they walked back across the bridge to the hotel. As they approached the entrance they saw Tom emerge through the doors with an elegant blonde. He helped her into a taxi and waved as the car drove off.

"Was she the news reporter?" Jim asked.

Tom nodded. "Mm. Nice lady. Anyway, did you enjoy your sightseeing?"

Susan groaned and staggered into the hotel foyer with her hand over her mouth.

Tom stared after her. "What's the matter with Susan?"

Jim shrugged. "I guess the sight of you with another woman was too much for her."

* * *

"It's too bad you couldn't make it to the show last night, Susan," Jim remarked. "We had quite a party in the dressing room, afterwards."

"I don't doubt that for one moment," she replied, brusquely.

"Are you feeling better today?" Joe asked. "We were worried about you."

"I'm all right now," she answered. "And it's nice to know that you care."

"He didn't say that we cared. He said that we were worried," said Jim. "Anyway, I've been studying Joe's guide book. If we go north on our way out of town we can visit a TV tower and take an elevator ride up to the top. It's so high that you can see across three countries. And at the top it even has a cafe that revolves. Won't that be nice?"

Susan glared at him and took a large sip of wine.

"Are you sure that woman yesterday was from the newspaper?" Pete said suspiciously, as he refilled his glass.

"Yes," Tom insisted. "Why doesn't anyone believe me?"

"Because you usually do interviews over the phone," said Jim. "And why were you waving goodbye to her as she went off in the taxi?"

"I was just being polite," Tom answered in an exasperated tone. "Why are you all giving me such a hard time?"

"Ignore them," Joe told him. "They're probably jealous because you had a woman in your room."

"In the future you won't need to find a woman at all," Susan said, thoughtfully. "All this virtual reality stuff is becoming so sophisticated that you'll soon be able to have virtual sex, using a computer."

"It'll probably be better than the real thing, for some of us," muttered Pete.

"No," Jim said vehemently. "Nothing will replace the real thing. Especially the first time. Nothing can compare with the first time." A look of rapture appeared on his face.

"I'm surprised you can remember that far back," Susan remarked.

Jim gave a nostalgic smile. "It's a memory that I will always treasure."

"Yeah, and he still has the receipt," chuckled Tom.

They were on the bus, heading for Budapest. They had picked up a few cases of red wine in Bratislava, and were having a wine-tasting party to pass the time.

Tom glanced around. "Are there any more of those peach pancakes left?"

"No, I just ate the last one," Susan told him, swirling the wine in her glass. "A bit full-bodied for my palate. What else have we got?"

"I bet the women will love it, though," mused Jim.

"Love what?" Tom asked, looking confused as he emptied his glass.

"Virtual sex," Jim explained. "They need never worry about contraception again."

"Ooh, I hadn't thought of that."

"Yeah," Jim continued, sinking into a low voice. "We'll probably have to offer them lots of money for the real thing."

"No!" gasped Tom. "Do you really think it could come to that?"

"Who knows? But it would be the end of swing parties, that's for sure."

"Swing parties?" echoed Susan. "What are they?"

"Sex orgies," Tom whispered to her.

"Don't say you've never been to one?" Jim said, sarcastically. "You don't know what you're missing."

Susan frowned. "The blokes at these sex orgies, are they slim, young, good-looking men, or are they fat old geriatrics?"

Jim contemplated for a moment. "Fat old geriatrics, mostly."

Susan shuddered. "If I was going to do that sort of thing, I'd want to be paid for it."

"How much would you charge?"

"I was speaking hypothetically. I wasn't offering you my services," she retorted.

Jim sighed. "Uh, pity."

* * *

They were woken by the sound of car horns tooting all around them. Janek was trying to negotiate the bus through the busy streets of Pest. At each junction he slowed down to read the street name, and the impatient motorists hooted, whilst Janek reciprocated with vigorous hand gestures. At last he found the street he was looking for, and turned right to follow the river. At the end of the street an imposing hotel loomed upwards, facing across the Danube.

"I hope our rooms have a view of the river," Joe said, eagerly.

"Ugh, my head hurts," Tom complained. "I think I overdid the in-flight complimentary drinks. Where are we, anyway?"

"Budapest, Queen of the Danube," Susan loftily informed him.

Pete frowned. "Is this a different country from this morning?"

"Yes," Susan replied, wearily.

"I guess I'd better throw all my coins away, again," he grumbled, as they staggered off the bus and into the luxury hotel.

They unpacked their bags and settled into their rooms. They had a large suite, and the lounge area overlooked the river, with an open view across to the grandiose buildings on the opposite bank.

"I must get some more film," Joe murmured. "I can take lots of great photos from our balcony. I wonder if I can get some rolls developed here?"

"This suite will cost us a fortune," Pete muttered.

"Oh, stop moaning," Tom replied. "I don't suppose we'll be here for long. Susan, what's on the itinerary this week?"

Susan pulled the creased paper from her bag and studied the list.

"I can't make head nor tail of it," she told him.

"Give it here," said Tom, snatching it from her impatiently. He read through it twice, then said glumly, "I can't understand it either. Let's hope that Terry shows up soon."

As if on cue, there was a knock at the door, and Terry and Ahmed strolled into the suite.

Terry smiled brightly at them all. "Hello again, luvvies. Sorry I had to love you and leave you in Prague. Did everything go all right? Sorry about the log cabins. It must have been hellish for you." He pouted sympathetically.

"Oh, it wasn't so bad," Tom replied, keen to keep the conversation away from their shows in Brno. "But I can't follow this itinerary that you've drawn up for us. Can we go through it in detail?"

"Mm, it's a bit of a pigs breakfast," Terry confessed. He sat down next to Tom and picked some bits of fluff from Tom's untidy jeans as he explained the route.

"The sponsors wanted maximum ticket sales, so I've split it into three sections. You'll do one show in Budapest, then go westwards to do shows in Gyor, Szombathely and Szekesfehervaar. Back to Buda for another show, then east to do concerts in Eger, Miskolc and Debrecen. Then back here for one more show, and then south to Kecskemet, Szeged and Pecs."

"The sponsors are certainly getting their money's-worth," muttered Susan, as she hastily wrote everything down.

Tom shifted uncomfortably. "Do I have to pronounce these place names when we're playing there?"

"Well, yes," said Terry, looking surprised. "Is that a problem?"

"I'm not sure that I can get my tongue around some of them."

Susan smirked. "Maybe you should sign up for electrocution lessons."

"I think you mean elocution lessons," Tom snapped.

She widened her eyes. "Do I?"

"Lucky you haven't got false teeth," chuckled Jim. "They'd end up in the front row."

Terry smiled benevolently. "Just do your best, luv. You've got lots of rest days here in Budapest," he continued. "I know you'll love it here. I wouldn't live anywhere else. The shopping is nearly as good as Paris, and the night-life is terrific. It can be bad for your waistline, though. Don't eat too many luscious cakes. And you must visit the thermal baths, the water is quite exhilarating."

He lowered his voice a fraction and carried on in a confidential hush, "But be careful who you talk to. Some of the people who go there are interested in more than just bathing. Isn't that right, Ahmed?"

Ahmed nodded in agreement, with a look of disapproval on his face.

Terry stood up and smoothed his trousers. "Oh yes!" he cried. He pointed at the large package in Ahmed's arms. "Silly me, I nearly forgot.

We've brought the tour merchandise with us. Baseball caps and tee shirts with the sponsor's name on the front, and your name on the back."

He wrinkled his nose and said thoughtfully, "I think that's all. Any questions, boys and girls?" He gave each of them his agony-aunt smile.

"How much is this suite gonna cost us?" demanded Pete.

"Oh, don't worry dear," Terry replied, with a flick of his wrist. "The manager here owes me a favour, so he's let you have the suite at a reduced rate." He gave them a conspiratorial wink.

Joe asked hopefully, "Are there any express photo labs around here?"

"Heaps," Terry assured him. "Just follow the tourist trails and you'll come across them."

"By the way," said Tom, "Do you have a phone number that we can reach you on?"

Terry clicked his tongue. "I'm having a few problems with my phone line at the moment. Just talk to the manager if you need to see me. He usually knows where to find me. Right then, my dears, we'll be off." He readjusted the designer purse on his wrist. "Can I just use your loo before we go?"

Tom nodded. "Sure, you can use my room."

When Terry returned a few minutes later he had a puzzled look on his face.

"I hope you don't mind me asking," he said quietly to Tom, "But why do you have a glue stick next to your razor? Do you use it on your skin when you nick yourself shaving?"

Tom frowned. "What are you talking about? What glue stick?"

Terry retraced his steps to the bathroom and came back carrying the item in question.

"That's my deodorant," Tom told him. "I got it in Prague."

"No, it's definitely a glue stick. Children use them for making scrapbooks and such-like."

Tom groaned. "I've been using it three times a day!"

Terry gave a sympathetic grimace. "Oh dear, I bet you've been having trouble with your arpeggios."

"Is that Hungarian for armpits?" Susan whispered to Joe.

"Don't worry luv," Terry continued. "I'll get you some proper deodorant sticks. Is Aramis all right for you?"

"Whatever," mumbled Tom.

"Toodleoo then. We can't stick around any longer." Terry and Ahmed giggled their way into the corridor.

Susan unpacked the bundle of merchandise and examined the contents. The black baseball caps had the Zblatov logo on the front, with Tom Banks picked out in gold thread on the back. She pulled a black tee shirt from its plastic bag and shook it out. The Zblatov logo covered most of the front. She glanced at the back, did a double-take, then grinned.

"Nice tee shirts. Shame about the spelling mistake."

"What spelling mistake?" asked Tom, peering at the front of the shirt.

"On the back. They've printed W instead of B."

CHAPTER 12

Next morning they were taking a leisurely stroll through a Pest shopping precinct.

"This search for a deodorant stick is turning into the quest for the Holy Grail," grumbled Pete.

"Terry said that he'd give you one of his," Susan reminded Tom. "Why bother to buy one?"

"Who knows when we'll see him again," Tom replied, sceptically. "Did you leave a message for him at the desk?"

Susan nodded her head. "I said that it was urgent, though I don't expect that he will be able to get any new tee shirts done in time for the shows. We'll have to make do with the baseball caps."

They came upon another pharmacy, and Susan went inside with Tom. Minutes later they emerged, looking jubilant.

Tom cried, "We found one, at last!"

Jim tilted his head dubiously. "Are you sure it's the right thing?"

"Of course I'm sure," Susan said, tartly. "I waved my elbows in the air and did under-arm strokes, and they knew immediately what I wanted. Women are always better at shopping than men. I don't know how you managed to pick up a glue stick," she added, derisively.

"Probably because I don't usually do my shopping in downtown Prague," Jim replied. "Though I did think at the time that it was a bit odd, having deodorants on the same shelf as writing paper."

Susan pressed her nose against a shop window. "Ooh, look at this." She had stopped outside a cafe, and was gazing at the tantalising display of cakes.

"You can't possibly be hungry," Tom remarked. "We've only just had breakfast."

"I don't need to be hungry to eat cream cakes," she replied. "Let's go in and try some. We've got to hang around for an hour before Joe's photos are ready, anyway."

They trooped inside and parked themselves in front of the counter. Inside a long glass cabinet there was a tempting array of luscious gateaux, topped with strawberries, black cherries, mandarin segments or slices of pineapple, and sprinkled with almonds or chocolate curls. Fresh cream fluffed out from between the triple layers of sponge cake.

Susan groaned in agony. "How can I possibly choose one? I want to try all of them." She pursed her lips, then exclaimed, " I know! If we all choose a different slice of cake, I can taste a piece of each one."

"Why don't you just order five pieces of cake for yourself?" Tom suggested.

"Don't be ridiculous," she retorted. "I can't sit at a table with five pieces of cake in front of me. I'm not a complete piggy."

"No, you're still practising," Jim muttered, as he followed her inside.

When the waitress brought the coffee and cakes, Susan subjected the band to one of her hard stares. "Don't start eating until I've had a spoonful from each plate."

"Don't worry," Tom sighed. "None of us actually likes cake!"

* * *

In the evening Janek turned up with the bus to take them to the venue.

"Come on Joe," Tom called. "Leave your picture book alone, it's time to go."

Joe had bought himself a large scrapbook, and had spent most of the day pasting his photos into it, using Tom's glue stick. Underneath each photo he was writing short notes to accompany the picture.

"Let me just finish this page," Joe murmured, his head bent down in concentration.

As the band exchanged impatient glances, Terry and Ahmed appeared in the doorway.

"I got your message," Terry said, breathlessly. "Something about the merchandise. We dashed over as soon as we could. What's the problem?"

"Susan will tell you about it," Tom said, as Joe finally closed his scrapbook. "We gotta make tracks to the venue."

As the band hurried out, Susan opened a bag of tee shirts, unfolded one and pointed at the misprint on the back.

"Ooh," gasped Terry, covering his mouth with both hands. "I never thought to check them. A friend of a friend did them for me." He wrinkled his nose in annoyance. "We'll take them away and see if they can do another batch in double-quick time. Is this all of them?"

"I've kept a couple as souvenirs," she told him. "I thought I'd send one to Tom as a Christmas present, as a reminder of the time that we've spent together."

Terry pouted. "Ooh, don't talk to me about Christmas. I sometimes think that I know too many people, with all the cards that I have to send."

Susan's memory was suddenly jogged, and she said, "I nearly forgot. There was a man looking for you at the show in Brno. Did he get in touch with you?"

Terry looked blank. "What was his name?"

"He didn't say. He was a rather creepy-looking bloke, but he had a nice cashmere coat."

Terry and Ahmed exchanged a quick glance.

"What did you say to him?"

"Not much. Just that he could probably find you in Budapest. He didn't seem keen to chat. He shot off fairly quickly when I told him that you weren't with us."

"Did the boys tell him anything?" Terry demanded, anxiously.

"They didn't see him. I was on my own when he turned up."

Terry frowned and was silent for a moment. Then he said to Susan, "I'd be grateful if you didn't mention it to the others. It's nothing to do with the tour. Could you do me another favour, too? I've got something that I need to keep in a safe place for a while. Would you look after it for me?"

Susan hesitated. "Well, I don't know. I've got enough on my plate as it is."

"I'll make it worth your while, luv. I don't expect favours for free."

"Okay. What is it?"

Terry unzipped his leather pouch and took out a small black book, then he pulled out a wad of bank notes. He handed them all to Susan, saying, "Keep the address book in a safe place, or I won't be sending any Christmas cards this year."

Ahmed gave a tiny chuckle.

Terry fished something else out of his leather pouch. "Here's the deodorant stick that I promised to Tom. I'll just put it in his bathroom, then we'll be off. Would you like a lift down to the show?"

"Yes please. I like to keep an eye on them. They usually get into trouble if I'm not around."

As they walked out of the hotel, Susan paused to admire the nearby illuminated bridge that spanned the ink-black Danube.

"It looks lovely at night," she murmured, and she strolled behind Terry and Ahmed, who were weighed down by the bags of tee shirts. They had halted beside a yellow Mercedes, and as Susan joined them she said in surprise, "What happened to your Porsche?"

"I decided that violet wasn't really my colour," Terry told her, "So I got rid of it."

Ahmed threw the tee shirts on to the back seat of the car, and Susan climbed in beside them. As Ahmed edged the car away from the kerb, Susan glanced over her shoulder to get another glimpse of the dazzling bridge. As she did so, she caught sight of a figure standing beneath a lamp-post on the other side of the street.

She peered harder and tried to focus more clearly, but Ahmed accelerated swiftly down the road, and the figure disappeared from sight. Maybe she was mistaken, but she felt sure that the street light had illuminated the sinister man in the cashmere coat. Susan's thoughts were interrupted by Terry's voice.

"I noticed that Tom has some hair-removal gel in his bathroom. I used that particular brand once, and it brought me out in the most awful rash."

"What hair-removal gel?" Susan asked, baffled. She knew that Tom's personal hygiene routine did not involve the removal of any body hair.

"The depilatory stick," Terry replied. "On the shelf, next to the razor. Where the glue stick used to be."

* * *

The next morning, Susan was startled awake by a yell that came from the direction of Tom's room. Several seconds later there was a rapid knocking at her door, and Tom called, "Let me in, quick! I need some ointment!"

Susan pulled on her dressing gown and opened the door. Tom dashed in, clad only in a bath towel.

"What's wrong?"

"I must be allergic to that new deodorant," he complained. "All the hair under my arms has fallen out, and my skin has come out in a livid rash. Look!" and he lifted each arm in turn to show her. "When I got into the shower, the water was stinging my armpits, and that's when I noticed that the hairs were gone!"

Susan grimaced. "Er, I meant to tell you last night. Never mind, they'll grow back again. You'd better throw that stick away, and use the one that Terry brought."

As she smoothed the antiseptic ointment on to Tom's inflamed skin, Jim appeared in the doorway, puzzled as to what was happening. After Tom had explained about his hair loss, Jim grinned and said, "It's a shame you can't find the hairs. You could have stuck them back on with the glue stick."

* * *

That afternoon they were panting up a hill.

"We're supposed to be sight-seeing," complained Susan. "Not mountaineering. My feet are killing me." She groaned and sat down on a wooden bench.

"You should have worn sensible shoes," Joe remarked.

"I haven't got any sensible shoes," she snapped at him. "And if I did have any, I'd take them to the charity shop!"

Tom sat down next to her. "I will never understand women, as long as I live. I remember once, my wife saying to me, "I've got some new shoes. What do you think of them?" I glanced at them, and they were fairly ordinary-looking shoes with low heels on them, so I replied, "Yeah, they're nice sensible-looking shoes." And she gave me a stony look and went out of the room. Then a few days later, I was sitting at my piano while the maid was dusting around, and I happened to notice her shoes. I said, "That's a coincidence, Mary. My wife has a pair of shoes just like yours." And Mary didn't say nothing, but she gave me one of those half-smiles that women give you when they're thinking to themselves, "Gee, this guy is an idiot." And it wasn't until ages afterwards that it suddenly dawned on me that it was just the one pair of shoes, and that my wife had given them to the maid."

"I'm surprised she didn't throw them at you, first," Susan retorted.

"Not every woman has a temper like yours," Tom replied. And he stood up to resume the uphill trudge.

Joe was consulting his guide book as he walked. "It says that this hill was named after a medieval priest who was thrown over the edge by his parishioners."

Pete shrugged. "They probably didn't like his sermon."

"Not so much the sermon "on" the mount, as the sermon "off" the mount," Jim commented.

As they approached the citadel on the summit, Joe darted about, taking photos from every vantage point.

Susan was lagging behind, and she fell into conversation with a group of back-packers. When she caught up with the band she said indignantly, "We could have got up here on a bus! Those Australians came up on it."

Tom gazed after them, and remarked idly, "Where do back-packers go in the winter?"

"They don't have winter," Susan told him. "When they go back to Australia, it's summer-time there."

Later that afternoon they were travelling back to the hotel on a tram, and Joe was pleading desperately, "But I really want to visit the Castle today. We still have time."

"We just saw a castle," Jim argued.

"No, that was a fortress," Joe corrected him. " The Castle is different. Well, it isn't really a castle. It's the historic part of Buda, at the top of this hill."

They were still arguing as they jumped off the tram at the bridge stop. A short walk across the bridge would take them back to their hotel on the opposite bank.

"We don't have to climb all the steps," Joe continued. "We can go up in the cable car."

"Susan won't like that," Jim countered.

"Since when have you cared about me," she murmured.

"Why don't you go and see this Castle place on your own?" Tom suggested. "We're kinda overdone on the sight-seeing stuff."

"It's no fun on my own," Joe complained. "And besides, I need someone to help me carry all my camera lenses."

Ten minutes later they were ascending the steep hillside above the river, riding on the funicular railway. Jim nudged Susan and said, "They have a ride just like this in Disney world. They crank the cars up to the top of a hill, then let them drop fifty feet into a pool of water!"

Two hours later they were trailing behind Joe in a weary procession.

"Well, we've seen the Castle, the Bastion, Gothic houses and baroque mansions. Where to next?" asked Tom.

"The Metro station," Jim said firmly.

"I need to go to the loo," Susan announced. "Let's find a cafe or something."

They made their way through Vienna Gate, and after a few minutes walk they spotted a small restaurant.

"Karl Marx Pizzeria," said Jim, reading the name above the door. "Will they let us in without a red card?"

They sat at a table and ordered coffee, while Susan darted off to find the rest room.

Pete studied the menu, and after a while he remarked, "I wonder what a "Gulag" pizza is like?"

Tom grimaced. "They probably serve it straight from the freezer."

Pete frowned as he continued to read the menu. "They have an "Anarchist" pizza here. I wonder what that has on it?"

"It has anything that you damn well want!" said Jim, leaning back in his chair as he watched the young waitress squeeze between the tables.

"How about the "Lenin" pizza?"

Tom curled his lip. "You probably have to share it with everyone else in the restaurant."

Susan got back to the table. "You haven't got time to eat. Hurry up and finish your coffee, or we'll be late for our moonlight boat trip on the Danube."

"I didn't want to eat here anyway," Jim told her. "We'd probably get the trotskies."

* * *

It was chilly and dark as they chugged up the Danube in a tourist boat.

"It's freezing out here," complained Susan. "Can't we go and sit inside?"

"You can't see anything if you sit inside," Joe replied.

Tom inhaled deeply. "Gee, I love to breathe the night air on a river."

Susan tugged her jacket tightly around her. "There's nothing nice about diesel fumes."

"Push her over the side," suggested Jim. "She'll only make a little splash."

Joe thrust his camera case in Susan's direction. "Hold this while I change the flash."

She gazed at the spectacular flood-lit buildings on the opposite bank. "Seems a bit pointless, using a flash to take photos of an illuminated building at night."

"You can be a real misery sometimes," Tom murmured.

"I'm worn out. Can't we go back to the hotel to eat?"

"No, we're going ethnic tonight. Goulash and gypsy music."

"I hope you're not going to join in with the musicians," Susan said, testily.

"As a matter of fact, I used to play in a Hungarian bar in New York," Tom recalled, in a nostalgic tone.

Jim chuckled. "Yeah, back in the days when you were working for Alcoholics Anonymous."

Susan raised her eyebrows in surprise. "Really?"

"No, it's Jim's little joke," Tom explained. "When I first started out, I played modern jazz. It wasn't to everyone's taste, but I persevered with it. Unfortunately, several of the bars that I played in went out of business. Lack of customers," he ended, glumly.

Jim grinned wickedly. "He could close down a bar faster than the vice squad."

CHAPTER 13

"Here, take a sip of this," Jim said, handing a round bottle to Susan.

They were sitting on the bus on Wednesday morning, on their way to Gyor. Susan was clutching her stomach and groaning.

She eyed it suspiciously. "What is it?"

"Hungarian brandy," he replied. "They say it puts hairs on your chest."

Susan put the bottle to her lips and tasted a mouthful.

"Ugh! Puts hairs on your tongue, more like!"

She took another sip, then muttered, "I could probably get used to it, though."

"It's not like you to share your booze," Pete remarked.

Jim wrinkled his nose. "It's got a strange herbal taste."

"I don't think I should have had the second plateful of goulash last night," Susan said, plaintively.

"I don't suppose the five desserts did you any good, either," Jim commented.

"Well, it seemed a shame to let them go to waste, as it was all included in the price."

"If you stay in Budapest much longer you'll have to buy some larger clothes."

"Shapeless clothes are all the fashion now, anyway," Susan retorted.

"Yeah," Jim agreed, despondently. "I've noticed. When we were in England I didn't see any girls who appealed to me at all. They were all wearing dismal, baggy clothes and big construction-worker boots. They looked ghastly. Why don't young girls wear pretty clothes any more?"

"It's a government plot," Susan replied. "They want to reduce the number of single mothers living on state benefits, so they've manipulated the fashion industry for their own ends. Young girls look so unattractive now that there's no risk of them becoming pregnant."

"I could almost believe that," Jim remarked, "If it wasn't for the fact that you always talk total rubbish."

"Huh. At least I know the difference between brandy and medicine," Susan scoffed, as she took another swig from the bottle.

"Are you two going to bicker all the way to Gyor?" demanded Tom. "I'm trying to do some work here."

"What are you composing?" Susan asked, gazing at his music pad with lack of comprehension.

"It's a little piece of modern jazz."

"Modern jazz," murmured Susan. "Music for emergencies."

Tom stared at her. "What do you mean? What kind of emergency?"

"If you're having a party in your house, and it's getting on for two in the morning, and you want everybody to leave, you just put a modern jazz album on the hi-fi, and everyone disappears like magic."

"I always use a folk music album for that," said Jim.

Susan shook her head. "No, you can't rely on folk music. People are liable to fall asleep where they sit, instead of getting up and leaving. But nobody can sleep through modern jazz. Not unless you hit them on the back of the head with an empty vodka bottle first."

"It can be arranged," muttered Tom, not looking up from his pad.

Susan disregarded his remark and continued to sip from Jim's bottle.

"This is good stuff," she informed them, with a small hiccup.

"I think you've had enough to cure your stomach ache," Jim told her, as he wrested the bottle from her grasp. "I must take some of this with me on the flight back home. It's the antidote for airline food."

"I don't know why everyone moans about airline food," Susan argued. "I worked in a travel shop once, doing the accounts. The air ticket booking clerk sat next to me, and I couldn't have done her job for anything. All those fussy people, bleating on about how they want a vegetarian meal, or how they can't eat dairy, or how they must have low-fat. Why can't they eat what they're given and like it? It's an airplane, not the Savoy bloody Grill!"

She tugged the brandy bottle from Jim's hand, took another sip and continued, "When I get on a plane, the only thing that I'm concerned about is getting to the other airport in one piece. I'm the one with the rosary beads, chanting, "Hail Mary, full of grace, get us safely to the other place.""

"And it's not just the food," she ranted. "They make such a fuss about where they want to sit on the plane. They want to sit by the window, or by the bulkhead, or next to the emergency exit. That really makes a lot of sense, doesn't it? Everyone knows that when a plane goes down, if you're lucky enough to be sitting next to the emergency exit, you just step out of the wreckage and walk away."

"The stewardess usually sits at the back of the plane," Jim said thoughtfully. "I guess that's because it's the safest place."

"Stewardesses get nervous, too," Tom told them. "I was on a domestic flight one time, aboard a small plane, and the turbulence was pretty bad. I was sitting at the back, and there was a vacant seat next to me. The turbulence got so rough that the stewardess sat down next to me and fastened up her seat belt. She looked real scared, so I thought I'd try and lighten things up a little. So I turned to her and said jokingly, "Do these things go down often?" She gave me a stony look and said, "No, only once."

"I kept my mouth shut after that!" Tom said, sadly.

* * *

As they drove into Gyor a couple of hours later, Tom nudged Susan awake.

"What's the name of the hotel?" he asked. "Janek doesn't know where to go next."

Susan hastily dug the creased itinerary out of her bag and peered at the directions.

"Have we gone past a big, white baroque building?" she asked.

"I don't have a degree in medieval architecture," he snapped.

"There was an imposing-looking white building a couple of blocks back," Joe said, helpfully.

"Tell Janek to turn right at the next intersection," Susan decided. "If we find the river we can follow the road along it."

Janek duly found the river-front street, and several minutes later they came to a halt outside a Gothic building that bore the name of the hotel.

"Odd-looking place," commented Tom. "It looks like a convent."

"There's a church next door," Susan remarked. "You can go in there and pray for your fingers to work properly tonight."

"My fingers always work properly. It's my brain that lets me down."

They checked into the hotel and had some lunch, while Janek drove off to find the venue.

"Do you think it's a good idea to put Janek in charge of selling the merchandise?" Pete asked doubtfully, as they were drinking coffee after lunch.

"Who else is there?" Tom argued. "Terry and Ahmed are never around. That only leaves Susan."

"I'm an accountant, not a sales girl," Susan said, brusquely. "And besides, I need to be backstage to make sure that the crew don't sell any of our equipment."

"Has everyone finished coffee?" Joe asked, brightly. "Good. Let's go outside for a group photo. The girl at reception told me that this place used to be a monastery, so I want it for my scrapbook."

Tom grinned. "It's about the closest that Jim will ever get to a celibate lifestyle."

* * *

That evening at the venue, Janek had set up a little stall just inside the entrance lobby, and was doing a brisk trade selling the baseball caps. Once the show had got under way, Susan came along to help him pack away, and lock up the cash.

"I stay here after show, sell more hats?" Janek offered.

"No, we need you out back to help load the gear," she told him. "We'll take this stuff back to the dressing room now."

They carried the merchandise backstage and stacked it in a corner of the dressing room. Susan counted up the money, then gave the cash box back to Janek to lock up in the bus, while she went off to watch the band perform.

* * *

"What happened to your backing vocals on Another Lover?" Tom complained, as they made their way back to the dressing room at the end of the show.

"You sang the last verse instead of the second verse," Joe protested. "I didn't know how to follow."

"Oh, sorry."

As he opened the dressing room door and stepped in, he gasped, "What's this!"

Susan squeezed into the doorway beside him, and raised her eyebrows in surprise. The baseball caps were strewn across the floor like lumpy confetti at a black-magic wedding.

"Who did this?" she cried. "It was tidy when I went out!"

They picked their way between the caps, and collected them all up.

"Some fans must have been in here," Tom surmised.

"They wouldn't do this," argued Susan. "They might nick a few, but most of your fans are too old to be into vandalism."

They carried the bags of caps out to the bus and returned to the hotel.

* * *

"It's very flat around here," Susan sighed, as they sped along the road to Szombathely on Thursday morning. "You can see for miles."

"I can see two oxen pulling a plough in a field over there," Joe said, in amazement.

Susan corrected him. "Bullocks."

"No, I definitely saw them," he insisted.

"I'm getting fed up of sitting on this bus," Susan grumbled. "I almost wish that I was back at work!"

Tom chuckled. "You wouldn't be much good as a new-age traveller."

"That's a bit rich, coming from "shower-cubicle man"," she retorted.

"Camper vans back home have all the modern conveniences," he asserted. "You drive into a trailer park and plug yourself into the water and electricity. Though not both at the same time," he added, hastily.

"Lots of retired people are doing that, these days," Joe told them. "They take to the road because they can't afford to pay their property taxes and heating bills. So they take off to New Mexico in a camper van."

"I suppose we should call them "old-age" travellers," Susan observed.

Pete frowned. "Why don't they drive to Florida and spend winter on the beach?"

"They don't fancy their chances against the British tourists," Jim told him.

"But I once spent a vacation at a Disney resort hotel in Orlando," said Joe, "And there weren't any Brits there at all."

"They don't like paying Disney prices," Jim explained. "They stay in the cheap hotels downtown. Places called Dunspendin and Cockroach Condos."

"My twins want to go back to Disney world for another vacation," sighed Joe. "It's very expensive, but I don't mind paying out for it. It's nice to have kids and do things for them. We tried for seven years before they were born."

"That's just typical, isn't it?" Susan remarked. "You wait ages for a baby, and then two come along at the same time."

* * *

When they reached their destination, Janek followed the directions to the town centre, and they found the hotel easily. It was a grand, ostentatious building that dominated the rest of the town square. As soon as they had checked in, Tom said, "Right, let's dump our bags and go down to the venue. I wasn't happy about last night's show. I think we could all use a couple hours practise."

"But I wanted to take some photos," protested Joe. "There's a reconstructed Egyptian temple here."

"You're kidding!"

"No," insisted Joe. "It's just a couple of blocks away."

"Well, bring your camera, and you can get some shots on the way back"

The band rushed off, and left Susan to her own devices at the hotel. In the peace and quiet of her room, she suddenly remembered the little black book that Terry had given to her for safe-keeping. She fished it out of her handbag, and flicked through the pages. Good grief, she muttered to herself. He wasn't joking when he said he knows a lot of people.

Each tiny page was neatly filled with unpronounceable names, obscure cities, and lengthy phone numbers. Susan frowned. There were no street names listed at all. How does he use this for his Christmas cards, she puzzled? When she came to the S page, she paused to study a string of numbers that filled an entire line. Bank account, she murmured. S for Swiss? No wonder he can afford to change his cars like hankies, lucky bugger!

She dropped the address-less book back into her bag, and stretched out on the bed to watch Hungarian afternoon television.

* * *

When the band returned in the early evening, Tom knocked at her door to call her for dinner.

"Are you coming to the gig tonight?" he asked, as they made their way to the hotel restaurant.

She nodded. "I want to count the takings from the merchandise stall.

111

Janek isn't very organised. And I'll make sure that the stuff goes straight on to the bus when the show kicks off. It's obviously not safe to leave it in the dressing room."

"It's kinda strange," Tom said, with a frown. "We haven't had any trouble like this before, but Joe swears that his camera case was rifled while we were rehearsing this afternoon. He left it backstage and told one of the crew to keep an eye on it. Nothing was stolen, but some of the lenses were put back into the wrong holes, so someone had definitely been checking it over."

Joe's camera case was like a small metal suitcase. It had a thick foam interior, with lots of different-shaped indentations for the lenses and bits to fit snugly into.

Their conversation broke off as they entered the restaurant, which was resplendent with Art Nouveau decor. They joined the others at a table, and Tom murmured, "We're certainly eating in style tonight."

"Don't be too hungry," Jim advised him. "The menu has no prices on it!"

* * *

"Come on Susan! Are you going to sleep all day!"

Jim was hammering on Susan's door early next morning.

Susan stretched. "Ugh, all right. I'm awake," she called back. She remembered that they had to make an early start for the long drive to Szekesfehervar, so she leapt out of bed and quickly washed and packed.

Ten minutes later Jim was knocking at her door again.

"Come on," he called. "Janek's waiting."

She opened the door and demanded, "What about breakfast?"

"No time. We'll eat on the bus."

As they hurried out of the hotel, Joe pleaded, "Wait! I need a group photo in front of the hotel."

They huddled together into a neat group whilst Joe put his camera on a tripod and set the automatic timer. As Susan was gazing bleary-eyed into the distance, she noticed a man on the other side of the square. He was standing with his hands in his coat pockets, staring intently at them. Before Susan could focus her eyes properly, Joe's camera went "click", and Tom grabbed her elbow and propelled her onto the bus.

After half an hour on the road, Janek pulled into a lay-by.

"Breakfast now?" he suggested.

"At last," grumbled Susan. She was desperate for a cup of coffee.

Janek set up his little camping stove a few yards from the bus, and emptied a handful of coffee grounds from a grubby brown paper bag into his tin coffee pot. He lit the gas and set the pot to boil, then lit up one of his black cheroots.

As he pushed his ornate cigarette case back into his pocket, Susan remarked, "Does you grandfather have his own jewellery business?"

Janek shook his head. "He work in steel mill, till too old."

"How did he learn enamelling, then?"

"His grandfather, he teach him when he young boy. He Russian, then."

"Where was he rushing?" she asked, somewhat confused.

"Moscow," he replied, and he dashed across to where the coffee pot was spluttering.

"Is the coffee done? Great. Let's find somewhere to sit, away from the road," she suggested.

There was a gate nearby, and they went through it into the adjoining field. A few yards away was a grassy knoll, shaded by a handful of trees, and partially screened by bushes and briars. They sat down on the lush grass, and Jim handed around the bread rolls that Janek had bought earlier. Janek brought the cups of coffee, then sat down beside them and puffed at his cheroot.

"Don't blow smoke over the food," Susan complained. "Take that smelly cigar somewhere else."

Janek stood up and mooched back to the gate. He leant against it while he enjoyed his smoke.

"We could take this opportunity of peace and quiet to practise the close harmony on Warm Rain," Tom said to Joe. "It sounded a bit off when we did it last night".

They emptied their coffee cups and began to sing. Tom sang half a verse, then Joe joined in and harmonised with higher notes.

After several minutes of the duet, they were startled by a low bellow, and a thumping noise in the background. A horned cow appeared from behind the bushes and stood a few yards away from them, staring and stamping its hoof.

Susan gasped, "Oh no, it's a bull!"

"Are you sure?" Jim asked in alarm.

"Yes," she insisted. "Bulls always stamp like that when they're annoyed!"

"We'd better take off," he decided.

"No, if we run, it will chase us!" she whispered. "We need to distract it."

Susan chewed her lower lip, then said quietly, "Something red would do the trick."

She turned to Janek at the gate, and hissed, "Quick! Get Tom's red shirt out of his bag, and bring it here."

"Why?"

"Just do it!"

Janek shrugged. He went back to the bus and returned with Tom's remaining scarlet shirt.

Susan gestured. "Throw it over to me."

Janek tossed the red shirt to her, and she tied it around a small branch that she had found nearby.

"Can any of you lot throw a javelin?" she asked quietly.

Tom nodded and said softly, "I used to be pretty good when I was at school."

"Throw this so that it lands a few feet behind the bull."

Tom held the branch aloft, then drew back his arm and launched the missile. The branch flew through the air in a graceful arc and hit the ground with a gentle thud.

The stamping creature turned its head to see what had landed from the sky. The red shirt drew its attention, and it ambled back towards the branch.

"Quick, let's go!" snapped Susan.

They retreated hastily through the gate and jumped on to the bus.

Janek had been watching with a bemused expression on his face. He shook his head in bewilderment, then casually dropped his cheroot on to the ground and extinguished it with the heel of his shoe. He strolled over to the grassy knoll and retrieved the coffee cups.

After a few moments of investigating the red shirt, the animal turned back around and stared at Janek.

Janek shook his head sadly. "Sorry little bullock, but nice singing is ended now."

The bullock lowered its head and trotted away across the field.

CHAPTER 14

"Susan, will you stop singing. It's getting on my nerves," Jim complained, testily. "What with you singing "Ten Green Bottles", and Tom practising his pronunciation of Szekesfehervar, we sound like The Idiot Family on a day out."

Tom mumbled, "I can't get the hang of this name at all."

"Just say, Good evening, Chicago," Jim suggested. "Don't worry about it."

Pete had been gazing out of the window, and he suddenly interrupted with, "I think this would be a good place to buy a couple of cases of wine. We've passed several roadside shacks that have been advertising their local wine for sale. It'll probably be real cheap."

It was nearly lunchtime on Friday, and they were travelling through a hilly district, where dense vineyards spread up the slopes, yielding to thick woodland along the ridge.

Pete spoke briefly to Janek, and after a few more miles they halted beside a low, white-washed building at the side of the road. Propped against the side wall was a hand-painted sign, depicting a wine bottle and glass.

They clambered off the bus, glad to stretch their legs after three hours on board. As they walked along to the entrance, a fierce barking suddenly erupted, and two large dogs poked their heads over a low wall nearby. The group stopped in their tracks, uncertain whether to continue or retreat to the bus, but the commotion had brought the owner out to the front, and he shouted the dogs into silence. He placed his hands on Susan's shoulders and steered her through the large, carved oak doorway.

Inside, there were heavy wooden chairs and laminate-topped tables. The owner pressed Susan down on to one of the chairs, and gestured to the others to sit down, before disappearing behind a door at the far end of the room. He re-emerged a few minutes later with an armful of wine bottles that clinked together as he strode towards them. He deposited the bottles in front of them, then bent down behind a small counter and brought out half a dozen small glass tumblers.

"Don't worry," said Pete, in a business-like voice. "We don't want to taste it, we want to buy. How much for two cases?"

The man merely smiled and nodded, and proceeded to uncork a wine bottle.

"Just take a sip," whispered Susan. "He won't let us go without tasting it."

He lined up the glasses in a row and poured a measure into each one in a single movement. They all took a sip, and nodded in appreciation.

Their host smiled and quaffed the contents of his glass, gesturing to the others to do the same. As the visitors obediently emptied their glasses, he opened another bottle, and poured a sample into each empty glass as before. They took small polite sips, and the Hungarian proceeded to uncork yet another bottle.

"We can't possibly taste all the bottles," Tom hissed anxiously at Pete. "We'll be hungover for the show!"

Pete said in an authoritative voice, "Thank you. We'll have one case of each," pointing to the two bottles that they had sampled.

Their host nodded and smiled once more, then emptied his glass and motioned to the others to do the same.

"Can't we just make a run for it?" murmured Tom.

"He might set the dogs on us," Susan replied, quietly.

Jim was entering into the spirit of the event, and was clinking his glass against the Hungarian's before each mouthful.

The patron suddenly leaned back in his chair and shouted at one of the doors in the wall behind them. There was a distant clatter of dishes, and shortly afterwards the door was pushed open by a stout woman who was carrying a tray loaded with plates and pancakes. She set it down on their table and smiled at each of them, then she scowled at their host and disappeared back behind the door.

The remaining bottles were duly opened and sampled.

Two hours later they staggered back on to the bus, and woke the sleeping Janek. He loaded eight boxes of wine, complaining loudly about not being included in the festivities.

As they resumed their journey, Tom mumbled, "I now understand what people mean when they talk about European hospitality." He closed his eyes and slumped down in his seat.

* * *

Susan woke up and realised that the bus had stopped moving. She glanced at her watch and saw that it was late in the afternoon. She looked out of the window and saw a fairy-tale castle, complete with turrets and battlements, set amidst a beautiful terraced garden that was interspersed with statues and edged with ornamental stone walls.

Tom also awoke, and gazed out of the window, transfixed by what he saw.

"Have I slept for a hundred years and turned into Prince Charming?" he murmured.

"Dream on!" retorted Susan. "It would take more than a two-hour nap to improve your looks!"

"What is this place?" Jim asked, blinking rapidly.

"It's a folly," answered Joe, who was assembling his camera equipment. "A bizarre amalgam of medieval architectural styles, according to the guide book. The guy built it to please his wife."

"Why didn't he just take her out dancing," muttered Pete.

Tom stirred himself. "Let's have a walk around the place, and clear our heads."

As they wandered through the grounds, Joe remarked, "This would be a great place for wedding photos, what with the lovely gardens and the castle as a backdrop."

"But an uninvited wicked relation might turn up and put a curse on the proceedings," Susan conjectured, with fairy-tale images in her mind.

"It happened to me, once," Jim said.

Susan frowned. "What are you talking about?"

"My ex-wife and her mother turned up at my second wedding."

"Did they throw confetti?"

"No," Jim replied. "The only things that they hurled were insults."

"Well, at least insults are painless," Susan observed. "At Italian weddings they throw pasta at the bride and groom. And not just the small pasta that you put in soup, but great big cannelloni tubes! You really feel it when one of those hits you on the back of the neck. It's quite dangerous, really," she continued. "You could take someone's head off if you threw a sheet of lasagne with enough force."

"I heard that the Germans throw crockery at weddings," Joe remarked.

"Yes, but not at the bride and groom," Susan explained. "They fling cups and plates at the couple's front door."

"My second wife's family did that," said Jim. "But they weren't German. And I'm fairly sure that they were aiming at me, not the door."

Tom glanced at his watch. "We'd better make tracks."

They drove the remaining short distance across town to the venue, and took their bags with them into the hall. They were returning to Budapest after the show, so the band used the dressing room to change their clothes and freshen up as best they could.

* * *

As the applause subsided at the end of the show, Susan commented to Tom, "They didn't seem to mind being called Chicago. But isn't it a bit risky, saying to the audience, "Any requests?" They might shout back, "Yes - get off!"

"It has been known," Pete muttered.

They collected their bags from the dressing room and were preparing to leave, when Tom suddenly frowned and stood still.

"That's odd," he murmured. "I'm sure that I left my sweatshirt on top of my bag, ready for me to put on."

He unzipped the bag and searched through the contents. The sweatshirt was right at the bottom of the bag.

"Susan, did you re-pack this for me?"

"No," she answered. "You must have put it back inside. You're always tidying up."

"My shirts have been folded," he continued, looking baffled. "I always roll my shirts up. Someone has definitely re-packed my bag."

"Well you haven't got anything worth stealing, so don't worry about it," said Jim.

They boarded the waiting bus and headed off towards the motorway.

"How long will it take to get to Budapest?" Tom asked Susan.

"About an hour."

"Don't let me fall asleep," he told her, "Or I won't be able to sleep properly when I get to bed."

They were driving through the darkness, a solitary vehicle on the highway, with no overhead street-lights to pierce the black night.

Susan suddenly noticed a strange blue glow up in the sky, and she grasped Tom's arm tightly.

"You don't have to pinch me," he complained. "Just talk to me to keep me awake."

"Look up there!" she cried. "It looks like a UFO!"

Tom followed the direction of her gaze and spotted a luminous object above them.

He sighed. "You really should get yourself a pair of spectacles. It's a Zeppelin. It's probably advertising light bulbs."

"It might be an alien spacecraft, cleverly disguised as an advertising airship," she argued.

"Why would aliens want to come here?"

"They come here to help us. Not everyone on planet Earth is a human being, you know," she said, in a mystic tone. "Alien creatures have travelled here from a distant galaxy, to carry out the tasks that we humans find difficult. The most skillful of them work as surgeons."

"Yeah, right. And how do you know this, exactly?"

"Well, have you ever met a surgeon who displays any human characteristics?"

Tom tilted his head in a thoughtful manner. "Mm, you have a point. So, what do the rest of them work as?"

"Mini-cab drivers."

* * *

They all slept until late on Saturday morning. Breakfast was brought up to their suite, and Tom was still yawning after his second cup of coffee.

"Are we playing in the same place as last time? That small hall in the middle of the park?" he asked Susan.

"No, it's a bigger venue, on the island. It's open-air, so let's hope it doesn't rain."

Tom clicked his tongue and shifted nervously in his seat. "We'd better get down there and check on the acoustics. These open-air places can be a real devil to get the sound level right."

The band disappeared soon after breakfast, leaving Susan alone to organise the laundry, study the following week's itinerary, and total up the takings from the merchandise stall.

Janek had brought the bags of caps up to the suite, so that Susan could do a stock-take. Before she could begin counting, there was a knock at the door, and she found Terry and Ahmed outside, weighed down by large bags of tee shirts.

"Here we are again, luv," Terry beamed at her. "These are the new tee shirts, all hunky-dory. Are the boys not here?" he asked, glancing around the empty suite.

"No, they've gone to the venue. Tom wasn't very happy when he found out that it was an open-air place. He thinks our equipment might not be up to it."

"He's such a worry-bucket, isn't he? Anyway, did everything go all right last week?"

"Er, yes." Susan decided that one worry bucket on the tour was probably enough for Terry, so she said nothing about the rummaged bags and lurking strangers.

"Good. I'll have my little black book back, please."

Susan delved into her bag and handed the address book to him.

Terry pressed his lips together in satisfaction. "Excellentay. Tell the boys we're sorry to have missed them."

"Do you want to take the merchandise money away with you?" Susan asked. "I don't know where to bank it."

"We'll pop back tomorrow night for it," he replied. "You'll probably sell a lot more stuff tonight."

"I'll draw up a sales schedule for you, showing the number of items sold, and the remaining stock."

"Don't bother with the formalities, luv," Terry answered, as he waved his hand in a gesture of disinterest. "We don't bother too much about paperwork."

After they had left, Susan decided to keep a proper record of all the merchandise sales, despite what Terry had said. She unpacked the tee shirts and checked a few over, then counted them up.

She had counted the caps before they had left Budapest, and had packed them in bags of fifty, but they had got into a mess since the incident at Gyor. She checked each one over for dusty footprints, and counted them all again. When she had finished writing down all the numbers, Susan frowned and chewed the end of her pencil. Either the cash was short, or they had lost some caps. She cursed softly, and came to the conclusion that the intruder in the Gyor dressing room had made off with a bag full.

* * *

When Janek arrived in the afternoon to collect his caps, he was delighted to find a large pile of tee shirts awaiting him. He grinned happily and said, "This very good. I sell many tonight. Big show."

"Can you manage the stall on your own?" Susan asked, dubiously. "You'll be busier now that we've got the tee shirts as well. I could give you a hand."

Janek shook his head vigorously and replied, "My friend Lazlo, he help."

Lazlo was one of the crew. He seemed to spend more time playing cards with Janek than wiring up the sound equipment, but as Susan had once seen him trying to force a two-pin plug into a three-hole socket, she had decided that it was probably safer if he spent his time gambling.

"Give the cash box to me at the end of the show," she told Janek. "Terry will collect it tomorrow."

Janek looked momentarily disconcerted, then nodded his assent and struggled out of the suite with an armful of bags.

Tom and the band hurried in as Janek staggered out.

"We've just about got time to eat and shower," Tom muttered, looking wild-eyed and apprehensive.

"What's the matter with you?" Susan asked. "You don't usually get so agitated before a show."

"The place is huge," he moaned. "We had to wire up every last speaker. When we start up we'll probably blow all the fuses in downtown Buda!"

* * *

"You certainly gave them value for money," Susan commented, as she climbed into the taxi with Tom. It was a half hour after the show had ended, and the crowd had mostly dispersed. A few people were still trickling along the streets, making their way off the island and back into the city. Their two taxis were the only vehicles on the street, which was normally reserved for buses only.

"Well, once we'd got going, and the power seemed to be holding out all right, I stopped worrying. Three hours ain't much to me. I could play all night, if people are happy to listen."

"Did you see where Janek went?" she asked him. "He was supposed to give me the cash box, but I couldn't find him anywhere."

"Maybe he's gone for a midnight swim. There's a nice thermal pool just down from here," Tom remarked, closing his eyes.

"By the way," she said, nudging him awake, "I nearly did some money laundering this afternoon."

"Howzat?" he replied, sleepily.

"I was sorting out the dirty clothes in your bag, and I found a couple of thousand dollars rolled up inside a pair of socks."

"Tck! The Brno cash! I forgot that I still had that in my bag. I did have something worth stealing, after all. Hungarian thieves must be pretty inept," he mumbled, before nodding off to sleep with his head on Susan's shoulder.

Susan thought that was fairly unlikely, but she kept her opinion to herself.

CHAPTER 15

"One day off isn't much," Pete grumbled, over breakfast next day. "I think I'll spend the rest of the day in bed."

"I was thinking along the same lines," murmured Jim, as his eyes followed the young waitress around the hotel dining room. "All work and no play, as they say."

Susan followed the direction of his gaze and said sharply, "You can play all you want, but can you afford to lose any more clothing?"

Jim winced at the memory of Krakow, and sipped his coffee despondently.

"You can't stay in the hotel all day," protested Joe. "We've still got lots of places to visit here. I was thinking of going to that thermal pool on the island, as it's a nice day."

"Is it a guys-only pool?" Jim asked.

Joe thumbed through his guide book, perused a page then said, "No, it's open to all. There's even a section for nude sun-bathing."

"Sounds good to me," Jim said enthusiastically, his face brightening with anticipation.

Susan protested, "But I haven't got a swimsuit."

"Break open your piggy-bank and go buy one," Tom told her. "The market is open on Sundays."

"I can't buy a swimsuit in the market," she snapped. "Where would I try it on!"

Joe said, "There are some clothes shops down by the express photo place. That street is always full of tourists and the shops seem to be open all the time. We could go along there. I have some rolls of film that I need to take in, anyway."

"Don't go into the clothes shop with her," Jim teased. "You'll end up paying for her swimwear!"

* * *

An hour later, Susan and Joe were strolling along a narrow street which was flanked by imposing buildings decorated with frescoes.

"It didn't take you long to choose a swimsuit," Joe remarked.

"The prices were making me feel dizzy," she replied, "So I just grabbed the cheapest one I could find. I hope it's not too revealing."

"It must be difficult for you, travelling with a group of men," Joe said thoughtfully. "Most women would feel intimidated."

Susan gave him a derisive look and echoed, "Intimidated? By a dim piano player, an incompetent sex-maniac, and two guitar pluckers? Do I look feeble-minded?"

"No, no, not at all," Joe said, hastily. "In your job, I suppose you must be used to competing with men."

"I don't bother to compete with men," she replied, tersely. "I tell them what to do, and they do it."

"Don't you ever get any sexual harassment?"

"Not as much as I'd like," she replied, wistfully. "Most English men are too reserved to even wink at a pretty girl. It's very depressing."

As they emerged from the photo shop with Joe's prints, Susan spotted the rest of the band coming along the street towards them.

"Where have you lot been?" she asked, as they drew level.

"Down to the market," Tom replied. "I needed another tee shirt."

"Let me see it."

Tom cautiously reached inside his plastic bag and brought out a plain white tee shirt.

Susan smiled with relief, then frowned and said, "Why spend money? You could wear one of the Zblatov tee shirts."

"I don't wear shirts with my name on them," he asserted. "I'm not that much of an egotist."

"What he means is, that it would leave him open to jokes about not being able to remember his own name," Jim explained, with a grin.

Back in the hotel suite, Susan disappeared into her room to find a pair of scissors to cut the price tag off her new swimsuit.

"Was the market any good for souvenirs?" Joe asked the others.

"They have some beautiful embroidered dolls," Tom replied. "I think I may go back there and get one for my niece. It would make a nice Christmas present."

"By the way," Tom continued, lowering his voice, "I bought the perfect Christmas gift for Susan. It's a tee shirt with the word "PEST" printed on it."

Joe raised his eyebrows doubtfully. "I'm not sure she would appreciate being handed a gift like that."

Tom looked momentarily alarmed, then muttered, "Mm. Maybe I'll mail it to her."

* * *

"I don't understand how a skinny girl like you can sink so deep," Tom remarked, as he fished Susan out of the water-chute landing pool.

She spluttered the water out of her nose and shook her head dry.

"I'm a strange shape. I always go down water slides like a rocket, and hit the water like a brick."

"I think that you're a very nice shape," Tom murmured, as he strolled a couple of paces behind Susan.

They walked back to where they had left their towels on the grass, and after a quick rub-down, they went off to the wave pool, where Pete and Joe were enjoying the surf.

"Isn't this great!" enthused Joe. "What a terrific idea, having a pleasure park on an island in the middle of the river."

Susan bounced upwards through a wave and replied, "If this was London or New York, it would be sold off for towering concrete office blocks."

"I've been looking everywhere for you all," said Jim, suddenly appearing beside them. "This place is so big, and everyone looks the same in bathing trunks."

"Did you get bored with nude sun-bathing?" Pete asked with surprise. "We didn't expect to see you again today."

"Life is full of disappointments," Jim said, morosely. "I scoured the whole area, and not one of the women in the nude section is under sixty-five. Why is it that young girls never take their clothes off in public?"

Susan grimaced and said, "The same reason that good-looking men are always married."

* * *

"How do you think they got the statue of Gabriel to the top of that column?" Joe pondered, as they sat at an outdoor restaurant.

"The same way that they got Nelson on to the top of his column, I expect," Susan told him. "They tied him to the pigeons and they lifted him up."

They had walked through a vast paved and windswept square that was dominated by a towering column looming skywards, lifting the archangel Gabriel towards heaven.

"All those statues of warriors were a bit grim," Tom remarked. "It's nicer here."

They were sitting at a table on the terrace, surrounded by verdant foliage, and listening to bird cries emanating from the nearby zoo. A bright yellow parasol sheltered them from the sun, and gave the place a slightly tropical air.

"I'm not sure that I fancy the Fine Arts museum," grumbled Susan. "I'd rather sit here and drink some more wine."

Jim and Pete nodded in agreement.

"But it's a wonderful collection," insisted Joe. "I'm sure you'll enjoy it, once you're inside. It's full of priceless treasures."

"I did the Vatican museum once," Susan recalled, glumly. "After two hours of walking around the priceless treasures, all that I wanted to see was the coffee bar."

Pest City Park was crowded on the sunny Sunday afternoon. After their swim at the outdoor pool, they had taken a taxi across town because Joe wanted to see a Rodin sculpture in the art museum.

"Tell you what," said Tom. "You go round the gallery, and we'll go around the botanical gardens. We'll meet up at Gabriel's column at six."

"There's an amusement park not far from here," Jim told them, as he flicked through Joe's guide-book. "Let's take Susan up for a spin on the big wheel."

Susan glared at him and snapped, "If it wasn't for the fact that you're a vegetarian, I'd give you a knuckle sandwich!"

"But I'm not a veggie" Jim began, then he stopped abruptly.

"You nearly walked right into that one," Pete sniggered.

Jim grunted. "Huh. Almost, but not quite."

* * *

When they got back to the hotel in the evening they were all exhausted.

"Shall we go out tonight or eat downstairs?" Tom asked.

"Let's stay here," Susan announced. "I've got to wait for Terry, though it seems pointless, as I haven't got the cash box to hand over to him. I don't know what Janek is playing at. I'll have strong words for him when he eventually re-appears!"

"Don't give him a hard time," Jim said quickly. "If you upset him, he might piss off back to Poland, and we'll be up the proverbial creek without a driver."

Susan stood with her hands on her hips, and scowled at Jim. "When do I ever upset people?"

"Uh, I think I'll take a shower now," mumbled Tom, as he hastily retreated to his bedroom.

Pete scuttled off, saying, "I've gotta go and count my Levis."

"I'd better check my prints," whispered Joe.

Jim glanced around at the deserted lounge, then leapt to his feet, saying, "Don't worry about Janek. I'll go and see if he's in the bar." And he sprinted out of the suite.

Moments later there was a knock at the door. As Susan let in Terry and Ahmed, she said apologetically, "I'm afraid this is a wasted visit for you. I haven't got the merchandise money here. Janek has still got it. I hope."

Terry beamed at her. "Never mind, dear. We can collect it some other time. I'm glad we've caught you on your own," he continued, his eyes darting furtively around the room. "There's a small favour that I'd like to ask. Could you take this with you on your travels tomorrow?"

Terry was carrying a brown crocodile-skin shoe box under his arm. As he handed it to Susan, she saw that it had the word "Gucci" printed on the lid in gold lettering. He whispered to her, "I have to deliver this to a friend in Debrecen, but I can't get there this week. We have some urgent business to attend to in Vienna. So, as you'll be in Debrecen on Wednesday, I was wondering if you could take it for me. My friend will collect it from you at your hotel."

"It's a bit bulky," Susan complained. "I'll have a job to get it in my suitcase."

"I'll pay for the inconvenience, of course." Terry extracted a large number of notes from his wallet. He pressed the cash into Susan's hand, and continued in a hushed voice, "Keep the box with you, wherever you go. Don't let it out of your sight. And don't mention it to anyone else. I'll give my friend in Debrecen a pass-word to use, so that you can identify him."

This all seemed rather elaborate to Susan, just for delivering a pair of shoes, but she nodded her assent and then said, "I know a good pass-word.

I'll say to him, "What do you call a musical fish?" And he's got to reply, "A piano tuna."

Terry raised his eyebrows and groaned, then replied, "All right. At least it's easy to remember."

As he and Ahmed took their leave, Terry said over his shoulder, "I'll see you back here on Friday. Good luck!" and he quietly closed the door behind him.

Susan went into her bedroom and counted up the notes that Terry had given her. She gasped as she realised that she had two thousand dollars in her hand.

Susan unzipped her overnight bag, took out her spare pair of shoes, and placed the box in the space. The shoes would easily fit into her suitcase, but it was a nuisance having to carry the overnight bag around with her.

She went into Tom's room, and said to him in a weary voice, "I'm too tired to go down to the restaurant. I'll get room service to bring me something to eat, though I'm not really very hungry." Then she shivered and said, "I feel cold. Can I borrow a pair of your socks to wear?"

"Sure," Tom answered, getting a clean pair of socks out of his bag. "I sure hope you're not going down with the flu."

She shook her head. "No. It's just that time of the month, you know."

He gave her a sympathetic smile. "Oh, I see."

Susan scampered back to her room. She rolled the cash up inside the socks and tucked them at the bottom of her overnight bag. Then she phoned room service and ordered fillet steak with fries and a bottle of French wine.

* * *

Later on that night, Susan was sitting on her bed watching television, when there was a tentative knock at her door. She leaned over the edge of the bed, rolled the empty wine bottle out of sight, and said in a small voice, "Come in."

Tom tiptoed in, and sat on the bed beside her.

"How are you feeling?" he asked, gently.

"Oh, not too bad," Susan replied, giving him what she hoped was a brave smile.

"We discovered what happened to Janek last night," he told her. "We found him and Lazlo in the bar when we went down for dinner. It turns out they were involved in an accident last night."

"Is Janek all right? Will he be able to drive the bus tomorrow?"

"Yeah, he's fine. It wasn't his accident. He and Lazlo were loading some of the gear on to the rig, after the show last night. Apparently, they were pushing one of the wheely-crates up the ramp, on to the truck, when they lost hold of it. My guess is that they were fooling around, or drunk, whatever. Anyway, the crate rolled back down the ramp and ran over the foot of some guy who happened to be standing there. He made a fuss, so they had to get an ambulance to take him to hospital, and Janek and Lazlo had to go along as well, to fill in some forms about how it happened."

Susan frowned. "Why was the bloke standing so close to the truck?"

"Dunno," Tom replied. "None of the crew had seen him there at all. He must have been lurking in the shadows."

"He was probably hoping to nick something," Susan concluded, as she turned her attention back to the television screen.

CHAPTER 16

They drove into Eger just before lunchtime the next day. The journey had been quick and easy because they had travelled along motorway for most of the route, but as Janek heaved the bus through the narrow streets in the old town, he became increasingly frustrated. They were looking for the market square, and the streets seemed to get tighter at each turn. When they eventually found it, Janek clicked his tongue in exasperation and shrugged his shoulders in despair. The whole of the square was paved and pedestrianised, so they had to climb off the bus and carry their luggage up to the hotel on the farthest corner of the plaza.

Janek drove off, carefully manoeuvering the large bus down the medieval roadway, and gesturing rudely at the pedestrians who persisted in stepping in front of him.

Joe gazed at the historic buildings with admiration and said, "They've done a good job of preserving these medieval places. I don't recall ever seeing such charming old architecture, not even in England."

"We pulled down all our medieval buildings to make the roads wider," Susan bluntly informed him.

The hotel was a squat, half-timbered building with a steep terracotta tiled roof. The walls were painted in chocolate and white, and the windows were flanked by ornately carved shutters, with long window boxes containing masses of colourful petunias on each ledge.

"My kids have a jigsaw puzzle that looks like this," Pete remarked.

They checked in, and carried their bags up the narrow wooden staircase to the tiny attic bedrooms.

Joe smiled. "What sweet little rooms."

"A lot of charm, but not much headroom," mumbled Tom, as he ducked through his doorway. "Lucky it's just for one night, or I'd end up looking like the Hunchback of Notre Dame."

"You'd probably get more fan-mail then," Susan observed.

Tom pursed his lips and continued, "Let's go across the square and get something to eat. We can sit outside and enjoy the sunshine."

Susan picked up her overnight bag and followed the others downstairs. Across from the hotel was a restaurant with wooden tables and benches set outside on the cobblestones. The dining area was enclosed by a decorative wooden trellis, with troughs of bright flowers fastened along the edges.

As the waiter seated them at a table, Susan fidgeted with her overnight bag, trying to squeeze it underneath the bench.

Jim watched her and said, "Why didn't you leave that in the hotel? Has it got the Crown Jewels in it?"

"No, just "womens" things," she replied archly, shifting uncomfortably on the hard seat.

"Oh, I see," muttered Jim, looking slightly embarrassed.

Tom studied the menu. "What shall we try?"

"Whatever we get, it will have bees in it," Pete said, as he swatted at the flower tub next to him, where the bees were busily diving from one bloom to another.

"Wasps are worse," Jim said. "They take a big interest in alcoholic drinks. Bees are usually teetotal."

Tom shuddered and said, "I was drinking a can of coke out in my back yard once, and I didn't notice that a wasp had crept inside the tin. I nearly swallowed the damn thing."

"I don't know which is more disgusting," Susan said disdainfully. "Drinking from a can, or drinking cola!"

Tom widened his eyes. "What have you got against cola? The whole world drinks it."

"Too true! You can go anywhere in the world and see empty cola tins lying in the gutter. I expect that after the nuclear holocaust, the only remnants of human civilisation will be the empty cola tins lying around."

"Nuclear war will never happen," Joe asserted. "People aren't that crazy."

Susan shook her head. "Corporations are. You know how cut-throat it is between Coke and Pepsi. They'll have a nuke button installed on their computers, and some dim marketing executive will press it, thinking it means "new advertising campaign". In their crusade to expand their markets, they'll expand the planet into thirty million fragments," she ended, dramatically.

"That would be terrible," Jim responded. "The cola would be warm!"

* * *

"I'm bored," Susan complained, as she sat in the dressing room, twiddling her thumbs.

They were back-stage in the concert hall, waiting for the audience to settle.

Tom was sitting cross-legged in a chair, with his eyes closed, pretending to relax, but his fingers kept making involuntary twitches as he practised some of the more difficult pieces in his mind.

Jim was thumbing through a girlie magazine, giving the appearance of being a waiting passenger at a railway station, while Pete was gazing vacantly at the wall.

"You could tune this acoustic for me," Joe said to her. He passed a guitar over to Susan and instructed, "Tune it off the lowest string. That one usually stays true. Hold the string down behind the fifth fret, and use that note to tune the next string. Do that until the second-to-last, then move up a fret, then down to the fifth again for the last string."

Joe disappeared into the bathroom as Susan studied the neck of the guitar and placed her fingers on the first string. She dutifully twanged the strings and twiddled the keys to adjust the pitch. After she had tuned three strings, she gave the guitar a strum, and winced.

"That doesn't sound right," she murmured.

Pete stopped gazing at the wall, and gazed with interest at Susan's fingers. Jim had stopped perusing his magazine, and he also studied Susan's hands with rapt attention.

Susan carried on tuning the last three strings, remembering to move up a fret as Joe had told her. When she had adjusted all six strings, she plucked them one by one, and wrinkled her nose in dissatisfaction.

"This sounds awful," she declared. "I don't think much of Joe's method of tuning a guitar."

Tom opened his eyes and gave her a pained look, while Pete and Jim grinned at each other.

"That's pretty good, considering you're a novice," Jim said to Susan. "Keep this up and we'll offer you a job. All the best bands have consultants who tour with them, solely to tune the guitars."

"Money for old string," Susan muttered scornfully, as she strummed.

Joe emerged from the bathroom, and winced as he heard the guitar.

"What have you done?" he shrieked.

"I just did what you told me," she snapped back.

"But you have your finger on the wrong side of the fret!"

"Only a woman would think that behind means in front," commented Jim.

Joe took the guitar away from Susan and whispered words of comfort to it as he gently re-tuned the strings.

"It's a pity that you can't do anything useful," Jim taunted Susan. "Most girls who travel with bands are good at something." He gave her an obvious wink.

"I'm not a born-again groupie," Susan retorted. "And anyway, I can do something useful. I'm a very good singer. I've got a voice that travels."

"And most of the places it gets to, it's not welcome," Tom murmured.

Susan glared at Tom. "And the only way that you can reach the high notes these days, is by standing on your piano stool!"

"Did anyone bring the bottles of mineral water?" Joe hastily cut in.

"Yes, I did. And I wish I had some salt tablets to drop into them! You lot never appreciate the things that I do," Susan grumbled.

"I think that sentence rates as the most frequently-uttered female phrase," Tom said, thoughtfully.

"No," said Jim. "That one's number three. Number one is, "These bathroom scales must be wrong," and number two is, "Are you going to sit there all day?"

Jim ducked as Susan threw a roll of toilet paper at him, then continued, "Women! All they do is nag. They even moan at you for sleeping at night! After our first child was born, my wife used to say to me, "What is wrong with your hearing? Have you become terminally deaf? You never hear the baby crying at night. It's always me who has to get up. We could have a jumbo jet land on the roof, or a controlled nuclear explosion in the back yard, or have the Mormon Tabernacle Choir singing in the bathroom, and you'd still be snoring soundly!"

"And she developed a mean streak after the third one was born," Jim said, grimly. "I woke up one morning with a bad headache, and when I looked at the clock I saw that it was nearly midday. The kids were all running around, screaming and yelling, and my wife was nowhere to be found. Then I found a note stuck to the refrigerator. It said, "I'm taking the day off. You can look after the kids for a change.""

"I couldn't understand why I'd slept so late, but when my wife got home that evening she admitted that she'd put some sleeping pills into my drink on the previous night, to make sure that she could get out of the house before I woke up. When I complained that she might have killed me, she just glared at me and said, "Maybe next time!"

"I don't know why women have kids," Jim concluded. "It makes them real bad-tempered."

* * *

They were standing at the bottom end of the square on Tuesday morning, waiting for Janek to arrive with the bus.

"He's late," Tom complained, looking at his watch and frowning, "Where did he get to after the show? I didn't appreciate having to walk back here after the gig last night!"

"Well it wasn't far," said Joe, "And at least it wasn't raining."

"It took me right back to the early days, when me and the wife used to load the drum kit on to the back of a pickup truck after a show," Jim said, nostalgically. "If I stopped to talk to the groupies, she'd drive off without me. I used to do quite some walking in those days."

"At last!" Tom exclaimed, as the bus drew into sight. It pulled up beside them and they scrambled on.

As Susan boarded the bus, Janek turned and spoke to her. "Which way you want to go to Miskolc? Long, flat road or short-cut through mountains?"

Susan was surprised to see that Janek had a black eye, and as she stared at the bruise, Tom ordered, "Take the short-cut. And step on it. We're late enough as it is!"

Janek scowled and muttered darkly under his breath, then accelerated quickly down the narrow street. Startled pedestrians leapt out of the way as Janek tooted his horn at them.

Susan sat down quickly and whispered to Jim, "He's got a black eye! Goodness knows what trouble he got into last night!"

Jim grimaced. "Maybe we should have told him to take the easy route."

"He's paid to drive," Tom said loudly. "He seems to forget that, sometimes."

As they drove northwards out of Eger, the gently rolling hills were gradually replaced by precipitous slopes densely covered with deciduous forest. The road climbed upwards and became narrower as it wound tightly around rocky crags in a dizzy sequence of hair-pin bends.

Janek had not seemed to notice the change of road conditions, and he swung the bus around the sharp corners at a reckless speed. Susan suddenly saw a rock-face rushing towards her, and she gave an involuntary shriek. Moments later, as Janek heaved the bus around the next bend, the road disappeared from her sight, and all that she could see was the sky above her and a cliff below. She closed her eyes and wished that she had brought her rosary beads.

The narrow road snaked its way through the mountains, and the bus lurched through ever more twists and turns, making Susan feel sea-sick from all the sideways movement. She groaned quietly and swallowed hard, trying to overcome the nausea.

Jim noticed that she had become ashen-faced, and he remarked cheerfully, "They have a ride just like this in Disneyworld, but they make you do it in total darkness!"

The road suddenly plunged downhill, and they dropped at a breathless speed into a small, wooded valley. Through the trees they could see a lake glimmering in the dappled sunlight. Looming above the water, and fringed with dense forest, was a turreted chateau of grandiose proportions. Janek slowed the bus, and turned off the road into a car park, the entrance of which was almost obscured by foliage.

"Where on earth are we?" demanded Tom.

"Maybe it's the hotel," Pete deduced, as he spotted a uniformed youth struggling with trolley full of suitcases.

Susan pulled the crumpled itinerary from her bag and handed it to Tom. She felt too sick to read.

"Yeah, it's the hotel all right. It says here that Miskolc is just a few miles down the road," Tom read aloud.

"What a strange place," said Joe. "It looks like something from a Gothic horror novel. I've never seen turrets on a hotel before. And those spikes on top are almost like minarets." He studied the eccentric architecture as the others staggered off the bus with their bags.

Half an hour later, Susan was lying on her bed when there was a knock at the door. Tom was outside.

"Are you coming into town with us? I want to get down to the hall early, so that we can rehearse this new piece that I've written. If it sounds all right, I'll include it in tonight's set."

Susan shook her head. "I think I'll stay here. I'm not feeling very well."

"You do look a bit pale."

Jim stepped out of his room as Tom was speaking, and he said, "There's a notice down at Reception about a "murder-mystery-whodunit" event that they're holding here tonight. They needed a volunteer to be the corpse, so I put Susan's name down."

* * *

Susan felt ravenously hungry on Wednesday morning, having not eaten anything since Eger. She phoned room service and ordered two cooked breakfasts. After twenty minutes there was a knock at the door and a shout in Hungarian, and Susan let in a waiter who was pushing a trolley of food and coffee. As she held the door open, Jim appeared from around a corner of the corridor, walking bare-footed and holding a pair of very muddy socks.

Susan looked at them with distaste. "Why are you carrying those filthy socks?"

"I didn't want to get the hotel carpets dirty," Jim replied, "So I took them off before I came inside. I thought that would've been obvious to a woman of your intellect."

Susan stared at him in bewilderment, then quickly closed the door as the waiter left. She didn't want to share her breakfast with a hungry drummer.

* * *

"That wasn't very sociable, having breakfast on your own," Tom complained, as they paid their bills at the front desk

"I was too hungry to wait for you lot," Susan countered. "I thought that you'd be sleeping late."

Susan was running out of excuses for eating alone in her room. The overnight bag was an encumbrance in hotel dining rooms, and she was looking forward to getting rid of the shoe box in Debrecen.

As they walked outside to the bus, Susan asked, "Did you find out how Janek got his black eye?"

Jim shook his head. "No, he won't talk about it. I guess it must have been a girl. If it was a guy that did it, he would've been bragging about how many punches he took."

"It's a shame that more people on this tour can't keep their minds on their jobs, and off of women," Tom said tetchily, as he stepped on to the bus.

"Why's he so bitchy this morning?" Susan muttered.

"He's sulking because his new piece didn't sound too good last night," Jim said, loudly.

"It would have sounded fine if you had concentrated on the music, instead of giving the eye to that plump blonde," Tom replied, curtly. "You were all over the place with your drumsticks."

Jim shrugged. "Well, what do you expect, writing stuff in nine-eight time? It's unnatural. And anyway, she wasn't plump. She was voluptuous."

"I hope she was worth the cost of a new pair of trainers," Pete remarked, as they drove out of the hotel car park.

Susan glanced down at Jim's feet and noticed that he was wearing deck shoes. She raised her eyebrows in surprise. "Don't tell me she stole your trainers?"

"Have you taken leave of your senses?" Tom cut in. "Who would want to steal Jim's smelly footwear!"

"What happened, then?"

"She invited me back to her place," Jim explained. "But first she took me to the Thrashing Showers, just outside of town. I was a bit dubious when she suggested it. I thought she might be into the painful stuff, you know. But it turns out to be a thermal shower in a cave. She works there, so she knows how to get in at night. It was pretty good there, I must admit. Anyway, after that, we went back to her place. Her old man was working night shift at the armaments factory. I didn't plan to stay too long, but what with the show and the warm-water bathing, I fell into a deep sleep."

"Next thing I know, she's shaking me awake 'cause she hears his key in the front door! So I pulled on my shorts and socks, she pushed me over to the bedroom window, and I had to jump out into the shrubbery. She tossed the rest of my clothes out after me. I waited for her to throw my trainers as well, but he must have come into the bedroom before she had a chance. So I got dressed in the bushes, and walked till I found a taxi-cab."

"You're supposed to collect souvenirs, not distribute them," Susan told him.

CHAPTER 17

"That's the worst game of I-Spy that I've ever played," grumbled Susan, glad to see the outskirts of Debrecen come into view. The two-hour bus journey had taken them over the flat, uninspiring plains, where wheat fields and pasture land stretched interminably into the distance. The desolate landscape was sprinkled with occasional isolated farmsteads, showing flaking whitewashed walls and sagging terracotta tiled roofs.

"I don't believe that your P was for pig," she said accusingly to Joe. "I never saw any pigs."

"There was one," Joe insisted. "It was snuffling around a derelict-looking shed along by the roadside."

"His eyesight is better than yours," Jim cut in. "If he maintains that he saw a pig, then I believe him."

"And how many different words are there for wheat?" Susan continued, in a tone of complaint. "I think it's cheating to say M for maize, C for corn, R for rye, and B for barley. We're not all horticultural experts, you know."

"Tomorrow we'll play for money," Jim told her, as he studied a map of the area in Joe's guidebook. "We have to re-cross this plain to get back to Budapest."

The bus suddenly swerved to the right as Janek swung out of the path of a tram which was rushing up behind them. Shortly afterwards they halted outside a hotel in the centre of the town. As they entered the spacious foyer, they were surprised by the crowds of people teeming about inside.

"This is a popular place. I think I'll dump my bags then mooch along to the bar," Jim announced, as he cast his gaze at a group of slender, dark-skinned young women who were chatting gaily on the other side of the foyer.

"This is obviously the in place to come for lunch," Tom observed. "We'll be lucky if we get a table."

"I'm not hungry, anyway," Susan lied. She felt obliged to go straight to her room and wait there until Terry's friend arrived for his shoe box.

"I think I'll go for a run in the park opposite," Tom decided. "I haven't had any exercise in days. I'd like to stretch my legs a little."

Joe wanted to write a letter home, and Pete elected to go to the bar with Jim, so they went their separate ways, arranging to meet in the foyer at five.

Alone in her room, Susan stood at the window and looked out at the twin towers of a church across the street. It had a gloomy, forbidding look to it, and it reminded her of a bad-tempered nun in her junior school days. She turned her eyes downwards to the small park that was in front of the church. A bright display of bedding plants showed a riot of cheerful colours in contrast to the dark church walls.

A tall, moving figure in the park caught her eye. Tom was jogging along a path which circled the flower beds. She watched him do several circuits, puzzling as to why he did an occasional leap into the air, when she was startled by a knock at the door.

She opened the door, then took an involuntary step backwards. The man standing in the corridor was wearing a black trench coat, dark glasses, and had a black felt hat pulled down over his forehead. A black document case was tucked under his arm.

"Are you Terry's friend?" she asked. Or the grim reaper, she thought.

He glared at her then quickly stepped inside the room, closing the door firmly behind him. "You have a package for me?" he rasped.

Susan nodded, and crossed the room to where her overnight bag was sitting on the floor. She unzipped the bag and pulled out the shoe box, and was about to hand it over to the stranger when she suddenly remembered that there was a password.

"What do you call a musical fish?"

"A piano tuner," he swiftly replied.

Well, I suppose that's close enough, she thought to herself.

Susan handed the shoe box to him, and he tried to lift the lid. When he saw that it was taped down, he muttered something under his breath, then took a penknife from his coat pocket. He deftly slit the sealing tape around three sides of the box, then he nicked his hand with the knife. The shoe box fell to the floor, spilling its contents in an untidy heap.

"Photos," Susan murmured in surprise. "I thought it was a pair of shoes."

On the floor was a mound of small photo albums, each page just large enough for a compact print. Some of the pictures had come loose from their pages, and as Susan bent to pick them up, she noticed that they were photographs of cars. A purple sports car caught her eye. "Ooh, nice colour," she remarked.

The man snatched the photos out of her hand, then he swiftly gathered up the albums and shoved them into his case. He hurried out of the room without another word.

What awful manners, Susan thought. He didn't even say thank you. It's obviously true what people say about second-hand car salesmen.

Susan decided that she would have a long, hot bath, then a long, cool drink in the bar.

* * *

At five-fifteen they were standing in the hotel foyer, waiting for Jim.

"Where the hell is he?" demanded Tom. "Are you sure he's not in his room?"

"He went out ages ago," Susan replied. "He said that he needed to go to the drug store. Maybe he stopped off to buy a pair of trainers, as well."

"We'll have to go," Tom declared, after glancing at his watch. "You wait here for him, and we'll send the bus back to collect both of you," he told Susan.

As he strode off, Susan ambled back into the bar and sat where she could scan the whole of the foyer. The throngs of drinkers had diminished since lunchtime, but the air was still heavy with cigarette smoke. The barman was washing glasses, and on the counter in front of him sat a whirring electric fan which was turning itself from left to right, like some alien creature that was looking up and down the bar for a pretty girl to talk to.

It could certainly learn a thing or two from Jim. When Susan had walked down to the bar that afternoon, Jim was on his way upstairs with a slim brunette. Pete had been glad of Susan's company, as Jim had only reappeared briefly to inform them that he had to go out to buy essential supplies.

It must be something to do with all the red meat that he eats, Susan was thinking to herself, when she spotted Jim dashing into the hotel foyer, clutching a large paper bag. She finished her drink and strolled out to the entrance, to catch him on his way out again.

"What took you so long?" she asked, as they went out to find the bus.

Jim looked rather sheepish, and answered, "I had to give payment in kind."

Susan frowned. "What do you mean?"

Jim paused, then said, "I went into the pharmacy, and there was a woman in a white coat behind the counter. She was fairly presentable, but no spring-chicken, if you catch my drift. She spoke good English, though, and I had no problem explaining what I wanted. She showed me a selection, then she winked at me and said that she had some good-quality American ones in the back room."

"I like to put my faith in US rubber," he continued, "So I followed her into the back room. You can guess the rest."

Susan rolled her eyes. "Well, they say that it's always wise to try before you buy!"

* * *

As the band came off the stage after the show that night, Joe asked, "What was all the commotion in the front rows?"

"Just a minor fracas," Susan explained. "There was an idiot whistling a bit too vigorously, and the bloke sitting in front of him got cheesed off, and laid one on him."

Joe chewed his lip anxiously. "I hate it when the audience starts fighting."

Pete sniffed. "Huh. It makes a change for them to entertain us."

"I didn't notice anything," Tom commented.

"You wouldn't notice if the stage caught fire," retorted Susan. "You only have eyes for your piano!"

"I did notice that the drumming wasn't all that it should have been," Tom observed in a caustic tone, giving Jim a sideways look.

"Sorry about that," mumbled Jim. "I've had a hard day."

* * *

Thursday afternoon found them back on the bus.

"Shall we play cards?" suggested Susan. "I don't want to play I-Spy again."

They had only been travelling for half an hour, but she was bored already.

"Why don't you read a book," Jim responded curtly, with his head back and his eyes shut.

"I get travel sick if I read."

"Damn," Tom muttered to himself. "I felt sure that I had it right this time." He took an eraser from his pocket and started scrubbing at a page.

"Are you still doing that same logic problem?" Susan asked, with incredulity.

Tom nodded his head and blew the rubbings off the page. The pencilled answers had been erased so many times that the paper was almost transparent.

"How long have you been working on it?"

"Three days."

Susan laughed derisively. "I can do one of those puzzles in twenty minutes. If you had a brain, you'd be dangerous."

"Leave the poor bastard alone," Jim cut in. "He enjoys sweating over logic puzzles. I've known him to spend an entire six-week tour trying to solve one. You don't understand the immense feeling of satisfaction he gets when he finally solves it."

Tom nodded fervently in agreement as he continued rubbing.

"And it's cheaper than drugs," Jim added.

* * *

Two hours later they had picked up the motorway to Budapest, and the smooth road lulled them to sleep. As the others dozed in their seats, Joe was sorting through his photographs, putting them into chronological order. He studied each picture, then wrote the location and date in pencil on the back. As he looked at the photos of Gyor and Szombathely, he frowned and examined them more closely.

"That's odd," he murmured to himself.

"What?" Pete asked, sleepily.

"Sorry. I didn't mean to wake you. I was surprised by something in my photos."

Pete was curious. "Show me."

Joe picked up a photo. "This is the hotel square in Gyor." He pointed to a figure in the background. "See this guy, with the coat?"

Joe showed another photo to Pete and pointed out, "There he is again. But I took this one the following day, at the Egyptian temple in Szombathely."

"Sure looks like the same guy," agreed Pete. "Maybe he's a fan, hoping to get Tom's autograph. He's a real snappy dresser," he added, as he studied the photos. "Those cashmere coats cost a fortune."

* * *

Susan was shaken roughly awake by Janek's hard fingers on her shoulder.

"Get off now, quick!" Janek was urging her.

Susan opened her eyes. She looked out of the window and saw that they were parked outside their hotel in Pest, on the banks of the Danube. The familiar lights of the Chain Bridge glinted a myriad of reflections in the dark river.

"What's the rush?" she complained, stretching her arms and legs.

"I go to wedding party," Janek reminded her. "Drive to Vienna tonight."

Susan looked around and saw that the band had already got off the bus and disappeared into the hotel. What gentlemen, she thought, as she struggled off the bus with her overnight bag. Janek threw her suitcase on to the pavement beside her, then jumped quickly back on to the bus and rumbled off down the street.

As Susan blinked rapidly to accustom her eyes to the darkness, a sleek red sports car glided to a stop alongside her. The electric window hummed open. Susan looked suspiciously into the car, and sighed with relief when she saw that it was Terry and Ahmed.

"I wish you wouldn't do that," she snapped. "I thought you were kerb-crawlers."

"Don't worry, luvvie," Terry replied. "You don't look glamorous enough to attract passing trade."

"I'm glad we caught you," he continued. "We've got to dash across to Romania for a couple of days, but you all know your way around pretty well by now, don't you?"

Susan nodded vaguely, then focused her eyes and asked, "What happened to the yellow Mercedes?"

"Primrose," Terry corrected her. "It showed the dirt horribly, so I got rid of it."

Susan bent down and unzipped her overnight bag. She pulled out the Gucci shoe box. "You can have this back," she said, handing the box to Terry. "Your friend collected the contents."

Terry looked at the box, then said disdainfully, "The corners are all crushed!"

"Sorry. It got a bit squashed in my bag."

"You can keep it as a souvenir, luv. It's probably the closest you'll ever get to owning designer goods."

Ahmed let the clutch up and the Ferrari surged smoothly away with a sensual purr. Susan was left standing alone with an indignant look on her face. She picked up her luggage and marched across to the hotel lobby, muttering quietly to herself. She did not notice the man standing in the shadows, on the other side of the street.

He had a cashmere coat, a pair of crutches, and a heavily bandaged foot.

* * *

"Why didn't you lot wake me up?" Susan complained loudly, as she entered the hotel suite.

Jim smirked. "We thought that Janek might want to take you with him to Vienna."

"He may be a crazy Pole, but he ain't that crazy," muttered Pete.

"Damn," Susan exclaimed, as she suddenly remembered something. "I was going to do a stock-check on the merchandise. Now Janek's gone off with it all in the bus."

"Nope," Tom cut in. "We carried it all up here for you, whilst you were sleeping on the bus. I was going to come back out to wake you up."

"Oh, I see." She smiled briefly at him before carrying her bags through to her bedroom.

"You're the original Virginia creeper," Jim commented, when Susan was out of earshot.

"I'd like to get back in her good books," Tom said. "She might be sweet to me again."

Jim stretched out his arms, as if flying, and disappeared into his bedroom, uttering a drawn-out "oink" as he went.

* * *

"What do you mean, you're going on a "spa" crawl?" Susan demanded irately, over breakfast on Friday morning.

"It doesn't have to be a crawl, it can be a breast-stroke," Pete mumbled.

"No, it can't. These are guys-only pools. That's why you can't come," Jim told Susan, as she gave him a hard stare. "Anyway, it was Joe's idea."

As Susan turned her glare on him, Joe said defensively, "It would be a unique experience, doing a tour of all the thermal baths here. But unfortunately, men and women aren't allowed in together."

"What am I supposed to do all day?" she snapped. "Organise the laundry again, I suppose!"

"It's very sweet of you to offer," Tom chipped in.

"And you can count all those tee-shirts, as well," Jim added. "We'll be back before you know it."

The band disappeared after breakfast to swim their way around Budapest, while Susan set to work, wishing verrucas upon them all. She emptied the money out of the cash box, and started counting. There were US dollars and German marks amongst the Hungarian forints, so all the currencies had to be separated, counted and converted. Then Susan set to work counting all the merchandise. It was a tedious job, and she was glad to get it finished.

She wrote down all the numbers, did a few quick calculations, then frowned. The numbers did not total up as she had expected. After a lengthy double-check of money and caps and tee shirts, she did the calculations again, and swore briefly. Maybe they had lost some more merchandise on their travels, and possibly her currency conversions weren't quite accurate. But as she studied the numbers again, she came to the conclusion that Janek and Lazlo were probably paying themselves a generous commission on all their sales.

* * *

Susan was watching television in the early evening when the band returned.

"You lot must be squeaky-clean," she said facetiously. "Was it an interesting experience?"

Jim sniggered. "We made several new friends."

"Only one place was like that," Joe countered. "And the ornate Turkish ceiling was well worth seeing."

"Yeah, right. That's why we were all doing backstroke," Tom remarked.

CHAPTER 18

"As this is our last show here in Budapest, do you think y'all can keep your minds on the music?" Tom harangued the rest of the band on Saturday morning.

"Make the most of it," Susan said. "It might be your last-ever show."

Jim gave her a sideways look. "Are you planning on poisoning us all by cooking breakfast tomorrow?"

Joe looked up from his photo scrapbook and said in a hurt tone, "We do keep our minds on the music. We're professionals."

Pete had jotted some figures down on a small notepad, and he returned Susan's calculator to her, saying, "I reckon trainers are the best bet. One of the guys on the front desk has a factory discount card. His brother works at the plant. He'll take me down there, for a small fee. I should be able to get nearly thirty pairs in my suitcase. He says that I'll get a good price for them across the border."

Tom cried, "Will you all pay attention!"

"Why will it be our last ever show?" Joe asked anxiously, as he caught up with the conversation.

"I've just been studying our route," Susan replied. "It seems that a couple of our destinations were front-line targets, before the cease-fire."

Jim frowned. "What do you mean, "front-line"?"

"Front-line, as in, people shooting at you," she replied, tersely.

"The sponsor told me that it's as safe as houses," Tom assured the others.

Susan grimaced. "A lot of the houses in former Yugoslavia have been demolished."

"Maybe we should tie a white flag to the front of the bus," Joe suggested.

"Yeah, sure," Jim retorted. "Maybe we should paint a bulls-eye on it, too."

"Could we get back to tonight," Tom insisted. "I can't think about more than one thing at a time. These Budapest audiences have been real great, so let's try and go out with a bang."

Joe winced. "I wish you'd chosen a different word."

* * *

"Come on Susan. Either you want to buy it or you don't," Tom complained, in an exasperated tone.

They were browsing around the stalls in the indoor market. It was getting near to lunch-time, and many of the stall-holders were starting to close up. Tom was clutching a plastic bag that contained a Hungarian folk-dress doll. It had only taken him a few minutes to choose the colourful rag doll. She was wearing a bright red patterned dress, richly embroidered with white, blue and red silks, and embellished with imitation pearls. Her head, hands and feet were porcelain, so Tom was holding the bag close to his chest, to keep her safe from the crush of shoppers around them.

"They're beautifully made," Susan commented, lifting corners of the woven throws and comparing colours. "But they're not really big enough for a bed-spread. And they're probably not washable. They might look nice on the bathroom floor. But the water splashes might make the colour run. Oh, I don't know," she ended, fretfully. "They're a bit pricey for what they are."

Tom sighed heavily and looked at his watch, then said, "I'll pay for it, if you want it."

"Oh, thank you, Tom," Susan answered quickly. "That's very kind of you."

She sorted through the sumptuous linens once more, then frowned. "I can't decide between the ivory and the green."

"Take both of them, and let's get out of here," Tom replied frantically, and he hastily dug into his pocket for some cash as a stream of heavily-laden shoppers pushed past him, their wicker baskets stabbing at the back of his legs.

As Tom and Susan made their way along the Danube embankment and back to the hotel, they passed a boarded-up building whose large, arched entrance seemed to be home for a group of down-and-outs.

"Shall I give them some coins?" Tom murmured.

Susan pulled a face. "Only if you want them to follow us all the way down the street."

"I can see that you're full of sympathy for homeless people. Maybe you should try living in a box for a while."

"Lots of people in England live in cardboard boxes these days," she replied. "In fact, it's almost de rigueur in some circles, especially amongst the mentally ill."

"That's not very nice," Tom responded. "The mentally ill should be in special homes, not boxes."

"They used to be, but the Government closed them down."

"Why?"

"Because they couldn't turn a profit. Though I'm surprised they didn't try to privatise the asylums. That's the current trend," she said, cynically.

"They aim to do it with prisons, back home."

Susan stared in disbelief. "You're kidding? What will they be called? Jails R Us? Or Cell-U-Like? And how will they run them at a profit?"

Tom shrugged. "I guess they'll fire the warders, and make the convicts look after themselves. More of a self-help organisation than a jail."

"Self-help themselves over the wall, more like," Susan muttered.

* * *

Later that afternoon, Janek appeared at the door of their suite. He sauntered casually inside, hands thrust deep into the pockets of an antique leather flying jacket that looked fresh from the store.

Jim glanced at Janek and remarked, "Vienna's a good place for shop-lifting, huh?"

"I pay for this jacket," Janek replied, indignantly.

And I bet I know where he got the money, thought Susan. She decided to keep her suspicions to herself, as Janek was the only person in the group who could ask for dry Martini in five different languages. There was no reason why he should have it all his own way, though.

As Janek picked up the merchandise to take down to the venue, Susan said, "I'll give you a hand on the stall tonight. You'll probably do a lot of sales as it's the last show in Budapest."

Janek looked dismayed, then he forced a smile and replied, "Very good. Yes. Thank you."

He ambled out of the suite looking unusually thoughtful.

* * *

As they climbed off the bus outside the venue that evening, Jim took hold of Susan's arm and steered her towards the stage door.

"I have a little job for you tonight," he told her.

Susan tried to free her arm. "I have to help Janek on the merchandise stall."

"He can manage without you. This is more important."

Susan scowled at him. "What's more important than that?"

"I need you to play the bongo drums."

"You haven't got any bongo drums."

"Yes I have," asserted Jim. "Tom wants to do a song tonight that needs them, and I can't play bongos and my drums at the same time. We usually have a backing singer who helps out. You can do it instead."

"I don't know how to play bongo drums."

"Oh, anyone can play these little bongos," Jim said airily. "I'll run through it with you. It's a piece of cake."

He guided her to the back of the stage where the drum kit was set up, and did a short demonstration of how to tap out a rhythm on the bongos.

"The song is about half-way through the running order, so you'll need to be here on stage all through the show," Jim told her.

Susan's mouth fell open. "What! You mean that I've got to stand here for two hours just to play the bongos for four minutes? That's absurd!"

Jim shrugged. "That's show-business, honey."

* * *

As the curtain pulled across the stage at the end of the show, Tom eased himself off his piano stool and walked across to the drums with a frown.

"I couldn't hear the bongos at all," he complained. "What went wrong?"

Susan looked at him blankly and replied, "I was hitting them. What else was I supposed to do?"

Jim bent down beside the bongos and exclaimed, "Hell, I forgot to mike them up! How stupid of me!"

Then he turned to Susan and said, "Never mind, sweetheart. You looked real good, even if we didn't hear nothing."

Susan clicked her tongue in exasperation and grumbled loudly, "What a waste of my time! I'm going to check on the merchandise stall. It's where I should have been in the first place!"

"Not so fast," Jim quickly cut in. "You have to tidy your kit away. Put the bongo drums back into their little boxes. Let's try and be professional here."

Susan glowered at him. "Where are the boxes?"

He gestured towards the rear of the stage. "At the back, somewhere."

Susan stepped gingerly over cables and junction boxes, and rummaged about in the gloomy recesses of the back stage wall.

"I can't see a damn thing," she muttered. "It's too dark."

After stumbling over two guitar cases and stubbing her toe on a power-breaker, she groped her way back to Jim at the drum kit and snapped, "I can't find the bloody things."

Jim was loading his drums into their boxes, and he suddenly cried, "Oh, here they are! I forgot that I had put them into my big drum box. Silly me!"

Susan eyed him suspiciously, then placed the small bongos into their boxes and made her way out to the bus.

Janek was sitting in the driver's seat, and as Susan boarded, he smiled broadly and announced, "Very good sales tonight. We do very well!"

Susan pursed her lips and slumped down into a seat. She closed her eyes to try and ease the thumping headache that had ensued from standing next to Jim's drums for two hours. She made a mental note to accidentally step on the little bongos the next time she saw them.

As Jim climbed on to the bus he paused briefly beside Janek, then moved on, hastily pushing a handful of notes into his pocket.

* * *

"Are we going to have lunch at the Hungaria Cafe?" Susan asked hopefully, the following morning.

Tom clicked his tongue. "We've only just had breakfast."

"Well, there isn't much to do on a Sunday," she countered. "We might as well make the most of good food before we hit the road again."

"We really should go there," agreed Joe. "I'd like some pictures of the interior. They say that the decor is immaculately preserved, just as it was at the turn of the century. Apparently, composers and intellectuals still meet there, to talk and work."

"In that case, they probably won't let us in," Jim observed.

Joe persisted. "We could have lunch there, then go to the park for the rest of the day."

"Yeah, all right," Tom agreed. "I don't want to sit in the hotel all day."

After studying Joe's street map, they decided that the cafe was within walking distance, so they set off on foot. A ten-minute stroll took them into an area that they had not visited before, as it was off the regular tourist route. The shops looked less expensive and slightly run-down.

As they passed a clothes shop, Joe paused and studied the window display.

"That's a nice dress," he remarked.

"Which one?" Susan asked, scanning the display of gaudy-looking evening dresses with distaste.

"The red satin one, with the lacy sleeves."

Susan curled her lip and said nothing.

"It would look really good on my wife," Joe continued. "She looks lovely in red, because she has such dark hair. I wonder how much it is? I'd like to buy it for her as an end-of-tour present."

"The shop's closed," Jim told him, after he had tried the door.

"I'll come back tomorrow morning," Joe decided, and he made a note of the street name on the inside cover of his guide book.

They reached the street where the cafe was located, and as they walked alongside the parked cars they passed one which had its lights flashing and an alarm wailing hysterically.

Susan put her fingers in her ears as they went by, and complained to the others, "Car alarms are a real nuisance. They should be banned."

"Doesn't your car have an alarm fitted?" Jim argued.

"I haven't got a car," she replied, curtly.

Joe raised his eyebrows in surprise. "How do you manage without one?"

"Blokes always have cars. Why should I bother with the expense."

"That's a real radical feminist view," mumbled Pete.

"I guess the broomstick is easier to park, anyway," Jim observed dryly, and he quickly side-stepped to avoid Susan's elbow.

Tom said in a nostalgic tone, "I can remember the days when you could jump on to the roof of a car and slide down the windscreen, and it wouldn't utter a word of complaint. Nowadays, if you brush against a parked car with your shopping cart, it starts wailing at you like a banshee. Some of them even try to order you about. They say stuff like, "Move away from the vehicle immediately." I usually stand there beside it and say, "Yeah, so make me.""

"Remind me not to go to the supermarket with you," Susan murmured.

Jim grinned and said, "Back home in Florida, there's an exotic bird which makes the same whooping noise that they use on car alarms. My cousin runs a hotel in Orlando, and he regularly sees the tourists wandering around the car park at the crack of dawn, trying to figure out which car alarm is screeching. It takes them a fair while to realise that it's a bird call."

Susan chewed her lip thoughtfully. "I wonder if there are any recorded cases of the bird trying to mate with the hood of a stolen car?"

Tom grimaced. "It sure wouldn't do your paintwork a whole heap of good."

* * *

"This place is awesome," Joe gasped, as they entered the cafe. "I feel that I should genuflect."

Richly ornamented marble columns rose up and arched beneath the cathedral-like ceiling, which was embellished with frescoes and adorned with opulent mouldings.

"Save your prayers for when they bring us the bill," Pete advised.

The soft murmur of voices echoed faintly around the vaulted coffee house, and as Tom sat gazing at the historic decor, Jim said to him, "Does all this stuff inspire you to compose something wonderful?"

Susan gave a derisive sniff. "We're only here for lunch, not for a two-week vacation."

Tom was silent for a moment, then he announced, "As it was Susan's idea to come here, I think that she should pick up the tab."

He smiled sweetly at Susan as she choked on a mouthful of coffee.

* * *

They spent a restful afternoon in the city park, then took a cab back to the hotel in the evening.

"I'm gonna miss this place," Tom said wistfully, as he gazed out of their lounge window. "This must be the best view in Europe." He disappeared into his bedroom to start packing.

Susan was buzzing around the rooms, organising their departure for the following day.

"Give me all your dirty clothes," she ordered. "The lady in charge of the laundry room said that she can have everything done by tomorrow morning. This is your last call for a clean shirt."

As Susan went into Tom's room, he was trying to pack the Hungarian doll into his suitcase.

"How can I do this?" he said, fretfully. "However I pack it, something else falls on top and squashes it. The little hands and feet will be broken by the time I get it back home!"

Susan paused for thought, then said, "I've got a box that you can put it in."

She fetched the Gucci shoe box from her room, and laid it on Tom's bed. Then she wrapped the doll inside two hotel hand towels, put it inside the shoe box, and taped the lid down securely with some sticking plasters from her first aid kit.

"That should get her home safely," she said, confidently. "If I put it in the middle of your case, like this, the clothes around it will cushion any knocks."

Tom smiled gratefully. "Gee, thanks. You're a star packer. I've got time for a long shower, now."

And he ambled into his bathroom, not giving even a second thought as to how the world's cheapest shopper happened to have a Gucci shoe box.

CHAPTER 19

On Monday morning the hotel suite was empty. Susan had disappeared to collect the laundry, Pete and Joe had gone out to buy the red dress, and the others had decided to re-stock the bus with bottles. They were due to be in Kecskemet for a gig that night, so they had all made an early start.

When Pete and Joe returned from their shopping trip they were in a subdued mood. They walked along without speaking, and as they approached their suite the door opened and a stranger emerged. He frowned when he saw the guitar players, and he limped quickly down the corridor away from them.

"Isn't that the guy in your photos?" Pete remarked. "He must have got an autograph off Tom at last." He inserted his card key and opened the door.

"That's odd," he murmured. "Where's Tom?"

As he spoke, there was a commotion out in the corridor. Tom and Janek appeared, laden with cardboard boxes, and Jim was a few paces behind them.

"Salami coming through," Tom announced. "Mind your backs."

"Mind your noses, more like," Jim grumbled. "I'm suffering garlic poisoning here."

Tom dropped the boxes on the floor and sniffed his fingers. "Ugh! I need to rinse my hands." He ambled into his bedroom. Moments later he dashed out again, clutching his Hungarian doll. The doll had a deep incision running the length of her body, and pieces of rag stuffing were protruding from the split. The pretty embroidered dress was hanging in two tattered halves, with frayed threads dangling across her gaping middle.

Jim stared in astonishment. "Did your rag dolly need an emergency appendectomy?"

"Some bastard has cut her up!" Tom seethed.

"Who would want to do that?"

Joe disappeared into his room and came back carrying his scrap-book photo album. He quickly found the photos that he had shown to Pete.

"This is the guy," he said, stabbing with his finger at the pictures of the man in the cashmere coat. "He was coming out of the suite as we came along the corridor, and we assumed that you were in here. We thought he was just an autograph hunter. Why would he cut up your doll? It don't make sense."

Janek shrugged. "He probably thief. Look for hidden jewellery." Then he glanced down at the photo and gasped with surprise. "This man we hit with wheely-crate! Maybe he want revenge!"

"If I catch up with him, I'll break both his arms, as well as his other foot!" Tom growled, and he stared hard at the photos, memorising the man's face.

* * *

When Susan returned to the suite shortly afterwards, she wrinkled her nose and said, "What's that awful smell?" Noticing the glum faces of the band she added, "Has someone died?"

"The rag dolly has been murdered," Jim told her, and he held up the sad remains of Tom's doll.

"Tck. All that careful packing for nothing," she muttered.

Joe told her the full story, and as he displayed the photos of the villain, Susan widened her eyes in surprise.

"We think that it was a revenge attack, for his injured foot," he concluded.

Susan nodded in agreement, but a sudden doubt flashed through her mind. If the cashmere coat man was in the Gyor and Szombathely photos, then maybe he was responsible for the scattered baseball caps and the searching of Joe's camera case and Tom's bag. But his wheely-crate injury had happened after those incidents. So what was he after? She chewed her lip nervously as she remembered Terry's little black book. Could he have been looking for it? Susan decided to keep quiet about it. Tom probably wouldn't be too pleased if he found out that she had been working a sideline as Terry's courier. It was Tom who suddenly interrupted her thoughts.

"You can have this back. I don't need it any more." He handed her the Gucci shoe box, and went back into his room to re-pack his suitcase.

Jim peered at the box and eyed her suspiciously. "Since when have you been buying Gucci shoes?"

"I got the box from Janek," she lied. "He bought some new shoes in Vienna."

Janek opened his mouth to contradict her, but Susan glared at him and said, "I must remember to tell Terry what an amazing job you're doing on the merchandise stall."

Janek promptly closed his mouth and started carrying bags down to the bus.

Half an hour later they were on board the bus, heading south along the motorway. The salami had been wrapped in hotel towels and stowed in the luggage compartments, and the new supply of bottles was chinking between the seats.

Tom had opened one of the bottles and was now feeling in a better mood. He suddenly remembered Joe's shopping trip, and he asked, "Did you get that red dress for your wife? I forgot all about it until now."

Joe looked embarrassed and replied, "No, I didn't get it."

"Didn't they have her size?"

"They didn't have any ladies sizes," Pete muttered, scornfully.

Jim was intrigued. "Explain," he demanded.

"Well," Joe began hesitantly, "We went into the shop, and the assistant didn't speak much English, but he was very friendly. So I pointed to the red dress in the window, and he nodded. Then he looked me up and down, and took one of the red dresses off a rack. He gave it to me, and waved me over to this little curtained-off section. I was thinking, maybe I have to go behind the curtain to pay, when suddenly this big ugly guy comes striding out from behind the curtain, wearing a skin-tight black evening dress. He picks up a pair of high-heel shoes, puts them on, then struts back behind the curtain."

"It was then that we realised that it was a transvestite dress shop, so I dropped the red dress on to the counter and we left in a hurry."

"I bet you guys will be real cross if I repeat this story," chuckled Jim.

Susan chipped in, "I used to think that cross-dressing is when a bloke can't find a pair of socks that match in the morning."

* * *

An hour later they pulled into Kecskemet.

"Thank goodness," sighed Susan, as they followed the town centre signs in search of their hotel. "I've had enough of agricultural I-Spy. How many types of fruit tree are there in this country? And how can Joe tell the difference between a greengage and a plum from a speeding bus? He's a freak."

"You're just pissed because you're crap at the game," Jim commented. "How could you not get A for apricot? The trees were laden with them."

"They all looked like apple trees to me."

Susan sulked while she consulted her tattered itinerary. Then she shouted to Janek, "Turn right when you see a building with an onion on the top."

"I know that this is a heavily agricultural area," said Tom, "But isn't it taking things a bit too far, putting vegetable produce on top of the buildings?"

"It's an architectural term," Joe enlightened him. "It's a type of dome."

"I bet Joe could tell us what type of onion it is," Susan muttered under her breath.

"Hey, there's a cinema opposite the hotel," Jim cried enthusiastically, as they turned into the street. "Maybe we could catch the matinee showing."

As they halted outside the hotel, Jim stared across at the cinema hoarding and groaned, "You'll never guess what's on."

"Are they showing "Gone With The Wind"?" Joe asked, hopefully.

"No," Jim replied. "The Piano."

Tom grinned. "They must have known that I was coming."

"Talking about pianos," Susan interrupted, "Can't you do something about all those grubby fingerprints on yours? It looks horrible when the stage lights shine on it. Dozens of sticky handprints suddenly appear. If I could find a can of furniture spray, I'd give it a good polish."

"Don't you lay a hand on my piano!" Tom exclaimed, in a panic-stricken voice. "It's a musical instrument, not a side-board!"

"My drum kit could do with a gentle buffing," Jim remarked. "And you could line the boxes with some of that fancy scented paper," he ended, sarcastically.

Susan glared at him. "There's nothing wrong with being neat and tidy."

"I'll get Lazlo to dust the piano over," Tom said hastily, as Susan climbed off the bus. "You don't need to worry about it. Please don't touch my piano," he called after her, as she headed into the hotel.

* * *

After lunch, Joe knocked at Susan's door and asked if she wanted to go sightseeing with him.

"The others have gone to do the sound check," he explained, "But Tom said that I could have some time off. There are some buildings here that I want to snap."

"All right," she agreed. "But I'm not carrying your lens case. It weighs a ton!"

"I wouldn't expect you to," Joe replied, looking offended. "Just keep your eye on it while I'm adjusting my camera. Make sure that no-one walks off with it."

They strolled into the paved square adjacent to the hotel, and paused outside an ornate Gothic-style building where a carillon was tinkling a piece of Mozart to chime the hour. As the bells ceased, a small knot of tourists moved out of the way, and Susan parked herself on a bench while Joe picked out a suitable lens for a wide-angle shot of the building.

Susan was gazing vacantly at the spiky red flowers that were planted in neat rows beside the pathways. The square was dotted with trees, which were casting dappled shadows around the bench. Susan screwed up her eyes against the sudden changes of light as the sun disappeared behind a cloud, then emerged again with harsh intensity. She suddenly focused on two figures sitting on a bench, some distance away. They had their backs to her, and she was puzzling as to why the two men were wearing heavy coats on such a sunny day, when they both stood up and walked off in opposite directions.

One man was wearing dark glasses and a black trench coat, and Susan had a vague notion that she knew him from somewhere. As she turned her gaze to the other figure, she was looking into the bright glare of the sun, and her eyes watered slightly. The man walked towards a clump of trees and was quickly lost in the shadows, but Susan had the distinct impression that he had been walking with a limp.

* * *

The concert hall was only two streets away from the hotel, so when Joe had finished his photography, he and Susan walked down there to meet up with the others. Inside the venue the stage was deserted, except for Lazlo, who was lolling against the piano and pushing a black duster over it in a languid manner.

"Make sure that your sweat doesn't drip on to the piano," Susan said, in a caustic tone.

"I finish now, anyway," Lazlo replied. He shook out his duster, then turned it right-way out to reveal that it was a Zblatov tee shirt. He folded it carelessly, then shoved it back inside the merchandise bag.

Susan and Joe went along to the dressing room, and found the others playing a game of cards with some of the crew.

"Have you done the sound check, or are you waiting for me?" Joe asked.

"We're waiting for Lazlo to finish his heavy breathing on the piano," Tom answered, without looking up from his hand.

Jim laughed. "He smokes too many cheroots to do any heavy breathing."

"It's just as well that the merchandise was black to start with," muttered Pete, "What with him and Janek dropping their cigar butts into everything."

Susan shuddered, and decided to give up doing stock-taking checks on the tee shirts and caps.

"Susan honey, could you do a small favour for us?" Tom asked, as they ended the game and packed away the cards. "Pete has left his harmonica in his hotel room. Could you run back and get it for him?"

"Why didn't you send one of the crew for it?" she grumbled.

"My suitcase is full of trainers," Pete told her. "The temptation would be too much for them."

Susan gave an exasperated sigh, took Pete's room key and set off again. As she approached the hotel entrance, a noisy car rattled down the street and halted beside her in a cloud of smelly exhaust fumes. She waved her hand in front of her face to clear the air, and was amazed to see Terry wave back at her from inside the decrepit car. He used both hands to wind down the wobbly window.

"Hello dearie. Can you spare us a few ticks? I'd like a quick word. Hop in the back."

Susan climbed into the back seat, too astonished to argue. She sank backwards into the spongy upholstery, and struggled to elbow herself upright.

"What a vile smell," she complained. "I think this foam seat has rotted."

"Very likely," Terry murmured, as he swivelled around to face her. "Anyway, I know it's a bit of an imposition, but I was wondering if you could do a small favour for me."

Susan groaned. "Not again. I'm getting a bit fed up of doing favours for you."

Terry nodded. "Mmm. I know I'm a bit of a pain. But I'm without a car at the moment. I borrowed this wreck from a neighbour, and he wants it back later today. Trouble is, a friend of mine will be in Szeged tomorrow, and he owes me some cash. I desperately need the money, but I won't get my new wheels for a couple of days. Would you be a luv and collect the money for me? I'll pay for the inconvenience, of course."

She chewed a fingernail. "I'm not keen on carrying cash around. Suppose I get mugged?"

"How could you get mugged? You're on the bus most of the time."

"Oh all right. What do I need to do."

"Same thing as in Debrecen. It's the same man, so you can use the same pass-word. We'll see you in Zagreb on Thursday."

Ahmed revved the car as Susan climbed out, and they chugged off down the street, leaving a cloud of toxic fumes in their wake.

CHAPTER 20

As they approached the centre of Szeged, late on Tuesday morning, Jim gazed out of the bus window and remarked, "The night-life here must be pretty good. This area is full of clubs and discos."

Janek dropped them outside a tall, concrete hotel which overlooked the river, then he continued down the road and parked outside the venue. As the band made their way through reception, Tom announced, "I'm going to catch a couple of hours sleep. I'll see you down here at four."

"Good idea," said Jim. "If we get some rest now, we could all go clubbing after the show. We haven't had a night on the town in a long while."

They all dispersed, and Susan ambled along to her room, wondering when Terry's friend would arrive. She dumped her bags on the bed, and decided that she couldn't be bothered to unpack. Life on the road was becoming increasingly tedious. She went to the window and looked out over the river, trying to remember which part of Hungary they were in. All these towns were beginning to look the same.

A rapid knocking at the door startled her. When she opened the door, there was a man in a black trench coat standing outside. He was wearing dark glasses and the same black hat as in Debrecen. He shoved her aside with his document case, and darted into the room.

"What you call musical fish?" he demanded.

"A piano tuna."

The man extracted a brown envelope from his case and handed it to Susan, then turned on his heel and strode swiftly from the room.

His manners haven't improved any, Susan murmured to herself. She opened the envelope and counted up the cash. Her eyes widened. No wonder Terry was keen to collect this. It was a huge sum, and in American dollars, too. She felt uneasy about carrying it around with her, but she was stuck with it now. She stowed the envelope at the bottom of her handbag and put a large, stiff-bristled hairbrush on top of it.

As Susan zipped up her bag she frowned, puzzling over a little nagging doubt at the back of her mind. He was definitely the man that she had seen in Kecskemet on the previous day. His black trench coat was distinctive. But if he was a friend of Terry's, why was he with the nasty limping man in the cashmere coat? It didn't seem likely that someone who attacked dolls would be a friend of the urbane Terry.

Susan switched on the television, then lay on the bed and closed her eyes. She fell asleep and dreamed that she was a sales assistant in Burberry's.

* * *

She was woken by a noisy hammering on the door.

"Susan, Susan, it's time to go!" Jim called.

Susan clambered off the bed and as she opened the door she asked, blearily, "Is it Wednesday already?"

Jim gave her a sideways look. "Have you been drinking?"

"Chance would be a fine thing," she muttered. "All this travelling has befuddled my brain."

"Well try and clear your head. Janek wants you to help out tonight. Apparently this is a university town, and he reckons that he can unload most of the merchandise here. Students love this kind of gear. They have no dress-sense at all."

Susan picked up her handbag and followed Jim down to the hotel restaurant, where the others were waiting for them.

"I think I'll use my fret-less bass tonight," Joe was saying to Tom. "It does a nice intro to Open Book."

"It's more like a coffee table than a guitar," Jim commented, as he sat down. "How can you cope with having a plank of wood strung across your chest?"

"It's easy to carry," Joe insisted. "I love that guitar. It goes everywhere with me."

"That reminds me of when my coffee table left home," murmured Tom.

As Susan gave him a baffled look, he recounted, "It was a few years back. My wife told me that she was going to stay with her sister for a few weeks, because she hadn't seen her in a while. But strange things started to happen. I came home one day and noticed that the coffee table had vanished. A few days later, one of the Persian rugs disappeared. The following week, a couple of paintings went missing."

"It turned out that she had moved in with a guitar player, and she was re-furnishing his apartment with my stuff. But she came back to me when he went off on a world tour," Tom concluded. "And she brought all of my things back."

"That's obviously why they call it "occasional furniture"," muttered Susan.

"He was nothing much to look at, either," complained Tom. "I said to her once, "What's he got that I haven't?" and she replied, "A wah-wah pedal in full working order." She could be real cruel, sometimes."

Susan was mystified. "What's a wah-wah pedal got to do with it? Am I missing something here?"

"Tom was having a few problems, down below," Joe answered, in a low tone.

"You mean, rats in the cellar?"

"Impotence," Pete told her bluntly.

"There's no such thing as impotence," asserted Jim. "There's just guys who don't feel in quite the right mood, from time to time."

* * *

The merchandise stall was totally hectic. Susan had been given the job of stock control. As Janek and Lazlo sold the gear, Susan would throw more shirts and caps on to the counter.

"Why can't we put all the stuff on to the table to start with?" Susan grumbled.

"Too easy to steal," Janek informed her. "Keep gear in plastic sack by feet."

This meant that Susan was constantly ducking up and down to reach for merchandise, with the other two crushing her fingers with their big feet. Her handbag was slung over her shoulder, satchel-style, and it got in the way all the time. By the time the show started and the crowd around the stall had dispersed, Susan was completely exhausted.

"You go rest," Janek told her firmly, and he pushed her towards the back-stage door. "Me and Lazlo count up."

Susan staggered away. She had given up caring about the accounts discrepancies on the stall. There didn't seem to be much stock left, and good riddance, she decided.

When the band finished their performance and came off stage, Jim berated Joe, "Why did you play the intro to Open Book twice?"

Joe looked sheepish and replied, "It sounded so nice the first time, I thought that I'd play it again. That bass has such a wonderful resonance, it gives me goose bumps."

"It takes a bit more than a guitar to get me excited," scoffed Jim. "Are we going straight on to the clubs?"

"I'm too tired," Susan said, yawning. "I'm going back to the hotel. You lot can please yourselves what you do."

"You can't run out on us!" exclaimed Jim. "Some of these places don't let all-male parties inside. Don't be such a misery."

"Yeah," agreed Pete. "And if we happen to stray into a gay bar by mistake, we'll be safe with you."

Susan groaned. "I can't believe that four big ugly men would need me as a chaperone. I'll come with you as long as you buy my drinks. I'm not paying club prices."

They found a taxi in the street behind the venue, and a five-minute drive took them to the slightly seedy area of town where most of the discos and bars were located.

"Let's have a few drinks before we hit the clubs," Jim suggested, and he steered them into the nearest bar.

The place was almost empty, so they perched on the bar stools and made themselves comfortable, with elbows resting on the counter. Susan placed her handbag on the bar, and looped the strap around her wrist so that no-one could snatch the bag away.

Jim ordered the drinks, then casually surveyed the room in search of any good-looking women. His eye was caught by a young blonde who was sitting alone at a table. He mooched over with his drink, and sat down next to her. After a few minutes of conversation, Jim and the blonde were joined by a hefty young man who had previously been playing on a video game at the far side of the room. The young man appeared to be in a bad temper, and Jim hastily left the table and returned to the others at the bar.

"Can't win them all," he remarked, as he sat down on his bar stool. "We'll try another place. It's too quiet here."

As Jim lifted his glass of beer to his lips he was suddenly shoved from behind, and the drink spilled over his shirt.

"Hey!" Jim cried angrily, and he turned to see the hefty young man pushing past, with his girlfriend.

The young man shrugged, and walked out of the bar.

"He did that on purpose!" seethed Jim.

"Well, what do you expect?" countered Tom. "You tried to pick up his girl."

"Susan, do you have any tissues?" Jim asked.

"Yes, in my bag," she replied, disentangling the strap from her wrist.

Jim grabbed the bag, unzipped it and plunged his hand inside

"Argh!" he shrieked. "What do you have in there? Piranha fish?" He sucked his fingertips and grimaced with pain.

"It's my hairbrush. Serves you right for being so impatient." She carefully moved the brush and pulled out some paper tissues, so that Jim could dab his shirt dry.

* * *

Several bars later, they made their way into a club that had a lurid neon sign and two sturdy bouncers at the door. Jim handed a wad of notes to the girl behind the desk, and they moved through to the disco area. The deafening music defeated any attempts at conversation, so Tom gestured to an empty table on the other side of the dance floor, and they squeezed through the lurching throng.

Susan sat down on a rickety cane chair and tucked her handbag behind her, then leaned back on it to keep it secure. The men crossed to the bar to fetch some drinks, while Susan shifted on her uncomfortable seat and winced at the thumping bass that was vibrating up through the floor.

There was barely enough light inside the club to see across the dance floor. Sporadic bursts of strobe lighting gave an occasional ghastly illumination, and reminded Susan of a Vietnam war film that she had once seen. She hoped that the others wouldn't want to stay too long. Jim's lack of success with the blonde had put him in a heavy drinking mood, and he could barely stand, let alone dance.

When the drinks arrived at the table, Susan held up her glass to study the minuscule quantity.

"Is there anything in here, apart from ice?" she shouted over the din.

"It's very good quality ice," Pete yelled back. "The most expensive that you can get."

Susan sipped her short measure and watched the writhing figures on the disco floor. As a strobe suddenly lit up the room, she glimpsed a man edging his way around the dance floor. She nudged Pete.

"Look at that pratt. Fancy wearing an overcoat in a club."

Blackness fell over them once more, and the man vanished into the shadows.

"Probably a pick-pocket," Pete replied.

"What?" Susan strained to hear him as another loud disco tune started up.

Pete shook his head, and mouthed, "Never mind."

Jim sank his beer in three gulps, and set off to the bar once more.

"Do you want to dance?" Tom bellowed in Susan's ear.

She shook her head, and looked down at her watch, squinting to try and see the hands in the semi-darkness.

Tom suddenly cursed, then leapt out of his seat and sprinted away. Pete dashed after him, and Susan stared in bewilderment as they disappeared across the room. A flash of white strobe gave her a clear sight of the bar for an instant, and she saw Jim grappling with another man. It looked like the same young man who had spilled beer over him in the other place. Tom and Pete lurched into the crowd at the bar, and she saw arms flailing through the smoky air. She leaned forward nervously in her seat. Then the room was plunged into darkness again. There was a stealthy movement behind her as a man crept up to her chair and deftly unzipped her handbag. He thrust his hand inside the bag, then swiftly withdrew it as a grimace of pain shot across his face.

A moment later there was the sound of breaking glass, and a woman screamed.

Joe tugged at Susan's arm. "Let's go!"

She hastily grabbed her bag and darted after him, side-stepping the bouncers who were pounding across the dance floor towards the bar. Joe caught Susan tightly around the waist, and they shoved their way through the heaving crowd until they got outside.

They paused to catch their breath, and moments later the other three came hurtling out of the club.

Susan clutched anxiously at Tom's arm. "Are you all right?"

He nodded and rubbed at his stomach. "Yeah. I got a smack in the ribs, but I'll live."

He looked Susan up and down, and brushed a smattering of cigarette ash off her shoulder. "Your purse is unzipped," he noticed. "Did it get broke in the crush?"

Susan ran the zip back and forth. "No, it's fine. I must have caught it on something." She felt around in the bottom of her bag, and gave an inward sigh of relief when her fingers came to rest on the money envelope.

As she closed the zipper, she turned to face Jim, and snapped angrily, "When you said that we were going clubbing, I didn't realise that you meant it literally!"

CHAPTER 21

They were half way to Pecs next morning before anyone spoke to Jim. Not that Jim cared. He had a bad hangover and was grateful for the silence.

The road meandered between gentle hills and quiet valleys. It was a dry, dusty day, and as the midday sun glared through the bus windows Jim stirred himself and spoke a few words to Janek. A few minutes later, Janek pulled the bus into a small lay-by and announced that he was making a coffee stop.

"Not feeling too good today, huh, Jim?" Susan jibed, as Jim staggered off the bus to breathe some fresh air.

He grunted. "I'll be just fine after a good dose of caffeine."

The sultry heat settled over them like a blanket, and the only noise that disturbed the air was the chirping of invisible cicadas.

Susan carefully inspected a patch of grass for ant nests, then spread out a large bath towel and sat down in the shade. She placed her handbag close beside her.

"Were you a bookie's runner in a previous existence?" Jim remarked, fixing Susan with a suspicious stare. "You and that bag are never parted. What do you have in there, apart from the piranha fish hairbrush?"

"I'm not going to bore everyone by counting up my emery boards and used bus tickets," Susan replied, cagily. "And anyway, do you know any women who go anywhere without a handbag? Apart from the heroines in Hollywood films, of course. They gad about without so much as a front-door key or a credit card in their pockets."

Susan sniffed disdainfully and continued, "You certainly can't go anywhere without a handbag when you've got a man in tow! They look at you all wide eyed and say innocently, "Can you fit this in your handbag?"

"And you turn around to see a four-pack of beer or a tyre lever being thrust at you! I reckon that the only reason men get married is to have some other silly fool to carry all their junk around."

"Yeah, right," mumbled Jim, massaging his throbbing temples. "Sorry I asked."

Meanwhile, Tom was doing physical jerks, and groaning as he stretched his back.

"My back has never been the same since I had an accident on my exercise bike," he complained.

Susan smirked. "What happened? Did the brakes fail when you were going downhill?"

Tom gave her a tight smile and replied, "I didn't adjust the saddle height correctly. I was in mid-pedal when the seat dropped a couple of notches. It jarred my spine. Amongst other things."

"It serves you right for trying to keep fit."

Tom shook his head at her. "Don't you take any exercise at all?"

"I've got an exercise TV," she told him.

"A what?"

"My television hasn't got a remote control," Susan explained. "If I want to change the channel, I have to get out of the chair, walk across the room, press a button, then walk back again."

"You should patent that idea," suggested Pete. "You could make a fortune from health freaks."

"And if it's a really bad programme," she added proudly, "I jog across the room."

"My brother-in-law jogged into the side of a bus, once," said Pete.

"He should have waited until the doors opened," Jim commented.

"It was going in the wrong direction. And he didn't have any money for the fare."

"Joggers never look where they're going," Susan said. "They're like over-sized hedgehogs. Roadkill just waiting to happen."

Joe nodded in agreement. "They never use pedestrian crossings. It's like they're daring the cars to hit them."

"Maybe they do it on purpose," Pete said, thoughtfully. "To get an insurance payout."

"Did your brother-in-law get any money out of the bus company?" Jim asked.

"Nah. They invoiced him for denting the bodywork."

* * *

It was mid-afternoon when they pulled into Pecs.

"What a tortuous drive," grumbled Jim. "The Romans obviously never laid any roads around here."

"Stop complaining and look for a man on a horse and a drinking fountain," Susan told him.

"I have a bottle of water here, if you're thirsty," Joe offered.

Pete was baffled. "Why do we need a man on a horse?"

"You lot are about as much use as a pair of jockey shorts at a Tom Jones concert," Susan said, scathingly. "They're landmarks. The hotel is just along from a statue of a man on a horse."

"Like the one that we just went past?" said Tom.

Susan groaned. "Why didn't you tell me before? Which side of the road was it on?"

"I dunno. I was looking backwards."

"Now I know why you have "Chesapeake Bears" printed on your sweatshirt," Susan said, sarcastically. "You probably couldn't find your way back home unless it was written on your clothing."

"Yeah, and next time I visit the Outer Banks, I'll get you a sweatshirt from Nag's Head," Tom muttered, as he stared out of the window.

"That's a nice place," Joe commented, as they drew level with an ornate art-nouveau building which had a pristine pastel facade. "Palatinus Hotel," he murmured, reading the sign.

"Where?" cried Susan, swiveling in her seat. "Janek! Stop the bus!"

Janek had spotted the hotel several moments before, and was already slowing down to find a parking space. He made a right turn into a side street, and drew up behind the band's equipment truck.

"I guess this is the venue," Tom observed. "You can have the night off, Janek. We can do without the bus tonight."

They gathered up their luggage and walked back around the corner to the hotel. The interior had elegant décor in turn-of-the-century style.

"Plush," murmured Jim. "I bet the bar is full of gorgeous career women."

"Don't even think about it," Susan cut in. "Not after all the trouble that you caused last night."

"That was a rough place," he countered. "This place is real sophisticated. Anyway, we should make the most of our last night in Hungary. We'll be dodging bullets and bandits for the rest of the tour."

Pete nodded sagely in agreement, as a group of girls walked past in short skirts. Their slim brown legs mesmerized him for a moment. "We've got to spend all our Hungarian money," he told the others. "They won't change it back to dollars."

Susan clicked her tongue. She knew that Pete was right, so she grudgingly conceded. "We'll certainly lose half the value if we re-convert, so we may as well spend it here."

As they went off to find their rooms, Jim punched the air in triumph, after checking that Susan was out of sight.

* * *

Later that evening, as the band waited in the dressing room before the show, Susan staggered in with a bag full of tee shirts and caps.

"Do you want these as souvenirs?" she asked, offering the bag around.

"Are you kidding?" muttered Pete.

Jim gave a disparaging sniff. "You told me that black wasn't my colour, so don't try and unload them onto me."

"They might come in useful for Trick or Treat," suggested Joe. "The kids are always looking for scary black clothes at that time of year."

Susan turned to Tom. "Would your fans back home want any?"

"His mom and dad would look kind of silly in this stuff," Jim said, facetiously.

"We might as well leave it here," Susan decided. "I've told Janek and Lazlo that when we get to ex-Yugoslavia their main duty is to look after the gear. The equipment is more important than a few tee shirts." She dumped the bag in a corner of the dressing room, and hoped that the theatre staff would help themselves.

* * *

At eleven-thirty that night they were sitting around a table in the hotel bar.

Tom took a long sip of beer. "What's the itinerary for next week?"

Susan dug into her handbag and found the crumpled itinerary. The paper was wearing thin along the creases, making some of the words difficult to decipher.

"Ex-Yugoslavia is a bit vague," she replied, glancing at the travel instructions. "Terry's got the hotel names and venues listed, but he hasn't given us any directions. Apparently, you can't get hold of any guide books. The publishers withdrew them all when war broke out. Let's just hope that some of the sign-posts are still standing."

"Why do you call it ex-Yugoslavia?" Joe asked.

"Because I can't remember all the names of the new countries. Life was simple under the Communists. There were only seven countries in eastern Europe. Now there's about thirteen. And Russia sub-divides itself on an regular basis. I have nightmares about the Eurovision Song Contest lasting for forty days and forty nights."

"I hope Terry will be travelling with us on the next leg," Tom said. "I don't fancy going it on our own."

Susan nodded. "He told me that he'd see us in Zagreb."

"Don't hold your breath waiting on him," Jim scoffed. "He ain't been keen to travel with us up to now."

Susan shrugged. "Well, if we get lost, we can stop and ask a soldier for directions."

Pete raised an eyebrow at her. "Get real. They'll probably set fire to the bus."

"The UN troops are there, and NATO as well. All we have to do is look for blue or white helmets."

Jim gave her a sideways look. "Blue and white helmets? What ever happened to camouflage? Do these guys enjoy being sitting ducks?"

"Let's have a few more drinks, and the situation may not seem quite so grim," Tom muttered, as he tilted his glass.

After an hour and a half they weren't feeling any happier. Joe was telling them how much he missed his wife and kids.

"I don't know why I go on the road," he sighed. "I hate being away from home. I always feel that people who've got no kids just don't know what they're missing."

"I'll tell them exactly what they're missing," Jim cut in. "Sobbing, vomiting, sticky fingerprints all over the furniture. And that's just the Christening party!"

* * *

On Thursday morning they were an hour out of Pecs when they came to the border with Croatia. A long line of traffic was waiting to cross through, and the border guards were doing unhurried checks on all the vehicles.

The bus moved slowly forwards, and as it drew level with the check-point, Tom murmured, "Do you think we'll be in trouble with all these bottles on board?"

"I think they're more interested in hand-grenades and rifles," Susan assured him.

A fresh-faced soldier with a sub-machine gun climbed on to the bus and motioned for them all to follow him outside. They trooped off silently, and after he had glanced at their passports he started a careful examination of the tour bus.

Janek opened up the baggage compartment and the soldier pushed the suitcases around, whilst keeping one hand firmly on his gun. A cigarette was propped on his lower lip, and as he bent forwards over the luggage the ash dropped down.

"Tck," complained Susan. "I thought they weren't supposed to smoke on duty."

The border guard pulled the salami boxes out from behind the suitcases. He frowned at the rolled-up towels and proceeded to unwrap one of them. Finding a salami in the middle, he nodded, then re-wrapped it untidily. He unwrapped three more, then pushed them back into the box, with cigarette ash falling on to the skin of the salami.

"That salami has already been smoked," Susan told him, irately.

The soldier gave her a blank stare, then ambled to the front of the bus and waved them back on board.

As they climbed back on to the bus, Tom gave Susan a severe nudge and whispered harshly, "I'd prefer it if you didn't try and pick a fight with these guys!"

"Don't be so nervous," she replied, tartly. "The gun probably isn't even loaded."

As they drove through the check point and into Croatia, Jim noticed a line of army jeeps parked near the border.

"Well, here we are in the war zone," he commented, uneasily. "What do we do if someone starts taking shots at us?"

"Just close your eyes and pretend you're in Miami," Pete replied.

"Huh. If we were in Miami, I could at least return fire."

CHAPTER 22

"It was a stroke of luck, coming up behind this military convoy," Jim said, as they wound their way slowly towards Zagreb later that morning.

"Luck?" cried Tom. "We'll barely have time to drop our bags and get to the venue. I hope that the big rig isn't caught in one of these queues!"

Joe nodded anxiously in agreement. They had no idea how far ahead the equipment truck was, and there was no way that anything could get past one of these army convoys, slowly jolting and grinding gears along the serpentine roads.

"Well at least we're safe," Jim countered. "I find it very comforting to have all those soldiers ahead of us."

"It looks like there's a stretch of freeway up ahead," Pete remarked, straining his eyes forwards.

Sure enough, the road swung around in a long loop, taking them down on to a wide motorway. Janek edged the bus into the outside lane and accelerated swiftly, passing the line of army trucks.

"We should have stayed with them," Jim complained, and he gazed wistfully over his shoulder as the convoy disappeared into the distance.

Joe tried to console him. "They're probably not going into Zagreb, anyway."

Susan made some clucking noises and waved her elbows up and down in an attempt to embarrass Jim.

"You're pretty good at chicken impersonations," Jim commented. "Do you keep chickens in your back yard, or have you been in touch with your feathered friends in Gora?"

"You can't keep chickens where I live," Susan replied. "You'd have to build the hen-house like Fort Knox, or else you might as well put a flashing neon sign on top of the coop, saying Foxy's Diner."

Tom frowned at her. "But you live in the city. You don't get foxes in the city."

"There's a big population of urban foxes in Bristol," Susan told him. "They used to scavenge from rubbish bags, but then the council gave us all wheely-bins for our garbage, so now people put food out for the foxes, to make sure that they don't go hungry."

Jim clicked his tongue. "You're making this up."

"I'm not. People from the University zoology department go out to catch the foxes, from time to time."

"Do they make them into fur coats?" Pete asked.

"No, they put little radio collars on them, then track them with a listening device," she replied.

"See," said Jim. "I told you she was talking rubbish."

An hour later they turned off the motorway at an exit that they hoped would take them into the centre of Zagreb. As the bus jolted over tram rails, Susan had an idea.

"Follow the tram lines," she shouted to Janek. "They must run into the town centre."

Janek followed her instructions, pausing at each junction where several sets of lines crossed each other. He chose the streets which had the most rail tracks running along them, stoically ignoring the short-tempered motorists who were tooting their horns as the bus blocked the junction. They went along until they came to a busy intersection, where the tram lines criss-crossed and then split off into four different directions.

Janek gave a loud groan of despair and lifted his hands into the air to appeal for heavenly guidance. Susan dashed to the front of the bus and looked frantically in every direction, trying to decide on the best way to go. She spotted a large, modern building down one of the streets, and pointed it out to Janek.

"Head for that place. Maybe we can get directions there."

Janek edged the bus along the street, hugging the kerb in an attempt to stay out of the path of noisy trams that rushed up behind them with bells clanging angrily. They halted outside the building, which proved to be a bus terminus. Susan darted away and followed the crowd of people who were going into the building.

She reappeared several minutes later, looking relieved.

"It's our lucky day," she told the others. "I met an Australian back-packer by the information counter. He said that the hotel is near the railway station, and if we follow a number six tram we should find it easily. It's a huge Neo-classical pile with Doric columns, so it should be easy to spot."

They waited at the kerbside until a number six tram came along, then

Janek swung the bus into the road and followed close behind. After a few minutes they reached the railway station, and as the number six tram made a right turn, Janek had to brake violently to avoid a number nine tram which was trying to cross their path. Janek shook his fist and yelled at the tram driver as the number nine veered off to the left.

"Look!" cried Joe. "I can see Doric columns down that street. Follow the number nine!"

As they drew up outside the palatial hotel, Susan gave a sigh of relief and remarked, "I'm not sure that being shot at is any worse than driving in this town!"

And they clambered quickly off the bus and headed for the hotel bar.

* * *

"We're going on down to the venue," Tom shouted through Susan's door later that evening. "Are you coming?"

Susan opened the door and shook her head. "I've got to wait for Terry," she replied. "There might be a change in the itinerary."

The band departed, and Susan sat in her room, uneasy at being alone. She wished that Terry would turn up soon and collect his cash. They had spent the afternoon in the nearby botanical gardens, trying to relax after the journey. As they had walked through a leafy corner of the park, Susan caught a glimpse of a figure lurking behind a tree, watching them. Or maybe it was just a trick of the light. None of the band had noticed anything. She muttered to herself, "I'm getting paranoid," when a sharp tapping at the door startled her.

"Who is it?" she called, with her hand on the door knob.

"It's Terry and Ahmed, luvvie. Open up."

She quickly let them in.

"Everything all right, dear?" Terry asked.

Susan nodded and promptly took the envelope of money out of her bag. Terry counted up the cash and smiled.

"Excellent," he purred. He then counted out a handful of notes and gave them to Susan. "I knew I could rely on you. You're a little gem. Anyway, I hope the boys won't be annoyed, but they'll have to do an extra show out here. Belgrade. After doing the two shows in Split and Dubrovnik, you'll have to retrace your route back to Zagreb, cross into Hungary, go along to Serbia, and drop down into Belgrade that way. I've written it all down for you, with a few directions as well."

Susan looked at the small map that Terry had brought with him.

"That's crazy," she complained. "Why do we have to go such a long way around to get to Belgrade?"

"It's the only way that we could get insurance," he explained. "We thought the borders might be open by now, but things are still a bit too risky in Bosnia. The sponsors didn't want to do Belgrade at all, what with all the sanctions. But then the Russian embassy out here found out about the tour, and they kicked up a fuss." Terry grimaced briefly. "I don't suppose they've even heard of Tom Banks. They're just being sulky because they've been left out. Anyway, I've got a permit for you to use while you're there. It means that your bus won't be searched by Serbian troops."

"That's comforting," Susan murmured, sarcastically.

"And we've hired some small lorries to take the equipment down the Dalmatian coast," Terry informed her. "The big articulated wagon won't get around the bends on that route. The new trucks and drivers should be waiting at the concert hall."

Susan frowned. "I'd better get down there and let everyone know what's happening. You know what our Polish crew are like. If they think that someone's trying to steal the gear, all hell will break loose!"

"Can we give you a lift?"

"Have you still got that smelly old rust-bucket?"

"No luv. We came here in something a bit more comfortable."

* * *

As Susan climbed out of the orange BMW, she remarked, "This is almost as big as a limo. You could have a TV set in the back."

"I don't think I'll keep it for long," Terry said, blithely. "Burnt orange is a bit severe. The only other colour that they had was black."

"Why didn't you get a black one, then?"

"Ooh no," Terry murmured, looking aghast. "Out here, if you drive a black BMW, people think that you're the Secret Police or a gangster. We'll see you in Belgrade," he called back to her, as they sped off into the distance.

Susan found her way to the stage door of the concert hall. The tour bus and equipment truck were parked just along the street, behind a line of small lorries. She found Janek inside, playing cards with Lazlo and a group of men that she hadn't seen before.

"Are these the new drivers?" she asked Janek, nodding at the five strangers.

"Yes, they good boys," he replied, still studying his cards.

"They look like refugees," Susan muttered, looking at their shabby clothes. "Don't take all their money off them, or we'll be in trouble with the Red Cross."

* * *

At the end of the show there was chaos out on the pavement, with different-sized crates being trundled between the five small trucks.

"It's like one of those game shows where you have to do problem solving," mused Joe, as he watched the gear being stowed away. "What happens if it doesn't all fit into the trucks?"

Pete shrugged. "They take it all out and try again, I suppose."

As Tom and Jim emerged through the stage door, Jim was complaining, "Why did you shout let go when we were only half-way through Too Late? You cut out my drum solo!"

"Sorry about that," Tom replied. "I lost track of where I was in the song."

"It's easier to follow a number six tram than to follow you, sometimes. Anyway, are we all gonna play roulette back at the hotel casino?"

"Not likely," Susan cut in. "We've got a ten-hour drive tomorrow, so we've got to be on the road by five-thirty. Everyone goes straight to bed. Janek, you stay here until all the trucks have loaded up. Make sure that they're on their way by midnight."

"We may as well drive off now and sleep on the bus," Joe suggested.

"I not drive that road in dark," Janek told him, dramatically. "We end tour in sea, maybe!"

Jim gave a scornful toss of his head. "The road can't be as bad as all that."

And they returned to the hotel to catch a few hours sleep.

* * *

At five the next morning, Tom knocked gently on Susan's door. "Rise and shine."

Susan flopped out of bed and fumbled for the light switch.

"Open up," Tom called softly. "I have something for you."

Susan unlocked the door and peered sleepily at Tom as he carried a large cardboard box into the room.

"What's that?" she yawned.

"It was outside your door. Can I open it? I love opening parcels." Tom quickly untied the string that was around the box. He opened up the cardboard flaps, and pulled out a black plastic bag. Tom looked inside the bag and groaned.

"What is it?" Susan asked.

"It's the merchandise that we left behind in the dressing room at Pecs. No-one ever sends me anything nice," Tom grumbled, and he mooched back to his own room.

Susan pushed the merchandise back into the box and dumped it inside the wardrobe. She opened up her overnight bag and added the money that Terry had given her to the stash in the rolled-up socks. "Quite a little nest-egg," she murmured happily, as she stowed the socks at the bottom of her bag.

Half an hour later they left the hotel, and drove off down the dark, empty streets of Zagreb. Janek retraced the route that he had taken the previous day, and by the time the bus was on the motorway, Susan and the band were fast asleep.

* * *

By nine o'clock they had woken up and were complaining bitterly.

Pete put his head between his knees and said, "I haven't had travel nausea since I was a kid."

"I think I'm going to be sick," Susan groaned.

"Just don't look out of the window, then maybe you won't feel so bad," Tom suggested.

"Is the road like this all the way?" Jim demanded. "It's worse than being on a boat!"

Joe gazed out of the window and murmured, "What wonderful scenery."

The road followed a rugged coastline, weaving around the rocky outcrops in a relentless series of hair-pin bends. Mountains loomed to the left of them, and to the right was a sheer drop down to the sea. The bus swayed from side to side as one curve followed closely upon another.

"This must be the worst road in the world," Jim protested to Janek. "There's got to be a better way than this."

"Other road have many Serbs," Janek told him. "No Serbs here."

"I can believe that," Jim retorted. "They probably all got queasy, and went back home again."

"Shall we stop for breakfast?" Tom proposed. "We might feel better if we have something inside our stomachs."

"We might as well just toss the food out by the roadside," Susan muttered. "Cut out the middle-man."

The road dipped down, and terracotta tiled roofs suddenly came into view. They drove into a small village which was set in a secluded bay. The houses were strung in a line on the narrow ribbon of flat land that edged the sea. Susan blinked as the sun glinted harshly off the white-washed walls, and she turned her gaze to the tranquil sapphire sea.

Janek eased the bus to a stop beside a petrol pump which stood in stark isolation, set slightly back from the roadway. A man appeared from a cafe further down the street, and ambled towards them. Janek climbed off the bus and hovered over the man whilst he filled the tank. Then he followed the man back to the cafe, and emerged several minutes later carrying a large, brown paper bag.

"Breakfast," he announced, as he climbed back on board. He drove a little way down the road and parked on an empty piece of ground next to a small jetty. He set the coffee pot on its stove, and told the others, "I eat now. You want food or no?"

The others stirred themselves and followed him off the bus slowly, with much stretching and groaning.

"Let's try some of the salami," Tom suggested, as he peered into the brown paper bag and saw that it contained a dozen bread rolls. Janek opened up the baggage compartment and took one of the salami out of its towel.

"This salami is getting stronger by the day," Jim complained, as he wrinkled his nose in distaste. "It might be a good idea to put our suitcases into the other compartment. I don't want the dogs at Miami airport all howling over my bags because of the smell!"

Tom nodded thoughtfully in agreement, and Janek moved the cases into the second compartment.

When the coffee had brewed, they sat on the edge of the jetty and ate breakfast, with a warm breeze blowing in from the sea helping to quell their nausea.

As Susan used Janek's Swiss army knife to hack another slice of salami, she remarked, "It has gone a bit sweaty, even with being kept in a towel. I suppose it's because there's no air circulating inside the baggage hold."

"Well it's not going inside with us," Jim stated, vehemently. "I don't mind eating it, but I don't want to live with it!"

After breakfast they set off down the road again.

"I hope the equipment trucks make it in good time," Tom fretted. "They may have to rig up our little generator if the electricity supply isn't good enough."

"They should be nearly there," Susan assured him. "Terry said that it's a wonderful concert hall, so stop worrying."

Tom chewed his lip anxiously. "We'll probably be playing in a field, because the concert hall has been shelled."

Susan gave an exasperated sigh. "Your trouble is, you're too used to the good life."

"It wasn't so many years ago that we used to set up our own gear," Tom said, defensively. "But I'm not sure that I can remember which wires go where, any more."

"As I recall," Jim interjected, "We never let you do any wiring. You blew up more speakers than we could afford."

Tom fell into a sulky silence.

Joe suddenly chuckled and said, "Do you remember that gig we did in a marquee in the middle of a field at a little music festival? The one that my cousin arranged?"

"How could we possibly forget," Jim groaned. "Why did he ask us to play there? Did you piss him off by making a pass at his wife?"

"He thought that he was doing us a favour," protested Joe. "We were always looking for gigs in those days."

"Why was it so bad?" Susan asked.

Tom forgot that he was sulking, and recounted with grim humour, "The acts ran so close together, that the stage manager said to us, "You've got twenty minutes to set up".

"I replied, "Twenty minutes! We're musicians, not hookers! And I remember Pete said, "Yeah, hookers get paid more than we do."

With a rueful smile, Tom continued, "All of the other bands there were playing folk music or hoe-down stuff, with fiddles and banjos. Then we plugged in and started blasting away with solid rock, and the tent emptied at a stroke! We were left playing to two small girls who were eating ice-creams, and a collection of ragamuffin little boys who were chasing each other around the tent poles!"

As Susan sniggered unsympathetically, Tom told her, "We stuck to playing in bars after that. The audience was usually too drunk to run away."

Pete shook his head. "You're forgetting how we regularly used to empty that bar down by the health club."

"Mmm, happy days," Jim murmured, as a fleeting smile rippled across his face.

As Susan gave him a quizzical look, Tom explained, "The girl who ran the bar was sweet on Jim. She used to hire us all the time. We'd get a hundred dollars a night, plus extra if the bar takings were up. Trouble was, the bar takings were usually down when we played there. Give Jim his due, though. She kept asking us back!"

CHAPTER 23

After several hours of travelling southwards, the sun had climbed high into the azure sky. As they drove through villages, green wooden shutters were tightly closed against the fierce rays. Susan and the band played cards to pass the time, though the game was hampered by the fact that Joe was gazing out at the offshore islands that thrust sparkling white peaks through the sapphire surface of the Adriatic.

"I wish that we could stop to take some photos," Joe lamented. "This coastline is exquisite."

"We haven't got time," Susan told him. "You'll have to wait until tomorrow."

The road skirted a section of low coastline and ran close to the shore. Joe looked across the rocks and suddenly gasped, "Oh my!" He peered more closely at the people sunbathing on the rocky beach, and remarked, "They could get seriously sun burnt!"

Tom gazed idly at the subjects of Joe's attention, and did a quick double-take as he realised that the sun-bathers were completely naked. The bus rounded a bend that took them away from the beach, and the naturists were lost from view.

Tom strained his neck to try and view the road ahead. "Do you think that the road will bend back towards the beach again?"

"What's so special about the beach, all of a sudden?" asked Jim, who had not lifted his eyes from his hand of cards.

"We just passed some nude sun-bathers," Tom explained.

Jim's eyes widened, and he cried petulantly, "Why didn't you tell me?" He scanned the road ahead and estimated, "We should be alongside the beach again just after the next bend. Maybe we should stop and give the salami an airing."

Susan wrinkled her nose at him. "Don't be vulgar!"

"I was talking about lunch!"

"We're not going to stop. Not under any circumstances."

There was much grumbling from the men, and the card game was abandoned in favour of staring out of the bus window and counting the sun-worshippers.

* * *

In late afternoon they rounded a wooded peninsula and the town of Split came into view. Sun-bleached mountain slopes loomed up beyond the outskirts of the town, and buildings squeezed together along the water-front on all the available flat ground.

"We'll go directly to the venue," Tom shouted to Janek.

"It should be on this road," Susan murmured, as she studied the hand-written note that Terry had given her the previous evening. "It's a classical primrose building. It should be easy to spot."

They found the concert hall in the old town, near the harbour, and the band disappeared inside to do the sound checks.

Susan made herself comfortable in a wicker chair at a nearby pavement cafe, and relaxed under the shade of a colourful sun-umbrella. She ordered a drink and sat idly watching the passers-by.

"Maybe a life on the road isn't so bad, after all," she murmured to herself.

The street was fairly quiet, and there seemed to be just a handful of tourists roaming about. Susan shifted her chair so that her face caught the gentle rays of the sinking sun. She closed her eyes and imagined that she was independently wealthy.

After an hour, the band emerged from the hall. Susan beckoned them over to her table and said, "It's nice here. Just like Italy, but cheaper."

"I'm so happy that you're having a nice time," Tom said, caustically. "Could we trouble you to get us to the hotel?"

Susan eased herself out of the wicker chair and picked up the beer mat on which the waiter had drawn directions to the hotel.

They drove past a small park, then skirted a large, bustling street market that seemed to stretch right down to the harbour.

"I wonder if the market will be here tomorrow morning?" Pete pondered. "I could sell the trainers out of my suitcase."

They left the old town behind and travelled through an area of high-rise apartment blocks. The modern hotel was situated near the beach, and looked in surprisingly pristine condition, with unblemished stonework and a canopy-covered front veranda.

Jim raised his eyebrows. "Didn't these places along the coast all get shelled?"

"They've done a good job of patching up the damage," Susan observed. "Maybe we could tempt them into English housing estates."

"They have a swimming pool here," Tom observed, as he looked across the terrace bar. "I'll have a dip later on tonight."

The hotel foyer was deserted. The receptionist seemed pleased to see them, and gave them rooms at the front, with a balcony and sea view.

"Are we the only guests here?" Tom asked her. "We were hoping to get a meal. Is your restaurant open?"

"Three other guests only," she replied, in husky broken English. "We cook you dinner, but only one meal on menu."

"Can we use the pool?"

"Of course."

As they rode the lift up to the fourth floor, Susan remarked, "It's a shame that we're only here for one night. It's the first time that I've been in a resort hotel where they can guarantee you a sun-bed by the pool."

* * *

When the band went off at seven to the venue, Susan decided to take a walk by the beach and enjoy the sea air. A stone path ran along the shore and curved around the bay into the distance. Several people were walking dogs, and a few joggers were gasping their way along the path, so Susan reckoned that it was safe to stroll down it alone. The evening air was still warm, and she was glad for the opportunity to stretch her legs after being cooped up in the bus all day.

By the time Susan returned to the town, dusk was deepening and the street lights were glowing pale amber. As she walked past a petrol station on her way back to the hotel, she noticed a large, black car at one of the pumps. The man filling the tank was bending over, his face hidden in shadow, and although the night was warm he was wrapped up in a heavy overcoat. Susan glanced briefly at him as she passed by, then she stared more closely as he limped across to the cashier's booth, in the gathering gloom. She hurried away down the street and sprinted into the hotel foyer, casting an anxious glance over her shoulder.

* * *

Susan was reading in her room when the band returned just before midnight. She could hear them singing along the corridor, and she opened her door to tell them off. Before she could say anything, Jim pre-empted her with, "We're not disturbing anyone. There's no-one else here."

"We're all going for a midnight swim," Tom called, as he disappeared into his room. "See you downstairs."

Susan put on her swimsuit, grabbed a towel and made her way down to the pool.

Jim had persuaded the receptionist to switch on the pool lights, and she had even unlocked the pool-side bar to provide him with a few bottles of beer.

The pool was nicely warm. Susan and Joe splashed about in the shallow end, and Tom was swimming lengths. Pete was sitting on the side with just his legs in the water, and Jim was plunging into the deep end, trying to impress the receptionist.

"It's dangerous to drink and dive," Susan shouted at Jim, as he took a sip of beer, then plummeted into the water again.

She turned back to Joe and continued their conversation about how to cook Italian food.

"To make a really good tomato sauce, you've got to use virgin olive oil and a little bit of butter to sweat the onion, garlic and celery."

Joe nodded as he listened. "Does it matter what kind of pan you use?"

"Yes, definitely," Susan replied. "I use a saucepan that I bought in Italy. It has a thick, heavy bottom."

Tom was swimming past, and he paused as if to speak.

"Don't even think about it," she told him, abruptly.

Tom closed his mouth and swam quickly away.

* * *

On Saturday morning, Susan was on her way out of her room to get breakfast. As she opened the door, she fell over a cardboard box which was sitting outside. She pulled it into the room and opened up the flaps.

"I don't believe it," she groaned. It was the left-over merchandise that she had abandoned in Zagreb. She pulled a face at it, then went down to the dining room.

Susan was surprised to see the band there, slurping coffee and gobbling bread rolls.

"What's the rush?" she asked, as she sat down at their table.

"We've got lots to do," Jim replied, spraying crumbs at her as he spoke. "Me and Pete are going down to the market to sell some trainers, and Joe wants to explore the Roman Palace."

"Do me a favour, and take the merchandise with you to the market. See if you can get rid of it."

Pete was un-enthusiastic. "I don't know," he said, doubtfully. "Shirts aren't really my line."

"You can keep the cash," Susan coaxed. "I've already given the merchandise takings to Terry, and he wasn't interested in the leftover stuff."

"All right then."

* * *

By eleven-thirty they were back on the bus, following the coast road southwards once more.

"I wish I'd had more time," Joe said, wistfully. "I only got half-way around the old town, and I didn't get any shots of the harbour." He fixed Susan with a direct stare and added, "Don't forget, you promised that we could stop somewhere along the coast today, so that I can get some shots of the island peaks."

"I'd sooner take a look at the peaks on the shore-line," Jim mumbled quietly to Tom, and they speculated on how many nudists they would see on the way down to Dubrovnik.

The coastal highway wound itself around a succession of inlets and peninsulas, making giant loops as it followed the serrated contours of the coastline.

At lunch time, Joe chose a stopping point on the tip of a promontory, and he set his camera on its tripod while the others set out some food.

"We're too high above the rocks, here," Jim complained. "I need to use binoculars to see the sun-bathers."

Susan gave him a sideways look. "I can't think of a quicker way to get arrested."

"Why don't you use Joe's zoom lens," suggested Pete.

"Yeah!" Jim cried, with delight. "I hadn't thought of that!"

Joe obligingly attached the huge lens to the camera, adjusted the focus for Jim's benefit, then sat down to have his lunch

Jim pressed his eye to the viewfinder and eagerly scanned the rocks below.

"Nice, nice," he murmured appreciatively, as he focused on two girls clad only in scanty bikini briefs.

As the rest of the band took turns in peering at the sun-bathers, Susan sighed wearily and remarked, "Don't they grow women where you lot come from?"

"Yeah, but they cover the fruit to prevent frost damage," Jim answered, as he wrested the eye-piece away from Pete.

"It's nice to see home-grown ones," Pete commented. "I don't much care for the artificial ones."

Susan said thoughtfully, "If you have breast enlargement surgery, I suppose it means that you'll never drown."

Tom frowned at her. "How do you work that out?"

"Well, they insert sacs of vegetable oil into the bosoms," she explained, "So it must act as a sort of life-jacket. After all, oil always floats on top of water."

Jim nodded in agreement. "It would explain why the Baywatch girls are such good swimmers."

When Joe had finished his bread and salami, he dismantled the zoom lens and set about taking his panoramic shots of the rugged coastline. The others stood around, gazing idly at the scenery, and watching distant cars snake their way along the quiet road. Janek had parked the bus on a gravelled rest area, which was shaded by a few trees, and partially screened from the road.

The silence was suddenly broken by the sound of racing engines. Two cars came into view from the south, travelling very fast and close together.

"What are those two idiots playing at?" Susan muttered, as she watched the cars approach the sharp curve around the promontory.

The car in front was a sleek sports car, and on his tail was a hefty black saloon, which was revving fiercely to stay close behind. They rounded the bend with a squeal of tyres, then accelerated away towards Split. The black saloon suddenly swung out, shot past the sports car, then served back to the right and braked hard, forcing the other car off the road and into the cliff face.

Moments later, the driver of the sports car clambered out of his vehicle, looking dazed. The driver of the black saloon immediately leapt on him, took hold of his neck, and started to shake him violently.

"Holy shit!" exclaimed Tom. He sprinted off down the road, with the others following at a less athletic pace.

As Tom neared the crash scene, he bellowed, "Are you crazy? What the hell are you doing?"

The driver of the black saloon jerked his head around, startled by Tom's unexpected intrusion.

Tom stopped in his tracks as he recognised the man in Joe's photographs.

"You bastard!" he yelled. "You're the one who cut up my rag dolly!" Tom lunged forwards in a furious run.

The man in the cashmere coat abruptly released his hold on the other driver, and hobbled hastily towards his car. The black BMW roared away into the distance, and Tom was left standing in the road, panting heavily and waving his fist in frustration.

Susan and the others dashed alongside moments later, and as the driver of the sports car massaged his neck and regained his composure, he blinked his eyes and muttered, "By gum! Susan, me old mucker! How be yer?"

Susan stood wide-eyed in surprise. "Phil!"

"You two know each other," Jim deduced.

She nodded. "We were at school together. Haven't seen each other in years."

"What brings yer to this here part of the world?" asked Phil, appearing coolly unaffected by his recent ordeal.

"I'm travelling with a band," Susan told him. "They're playing a couple of concerts here."

"Well, stone the crows!" Phil exclaimed, looking impressed. He stared at the band, then whispered to Susan, "Is they famous? I doesn't recognise any of them."

"They don't get to England very often," she told him. "This is Tom Banks. He's a piano player."

"How do, Tom?" said Phil, shaking Tom's hand vigorously. "I always wanted ter play the pianer, but when I were a nipper, all the other lads would say as you was a nancy-boy if you did summat like that."

"Excuse me?" Tom responded, looking completely bewildered.

Phil asked innocently, "Doesn't yer understand English?"

Tom gave him a hostile glare. "I always used to think that I did, but obviously I was wrong."

Susan cut in, "They're Americans."

"Yankees, eh?" Phil remarked, with a broad grin.

"I'm not a Yankee!" Tom hissed from between clenched teeth.

"My father were a Yankee," Phil continued, blithely. "So me mother says, anyhow. I never met me dad."

"Do you know that guy in the black BMW?" Tom demanded.

"I never seen him before," Phil replied, looking baffled. "I went by him down the road a-ways, and he suddenly swung round and come chasing up after me, silly bugger!"

"Your car's a bit of a mess," Pete said, as he surveyed the crumpled front wing of the Porsche.

"It's an unusual car," remarked Jim. "You don't often see a violet Porsche."

"Ar, horrible colour, isn't her," Phil mumbled. "I reckon that's why I got her so cheap. That, and the steering wheel being on the right-hand side."

"It must be difficult to drive, with the wheel on the wrong side," Joe said. "How can you see when it's safe to pass?"

"I mostly drives in the middle of the road," Phil replied.

Joe was aghast. "Isn't that dangerous?"

"Only if you meets a tank."

"We'll give you a lift to Dubrovnik," Susan offered. "You can send a tow-truck out for your car."

Phil pulled a glum face. "I'll have ter count up me pennies, first."

"At least the insurance company will pay for the repairs," Joe consoled him.

"Insurance?" echoed Phil, sounding confused. "Oh ar, insurance," he repeated, in an unhappy voice.

"Let's get going," Tom announced, and he headed back towards the bus.

Phil took his car keys out of the ignition and opened the boot of the Porsche. There was a holdall and a small, square wooden crate inside. Phil carefully lifted out the crate and cradled it in his arms, while Joe picked up the holdall for him.

"What's in the box?" Jim asked, intrigued by the way that Phil was cautiously carrying it.

"It's my mate Luigi," Phil replied. "He died sudden. He been cremated, so I were taking his ashes to his family. They lives near Trieste."

Joe widened his eyes in sympathy. "Was it a road accident?"

"Oh ar. Summat like that," Phil answered, vaguely.

When they returned to the bus, Janek opened up both baggage compartments. He put the salami back into its box, and then he placed Joe's tripod into the other hold, with the suitcases.

Phil gazed at the large compartments and remarked, "You got a good lot of luggage space on this here bus of yours. Where's all the musical instruments, and such-like?"

"All the instruments go on a truck, with the electrical gear and amplifiers," Susan explained. "It has to be secure, for insurance reasons."

Phil nodded thoughtfully, and he remained quiet and pensive as they resumed their journey to Dubrovnik.

CHAPTER 24

Later that afternoon, the road traced its way along a sinuous ribbon of sea that seemed to snake interminably inland. The expanse of water eventually narrowed, and a bridge finally appeared to take them over on to the other side of the inlet. As they drove past a marina crowded with small yachts, Phil announced, "Dubrovnik is just the other side of this here tump of mountain."

"There is something excruciatingly frustrating about travelling along a road that zigzags in such a tortuous manner," Jim proclaimed, with unusual eloquence. "I'll be real glad not to do this journey again!"

Susan winced and remained silent. She hadn't told the band that they had to return via the same road. She decided that she would tell them after the show that night, when they were in the bar, feeling happy.

"Do you know your way around Dubrovnik?" Tom asked Phil.

Phil nodded. "I knows this place like the back of me hand."

"The venue is the Marina Theatre," Susan said, looking at her list. "Can you direct us there?"

"Oh ar," Phil assured her. "But we'll have ter go careful like, or we'll fetch up in the harbour."

As they swung around the head of the peninsula they could see the terracotta roofs of Dubrovnik stretching out below them, squeezed between the mountain slopes and the sea. Phil directed Janek through the tree-lined streets, until they reached the massive stone walls of the old town. They skirted the ancient fortifications, then turned into a narrow street that led down to the harbour.

"Does this road have a dry ending?" Jim demanded anxiously, as the street became a jetty, with water lapping on both sides.

Janek slowed the bus to a crawl, and carefully eased forwards up a ramp and on to a narrow metal bridge which straddled a corner of the harbour and linked to the main quayside. They traversed the juddering span, bumped down a ramp, and pulled into a courtyard where the equipment trucks were parked in a line.

An archway in the courtyard wall led into the rear of the concert hall, and the band ambled inside to find the crew. Susan stood on the quayside for a while, surveying the flotilla of small boats in the harbour, but the hot sun beat down uncomfortably on her head, so she ventured through the archway in search of shade. She wandered about backstage, and found her way into the wings. Tom spotted her, and he called out, "Small, but beautifully formed."

Susan smiled at the compliment. "Thank you, Tom. You haven't said anything nice to me for ages."

"I was talking about the hall."

Susan walked on to the stage, and gazed around. The concert hall was small and oval, with a compact seating area. To compensate for limited floor space, a dazzling three-tier balcony edged the auditorium, with a sweep of graceful arches curving between the stuccoed pillars. The arches were decorated in gold leaf, and sumptuous velvet drapes hung at the sides.

"Go and find Joe," Tom told her. "He's out front, admiring the architecture."

Susan wandered out through the velvet curtains, and found her way to the front entrance of the concert hall. Dark blue canopies shaded the front steps, where a pavement cafe was set out. Susan squinted as she stepped into the sunlight and scanned the picturesque street. She saw Joe just a few yards away, admiring a colonnaded portico. As she approached him, he enthused, "This is wonderful! It's like stepping back into Renaissance Italy!"

"They need you inside," Susan told him, as she looked about her, wide-eyed. The Baroque white-stone buildings were huddled close together within the protective ramparts of the ancient city walls. The narrow streets were paved with pale cobblestones, and there were no vehicles to spoil the air of antiquity inside the medieval enclave.

"They say that you can walk around on top of the city walls," Joe said, eagerly. "It's fortunate that the Serbs were such poor shots," he continued. Then he frowned and murmured, "Or maybe they didn't want to destroy this beautiful place."

"Ask them, the next time you see them," Susan said tersely, as she dragged Joe back inside the hall.

* * *

After the rehearsal, Phil went with them to the hotel, giving directions to Janek as they drove out of the town and along the adjacent peninsula. The modern holiday hotel complex was set beside a bay, and hemmed in by wooded slopes.

The hotel seemed devoid of guests, and the tiled floor of the foyer gave an eerie echo to their footsteps. As they checked in, Phil disappeared into the bar, and emerged with a bag that clinked as he walked. They rode the lift up to the top floor, and as they stepped into the corridor Phil announced, "I got you summat in return for me bus ride. Nuthin fancy. Just a few bottles of local vodker and a bag of ice. But don't have too much ice. The water hereabouts will likely give yer the runs."

Tom took the bag, and paused to hand a bottle each to Pete and Jim. Phil moved off to follow Joe, saying to the others, "Joe said that I could go along ter his room to have a baf."

Tom clicked his tongue in exasperation. "There's no F in bath."

"Bain't there? I'll have ter wash in the sink, then," Phil grumbled, as he disappeared into Joe's room.

Tom and Jim exchanged puzzled glances, while Pete muttered, "I can't understand a word he says."

"He has a real strange accent," Jim agreed. "He puts an R into every word."

"It's just an ordinary West-Country accent," Susan said, defensively.

"No-one in your office talks like that," Tom argued.

"Media people aren't allowed to have accents," Susan answered, curtly. "The Boss often tells me off for rolling my R's."

"You shouldn't wear such tight skirts," Jim replied, with a grin.

Susan gave a disdainful sniff and marched into her room. "Don't disturb me," she called back over her shoulder. "I'm going to have a nice long shower."

* * *

Fifteen minutes later, Susan was nicely soaped up in an invigorating hot shower. She was shampooing her hair and humming a tune, when she noticed that the torrent of water was becoming weaker. Before she had time to rinse her hair, the cascade of water had diminished to a mere trickle, and a moment later the shower was reduced to a few solitary drips.

Susan turned the shower lever back and forth, but no water emerged. She tried the bath taps, then the basin taps, but they remained resolutely dry. Susan cursed loudly, and surveyed her sudsy head in the bathroom mirror. She hurriedly wrapped a large towel around her soapy body, grabbed her room key, dashed out into the corridor and hammered noisily on Joe's door. He opened the door and stared at her with astonishment.

"Is Phil still in the bath?" she demanded.

"No, he went out a few minutes ago."

"Damn!"

As Joe stood gaping, Jim's voice came from across the corridor, "Susan, honey, if you're that eager for a naked man, I'll be happy to oblige you."

"Bugger off!" she snapped. "What about Pete? Is he in the bath?"

"No, he's here in my room, doing damage to a bottle of vodka," Jim replied, still smiling willingly at her.

"And Tom always takes a shower," Susan wailed. "What am I going to do? The water supply has dried up!"

"I heard Tom swearing through the wall, a little while ago," said Joe. "He was cussing because his shower wasn't working, so maybe he ran a bath."

"Go and shout through the wall at him," Susan ordered. "Tell him to let me into his room, and tell him not to pull the plug out of his bath. Quick, I'm desperate!"

Joe went back into his room and shouted, "Tom, don't empty your bath water. And let Susan into your room. She's desperate."

"That's the best news I've had in ages!" Tom yelled in reply.

A few moments later, Tom opened his door and Susan darted into the room, saying, "Can I get into your bath and rinse myself off?"

Tom was clad only in his dressing gown. He folded his arms, grinned at her and responded, "What's it worth?"

"A smack in the mouth if you say no!"

"Your feminine charms and powers of persuasion are too much for me to resist," he said, sardonically. "Feel free to climb into my bath tub and hold your head under the water for as long as you desire."

Susan scurried into the bathroom and quickly immersed herself in the deep bath. She closed her eyes and swirled her hair under the water. When Susan opened her eyes again, she saw Tom gazing wistfully at her body.

"You're lucky, being able to stretch out in the bath and still be completely submerged," he said, enviously. "I haven't been able to do that since I was ten years old. It's not much fun taking a bath when you have three feet of leg sticking out of the water."

"Three feet of leg?" echoed Susan. "You have a wonderful way with words, Tom. I can see why you're a songwriter."

"You're so hurtful sometimes," he pouted playfully. "How about a drink to sweeten you up?"

"Go on then. I'll have a vodka on the rocks."

"How come you never have a mixer in your drinks?" Tom called at her from the bedroom.

"I was taken with that advert on the telly, the one that says, "Why take two bottles into the shower?" So I don't bother with the tonic anymore."

Tom handed her a glass. She sipped, then grimaced. "Are you sure this is vodka? It tastes more like turnip colada!"

"Maybe it's the ice that tastes strange. Phil warned us not to use too much." Tom paused, then asked, "Was he your boyfriend when you were at school?"

"Not exactly. We were good mates, but we lost touch after he was expelled."

Tom pulled a face. "What did he do to get expelled?"

"He tried to thump the head, and she got really pissed off about it. Nuns take it very personally when you smack them."

Tom raised his eyebrows, then groaned. "Great! We pick up a hitchhiker and he turns out to be a psycho!"

* * *

In the early evening they had a hurried dinner in the cavernous hotel dining room, and then the band returned to the concert hall. Susan sat in the deserted restaurant for a while, sipping a leisurely cup of coffee and gazing out over the bay. She returned to her room and began to study the route to Belgrade. When a knock sounded at her door, she was momentarily disconcerted.

"Who is it?"

"It be me. Phil."

Susan opened the door and Phil walked in, carrying his wooden box.

"We missed you at dinner," Susan commented. "Where did you disappear to?"

"I were trying to get me car sorted out," he replied. "They wants a hefty sum of money to bring her back. I were wondering if you could lend me a few bob?"

Susan wrinkled her nose. "If I lend you some money, when will you be able to repay me?"

"I can pay yer back just as soon as I sells Luigi."

"Sell Luigi? Are you planning on selling his ashes to his family?" she asked, incredulously.

Phil guffawed heartily, and proceeded to take the lid off his small crate. He rummaged inside the box, and groped amongst the protective wood shavings. Then he extracted an object and presented it to Susan. Her eyes widened in astonishment as she stared at a jewel-encrusted golden goblet. Susan took the goblet from Phil, and nearly dropped it as the weight surprised her.

"It feels like solid gold!" she gasped.

"Her's got a mate, and all," Phil muttered, as he dug around in the box once more. He pulled out a small gold ewer, also emblazoned with precious stones.

"These must be worth a fortune," Susan murmured.

"Ar, I reckon so," Phil agreed, cheerily. "I were taking them to Trieste, to sell them. Now I got ter wait for me car to get ment."

Susan looked thoughtfully at the treasures, then quizzed Phil, "Is this why you were being chased?"

"It's hard ter say," he said, evasively.

Susan recalled what Terry had said to her at their last meeting, and she said to Phil, "What do you reckon about that bloke in the black BMW? Is he a gangster or a policeman?"

Phil shrugged. "It don't make no difference to me."

Susan frowned. "What do you mean?"

"If he's a gangster, he'll shoot me, and if he's a copper, he'll put I in prison."

"Is this stuff stolen?" she demanded.

"I paid fer it!" Phil asserted. "Didn't pay much, though," he grudgingly admitted, as Susan gave him a hard stare.

"They look like religious artefacts," Susan murmured, as she examined the gold cup and jug. "They were probably plundered from a museum or a church. We should return them to the rightful owners."

"And who would they be? I got these here pots in Bosnia. There be no knowing who it belongs to. And you know what them people are like for squabbling over things. Finders, keepers, I says."

"You've got a point," Susan conceded. "I suppose if you sell them out here, they might find their way back to the owners."

Phil idly glanced at the papers that Susan had strewn on the bed, then bent his head down to take a closer look.

"You off ter Belgrade, then? Joe didn't say nuthin about Belgrade ter me."

Susan sighed heavily. "I haven't told them yet. They won't be too pleased about it, because it means going back on that awful road. The only good thing is that we've got a special permit. We can cross into Serbia without being searched."

"I could get shot of Luigi in Belgrade," Phil said quickly. "I got a mate there. He buys and sells all manner of stuff. If you gives me a ride to Belgrade in that there bus of yours, I'll give you half the money I gets from selling these here trinkets. And they be worth a few bob, I reckon."

Susan did a quick mental calculation, and nodded her agreement.

"So can I have me loan now?" Phil pleaded. "To pay fer the tow-truck?"

"I suppose so." Susan delved into her overnight bag and brought out the pair of socks that held her cash. Taking out the roll of notes, she peeled off a few and handed them to Phil. As he made for the door, Susan called to him in a loud whisper, "Don't tell the others about Luigi. It'll make them nervous!"

* * *

Susan was sitting in the hotel bar at eleven that night, waiting for the band to return. She had the place to herself, and she was taking full advantage of the low prices. When the band came bustling noisily into the bar, Susan was surprised to see Phil with them.

"It be right kind of you ter share yer room wif me," Phil was saying to Joe. "I could'a kipped on the bus. I b'aint fussy where I sleeps."

"Janek is very protective about the bus," Joe told him.

Jim smirked. "Yeah, he likes to have the place to himself, in case he gets lucky."

Susan waited until they had sunk a few drinks, then she broke the news that they had to retrace the tortuous road back to Zagreb.

"I guess this means an early start tomorrow," Tom groaned into his glass of beer.

"The journey round to Belgrade will take about three days," Susan estimated. "We have to be there by Wednesday afternoon, so we'll have to be out of here by lunchtime tomorrow."

"Three days!" exclaimed Jim. "Have we got enough booze on the bus to last that long? I can't travel that road again if I'm sober!"

"What about the market?" Pete complained. "They don't have one tomorrow, 'cause it's Sunday. I wanted to stay until Monday, to sell the rest of my trainers."

"We can't possibly leave tomorrow!" wailed Joe. "This is the most wonderfully historic place I've ever been! I want to photograph all the old town, and walk around the city walls, and take a boat trip to one of the islands. I have it all planned out!"

"You don't have ter go the long way round," Phil chipped in. "I knows a way ter Belgrade from here what only takes a day."

"Why don't we go that way, then?" Joe pleaded with Susan.

"Terry said that we couldn't get insurance," she replied. "It's obviously not a safe route."

"It be safe enough," insisted Phil. "I used to do it regular. You goes up to Mostar, across the mountains into Montenegro, then cut through Kosovo and you're on the motorway up to Belgrade."

Jim frowned. "How come you know the country so well?"

"I runs a transport business here," Phil explained. "Used ter, anyhow, till the UN took me lorry."

Joe shook his head sympathetically. "Why did they take your truck?"

"Said as they needed it for urgent supplies," Phil grumbled.

"So, what sort of stuff do you transport?" Jim probed.

"Wooden floor lamps," Phil told them. "All carved and decorated by the locals round here. They makes a lot of wooden stuff. It's their livelihood. Now they can't sell none because I can't shift them."

"That's awful," said Joe. "I wish we could do something to help. These people have had a very bad time."

"Ar, it's a crying shame," Phil complained. "If I could only get these lamp stands across to Romania, I got a mate there what ships them out. I got a ton of boxes piled up in me warehouse in Mostar. They'll be stuck there till I gets me lorry back."

"We could help!" Joe exclaimed. "If we take this short cut of yours, we could collect your lamp stands on the way and take them on to Romania."

"Oh ar. That be a right good idear," Phil responded, cheerfully.

Joe turned to Tom. "Is this okay with you?"

Tom gave a non-committal shrug. "I guess so. It don't seem as hazardous out here as we all thought. The equipment trucks will have to go back the original route, 'cause of the insurance. But I don't really care which way the bus goes."

"It's a great idea," Jim interjected. "I don't need three days on the bus. I could be happily occupied here for a couple of days," his voice trailed off as his eyes followed a voluptuous waitress who was swaying past.

Susan gave an inward sigh of relief, and mentally dismissed the story she had been inventing to explain Phil's presence on the bus to Belgrade.

"It's a great opportunity to do something worthwhile," Joe enthused. "It's not often that we can make an impact on an international problem. It gives me a warm glow inside."

"Take more ice with it," Pete murmured.

CHAPTER 25

On Tuesday afternoon Jim and Pete sprinted out of the lift and across the foyer to the reception desk. They had spent the morning in Dubrovnik market, selling the last few pairs of trainers and giving away the tour tee shirts. They barely had time to pack their bags ready for their departure to Mostar.

"I didn't even have time to say goodbye to my friend," Jim murmured, as he cast his glance around the foyer, hoping to see the sultry waitress who had been his companion for two days. "I feel like a louse."

"You'll have to make do with bread and salami," Susan remarked, as she walked up behind him.

Jim turned to reply, and did a quick double-take. "How did you get such a good tan? I'm nowhere near that colour."

"It's difficult to get a sun-tan in your bedroom," she retorted, as they heaved their bags out into the sunny forecourt.

Janek and Phil were leaning against the bus, smoking and exchanging small talk.

"Did you fill up with petrol?" Susan asked.

"Oh ar. We got a tank-full. It'll likely get us all the way," Phil assured her.

Phil had advised that they should start the journey with as much fuel as the bus could hold, as petrol was still in short supply on the other side of the mountains.

They loaded their suitcases and bags inside the bus, leaving the luggage compartments free for Phil's lamp stands. The boxes of salami remained in the hold, as Jim steadfastly refused to allow them into his air space.

They drove northwards back up the coast, then turned inland to follow a river valley which cut a dramatic course between the steep mountain slopes.

"The roads be narrow and bendy all the way on from Mostar," Phil told them, "So me and Janek agreed that I does most of the driving tonight. These mountain roads be a bit of a bugger in the dark."

Susan nodded vaguely in agreement. She was still feeling nicely relaxed from her two days on the beach. Joe had cajoled them into walking around the ancient city walls on Sunday morning, but when he entered the cathedral to attend the noon service, the rest of them had dashed off to get a taxi back to the hotel.

Jim had gone off in search of the sexy waitress, and Pete had hired a boat and disappeared across the bay. Susan had stretched out on the beach, sitting up occasionally to laugh at Tom, who was wrestling with a wind-surf board.

On Monday, Pete had returned to his retail side-line at the local market, whilst Tom accompanied Joe on his island trip, having given up the unequal struggle with the wind-surf board, and Susan had been left in peace to improve her tan.

* * *

Just before five that evening they drove into Mostar. Stark, grey mountain peaks provided an intimidating backdrop to the town, which nestled in a fertile valley, with buildings hugging the river closely on both sides. They had decided to travel through the night, working on the hopeful theory that snipers would have a less accurate aim in the dark.

Phil directed Janek through the empty streets, and they halted outside a grey stone building that looked like a low barn.

"It'll take me an hour or so to load up," Phil announced. "You might as well take a stroll about the town. Though there b'aint much ter see, no more. Most of the nice places been shelled to buggery."

"Can I take a look at your lamp stands?" Joe asked, eagerly. "I'm interested in ethnic artifacts."

A look of alarm flashed across Phil's face, then he replied casually, "Right-oh. I'll just go in and fetch one out fer you to see."

He unlocked the heavy wooden door and darted into the barn, locking the door again behind him. After several minutes Phil re-emerged, carrying a crudely made wooden lamp stand. Jim peered over Phil's shoulder into the gloomy window-less warehouse, and saw a stack of oblong wooden crates in the middle of the floor.

"Will all of those boxes fit into the baggage hold?" Jim pondered, doubtfully.

"Oh ar," Phil assured him. "I knows how ter pack them in tight."

When Joe had finished admiring the rough woodwork, Phil commanded, "You come back here in an hour, and I'll be ready ter go."

Janek settled comfortably into his driving seat, lit up a cheroot and read his newspaper, while the others strolled off down the street.

They turned the corner into a wider street, which led them further into the town centre. After wandering around aimlessly for ten minutes, they noticed a bar that had a sign outside which read, "English Spokon Heer", so they mooched inside.

The interior was narrow, and unexpectedly crowded. Lean, muscular young men in military uniforms were crammed around small wooden tables. They were all sitting facing in the same direction, staring at a television set which was perched on a ledge in a corner of the room.

Susan and the band edged between the crowded tables and perched on rickety bar stools which were squeezed alongside the counter. As Jim ordered the drinks, Joe said happily, "We couldn't have chosen a better place. All the peace-keeping guys are here."

Susan glanced around the room and noticed that there was a helmet under each occupied chair. On one side of the room the helmets were blue, and on the other side they were white.

"This is a lively place," Tom remarked, looking around at all the young men who were talking in an animated fashion whilst watching the television.

Susan studied the TV screen for several minutes, watching men in white shirts playing a game of soccer with a team in orange shirts. She glanced uneasily over her shoulder at the ranks of young men. Some were lolling backwards, beer glass in hand, their chairs propped against the wall. Others were sitting slouched down in their seats, with glasses of beer lined up on the tables in front of them. They looked as if they had been in the bar for some time. Discarded beer bottles were heaped under the tables. The bar keeper had obviously given up trying to squeeze between the dense throng in order to collect the empties.

Susan listened to the conversations that were rumbling between the tables, and after she had taken a few sips of her drink, she whispered to her companions, "I'm not sure that this is a good place to be."

Jim clicked his tongue in exasperation. "You're always moaning. What's wrong with this place?"

She nodded her head sideways, and muttered, "That lot over there with the blue United Nations helmets, they're Dutch." Then she nodded her head in the opposite direction and said, "That bunch with white NATO helmets are British."

Jim shrugged. "So what?"

"The football game that they're watching is a World Cup qualifying match between Holland and England. There could be trouble."

"It's just a soccer game," Joe commented. "Why should there be any trouble?"

Susan gave a derisive sniff. "Well, don't say I didn't warn you." And she turned her attention back to the television screen.

The match appeared to be a tense one. According to the digital display, neither side had scored a goal, and there were only ten minutes left to play. There was a rumble of excitement from the English soldiers as a white-shirted player made a sudden desperate dash towards the goal. As he drew back his foot to strike the ball, an orange-shirted opponent cannoned into him, they both crashed to the ground.

The referee ran across to them, put his whistle to his mouth and pointed to a white spot on the ground in front of the goal mouth.

On the white-helmet side of the room cheers rang out and fists punched the air.

"What's happening?" Joe asked Susan.

"England have been awarded a penalty kick. They should score from this."

Meanwhile, on the television screen, a large orange-shirted man was trying to shove the referee away from the white spot on the turf.

"That's not very polite," remarked Joe.

The referee deftly reached into his pocket and extracted a yellow card and a red card, and he proceeded to brandish them in the face of his assailant.

Pete frowned. "Why is he waving those coloured cards?"

"Well, they ain't playing Happy Families, that's for sure," Jim observed.

There was jubilation amongst the English soldiers, whilst the Dutch sat holding their heads in their hands and aiming angry kicks at their blue helmets.

A hush descended over the room as a white-shirted player placed the football on the white spot that had been so jealously guarded by the referee. He took three paces backwards, then ran forwards and kicked the ball. The football rocketed skywards and disappeared amongst the spectators.

The groans of anguish from the English soldiers were drowned by jeers of derision from the relieved Dutch. One gloating soldier picked up his blue helmet and kicked it wildly across the room. It landed on an English table and knocked beer glasses down like skittles. The occupants of the table rose as one, picked up their white helmets and hurled them at the opposition.

Susan gulped her drink and leapt briskly off the bar stool. The others hastily followed, and they dashed outside with the sound of breaking glass and splintering wood echoing in their ears.

* * *

They walked around the quiet streets until an hour had almost passed, and when they came across a small supermarket they went inside to buy some food for dinner. They browsed along the shelves, picking up bread, meat pies, fruit and beer. As they approached the check-out, Pete said to Susan, "Any idea what currency they use here?"

Susan frowned pensively and replied, "We'll try using the Croatian notes, and if they won't take them, offer dollars."

The check-out girl took their Croatian money without a second glance, and they carried their bags of shopping back to the bus.

Phil was in the driving seat, and Janek was lounging next to him, sulking because he was temporarily redundant. Jim gave him some food and a few bottles of beer, and he brightened up. Phil slowly manoeuvered the bus through the town, and speeded up gradually as he became accustomed to the power steering and automatic gears.

"This be nice and smooth," he remarked to Janek. "With my old truck, I has to wrestle her round the corners. I think the tracking be buggered."

As they ate their dinner, Joe said, "I'm confused. Why do they use Croatian money here? Isn't this Bosnia?"

"The people here are Croats," Susan explained.

"So, who's fighting who in this country?"

She waved her hands in the air in a global gesture. "Everyone is fighting everyone else."

"I don't understand all this in-fighting," Joe said, in a perplexed tone.

"I can understand it perfectly," asserted Jim. "But that's probably because I have three sets of Appalachian in-laws."

Susan shook her head. "You've divorced them all, so they're not in-laws, they're out-laws."

Jim grimaced. "That's a very accurate description."

"Europeans are such aggressive people," Joe commented. "In America we always do our utmost to avoid fighting in wars."

"That's because you're no good at it," Susan replied, curtly.

Jim sneered, "The Italians aren't exactly renowned for their military prowess."

"Well, you have to know when to call it a day," Susan countered. "In the average prisoner of war camp in the last war, the British were digging holes in the ground to try and escape, and the Italians were digging the ground to grow tomatoes. Which would you prefer to do?"

"The Italian tomatoes get my vote," Tom chipped in. "They used to play soccer in the prisoner-of-war camps, didn't they?" he added. "Soccer and fighting are obviously part of European culture."

"My grandfather was in a POW camp in the first war," Susan told them. "He was in the German army, and he was captured by the British and held prisoner in France. When my dad was called up into the German infantry in the second war, granddad said to him, "Good luck, son. I hope you come back home safely. And if you're unlucky enough to be captured by the English, whatever you do, don't play football with them. They kick your legs something awful!""

"European traditions are so quaint," Tom remarked, as he drank his beer.

* * *

They were two hours out of Mostar, and the road had become a twisting, narrow pass that snaked its way through the mountains. Dense forest stretched into the hilly distance, and the overhanging branches of roadside trees seemed to hasten the descent of twilight. In the deepening dusk, the wooded slopes looked inhospitable and faintly menacing. No other vehicles were on the road, and the isolated stone cottages that were discernible through intermittent clearings were all tightly shuttered, with an uninviting aspect.

"Are the people around here friendly?" Jim asked anxiously, as he caught sight of some figures moving stealthily through the woods just ahead of them.

"They be mostly Moslems, hereabouts," Phil answered. "They b'aint so trigger-happy as them other lot."

Jim did not feel reassured, and his worst fears were realised when a group of men emerged from the shadow of trees and stood determinedly in the middle of the road as the bus approached.

Phil eased the bus to a halt, and grumbled to the others, "I'd best find out what they be after. You sit quiet."

He climbed off the bus and walked calmly up to the band of unshaven, shabbily-dressed men. After several minutes of gesticulation on their part, and non-committal shrugs from Phil, he returned to the bus and took the ignition keys.

"They says as they be hungry," Phil told the others. "I'll give them a couple of your salami."

As Phil went back outside to unlock the baggage compartment, Joe murmured doubtfully, "Do Moslems eat salami?"

The murky gloom had banished the last vestiges of daylight, and as the bus passengers peered out of the windows, they could just perceive the group of men scuttling furtively away, carrying a crate of Phil's lamp stands. The forest shadows enveloped them, and they swiftly vanished from sight.

Phil returned to his driving seat, appearing unperturbed by the incident. Jim voiced their communal curiosity.

"Why did you give them a box of lamp stands? Are "Homes and Gardens" doing a feature article on their village?"

Phil paused before he gave a reply, checking his headlights and adjusting the mirrors as he drove off. Then he answered casually, "They wants to learn how ter make them, so I gave them a few to copy off of. By the way, the Serbia border crossing be just around this next bend."

Joe looked perplexed. "I thought we were going to Montenegro?"

"Montenegro be a province of Serbia. Kosovo be a province too, but they wants to be on their own." Phil suddenly rummaged in his trouser pocket and exclaimed, "Bugger! I must'a dropped me lighter on the road back there. I thought as I heard summat drop to the ground, but I didn't pay no mind to it. I'll have ter go back and find her. She were a present from me old mum."

He stopped the bus and jumped off, saying, "I'll see yer on the other side. I knows me way through these here woods, so I'll cut through and meet yer on the road again just past the sentry post." Then he disappeared into the darkness before the others could raise a protest.

"Well this is just terrific," complained Tom. "Janek, how many beers have you had?"

Janek held up three fingers, and climbed into the vacant driver's seat.

"There don't appear to be a huge number of traffic cops around here," Jim muttered. "Drunk driving is probably the least of our worries."

They rounded a curve and encountered a wooden barrier that blocked the road. Two soldiers were huddled inside a poky sentry box adjacent to the barrier. The border guards seemed startled by the sudden appearance of a large bus. They stubbed out their cigarettes, donned helmets, slung rifles over their shoulders and sauntered across to the bus with an unhurried air.

Susan quickly extracted the Serbian permit from her bag, and she climbed off the bus, smiling sweetly at the two soldiers. Janek followed close behind her, trying to breathe without opening his mouth.

"Do you speak English?" Susan asked, in her most polite voice.

They exchanged puzzled glances, and stared at Susan with undisguised suspicion. She thrust the permit at them, and one of the guards scrutinised it closely, while the other soldier ambled around the bus, studying the occupants. The two soldiers exchanged a few guttural words, then the one holding the permit went back inside the booth. He picked up a telephone receiver and punched some numbers. After several minutes he slammed the receiver back down on to its cradle and stamped out of the booth, muttering to himself. He mumbled some brief words at his companion, who shrugged his shoulders in a non-committal manner. Janek darted inside the bus, and returned with two bottles of Tom's favourite scotch. This seemed to please the guards. One of them grabbed the bottles, the other pushed Susan's permit back at her and moved back to the barrier. He turned a wheel that lifted the barrier, and waved at them to go through.

Susan and Janek quickly climbed back inside the bus, and they drove off. As the frontier barrier swung down again behind them, Susan asked, "Who did they phone? Was there a problem?"

Janek replied, "They phone headquarters, to check permit, but nobody answer telephone. They not know what to do."

Tom grumbled, "I hoped that Phil would be helpful here, seeing as he's done this route before."

As Tom spoke, a figure appeared in the road ahead, waving them down. The bus halted, and Janek opened the door to let Phil aboard. He was in a cheerful mood.

"Yer got through all right, then?" he remarked, brightly.

Tom sniffed. "Yeah, no thanks to you."

"Did you find your lighter?" Joe asked.

"What? Oh, ar," Phil replied, vaguely. As he climbed back into the driving seat, he told them, "You can close yer eyes now and have a kip. I'll have yer across these mountains in no time. It be downhill the rest of the way."

CHAPTER 26

After three more hours of dark mountain roads, the band was asleep. Susan fidgeted restlessly in her seat. She could not get comfortable. As Phil swung the bus around each bend, she slid sideways and had to readjust her position. Susan decided to pay a visit to the tiny bathroom, thinking that it might help her settle to sleep. While she was inside the toilet, the bus eased to a stop, then moved off again after a few moments. When Susan returned to her seat she noticed with surprise that Janek was now driving, and that Phil was nowhere to be seen.

Susan went forwards and whispered to Janek, "Where's Phil gone?"

"He need a smoke, so he get off."

"How will he catch us up?"

Janek shrugged. "He say he know short-cut down hill."

The bus rounded yet another curve, and Susan blinked in surprise. A section of the highway ahead was illuminated with dazzling arc lights. As they approached the brightly-lit area, she saw that a military jeep was parked across the road. Janek slowed the bus and halted gently. Two soldiers jumped out of the jeep, carrying their semi-automatic rifles in the ready-to-fire position.

"I'm beginning to understand why Terry told us to go the long way round," Susan muttered to Janek, as she unfolded the Serbian travel permit once more. She stepped off the bus and decided not to make any attempt at conversation. She held out her piece of paper to one of the soldiers. He glanced down at it, then passed it to his companion.

A dog suddenly started barking nearby, and both soldiers turned to scan the dark wooded field that lay beyond the reach of their floodlights. After several nervous moments, they turned their attention back to Susan and her permit.

They eventually nodded at each other, and one soldier got back into the jeep and swung it to one side of the road, whilst the other motioned

Janek to move forward. Susan climbed back on to the bus and sighed with relief.

"You'd better go slowly," she said to Janek, "Or we'll leave Phil behind."

As the road wound itself downhill, a tiny red light appeared, waving back and forth in the middle of the road. Janek stepped on the brakes and the bus halted with a soft hiss. Phil was standing in the middle of the road, smoking a cigarette.

As he boarded the bus, Susan scolded him. "What are you playing at? You'll get run over, standing in the middle of the road like that!"

He shook his head. "No-one be out on the roads after dark. There's a curfew here in Kosovo province. And the Serbian patrols be a tad nervy with their trigger fingers."

Phil reclaimed the driving seat, and Susan helped herself to a large measure from Tom's whisky bottle, in an attempt to calm her nerves.

* * *

The road began a gradual descent from the mountains, and as the bends diminished, Susan fell into a fitful sleep. A sudden noise nearby startled her awake, and as she stretched her arms and legs, she realised that the bus was not moving. She peered closely at her watch, and saw that it was about one in the morning. Susan pulled the permit from her bag and stumbled to the open door of the bus. It was a pitch-black moonless night, and as she blinked her eyes into focus she saw Phil standing by an open baggage compartment, and half a dozen other figures who appeared to be unloading some of the boxes.

The men worked without making a sound, carrying the crates away to an invisible destination. A weak beam of light shone from a torch in Phil's hand, and as Susan strained her eyes, she noticed that all the men were bare-foot.

After a few minutes, all the strangers had evaporated into the darkness, and Phil gently closed and locked the baggage hold. As he climbed back on to the bus he noticed Susan, and gave a soft exclamation of surprise.

"I thought as everyone was fast asleep," he remarked, looking uneasy.

"A noise woke me up."

"It must'a been when I dropped me torch," Phil said, as he hastily pushed a wad of notes into his pocket.

Susan yawned. "Why were those men taking some of your lamp stands?"

"They puts some fancy Albanian carvings on them."

"Albanian?" echoed Susan. "But we're still in Serbia, aren't we?"

"Oh ar. But they all be Albanians what lives here in Kosovo."

"But why did they give you money?" she continued, confused by the transaction.

Phil chewed his lip briefly before replying. "It's me only guarantee that they does the work. When I comes back for me lamp stands, I'll give them the money back, with a bit extra for their wages."

"Strange way of doing business," Susan murmured drowsily, and she crept back to her seat and quickly nodded off again.

* * *

Susan was in a deep sleep when Janek shook her roughly on the shoulder at three in the morning.

"What is it?" she mumbled, her mouth so dry that she could hardly open her lips.

"I need permit," he hissed softly. "More soldiers here."

Susan swore under her breath and roused herself. As she staggered to the front of the bus she noticed that Phil had vanished again.

The bus had halted at yet another checkpoint. Flood-lights glared into Susan's eyes as she approached the jeep which was blocking the road. A sleepy soldier grudgingly hoisted himself out of his vehicle and scanned the piece of paper that Susan thrust at him. He glanced at the bus with indifference, then spoke briefly to his companion behind the wheel. The jeep reversed noisily out of the way, and Susan was dismissed with a peremptory nod.

Susan clambered back on to the bus, and as Janek accelerated away down the road, she asked wearily, "Where's Phil disappeared to?"

"He feel sick," Janek told her. "Meat pie upset him. He want fresh air."

Janek stopped the bus when they were a good distance away from the Serbian army jeep, and a few moments later Phil appeared, scrambling through a hedge alongside the road. He boarded the bus, red-faced and breathless, brushing twigs and leaves off his clothes.

"How many check-points are there along this road?" Susan demanded. "I'm fed-up of being woken up!"

"We be all clear, now that we're out of Kosovo province," he assured her. "The rest of the country b'aint so twitchy."

Phil settled back into the driving seat, and Susan groped her way back to her own seat and wrapped herself in a cocoon of blankets, craving some undisturbed sleep.

* * *

"Do you think that we should save some food for Susan?" pondered Joe, as the band munched their way through the previous day's leftovers.

"She won't want meat pie for breakfast," Tom responded. "And anyway, Phil has just taken the last piece."

It was eight o' clock on Wednesday morning, and they were travelling along a toll road, approaching Belgrade. Phil had relinquished the driving seat to Janek when they had joined the motorway at dawn, and he was now relaxing with the assistance of Mostar beer.

"We'll have to wake her up soon," Jim remarked, glumly. "She's got the directions to the hotel in her bag."

Tom studied the sleeping mound that was Susan. "Maybe we could ease it out from underneath her."

Jim raised a sceptical eyebrow. "Are you volunteering?"

Tom hastily shook his head. "I need my fingers intact."

Jim broke off some pieces of stale bread and lobbed them carefully at Susan's slumbering head. As bits of dry bread rained down on her, Susan jerked awake and opened her eyes.

"What are you playing at?" she snapped at Jim.

"I'm giving you breakfast in bed. I shan't bother again, if it makes you so tetchy."

"Where are we?" she mumbled, disentangling herself from the swathe of blankets.

"We're just running into Belgrade," Tom replied. "We need directions to the hotel."

Susan rummaged in her bag and found the piece of paper. She frowned. "It's an autocamp. Terry obviously couldn't get us a hotel at short notice. Follow the signs to the horse-racing track," she called to Janek. "And try to get behind a number twelve tram."

As they approached Belgrade they spotted an exit sign depicting galloping horses, so they turned off the motorway and drove away from the city. On the road up ahead they could see a tram winding its way through the suburbs of Belgrade. Janek accelerated to catch up with it, then settled neatly behind the number twelve, halting whenever the tram stopped. The tram led them to the race-track, and from there they followed a sign post to the campsite.

"Maybe we could spend a day at the races," suggested Jim, as they entered a wooded field that was dotted with tiny bungalows.

"A day in bed would suit me," Susan grumbled. "My back aches in five different places. How can you lot sleep so well on a bus?" she demanded, massaging her stiff neck.

"Years of practise," Tom answered. "And a good supply of beer."

* * *

"I'm glad you gave us the permit," Tom told Susan. "We've had no end of hassle."

"It comes as no surprise," she replied, in a resigned tone.

It was six in the evening, and they were eating dinner in the campsite restaurant. The bungalows were surprisingly comfortable, but the receptionist had made a big fuss about their passports when they had checked in. Susan had waved her permit at the girl and had steadfastly refused to hand over their passports. The manager had arrived on the scene, and he eventually abandoned his attempt at passport requisition when he was satisfied that the new arrivals were not Croatian or Turkish.

Susan had staggered off to bed, while the band had gone down to the venue to check that all the equipment had arrived safely.

"As soon as Janek parked the bus, two policemen appeared and wanted to know what we were doing there," Tom continued. "It seems that they had already searched the big rig."

"I bet that really pleased the crew," Susan murmured.

"They took off after they had read the permit," Tom ended, "But not before they had taken a good look at our passports."

"How did Phil manage to duck out without showing his passport?" Jim cut in. "I reckon he's related to Harry Houdini. He was off the bus and away down the street before anyone noticed the going of him and his box."

"Maybe his friend Luigi had an urgent business appointment," Pete said, facetiously.

As the others laughed, Susan smiled at the ironic accuracy of Pete's remark. She had been eagerly awaiting Phil's return, hopeful that he had been able to sell the contents of his box, but Phil had not yet reappeared.

"Are you coming down to the hall with us?" Tom asked her.

Susan shook her head. "Terry said that he'd see me here." She frowned briefly, suddenly worried that Terry might appear as Phil was handing over her half-share in Luigi. Then she caught sight of Phil. He was making his way into the adjoining bar, and he was carrying his box. She groaned inwardly, and finished eating her dinner in a disappointed mood as Tom gave instructions to the band.

"I don't think it's a good idea to pick up any girls," he lectured Jim. "It don't strike me as being an easy-going sort of town."

Jim nodded in agreement, and declared, "I wouldn't bring a playmate back here anyway. They have nylon sheets on the bed. If you get up to anything frisky during the night, you're liable to suffer death due to static electrocution!"

The band trooped off to do their show, and Susan hurried into the bar to find Phil. She sat down opposite him and hissed, "How come you've still got Luigi? You said that your friend would buy him!"

Phil shifted uneasily and replied, "He b'aint here no more. He gone off ter Romania. He'll buy it off me for sure, if I takes it there."

Susan clicked her tongue in annoyance then conceded, "Well, I suppose a few more days won't make any difference. Are you sure that you know where he's gone?"

"Oh ar. I knows where to find him. Don't you fret none. I'll see yer tomorrow, on the bus." He picked up Luigi and made an abrupt departure from the bar.

Susan returned to her bungalow and decided to study the route for the following week. She turned to the final page of the crumpled itinerary, and sighed as she counted up the remaining days of the tour. Her thoughts were interrupted by a knock at the door. Terry was standing outside, clutching two large carrier bags. He stepped into the room, and pushed a bag at her. "I've brought you a few loo rolls. You won't be able to find any in Romania."

Susan smiled gratefully. Her own supply of toilet paper was dwindling rapidly. Terry handed her another bag that clinked as he moved.

"And I've got you some good vermouth," he continued. "I know that you like the proper stuff."

"That's very nice of you," Susan replied, grabbing eagerly at the bag. As she looked inside, she noticed a large, bulky envelope tucked in between the bottles.

"What's this?" she asked, pulling it out for a closer examination.

Terry fixed her with a dazzling smile. "I was hoping that you could take it with you on the bus. It'll save me having to go to Romania next week. Could you do it for me, luvvie? I'll make it worth your while, of course," he whispered, giving her a knowing wink.

"It's not cash, is it?" she asked, warily. "I don't like carrying money around."

"No, it's just a few bits of paper. Nothing to worry about. My friend will collect it from you at the hotel, depending which day he can get there. I've given him a copy of your route, so he knows where you'll be."

"How will I know him?"

"It's the man that you've met before, the musical fish person. He may have a bit of cash to pass on to you, but I'll collect it from you at the airport before you fly out." He glanced down at his watch. "I've left Ahmed on a double-yellow, so I'll have to love you and leave you." He blew her an extravagant kiss and skipped smartly out of the room before Susan could utter any protest.

"Crafty bugger!" she exclaimed. "I told him I didn't want to carry any cash!" She flung the package to the floor in a fit of pique. The envelope split open and spilled its contents on to the coarse carpet.

Susan bent down and gathered up the assortment of photos and papers that were strewn on the floor. She idly glanced at the snapshots of flashy cars, then paused to look more closely at a handful of photocopied pages. They appeared to be pages from a cash book. The first column contained a string of numbers written in an untidy scrawl, the second had a date, the next one had an amount, and the final column had a smaller amount, and a percentage sign at the head of the column. Most of the numbers were close to indecipherable.

"Hmph," she murmured. "What a tatty sales book." She examined the envelope, and frowned at the ripped edges. "I can't hand it over like this. The photos will all tip out." Susan suddenly remembered that she still had the Gucci shoe box in her suitcase. She slipped the damaged envelope into the box, taped the edges down with sticking plaster, then returned to her perusal of the Romanian section of the itinerary.

* * *

"Is meat pie the only thing on the breakfast menu?" Joe complained, next morning.

"They didn't show us a menu," Pete told him, tersely. "They brought this straight out."

"I could murder a bowl of cornflakes," Jim said, longingly.

Susan tilted her head thoughtfully. "Would that make you a cereal killer?"

"Only if I had several bowls," he replied.

Tom grumbled, "I can't even drink the coffee."

"Is it coffee?" Jim asked, in amazement. "I thought it was a chocolate spread to put on bread."

"It's Turkish coffee," Susan told them. "You have to be fairly determined to swallow it."

Tom raised an eyebrow in Susan's direction. "Will you tell us off if we have beer for breakfast?"

"You could always break the habit of a lifetime and drink water," she said, caustically.

"I don't know why you bother speaking to her," Jim muttered sideways to Tom. "She never talks any sense at all!"

* * *

"Should we fill up with petrol on the way out of Belgrade?" Susan asked Phil, as they boarded the bus later in the morning.

"No, it be cheaper over the border," Phil told her. "We might have ter pay in dollars, though. They'll know as we b'aint locals, so they'll likely take advantage."

They drove eastwards, across flat, uninspiring countryside, and after an hour they came to a halt at the end of a long queue of cars.

"This be the border," stated Phil. "Make yerselves comfy. We'll likely be here for a good while."

The line of traffic was edging slowly forwards, and they could see the sentry booth up ahead in the distance.

"Maybe I could take some photos while we're waiting here," Joe proposed.

"No you won't. We're still inside Serbia. Your wife will never forgive me if you get thrown in jail," Tom said, sternly.

Susan nodded vehemently in agreement, and commanded, "Don't touch that camera. If you get hauled away, you're on your own!"

Joe cringed into his seat, suitably discouraged.

Janek climbed off the bus and set about brewing some coffee. The others followed him outside, and strolled around the bus, trying to estimate the length of time to the front of the queue.

An hour later, they were only six cars away from the border crossing.

Susan noticed that the sentries appeared to be confiscating various items from the travellers as they passed through.

"What are they taking off those people?" Susan asked Janek. "There seem to be a lot of illegal goods."

"Guards take what they like," Janek answered, bluntly. "It good idea to give them gift."

Susan searched for a large carrier bag, and hastily filled it with four toilet rolls, two Budapest hotel towels, and two bottles of scotch. She handed it to Janek, and he nodded in approval and put it beside his driver's seat.

As they got nearer to the frontier post, Phil announced, "I'll just take meself off for five minutes. That coffee has made me insides a bit windy." He swiftly disappeared into a small copse of trees alongside the road.

Ten minutes later the bus was at the crossing point, and two unkempt Romanian soldiers climbed aboard, eyeing the occupants with undisguised curiosity. Susan handed over the passports for examination, but the guards seemed more interested in the luxurious interior of the bus. One of them pointed to the folded drapes at the windows, and said a few words to his companion.

Janek quickly picked up the carrier bag that Susan had provided, and offered it to the soldiers. They inspected the contents, then after fingering the plush seat upholstery in an admiring manner, they climbed off the bus and waved them through the frontier.

As Janek drove off speedily, Susan asked, "Did they want the curtains?"

Janek nodded and replied, "Nice cloth hard to get in Romania. They like towels, so we lucky."

Susan suddenly remembered Phil, and they pulled into the side of the road to await his appearance.

"Do you think he's all right?" Joe asked, with concern. "Maybe we shouldn't have driven away without him."

As Joe spoke, they saw Phil sauntering towards them across an adjacent field, carrying a bag in his hand. When he boarded the bus he was whistling a cheerful tune, and he handed a bag of fresh bread to Susan, saying, "It be a nice day, so I had a little walk about. I thought as I'd pick up a few groceries on me way over."

And he settled back into his seat as they followed the bumpy road towards Timisoara.

CHAPTER 27

It was Thursday lunchtime when they neared Timisoara, and on the outskirts of town they spotted a petrol station. Janek sighed with relief and pulled into the forecourt, which was congested with two lines of cars, bumper to bumper, queuing for fuel.

Jim groaned when he saw all the waiting cars in front of them.

"We'll be here forever," he grumbled. "Maybe we should drive on to the next gas station."

Janek shook his head resolutely and stated, "They all like this. Long lines everywhere."

"I wonder if they'll let us fill the tank?" Susan mused, anxiously.

"What? You mean they might only let us have a couple of gallons?" exclaimed Tom. "That's bad news. We have a lot of miles to cover this week."

"You'll have ter offer them hard money," Phil muttered.

Tom took out his wallet and began counting out dollar bills.

Phil stared at the wad of notes. "Don't offer them too much, though. Does yer know how ter haggle a price?"

"Haggle?" echoed Tom. "Isn't the price of gas written on the pump?"

Phil gave a disdainful sniff. "Makes no difference what be written. You'd best let Janek do it."

Janek took Tom's dollars and pushed them deep into his pocket. When they drew alongside the pump, he jumped off the bus and had a furtive conversation with the petrol pump attendant. They exchanged nods, then Janek stood with his hands in his pockets as the tank was filled. After the nozzle was withdrawn, Janek surreptitiously passed the agreed amount to the petrol pump attendant.

"I've seem people selling drugs in a less covert manner than that," Jim observed, as they drove away.

* * *

"This is a pretty place," remarked Joe, as they drove into the centre of Timisoara. Small parks abutted both sides of the road, giving the town a rural air.

"The hotel is next to a park," Susan murmured, puzzling over the directions on her itinerary. "But which park? We'll have to stop and ask someone."

As they drew level with a queue of people at a tram stop, Janek stopped the bus and Susan stepped off. She showed her itinerary to the woman at the head of the line, and pointed to the hotel name and address. The Romanian woman smiled and nodded in a friendly manner, then she grabbed Susan's elbow and propelled her back on to the bus, following her aboard. The other people in the queue started yelling and gesticulating angrily at the woman, but she curled her lip at them, then tapped Janek on the shoulder and pointed down the street.

The woman directed Janek up a tree-lined boulevard, then guided him around the outskirts of a small park. As they rounded a corner, the woman pointed at a building which was set just inside the grounds of the park, and she rasped out the name of the hotel several times, to make sure they had got the message.

She got off the bus and went on her way, then Janek maneuvered slowly along a small road that led into the park, and drew up outside the hotel.

"What was the tram queue complaining about?" Tom said to him, as he got off the bus.

"They all want hitch lift," Janek explained. "Long wait for tram."

* * *

Five minutes later, the band were shuffling around inside the hotel foyer, whilst Susan shouted at the reception desk.

"What do you mean, you don't have our reservation? I've got written confirmation. Look!" Susan shoved the itinerary at the girl behind the desk. The receptionist reluctantly took the paper and studied it intently, then disappeared into a back room. She returned several minutes later with a middle-aged man, who smiled at them, then shrugged apologetically and spread his hands.

"Very sorry. We all full today. You try Hotel Nord."

Jim nudged Tom. "Wave some dollar bills at him."

Tom quickly extracted his wallet and offered a twenty dollar note to the man. He gazed wistfully at it, then shook his head sadly and repeated, "Very sorry. All full."

Susan sighed heavily, then said, "So where is this other hotel?"

"Near railway station. I give you map." The manager drew a little street map on a sheet of hotel paper, and handed it to Susan.

"That's a shame," Joe said, as they heaved their bags back outside. "This looks like such a nice place."

Janek had parked the bus behind the hotel, and he and Phil were surprised to see Susan and the band traipsing back towards them with their bags.

"Where we off to, then?" Phil enquired.

"We're playing "hunt the hotel"," Jim retorted, as they climbed back on to the bus.

They drove back around the park, and through the centre of town.

"There's the venue," Susan observed, as they passed the grand opera house.

"Mark it on the map," Tom told her, "Or we'll probably never find it again."

They drove past yet another park, made a few turns, and eventually found the hotel in a dingy street close to the railway track.

Tom groaned as he surveyed the shabby-looking hotel, but he brightened up when the receptionist offered them all a single room with bath.

"I'm gonna freshen up," Tom announced, as they went along the corridor.

"We need to change some dollars into Romanian notes," Susan reminded him. "Phil said that if you flash your dollars around too much, you get overcharged."

"I'll do that," Joe volunteered. "I can wander around and take some photos before we do the sound check."

"I'll come with you," Susan insisted. "You Americans haven't got a clue about exchange rates."

* * *

Half an hour later, Joe and Susan took a taxi into town, and hunted for an exchange office. There were long queues inside the first place that they found, but they decided to take their place at the end of the line, rather than trudge around the streets any more. As they stood there, Susan noticed a pair of seedy-looking men who were walking alongside the queue, murmuring something to the waiting customers. As each person shook his head, the men moved along, eyeing the next customer with an intimidating glare.

"Be quiet and keep your hands in your pockets!" Susan quickly hissed at Joe.

Joe looked confused, but did as he was told. As the shifty men approached, Susan stared down at the floor, and when they whispered gruffly to her, she shook her head without looking at them, and they continued along the line.

"What was that all about?" Joe asked, mystified.

Susan shrugged. "I don't know, but they look like villains. When we get to the counter, keep the dollars inside your hand, so that no-one else can see what we've got."

Joe stiffened in alarm, and he clutched the dollars tightly in his pocket, glancing over his shoulder with a nervous air.

They converted their cash without any trouble, and set off to photograph the baroque architecture in the town square. Passers-by stared as Joe wandered about, with his camera in his hand, judging the best angles for his pictures. Susan was strolling a short distance behind him, gazing vacantly about her, when someone barged into her. Susan gasped in surprise, and the man who had knocked her sideways gave a curt nod, then hurried away down the street.

Susan unzipped her handbag and hastily checked the contents, to make sure that she hadn't been robbed, then she scuttled over to Joe.

"Get a move on! If we stand here any longer, we'll probably be mugged!"

Joe scanned the street, and noticed several scruffy men who were skulking in doorways.

"Right," he agreed. "Maybe we should get Phil to come with us next time we go sightseeing. He seems like a street-wise kinda guy. Might help us stay outta trouble."

They walked briskly along to the next ancient church, with Joe re-focusing his camera as he went.

When they got back to the hotel the rest of the band were waiting on the bus, and after Susan and Joe had climbed aboard, Janek drove off to the concert hall.

"What was it like in town?" Tom asked Susan.

"Eventful," she replied, tersely.

"I wish I'd come with you," he said, glumly. "I found two dead mice in my bathroom."

Susan smirked. "Maybe you should change your deodorant."

* * *

At the venue there was complete chaos. The Polish crew were having a heated argument with the Romanian stage hands, and the equipment was scattered about the stage in a disorderly fashion.

"What's going on?" Tom demanded, aghast at the sight of amplifiers lying under a heap of junction boxes.

Janek spoke briefly to Lazlo, who waved his hands heavenwards in a gesture of despair, nearly impaling another electrician with his large screwdriver.

"They lose two drums of cable," Janek told the band. "Disappeared. No-one know where."

Tom cursed heartily. "I guess we'll have to do without a couple of the treble speakers. There's no way that we can wire them all up without the cable."

Phil was lurking in the wings, watching the pandemonium. He sauntered across to Tom, and muttered quietly, "I think as I can get yer wire for you. Give I a few of them dollar bills."

Tom frowned doubtfully, but then he stealthily pulled a few notes from his pocket and handed them to Phil. Phil disappeared backstage, taking two of the Romanian stagehands with him. Five minutes later they returned, carrying two hefty drums of electric cable.

"They got this out'a their store-room," Phil explained to Tom. "Seems as they didn't want ter be helpful, because the Poles had accused them of nicking the stuff off the lorry."

Tom gave an exasperated sigh. "Let's go and get something to eat. We can't do anything here."

"Me and Janek will hang on here, and give the sparks a hand," Phil offered.

As Tom and the band made their way out of the hall, Susan pulled Phil to one side and whispered urgently, "Where have you put Luigi? We don't want him stolen!"

"I locked him in the first aid cabinet on the bus," Phil answered. "He be safe enough in there."

* * *

Across the square from the opera house there was an elegant-looking restaurant, which Tom headed towards. Pete lingered by the entrance and complained, "They don't have a menu in the window."

"I'm past caring about money," Tom mumbled, despondently. "Do you think they'll have all the gear set up by eight?"

"Yeah, don't worry," Jim replied. "We've had tighter gigs than this."

Tom winced. "Like New York? Thanks for reminding me."

The restaurant was almost empty, and two waiters bustled up to them from opposite directions.

Tom looked from one to the other. "Do you speak English?"

One of the waiters nodded gleefully, and he ushered them to a table that was sparkling with silverware, while the other waiter mooched away with a sulky stare.

"Could we see the menu?" Tom asked, as the waiter stood motionless beside their table.

The waiter looked slightly disconcerted, but he promptly dashed away to a far corner of the room and returned with a yellowing sheet of cardboard, which was dog-eared and dusty. He adroitly brushed the dust away with his sleeve, and handed the menu to Tom with a flourish.

As Tom studied the menu, Pete leaned over to take a look.

"There are no prices on it," Pete grumbled. "They'll rip us off, for sure."

Tom was too busy deciphering the English translations to listen to Pete's remark.

"Soap and balls," Tom read aloud, in a baffled tone. "Do you think that means soup and meatballs?" He turned to the waiter and said, "I'll have soup to start, then fish, please."

The waiter shook his head. "No fish."

Tom sighed and looked at the menu once more.

"Okay. I'll have roast chicken."

The waiter shrugged his shoulders, and shook his head again.

Jim smirked. "Looks like the menu is a work of fiction."

"What exactly is available?" Tom demanded.

"Pork and french fry," the waiter responded, brightly.

"That'll do just fine," said Tom. "And bring two bottles of red wine."

Joe cut in, "Do you have any vegetarian meals?"

The waiter gave him a sideways look and raised an eyebrow.

"How about salad?" Joe persisted.

The waiter nodded and went away, taking the out-of-date menu with him.

Susan turned to speak to Joe. "You can have my share of fries. I'm not all that hungry."

After ten minutes the waiter returned with the wine and five bowls of soup.

"You'll have to pick the meatballs out of yours," Jim advised Joe, as he started eating.

Joe carefully extracted his floating meatballs, and shared them out amongst the others.

Twenty minutes later, the waiter came back with a dish of thick pork chops and a deep wicker basket which contained a mountain of fries. He also brought a plate of pickles, which he deposited in front of Joe.

As Joe looked at the plate in dismay, Susan said cheerily, "Pickles go quite well with pork. I'll have them if you don't want them. Mm. These fries are very tempting. Maybe I'll just have a few."

Jim grabbed the waiter's elbow as he sidled past.

"He doesn't want pickles. He wants salad. Tomato, lettuce, that kinda stuff."

The waiter looked confused, and dashed away. He came back five minutes later with a large oval platter which was laden with sliced tomatoes and chunks of white, crumbly cheese, and sprinkled with lots of chopped basil.

"That looks nice," Susan said, and she helped herself to a large portion.

Jim stared in disbelief. "You said you weren't hungry, and now you're eating Joe's dinner!"

"It don't matter none," Joe hastily chipped in. "There's plenty for all of us."

"Susan, will you leave some fries for the rest of us, please," Jim said testily, as he pulled the wicker basket away from her.

Two hours later, after a pastry dessert and some strong coffee, Tom glanced at his watch, then beckoned the waiter. The waiter sprinted over with the bill, and Pete picked it up to check it over. He frowned at the huge total, and borrowed Susan's calculator to make sense of the numbers. Pete smiled.

"About twenty dollars, I reckon. Good value, huh?"

Joe picked up the bill and said to the waiter. "This can't be right. I think you should check it over."

The waiter took the bill, and hurried away with a worried look on his face. He returned several minutes later, murmuring, "So sorry."

Pete checked the bill once more, then chuckled briefly and said to Joe, "Nice work. He's knocked it down to fifteen bucks."

Joe gave a horrified gasp, but before he could speak, Susan commanded, "Don't say any more, or he'll probably end up paying us!"

As they left the restaurant, Joe salved his conscience by slipping a twenty dollar bill to the bemused waiter.

CHAPTER 28

When Susan went into the hotel dining room on Friday morning, Joe was sitting at a table with Phil, who was munching his way through a mound of toast and omelette.

"Isn't Janek having any breakfast?" Susan asked.

Phil nodded, then as he paused to drink his tea, he told her, "We been taking it in turn to stay awake on the bus, overnight. There be a few nasty looking blokes what I spotted prowling around. Can't be too careful. When I goes back ter the bus, Janek'll come in."

The rest of the band shuffled into the dining room, looking bleary-eyed and haggard.

Susan stared at them. "What time did you lot get back last night?"

Tom yawned. "It was morning. Why didn't you stay to the end of the party?"

Susan shuddered and replied, "I got tired of fending off the amorous natives."

"Who was that guy who was glued to you after the show?" Jim asked.

"I've no idea," she said, tersely. "But you could probably trace him from all the fingerprints that he left on me."

When their breakfasts arrived at the table, Jim swallowed his cup of Turkish coffee in one gulp.

"Intravenous caffeine," he mumbled, as his eyes glazed over from the sudden rush of stimulant.

As Phil finished eating and pushed his plate away, Tom said to him, "Whereabouts in Romania do you need to take your lamp stands? Is it on our route?"

"Constanta is where I be headed for. It's on the Black Sea. I can ship them from there. I got a lot of mates over in Constanta." Phil turned towards Susan and gave her a sly wink.

Tom frowned. "We're not doing any concerts on the Black Sea coast.

226

You'll have to get there after we've done our last show, in Bucharest. That gig is a week from now. It'll be kinda tedious for you to have to hang around that long."

"It b'aint a problem," Phil assured him. "I can make meself useful along the way. I don't mind being night-watchman on the bus, and I can give a helping hand to the crew." He stood up and darted out of the dining room before anyone could raise an objection.

* * *

They were on the bus by nine, having estimated that it would take seven hours to reach their next destination, the Transylvanian town of Cluj. The road was flat and straight to start with, but when they turned eastwards into the rolling foothills of the Carpathian mountains, the road twisted slowly around endless slopes of dark green trees, following the meandering course of a river that had cut a gentle valley through the wooded landscape.

After several hours of driving beside the river, Janek halted the bus at a cross-road and shouted over his shoulder, "Which way now?"

Susan went to the front of the bus with her tattered itinerary.

"We follow the road to Deva, then on through Alba, and up to Cluj," she instructed.

Janek gestured towards the signpost at the side of the road. One sign was pointing straight ahead to Deva, and another board was pointing left to Alba.

"Follow the Alba sign," she decided. "It must be a shorter route."

They turned left, and the road climbed gradually as they left the river valley behind them. The bus ascended through lonely wooded hillsides, on a road that was glistening with smooth, black tarmac which looked as if it had been newly-laid. They saw no villages along the way as the road led further upwards, and scenic vistas came into view as the trees diminished in number on the higher slopes. Verdant pastures were sprinkled with vivid wild flowers, and looming mountain peaks rose majestically in the distance.

"Gee, what a fabulous view," murmured Joe.

Janek braked sharply, and the passengers were thrown about in their seats as the bus bumped over rough ground.

Jim bellowed, "Janek! What the hell you doing!"

"Road gone!"

Jim stumbled to the front of the bus and saw that the road had become a rocky trail. After bouncing along uncomfortably for half a mile, they came to a cross-road that had no signpost. The band congregated at the front of the bus to decide on a direction.

"Turn right," Tom said. "That way has tarmac."

Jim gave a derisive sniff. "For how far?"

Joe asked hesitantly, "Do we know whereabouts we are?"

"We're in Romania," Susan said, tartly.

Jim turned to her and said accusingly, "This is your fault. You told Janek to come this way."

"If you're so clever, how come you didn't pack some spare tarmac!" she snapped back at him.

"But which way we go?" Janek persisted.

"Let's take a vote," suggested Joe.

"I'm not voting," Susan said, sulkily. "You lot can take the blame for the next disaster."

They voted to turn on to the tarmac road, and Janek drove off, seemingly unperturbed about being lost in the mountains. He was singing to himself, and after a couple of miles he suddenly cut off his tune and shouted over his shoulder, "You want stop for hitchhikers?"

Susan stared at the road ahead, and saw a pair of young men with rucksacks standing on the grass verge, waving their thumbs hopefully.

"These guys are crazy," Jim muttered. "How do they think they're gonna find a ride in the middle of nowhere!"

As they got closer, Susan spotted a toy kangaroo dangling from one of the rucksacks. "They're Australian. Stop and pick them up," she told Janek.

As the two backpackers clambered aboard the bus, they were effusive with thanks.

"Gudday mates. Thanks for stopping," said the first hiker.

"We have an ulterior motive," Susan told him. "We're lost."

"We can put you right, no probs," the Australian breezily assured them. "I'm Bruce, and this is my mate, Billy."

After vigorous handshakes all round, Bruce continued, "We're up here with an orienteering group, but our map got blown away when we stopped for a tinny. Safest thing to do is get to the nearest road. We couldn't believe our luck when your bus came into sight! Where are you making for?"

"Cluj," Susan told him. "We took the turning for Alba."

"You should have gone to Deva," Billy told her, nodding sagely. "They haven't finished building the Alba road."

"Yeah, we noticed," murmured Pete.

Billy sat next to Janek, and gave him directions at each unmarked crossroad they came to, while Bruce chatted with the band.

"Which hotel are you stopping at in Cluj?" he asked.

Susan consulted her itinerary. "Hotel Transylvania."

"Streuth! You blokes must have more money than sense!"

Tom frowned. "Is it an expensive place?"

"Eighty dollars a night, mate!" Bruce said, shaking his head in disapproval. "That's US dollars, not Australian."

Susan said, "We only paid eighteen at the last place."

"I paid less than that," Tom added. "I got a discount on account of the dead mice."

"You should have brought them along," Pete muttered. "You could have used them to get a discount at the next hotel."

As Susan shuddered, Bruce continued, "We know a cheap hotel in Cluj. I'll give you a map."

"Hey look! There's the mob!" Billy suddenly cried, pointing to a group of hikers striding down a mountain slope.

"Aw, we can't get off now," Bruce remonstrated. "These nice people will never get back to the road if we don't show them the way."

"You're right," Billy agreed. "We'll hitch a lift back again, afterwards."

As the bus followed a tortuous route of abrupt left and right hand turns, Bruce was instructing the band in Romanian etiquette.

"Always ask what the rates are before you check into a hotel. Some of them are a total rip-off. And if you're in a queue, don't leave any space in front of you, or someone will push into it. And don't talk to the black market money changers that hang around the exchange offices. They'll rob you blind. A mate of mine got fleeced by them in Constanta. That place is heaving with crooks, isn't that right, Billy?"

"Streuth, I'll say!" Billy agreed. "I know three blokes that lost all their bread in Constanta." He bowed his head as a mark of respect.

Bruce suddenly clapped Janek on the shoulder. "Here we are mates. This is the road you want. Stay on this one, sport, and you can't go wrong. Two hours should take you into Cluj."

The Australian duo departed, after refusing to take the money that Tom offered them. They strode away back down the road, with optimistic thumbs extended.

* * *

When the bus got to Cluj, they found the cheap hotel that the hikers had recommended close to the town centre. It was busy at the reception desk, and Joe said, "If they don't have rooms here, could we go back along to our original hotel? It looked very comfortable."

The bus had driven past the expensive hotel on the way into Cluj. It was situated on a hill overlooking the city, embraced by the fortifications of an ancient citadel.

"I would prefer to part company with a little less cash," Tom replied, flatly. "No-one told me just how much it would cost to oil the wheels of enterprise in this country."

The desk clerk eventually gave them his attention, and said briskly, "If you like single room, you go to second floor. On top floor you share, and no have bathroom."

"We'll take the singles," Tom swiftly replied.

They quickly dumped their luggage in the rooms, then rushed back on to the bus. It was late afternoon, and Tom wanted to make sure that everything was in place at the hall.

"I wonder if we'll be besieged after the show again?" pondered Jim, frowning anxiously.

Susan raised a surprised eyebrow. "What's your problem? I thought you enjoyed having girls climbing all over you."

"Of course I do!" he replied, indignantly. "But I'm getting low on rubbers. Those Australian guys said that you can't find them here at all. They wanted to buy some off me."

Pete clicked his tongue in annoyance. "I wish I'd known. I would have got some when we were in Buda. I could have made a tidy profit selling them out here."

Susan turned to Jim and said sarcastically, "You could try using plastic bags. They're easy to get hold of, and recyclable."

"My wife uses supermarket bags as pedal-bin liners," Joe chipped in, "To save resources. She always turns them inside-out, so that the colours don't rub off on to the bin."

"Hmm, maybe it's not such a good idea, after all," Susan said. "You could end up with Savemart printed on your private parts." Then she frowned thoughtfully, and added, "No, it would probably just be "art"."

* * *

Down at the venue, everyone disappeared backstage, and Susan made herself comfortable in the front row, her mind dwelling fretfully on the hikers comments about Constanta. When Phil emerged from behind the fire exit curtains, she beckoned him over and said in a perturbed voice, "Are you going to sell Luigi in Constanta? It doesn't sound like a suitable place, to me."

"I can't see as I got a lot of choice," declared Phil. "That's where my mate be. I could always take Luigi back up to Italy to sell, but you'd be gone home by then."

Susan gave an unhappy sigh, and Phil assured her confidently, "Don't you worry. I can look after Luigi. I got him this far, haven't I?"

As Susan and Phil sat whispering furtively, the band came on stage to begin their rehearsal. Pete prowled backwards and forwards, scanning the floor around his guitar stand.

"Where's my pedal?" he demanded. "Has anyone seen my wah-wah?"

Two of the crew scurried away to look for it, but they returned from the truck empty-handed.

"I guess my guitar is gonna sound a bit flat, tonight," Pete grumbled.

Tom scowled. "Don't you have a spare?"

"I had two spares. I sold one to Janek's brother, and the other one got broke when Lazlo dropped an amplifier on it."

Tom smacked the piano keys in a fit of temper. "Holy shit! I don't believe this! What good is a lead guitar without any oomph!"

Phil leapt out of his seat and made his way on to the stage. He muttered briefly to Tom, who reached into his pocket and brought out a handful of notes. Phil sloped away, and when he came back ten minutes later, he was carrying an oblong cardboard box.

"Is this what you be after?" he said, handing the box to Pete.

"Yeah, that's mine. Where did you find it?"

"One of the stagehands took a fancy to it," Phil explained. "I had ter buy it back off him."

Pete shook his head. "Tck. If this was our last show, I would've sold it to him."

"OK, here we go," Tom called, as his fingers pounded the piano keyboard.

* * *

At eight-thirty on Saturday morning, Jim was thumping on Tom's door.

Tom eventually opened his door, and leaned against it, yawning and groaning.

"I only just got to sleep," he complained. "Those morons downstairs were playing that damn video game until three a.m."

"Really? We didn't hear anything," Jim remarked, casually.

As Tom focused his bleary eyes, he noticed a small brunette slinking away down the corridor.

Jim followed Tom into his room, to make sure that he didn't climb back into bed.

"I never used to believe in Hell," Tom declared solemnly, as he slumped on to the bed, "But after lying here all night listening to laser guns firing and missiles exploding and aliens shrieking, I know exactly what hell will be. It'll be spending eternity trapped inside a video games arcade."

"Quit bleating. You can sleep on the bus," Jim said bluntly, as he started to pack Tom's suitcase.

Joe's head appeared around the door, and he trotted into the room, looking bright-eyed and refreshed.

"How come you're not ready?" he asked Tom. "What's up?"

"Earthlings shall not rest until the foes on planet Zargon have been obliterated," Tom told him, in a grim tone.

Joe looked bemused, then continued, "I just passed Susan in the corridor. She's already eaten breakfast. She said that she'll be waiting on the bus for us. She wanted to have a few words with Phil."

Tom frowned. "Is it my imagination, or are those two spending a good deal of time whispering together?"

"He winked at her over breakfast, yesterday," Jim stated, in a meaningful tone.

"I don't know what she sees in him," Tom muttered. "He ain't even good-looking."

Joe murmured, "I think he looks a bit like you."

"He does not!"

"There is some resemblance," Jim ventured, with a sideways grin. "He claims that his father was an American. Maybe he's a long-lost relative of yours."

Tom snorted in disdain, and then shuffled away into the bathroom.

* * *

"It's not fair," protested Joe. "It's on our way. Why can't we stop and have a look around?"

"We haven't got time," Tom insisted. "It's a long way to Brasov."

"But Sighisoara is about half-way," Joe persisted. "We could stop there for lunch. While the rest of you eat, I could dash about and take some photos. It's supposed to be the quaintest town in Romania," he pleaded, in a desperate voice.

"He only wants to see the place because Dracula was born there," Jim mocked.

"That's not true," Joe responded, looking hurt. "It's an unspoilt medieval town with original fortifications. And if Janek could drive a bit faster, I'm sure we'd have time to visit it."

"And if we blow a tyre through hitting a pot-hole, you'll have plenty of time to take pictures," Tom curtly replied.

"We're making pretty good time," Susan cut in. "If we get to Sighisoara by midday, we could spend an hour there."

Joe bounced happily in his seat, and Susan picked up his guide book to look through.

"I'm confused," she announced, after leafing through the book. "It says that Bram Stoker's Dracula had a castle in northern Transylvania, but the Romanian tourist board say that Dracula's castle is in southern Transylvania at Bran, and another bloke says that it's somewhere else entirely."

"Maybe he had to keep moving on, because he was draining the local resources," Jim suggested.

"I'd stake money on that," added Pete.

"When he left a place, I wonder if the locals sang, "Fangs for the memory" as he drove away," mused Tom, as he chewed the end of his pencil.

"What are you working on?" Susan asked, noticing the sheet of paper filled with his untidy handwriting.

"A new song. Transylvanian Homesick Blues. I'll sing some of it to you."

Tom started to sing in a mellow blues tone.

> "Well I went to sleep this morning
> Stretched out in my crate
> I was up all last night
> Had a heavy date
> Took my girlfriend out dancing
> Didn't get home till late."

"She said that she was hungry
Fancied steak with fries
So I took her to a diner
Just before sunrise
That cruel lil' woman
She never treats me right
She ate garlic mushrooms
And I didn't get a bite."

"What do you think?" Tom said, proudly.

Jim gestured at his mouth with two fingers, but Susan murmured, "It has a certain Je ne sais quoi."

"Is that French? What does it mean?" Pete asked.

"I don't know what," she replied.

"You shouldn't use foreign words if you don't know what they mean," Jim said.

"Je ne sais quoi" means "I don't know what," Susan explained, with a long-suffering sigh.

"I knew that," taunted Jim. "I was just trying to irritate you."

"You could get a doctorate in that," she muttered under her breath. " But if it's a blues song," she said to Tom, "Shouldn't it begin with, "Well I woke up this morning"?"

"He's a vampire, so he wakes up at night. Oh, I dunno. I sometimes think that I should stick to writing instrumental music," Tom reflected, morosely.

Jim pulled a face. "People usually complain when you try and play like Monk."

Susan chipped in, "Do they have pianos in monasteries?"

As Tom gave Susan a sideways look, Jim smirked and declared, "It's not her fault. If God had meant for women to be clever, he would have given them a brain."

Joe quickly whispered to Susan, "He was talking about Thelonious Monk."

"I knew that," she snapped. "I was just trying to irritate him."

Tom smiled nostalgically and he recounted to the others, "When I was a teenager, learning to play the piano, I got myself some Thelonious Monk sheet music. When my mom caught sight of it, she said, "Wait until I'm out of the house before you play that stuff. The only thing worse than hearing Monk, is hearing Monk being played badly!"

Susan frowned thoughtfully and said, "How could you possibly tell if it was being played badly?"

* * *

Shortly before lunch time, the bus came to a halt in a small square just below the walled citadel of Sighisoara.

"You've got sixty minutes to see everything," Jim commanded, as Joe climbed off the bus, with his camera dangling around his neck. "On your marks, get set, go!"

Joe sprinted across the square, and up the steep, cobbled alley that led to the medieval hilltop town.

"He should be able to do it," Tom decided, as Joe disappeared between the historic buildings. "It's quite a small place."

"But it's uphill all the way," Susan said, tilting her head backwards as she surveyed the gothic church that topped the wooded mount.

Janek returned from his expedition to the local shops, and told the others, "No bread. Only pastries."

Susan examined the contents of his paper bag. "They look like croissants. I suppose they'll be all right with salami. Should we wake Phil?"

Phil was sleeping, stretched out on the back seat, having spent the previous night guarding the bus.

Tom shook his head. "Let him sleep. We need him to be alert at night. The crime stories those hikers told us have put the wind up me."

They found a bench nearby, and sat down to eat lunch.

Tom was gazing vacantly at a clock tower on the hill up above them. His eyes suddenly focused on a figure leaning over the parapet, just below the tower's spire.

"Is that Joe waving at us?" he murmured, staring at the distant human speck.

Susan squinted up at the tower, and remarked, "He'd have to be wearing a fluorescent coat and waving the Stars and Stripes before I could see him, at this distance."

"If he had a cell phone, we could call him and find out," said Pete.

"I hate those things," Tom grumbled. "They're so intrusive."

"I enjoy watching people using them," Susan chuckled, "Especially when they inadvertently stick the aerial in their ear."

"That's obviously why you haven't got one," Jim said, spitefully. "The shape of your ears would make it a hazardous enterprise."

As Susan clenched her teeth, Jim continued, "I might get myself one of those cell phones that vibrates in your hip pocket, instead of ringing."

"Well, we wouldn't phone you up on it," Susan retorted. "You'd enjoy it too much."

An hour later, Joe came sprinting back down the hill, flush-faced and panting heavily, and they climbed aboard the bus once more.

"Was it quaint and picturesque?" demanded Jim. "Tell me all about it," he pressed, as Joe tried to catch his breath and talk at the same time.

"Leave the poor bugger alone," said Susan. "You'll give him a heart-attack."

But Joe was keen to narrate his sight-seeing route, and he puffed excitedly, "I got to the top of the clock tower - wonderful view - then past the Dracula house - and up a bizarre covered wooden staircase to the church at the top of the hill. Did you see me waving from the top of the tower?" he asked, breathlessly. "I took a photo of you all."

Jim sniggered. "Susan could use that picture in her modelling portfolio. Half a mile away and forty-five degrees up, is probably her best angle. It minimises her jug ears."

"That's not very nice," Joe protested. "You'll hurt Susan's feelings."

"You'd need a half-brick to do that," muttered Pete.

"I'm sorry, Susan," Jim said, in an insincere tone. "Does it worry you that you've got big ears?"

"I haven't got him any more," Susan replied, tersely. "Noddy paid the ransom!"

CHAPTER 29

"See, we had plenty of time," Joe said, as they drove into the medieval centre of Brasov on Saturday afternoon.

Janek had become adept at swinging the bus around pot-holes, and now he was using the same skill to avoid pedestrians who were spilling off crowded pavements in the narrow streets of the old town. The historic centre was enclosed by forested hills, which hid the modern urban concrete sprawl from view.

"These directions are rather vague," Susan complained, as she studied her crumpled itinerary. "And there's a crease right over the hotel address."

As they drove past an ice-cream parlour, Susan noticed a huddle of back-packers standing outside, slowly licking ice-cream cones.

"Stop here," she ordered Janek. "I'll try and get directions to the hotel."

She approached the group and asked, loudly, "Can anyone direct me to the Aro hotel?"

A young man with a toy kangaroo attached to his sun hat, responded, "The Aro, sport? Yeh - no probs." And he gave Susan a brief set of instructions, which she quickly jotted down.

Five minutes later they found the hotel, tucked in the corner of a side street. Pete went inside to check on the prices, and he returned to the bus, muttering, "Twenty bucks." They collected their bags and hurried into the hotel foyer, whilst Janek and Phil drove away to find the venue.

The desk clerk seemed slightly surprised by their arrival, but he handed out the room keys with an air of indifference, then went back to reading his newspaper.

* * *

"It's a bit basic," Tom grumbled, as he surveyed his room.

"At least it's cheap," Susan reminded him.

Pete suddenly appeared from a doorway in the corner of Tom's room. Tom gasped in surprise. "How did you get there?"

"We share a bathroom," Pete explained. "I'm next door."

"Well I want first shower," Tom quickly insisted.

Susan frowned. "Shared bathrooms! Pete, I'll have your room. I'm not sharing my bathroom with a total stranger. At least I know all of Tom's unsavoury habits."

Pete dutifully handed his key to Susan, and moved his bags down the corridor, muttering discontentedly as he went.

Half an hour later, they re-grouped in Tom's room, waiting for Janek to come and collect them for the sound check. Jim had found an ice machine down the hallway, and he had filled a bag and brought it along.

"Wonderful," Susan enthused. "I haven't had any ice in my martini since Dubrovnik." She scooped a large cube out of the bag and dropped it into her drink.

The band were idly chatting about the running order for that night's show, and Susan was gazing abstractedly into her glass of vermouth. She suddenly shrieked, and held the glass up close to her eyes.

"Arghh! Gross!" Susan frantically fished the ice cube out of her drink, and stared at it, aghast.

"There's a cockroach inside this ice cube!"

"What are you complaining about?" Jim scoffed. "You're not a vegetarian. A little fresh meat never hurt anyone."

"It's not fresh, it's frozen," Pete corrected him.

Susan flung the ice cube to the floor.

"Do you do this at home?" complained Tom. "Who do you expect to clear up after you?" He picked up the ice cube, then paused. "What shall I do with it?"

"Flush it down the toilet," Susan told him.

"It probably won't sink," Tom argued. "I don't want to look at a dead cockroach every time I take a leak."

"It may not be dead," Joe said, thoughtfully. "It may have gone through a rapid freezing process, and be in a state of suspended animation."

"Yuk! It's melting in my hand!" Tom wailed.

"Chuck it out into the corridor. Then if it thaws and comes back to life, it can walk home to its loved ones," Susan said, sarcastically.

Tom strode to the door and lobbed the ice cube out into the hallway.

Joe smiled at Susan and said, "I think that shows great sensitivity on your part, to be concerned about that little creature's family."

Before Susan could disillusion Joe, there was a brisk rapping at the door as Janek shouted his arrival. They all trooped outside, and on to the bus. They drove around the block to pick up the main road, and as the bus swung into a busy boulevard, Joe remarked, "Look, there's another hotel called the Aro." After a second glance he added, "No, that one is the Aro Palace. Ours is the Aro Sport, isn't it?" he queried, looking at Susan.

Susan frowned as she recalled her brief conversation with the Australian outside the ice cream parlour, and she fished the itinerary out of her handbag. She scanned the paper, then muttered peevishly, "Shit! We checked into the wrong hotel. We're supposed to be at the Aro Palace."

Joe gave her a reproachful glance as the luxurious Palace hotel slid past the bus windows, but Tom merely remarked, "That place looks horribly expensive. We'll stay put."

* * *

At the concert hall, Phil was waiting at the backstage door to guide the band to the stage. A maze of corridors led through the cavernous building, with identical doors set along each wall. As Phil led them through the backstage labyrinth, he remarked, "We left a wheely-crate outside of yer dressing room, so as we could find it again. Most of these other rooms be locked up."

They rounded a corner and saw Lazlo sitting on the crate, smoking. He jumped off as he caught sight of them, and hastily extinguished his cigarette as he followed the others along a further network of corridors, and then on to the stage.

Tom approached his piano, then stood still and demanded, "All right. Where have you jokers put my piano stool?"

The crew responded with blank stares, and Phil suggested, "It might be in the wheely-crate what we left outside yer dressing room. I'll go and have a look." And he darted off the stage.

Phil returned a few minutes later with a perplexed look on his face.

"Some silly bugger has moved the crate," he complained. "I can't find her anywhere. One of the stage hands must have pushed it into a store-room. I'll have ter get the caretaker to unlock all the rooms for us. He won't be very happy about it. Can yer give I a bit of cash ter soften him up?"

Tom groaned, and dug his hand into his pocket, pulling out an assortment of notes. As Phil dashed off with the cash, Susan commented, "Why can't you sit on a chair? You're too fussy."

"I need to be able to move sideways," he snapped back at her.

"He'd probably topple off a chair," Jim chuckled. "He gets carried away with his prestissimos."

"You could incorporate it as part of your act," Susan suggested. "To liven things up a bit when the show isn't going too well."

Tom folded his arms in a sulky pose, while the rest of the band giggled at the thought of Tom crashing to the floor as he over-stretched for the low notes.

Ten minutes later Phil struggled on to the stage, carrying the heavy piano stool.

"About time," grumbled Tom. "Where was it?"

"One of the backstage staff thought as it were a dressing-table stool," Phil explained, "So he shoved it into the ladies room."

Tom gave an exasperated grunt as he perched on his padded seat, then commenced thumping the piano.

* * *

As Phil was helping to dismantle the speakers after the show, Susan said, "Try and get some sleep tonight. I want you to come with us when Joe and me go sight-seeing tomorrow."

Phil nodded his assent, then ducked smartly as Lazlo went past wielding a microphone stand above his head.

Joe was packing away his guitars into their sturdy cases. As he unplugged the fret-less bass, he kissed it gently before laying it down. He caught sight of Susan's sideways look, and he explained, "I always kiss her before I put her to bed. She's my favourite."

Jim rolled his eyes heavenwards as he straightened up from his crouching position on the floor, where he was doing a quick examination of Joe's amplifier switch.

"Yeah, she's real cute. I always bang her strings when you ain't around. Anyway, either the foot switch has a dodgy connection," Jim declared, "Or you knocked the jack-plug loose when you changed guitars."

Joe had lost his output briefly at the start of one of the songs, and Jim was trying to trace the fault.

"We only have two more gigs," Tom stated. "Don't worry too much. Just make sure that Lazlo doesn't try and fix it."

Susan disappeared out to the bus, and Jim gave Phil a hand lifting the speakers into the crates, taking the opportunity to probe into his family history.

"Phil, you know, I don't recall that you've ever told us your family name?" Jim remarked, casually.

"I mostly calls meself Mister Smith," Phil replied, coolly. "People has trouble pronouncing me surname, what with it being Polish, so I don't use it much."

"Jim, we're ready to go," Tom called from the wings. "Get a move on."

Jim followed the rest of the band as they made their way out of the hall.

"Do you have any Poles in your family?" Jim asked Tom, as he caught up.

Tom shook his head, and answered, "Not as far as I know. Why?"

"Phil's dad has a Polish name."

"See. I told you he was no relation of mine." Tom sniffed haughtily, and they boarded the bus once more to return to their uncomfortable hotel.

* * *

Tom slept in late on Sunday morning, and when he went along to find the others, there was no reply to his knock at any of the doors. He went back into his own room, and through the bathroom into Susan's room, but there was no sign of her. He grumbled to himself, and went downstairs to have a lonely breakfast.

Afterwards, he decided to go and check that the bus was still parked down the street. Even though he had seen Susan's bags in her room, he had a sudden panic attack about being abandoned in the middle of Transylvania. He was relieved to see that it was still there, with Janek dozing serenely in the driver's seat.

Tom knocked sharply on the door, and Janek was startled awake.

"Where is everyone?" Tom asked, as he stepped aboard.

"Susan, Joe and Phil go sight-seeing," Janek told him. "Pete and Jim go out for breakfast."

"Well that's nice," Tom mumbled, crossly. "Where did they go?"

"Aro Palace," Janek replied with indifference, and he closed his eyes again.

Tom got off the bus and walked around the block to look for them. As he reached the corner he saw Pete coming towards him, alone.

"Did y'all enjoy your breakfast?" Tom asked, sourly.

"Yeah, the Palace has real good food."

"Is Jim still there?"

"No, we came out together, then he saw a good-looking girl hanging around outside, and he fell into conversation with her. Then they went off together," Pete ended, with a resigned shrug.

"We have to check out in a half-hour," Tom muttered. "They'd better all be back by then!"

* * *

Just before noon, Susan and Joe dashed into the hotel foyer, as Tom and Pete were paying their bills.

"The wanderers return. Did you have a nice time, looking around?" he asked coldly, still peeved at Phil's inclusion in their jaunt.

"We couldn't go inside the Black Church," Joe lamented, "But we saw just about everything else. It's quite a picturesque little town."

"The beggars on the pavement weren't particularly picturesque," Susan muttered. "Especially not the ones who swore at us."

"You don't know for sure that they were swearing at us," Joe argued. "You don't speak Romanian."

"Well I'm fairly certain that they weren't saying, "Have a nice day"," Susan retorted.

Tom interrupted their debate, saying to Joe, "You'd better get Jim's stuff out of his room if you can, or he'll end up paying extra."

Susan and Joe darted upstairs to collect their luggage, while Tom looked at his watch and sighed impatiently. Susan was back down a couple of minutes later, and Joe staggered along shortly afterwards, weighed down by two sets of bags.

"He left his bathroom door open, so I collected his stuff. I hope I didn't miss anything. Where is Jim, anyway?"

"He took off with some girl," Tom answered abruptly, as he paid Jim's bill. "I guess we'd better wait for him on the bus."

* * *

At one thirty a taxi pulled up with a screech of brakes in front of the bus. Jim leapt out, hastily paid the driver, then sprinted aboard.

Tom exploded. "Do you think that we have nothing better to do than dance attendance on your sexual exploits!"

"I hope she was worth it," murmured Pete.

"I can understand why you're pissed," Jim responded, in a conciliatory tone, "But it wasn't really my fault."

"Did she kidnap you?" Tom demanded, sarcastically.

"She took me away under false pretences, so you could put it like that."

Tom's curiosity got the better of his bad mood. "What exactly happened?"

"Well," Jim began, "Me and Pete were walking away from the Palace hotel, when I noticed this pretty girl smiling at me. She beckoned me over, so I went up to her, and she said, "You come home with me? Nice room. Very cheap.""

"So I nodded and said yes. I don't mind paying for it from time to time. Needs must when the devil drives, and all that. And she was real cute."

"So we got on a bus, and went a good distance into the suburbs. She took me to her apartment in one of those big, concrete blocks way over on the other side of town. Imagine my surprise when she takes me into the living room and introduces me to her mom and dad! I was a little embarrassed. Then she took me into a bedroom and said, "This your room. Only two dollars a night. Breakfast one dollar. How many nights you stay?""

"It was then that I realised that she was offering me the room, and not her body. I panicked a little, because her dad was a beefy guy with big hands, looked like he works in a tractor factory. So I smiled sweetly at her and asked for a glass of water, then when she disappeared into the kitchen, I legged it out of the front door."

"I had to walk for a half-hour before I found a cab, and then two guys tried to mug me as I climbed inside. I clung to my wallet and the cab driver took off real fast. What a nightmare!"

Tom gave him a stern look. "Well I hope this will be a lesson to you."

"Most definitely."

"You'll have forgotten all about it by tomorrow," Pete scoffed quietly, as Jim slid into the seat beside him.

"True. One strange thing, though," Jim said, frowning. "As the cab went past the Palace hotel just now, I'm sure that I saw the guy who did the malpractice surgery on Tom's rag dolly."

"Don't mention it to Tom, or he'll stop the bus and go off to hunt him down."

But Tom was preoccupied with moaning miserably to Susan.

"Can you believe this place? The roads are full of pot-holes, the sidewalks are full of beggars, and everyone tries to rob you!"

"Yes," Susan said, with a nostalgic smile. "It's just like home."

* * *

Four hours later, Tom was still in a bad mood.

"Have you taken us the scenic route on purpose?" he demanded, glaring at Susan.

"This is the main road," she snapped back.

"Then how come there aren't any signposts?"

"They probably didn't expect a bus full of American idiots to come here."

"She's right," Joe chipped in. "It's shown as a major route in my guide book."

The road had twisted eastwards through the mountains after they left Brasov, giving them wonderful vistas of forested slopes and craggy summits, but making their progress painfully slow.

Tom shook his head despondently. "We ain't gonna get to Iasi by nightfall. What we gonna do?"

"Joe, could I borrow your gold chain and crucifix?" Jim asked. "Better to be safe than sorry," he explained, as Tom shot him a quizzical glance. "After all, this is Transylvania."

Tom gave an exasperated sigh. "We don't even know if we're on the right road. We haven't seen a village for two hours or more."

"Once it gets dark, we probably won't even see the road," Jim commented, in a sepulchral tone of foreboding.

"In that case, we'll have to pull off the road and park in the forest for the night," Susan stated.

"Does the salami have garlic in it?" Jim pondered. "Maybe we should fetch some out of the baggage compartment."

The bus suddenly hit a pot-hole, and they all bounced upwards in their seats.

"Sorry!" Janek shouted over his shoulder. "I not see it till too late!"

Phil had been asleep for most of the journey, but the jolt woke him up, and as he stretched himself, he commented, "We'd best find somewhere ter stop for the night."

"Is there a Holiday Inn around the next bend?" Tom asked, facetiously.

"No, but there be a farm over yonder," Phil replied. "I can see the wood-smoke through the trees."

The secluded, rambling farmhouse was tucked at the end of a rough, rutted track. As the bus came to a halt, the heavy wooden front door opened, and a sturdy woman in a colourful apron and matching headscarf gaped at them in astonishment.

* * *

"I guess they don't have too many visitors here," Tom remarked, as they sat around a huge, hewn wooden table.

The lady of the house had invited them inside with vociferous enthusiasm, and had pushed them on to wooden settles, before disappearing into another room. She swiftly returned carrying a tin tray laden with small glasses, and a dusty bottle that had no label and a tenacious cork. As the woman filled their glasses, several small children crept into the room, and they stared at the unexpected guests as if they had stepped from a flying saucer.

They scampered away as heavy footsteps approached from behind another door. A succession of young men, girls, and elderly men were introduced, followed by a collection of old ladies. They shook hands heartily, then the occupants of the farm all trooped back outside to carry on with their work.

"Conversation is gonna be a touch difficult," mused Tom. "Can you ask them if we can have accommodation for the night, Janek? You can speak a good deal of Romanian."

"They not speak Romanian," Janek replied. "They speak old German."

When the farmer's wife returned with a tray full of biscuits and fruit, Janek spoke a few words, and she hurried out of the room again. Shortly afterwards, there was a commotion as feet clattered up the bare boards of the stairs. The feet came clumping back down again, and the heavy wooden front door creaked open.

Jim crossed to the window to investigate the flurry of activity, and he saw a handful of children and two young men bounding across the yard towards a small barn, all carrying an armful of bedding.

Twenty minutes later, the farmers wife came back into the parlour, beamed at her guests, then led them upstairs to their bedrooms.

* * *

The spacious farmhouse had ornate wooden balconies outside the upper windows, with intricate carvings on the balustrades. The guests had been given rooms at the back of the house, overlooking a small courtyard. Joe was leaning on his balcony, admiring the fretwork and gazing at sunset over the majestic mountains. Susan was also on her balcony, surveying the domestic scenes below. Someone was carrying wood into the kitchen, and an unseen hand threw some vegetable scraps out of the door, to where a tethered goat stood, nibbling.

Joe noticed the creature, and said critically, "That's not very hygienic, having a goat tied up right by the kitchen door."

"It's environmentally friendly," Susan lectured him. "The goat is a waste-disposal unit."

Either that, or it's our dinner tonight, she thought to herself.

CHAPTER 30

Next morning, the farmer's wife provided them with a hearty breakfast, and steadfastly refused to accept the dollar bills that Tom offered as payment for their night's accommodation.

"Why won't she take it?" Tom whispered to Susan, bemused by the rural etiquette. "They could sure use the cash. None of the kids are wearing shoes."

"You can't pay for hospitality," Susan told him. "They'd regard it as an insult. Give the kids a few dollars each when she's not looking."

Tom surreptitiously distributed the notes as breakfast was cleared away, and then the band prepared to continue their journey to Iasi.

As they carried their bags out to the bus, Joe grimaced and clutched at his stomach, saying to Susan, "Could I have some of your indigestion pills? I'm not feeling too good."

"You should have told them that you're a vegetarian," Pete scolded him. "Why did you eat that big bowl of stew last night?"

"I thought that it would seem churlish to refuse it," Joe explained. "They went to so much trouble to cook that huge meal for us. It was a bit rich for me, though. I'm not used to eating so much meat."

Susan handed Joe her carton of indigestion pills, and after he had swallowed a few, he assembled his camera and dashed away.

"I won't be long," he called over his shoulder. "I want to get some shots of this place. It's very ethnic." And he disappeared round the back of the farmhouse.

The others climbed aboard the bus, and chatted idly as they waited for Joe.

Jim gazed out of the window, and puzzled aloud, "Why are the kids picking up feathers in the yard? That's kinda obsessively tidy, don't you think?"

"Maybe they collect them up to make feather beds," Susan suggested.

247

"That's a long-term hobby," mumbled Tom. "I've only seen a couple of geese here. Maybe they have some ducks behind the barn."

"Why do people keep ducks?" pondered Susan. "Their eggs are no good, and there's not much meat on them."

"They make the ponds look pretty," Tom told her.

"My son has a duck soft toy," Pete informed them. "But it ain't one of these cute yellow fluffy things. It's done up as a Biker, in full motorcycle gear - black cap, black shades, red neckerchief, black jacket and black boots."

"Does it have a knife, too?" Jim asked, tongue in cheek.

"When was the last time you saw a duck with a knife?" Susan said, scornfully. "You've definitely been on the road too long."

Joe suddenly reappeared, and boarded the bus, looking perplexed.

"Got all your photos?" Tom enquired.

"Yes, but I wanted to take one of the goat that was tied up by the kitchen door yesterday," Joe replied, frowning. "It's not there now, and when I asked the kitchen hand where I could find it, he pointed towards the refrigerator. I'm a bit puzzled."

"His English isn't very good," Susan said, hastily. "He probably misunderstood you. Let's get going now, anyway."

And she shouted at Janek to start the bus, before Joe could resume his fruitless search for the goat.

* * *

After half an hour, the tortuous mountain road began a gentle descent into a river valley, and Janek was able to move the bus into top gear. They sped northwards, following the course of the river through its wide valley, then they turned east towards Iasi, with the lofty Carpathian mountains becoming a distant shadow behind them. The road became flat and dull, and they arrived in Iasi much sooner than they had expected.

"What are we gonna do with ourselves for two days?" Jim grumbled. "This place is the back of beyond."

As the bus wound its way through the busy streets near the town centre, the local residents seemed to be surprised by its appearance, and they stared with interest at the luxury coach which was so obviously from the West.

"Haven't these people ever seen a bus before?" Pete muttered, as he noticed the inquisitive pedestrians.

"Maybe not," Susan commented. "We're a good way east. If you chuck a stone, it will probably land in Russia."

As Pete grimaced, Joe eagerly suggested, "Could we visit the border? I'd like to get some pictures of Russia."

Phil, who was seemingly dozing, spoke casually without opening his eyes. "They b'aint too keen on frontier photography, hereabouts. You'll likely get arrested, or shot at by some bad-tempered sentry."

Joe tightened his lips. "I think I'll limit my sightseeing to the town."

"We could go out tonight and look for the local hot-spots," Jim proposed.

"The clubs are usually closed on Monday nights," Susan responded, keen to dampen his enthusiasm. "You could all get an early night. You'd be fresher for the gig, tomorrow."

"I play better when I'm half asleep," Jim countered. "I prefer to be one step behind the piano player, so that I can tell which direction he's going in."

Janek had been making haphazard left and right turns, in a vague attempt to find the town square which held their hotel. The bus suddenly lurched upwards, and rumbled noisily over cobblestones. As passers-by gestured rudely at him, Janek shrugged his shoulders dismissively and continued to drive along the pedestrianised paving until he reached the square that he was looking for. The bus rattled back down on to the road surface, and halted outside their hotel.

"I find it!" Janek shouted, triumphantly.

"Were we breaking the law just then?" Joe murmured, nervously.

"We didn't see a no-entry sign," Jim argued. "If they don't want vehicles to use a street, they should put up a sign."

Janek nodded vehemently in agreement, and Susan sighed as she gathered up her bags.

They trooped into the hotel, which was a majestic turn-of-the-century edifice, with a cavernous lobby and a high, echoing ceiling. Tom was leading the way to the desk, when he stopped abruptly in his tracks, and groaned loudly.

"We ain't staying here," he announced curtly, and he promptly turned around and retraced his steps.

Susan followed him and demanded, "What's got into you?"

Tom nodded brusquely at the side walls of the hotel lobby, which were lined with ranks of video game machines, flashing coloured lights and emitting eerie noises.

"I'm not going to suffer a night in Hell, again," Tom muttered, as he shuddered at the memory of the hotel in Cluj. "We'll find another place to stay." And he marched determinedly out of the lobby.

On the opposite side of the street was a concrete high-rise block, with a hotel name stretching down one grey flank in huge neon letters. Tom set off towards it, and the others followed behind, with mutinous grumblings.

"I don't like modern hotels," Joe murmured. "They have no character at all. That old place looked interesting."

"It seemed like a nice enough place to me, too," Susan added, as she struggled with her heavy bags. "He can be a real old woman, at times," she ended, in a loud whisper.

Tom disregarded the rumblings of dissatisfaction, and led the way into the plushly carpeted foyer of the towering hotel. The lobby held a floor display of potted plants, and some deeply upholstered sofas. No devilish artefacts of computerised entertainment were visible.

Tom smiled happily. "This is just fine." And he gratefully accepted the second floor rooms that the desk clerk offered.

* * *

In the evening they assembled in the hotel dining room. Susan had spent the afternoon washing underwear, and Joe had gone out to take photos, leaving the others to play cards. They sat at a table, waiting for Joe to arrive before they ordered dinner.

"You don't suppose he's gone off to take snaps of the border?" Tom fretted.

"Phil went out with him," Susan assured Tom. "He won't let Joe stray too far away."

Joe came dashing into the room ten minutes later, apologising profusely for keeping them all waiting.

"I ran out of film," he explained, breathlessly, "And I had to try several shops before I found some good quality rolls."

"You ought to get yourself a video camera," Susan remarked. "Then you could have a complete moving record of your tours."

"I tried that once," Joe replied, "But the guys wouldn't co-operate. They kept walking backwards, to make it look like the video was stuck on rewind."

As the waiter brought a handful of menus to their table, Jim asked, "Are Janek and Phil eating somewhere else?"

Joe nodded and answered, "Phil said that he has some things to do at the venue, so Janek took him down there."

Jim frowned briefly. "The crew won't be setting up till tomorrow."

"They probably have a poker game running," Pete deduced.

Susan was studying the menu. "Roast pork with red cabbage," she declared, with relish. "I hope they cook it Polish-style. Phil's mother used to make a wonderful Polish red cabbage."

"Was his mother Polish as well?" Jim enquired.

"As well as what?"

"As well as his father."

"His father was American," Susan replied, with a derisive look. "I thought that even you had managed to grasp that much."

Jim tightened his lips. "Then how come he has a Polish name?"

Susan shrugged. "I assume he took his mother's surname because she wasn't married to his dad."

"So what was his father's surname?" Jim persisted.

"I've no idea. No-one ever knew who he was, except Phil's mum, of course. There were rumours that he was in the US air force, stationed in England just after the war. Presumably, he returned to America. Phil never talks about him. Why are you so interested, anyway?" she asked, suspiciously.

Tom adroitly kicked Jim's ankle under the table, so that the only reply forthcoming was, "Argh - just idle - ouch - curiosity."

Joe suddenly blurted out, "Oh, I nearly forgot to tell you. A cinema down the street is showing "Gone With The Wind". I thought that maybe we could go and see it this evening."

Jim groaned and pulled a face, but Tom nodded, saying, "Yeah, why not. We don't have any other plans for tonight. It might be a laugh."

* * *

A couple of hours later, they filed into the cinema and joined the short ticket queue.

"I can smell popcorn," Joe said, glancing eagerly about. He spotted the popcorn stand, and told the others, "Get my ticket for me, and I'll go for the popcorn. Who wants some?"

"I'll have a bag," Tom answered.

"Me too," Jim concurred. "It'll help to alleviate the boredom."

Pete shook his head. "I'll pass. The hard bits play havoc with my bridge-work."

"I won't have a bag," Susan decided. "It's very fattening. I'll pinch some off you lot if I feel like nibbling."

"You won't want any of mine," Jim stated. "I always spit the hard bits back into the bag."

"Why am I not surprised by that," Susan murmured.

They mooched into the sparsely filled auditorium and chose their seats. Susan strategically placed herself between Joe and Tom, so that she had two bags of popcorn to choose from. The house lights were quite bright, and as Susan gazed around at the other occupants of the cinema, she noticed a group of leather-clad men sitting in the back row. She nudged Tom sharply. The top layer of popcorn flew out of his carton, and he gave her a petulant look.

Susan nodded her head surreptitiously backwards, and remarked, "They look as if they should be watching Easy Rider."

Tom glanced over his shoulder, then diplomatically averted his gaze. "I didn't know that Gone With The Wind was a cult movie for bikers."

His remark drew the attention of Jim, who swivelled discreetly to look at the bikers, then declared, "I bet they know all the dialogue, chapter and verse."

As he turned in his seat, he knocked his jacket on to the floor. He bent down to retrieve it, and came face to face with a furry black rodent with yellow beady eyes. He straightened up abruptly, and said to the others, "You'll never guess what I've just seen!"

"A mallard with a flick-knife?" Susan retorted. She chuckled at her quick wit, while Jim smiled smugly with mordant anticipation.

The house lights dimmed, and the opening titles flashed on to the screen. Jim hoisted his feet on to the empty seat in front of him, and furtively scattered a handful of popcorn on to the floor. Moments later, Susan felt several small objects brushing speedily against her ankles. She gave a piercing shriek and immediately leapt out of her seat.

"There's mice in here!"

"No, they're rats," Jim assured her. "You don't get black mice. The thing that I saw was definitely black."

Susan gave a hysterical wail, and trampled over Tom's feet in a desperate lunge to get out of the row of seats.

"They have a show just like this in Disneyworld," Jim called after her, as she sprinted up the dark aisle.

"I didn't know she could move so fast," mumbled Pete, as he perched his feet on a seat-back.

Joe said anxiously, "Shouldn't we go after her? She seems a bit upset."

Tom heaved his long legs up on to the seat in front of him and remarked, "It's an ill wind that she's gone with. We don't have to share our popcorn now."

* * *

On Tuesday morning, Tom was already eating breakfast when the others wandered into the dining room.

"Who pushed you out of bed?" Susan remarked, surprised to see Tom up so early.

"The trams woke me up," he complained. "My room is at the front, and the damn things started rattling underneath my window at five a.m. Still, the video games at the other hotel would probably have been worse," he ended, trying to console himself. "Where did you get to last night, anyway? When we came back from the cinema I tapped on your door, but there was no reply."

"I went to a bar on the other side of the square," Susan explained. "They've got a casino upstairs, so I hung around there, watching seedy-looking blokes throwing their money away. I didn't pay for any of my drinks, so it was quite a good night."

Tom gave her a disapproving stare. "I don't think you should frequent those kind of places on your own. You might get into trouble."

"No I won't," Susan replied. "I carry a good supply of supermarket bags with me."

"Gross!" exclaimed Jim.

"Not that many!" She retorted, indignantly.

* * *

"I thought that you saw all of these places yesterday," Jim grumbled, as Joe led them through a maze of streets later that morning.

"The Palace of Culture was closed yesterday," Joe explained. "It has four museums that we can visit."

As the others groaned in unison, Joe turned into a small square which held a teeming open-air market. Women with weather-beaten faces and tightly-welded headscarves shoved through the queues with relentless determination, using their stout wicker baskets to fend off any retaliatory elbows.

The stalls were heaped with soil-encrusted root vegetables, and objects that were probably cabbages before the hot sun had wilted them. Draped around the edges of one small stall were ornate tasseled rugs depicting the Nativity scene. Plaster statues of the Virgin Mary were perched between handfuls of rosary beads, and behind these were boxes containing prayer cards and coloured pictures of the saints.

"I wonder if they still make luminous statues of the Virgin Mary?" murmured Joe.

"I had one of those in my bedroom when I was a kid," recalled Pete. "I used to put a handkerchief over it every night, 'cause the luminous glow frightened me."

"That act of cowardice probably saved you from radiation sickness," Jim remarked, sagely.

As they skirted the edge of the market, Joe enthused, "I love the medieval atmosphere that these historic European towns have. It brings to mind the old days when people used to come from far and wide with their paltry goods, to trade and exchange by barter, to avoid paying exorbitant taxes."

"That tradition still exists in England today," Susan told him. "We call it a car boot sale."

An overpowering smell of fish suddenly assaulted their nostrils, and they noticed a stall that had several shiny, black eels twisted on display.

"Ugh!" Susan exclaimed. "They look like soft snakes!"

Jim clicked his tongue and replied, "All you ever do is carp and moan."

"Susan, you look a bit pale. What's the mackerel?" Tom quipped, as Susan walked quickly away from the stall.

"You'll have to speak up, she's a little hard of herring," Jim announced.

"I've haddock enough of this plaice," Tom decided. "We'd better get our skates on if we want to see the museum."

"I'm not sure I want to go round the museum," Pete responded. "I'll have to mullet over."

As Joe lingered with fascination at the eel stall, Jim called, "Come on, we're not whiting for you any conger."

"The smell has made me feel queasy," Susan complained to Tom.

"Perch here on this bench," he suggested, with a snigger.

Susan curled her lip, and Jim remarked, "I think she's brisling with indignation."

"Only three more days and I'll be shot of you lot," Susan murmured, thankfully.

Tom chuckled. "Dace, that's a good one."

Two streets later, they reached the neo-gothic Palace of Culture. Joe sprinted inside, keen to view as many exhibits as possible, while the others ambled about with studied indifference. Stained glass leaded windows gave the building a cathedral-type atmosphere, and the high, vaulted ceiling echoed severely, discouraging any conversation. They wandered slowly and aimlessly in silence, lost in their own thoughts.

Tom stood admiring the ornate leaded windows of the gothic palace. His absorbed gaze drew Susan's attention, and she asked him, "What's so fascinating up there?"

"The arched windows have a perfect symmetry," he replied. "I always enjoy symmetry in architecture, it's very pleasing to the eye. I try to observe symmetrical designs wherever I go."

"I always count squares wherever I go," Susan confessed. "It's a compulsion that I have. Whenever I see panes of glass or panelled wood-work, I've got to count up the squares."

Jim overheard their conversation, and he gave them a sideways look, saying sarcastically, "You two really know how to have a good time, don't you? You should have met through a lonely hearts column - "Desperately Seeking Symmetry desires relationship with Countess Count.""

And he sauntered away with a derisory smirk.

* * *

They went back to the hotel for lunch, and they lingered in the top-floor cafe, sipping drinks whilst admiring the view across the city, and killing time until they were due at the venue for the sound check.

"Three more days," Tom mused, as he remembered Susan's remark at the market. "It doesn't seem like six weeks have gone by."

"Seems more like six months," Pete muttered, darkly.

"I guess you'll be glad to get back to work?" Tom said to Susan, in a sad tone.

Susan grimaced and shook her head.

"Me and the boss have never really hit it off. And things got worse after he introduced those awful personal computers into the office. He came along one morning to see how I was coping with mine. When I saw him coming along the corridor, I put the mouse on the floor, beside my foot. He breezed in and demanded, "How are you getting on with this wonderful new PC?""

"And I replied, "There's something wrong with it. I can't get the foot pedal to work." Then I pressed the button to open the CD Rom tray, and I said to him, "I like this cup-holder, though. It's really handy, being able to put my cup of coffee out of the way of the keyboard.""

"And he went ballistic! Put a screwdriver in his hand and he could have done repairs on the Mir space station. Humourless git!""

"Computers baffle me," Tom confessed. "Like, what does the "Rom" in CD Rom actually mean?"

"It's short for Romulus," Susan told him, tongue in cheek. "That's the name of the bloke who invented it. He works for Philips in Eindhoven."

Tom nodded blankly, and looked impressed.

"And I suppose the video cassette was invented by a guy named "Remus", huh, Susan?" Jim said, sardonically.

"That's right," she responded, blithely. "Romulus and Remus, those two famous Dutchmen."

As Joe gave a perplexed frown, Tom remarked to Susan, "You're very knowledgeable. I think you're a closet intellectual."

"Yeah - water closet," Jim scoffed. "She talks a load of sh-"

"Shouldn't we be getting down to the venue?" Joe hastily interrupted.

Tom glanced at his watch and nodded in assent, then gulped down the remainder of his beer.

CHAPTER 31

"Where has Joe disappeared to?" Tom demanded impatiently, as he sat at his piano, ready to start the run-through that afternoon.

"He went out front, to get a look at the baroque facade," Pete informed him, with erudite boredom.

"Do we get a diploma at the end of this tour?" Jim pondered. "I feel like we've done a six-week course in European architecture. Even Pete has learned this stuff, and he used to think that a flying buttress was an airplane."

Joe suddenly bounded on to the stage, saying, "This is a beautiful hall. It's wonderful how they've managed to preserve it so well. I really like the" he broke off abruptly as he approached his guitar stands. He glanced anxiously about. "Where's my fret-less? The guys know they're supposed to put it beside my regular bass?"

Pete shook off his vacuous lethargy and glanced at the equipment that was adjacent to Joe's microphone. Only one guitar rested there. The other stand was forlornly vacant.

"Shit. I should have noticed that."

"It's probably still in the truck," Tom responded. "You can fetch it later." And he poised his fingers over the keyboard.

Joe stood quite still, with a look of panic on his face. "I'll go now. I won't be able to play if I'm worrying about her." And he dashed off the stage to look for the wheely-crate that held his beloved guitar.

"Just as well we got here early," Tom grumbled, as he sat fidgeting.

After fifteen minutes they heard Joe returning, his voice raised in altercation with one of the crew. He walked back on to the stage with a dazed look on his face.

"I can't find her," he breathed, in a hoarse whisper. "She's not in the crate. The crew have searched everywhere."

"It must be on the truck," Pete insisted. "I saw you pack it after the Brasov gig."

"She's gone," Joe whimpered. "I'll never see her again." And his face crumpled, as if the tears were about to flow.

Susan had perched beside Tom on his piano stool while Joe was speaking, and she whispered, "He couldn't be more upset if he'd heard that his wife had been hit by a train!"

As Joe stood with his head in his hands, Phil appeared from backstage.

"Who be dead, then?" Phil asked, nodding towards Joe.

"His favourite guitar has gone missing," Susan hissed at him.

"Well bugger me! There's always summat to sort out, b'aint there? I bet I knows where her is, but I reckon as I'll need a few bob to get her back." Phil turned a meaningful glance towards Tom.

Tom pursed his lips, then thrust his hand into his pocket and handed over the customary notes. Phil went off clutching the money, saying cheerfully to Joe, "I'll find her, don't you worry yerself."

"I've looked everywhere," Joe moaned plaintively, after Phil had gone. "She's been stolen, I can just feel it. This is the worst night of my life." He hurled himself off the stage and slumped into a front row seat, chewing anxiously at his fingernails.

Half an hour later, Phil strode on to the stage carrying a guitar case. Joe jumped up and clambered back on to the stage.

"Oh Lord, please let it be her," he pleaded, as he undid the catches. The glossy dark wood body of the guitar was revealed, and Joe sank to his knees in relief. "Where did you find her?" he murmured, with fervent gratitude.

"We was playing cards with some of these-here stage hands last night, and one of them had his brother-in-law in the game, and he saw the guitar and took a fancy to it, him being a musician and all. He borrowed it fer the night, to have a bit of a play on, and forgot to bring her back. It were still in the boot of his car, a few miles from here. I had ter get a taxi there and back."

"Couldn't Janek have taken you there?" Jim asked, with a thoughtful frown.

Phil glibly replied, "He gone out fer pizza, and took the bus keys with him."

"Let's get this show on the road," Tom called impatiently, and he glared sulkily at Phil's departing back as he and Susan went backstage deep in conversation.

* * *

After the show, Tom was alone in the dressing room, pulling on a dry shirt before the bus journey back to the hotel. Jim came into the room and sidled up to Tom, saying, "Take a look at this." He opened his hand to reveal a small card.

"It looks like a dentist's appointment card," Tom remarked. "So what?"

"The clinic address is some place in Dubrovnik," Jim pointed out. "I'm pretty sure that this fell out of Phil's pocket. No-one else in the crew is likely to have a dentist in Dubrovnik."

Tom studied the card more closely, and his eyes widened with surprise as he read the patient's name.

"Wasn't that your mom's family name before she got married?" Jim probed.

As Tom nodded reluctantly, Jim continued, "And don't you have an uncle George who was in the US air force, years back?"

Tom frowned pensively, then nodded again, briefly.

Jim raised his eyebrows and lowered the corners of his mouth in mock sympathy, then remarked in a rueful tone, "I told you there was a resemblance between you and Phil. I reckon you should be calling him "cuz"."

"That's absurd," Tom said quickly. "Lots of people share the same name. And how do you know that this card fell out of Phil's pocket?"

"It was on the floor down at the front of the aisle, where those guys were fighting," Jim answered.

"They're supposed to dance in the aisle, not fight," Tom grumbled, sourly.

"They started off dancing," Jim explained. "But one guy was over-enthusiastic, flinging his arms around like a deranged John Travolta. Some other guy was edging up the aisle, to go to the bathroom I guess, and the demented dancer caught him smack on the temple as he squeezed past. The poor bastard ended up stretched out across some girl's lap, and her boyfriend got pissed off. Things got out of hand, so Phil and a couple of heavies went down to sort it out. The card must have fallen out of his pocket in the fracas."

"He ain't no cousin of mine," Tom said irately, trying to recall the stories that his Uncle George used to tell about the war.

"Well, no matter," Jim concluded. "Me and Pete are gonna have a few drinks. Are you coming along?"

Tom shook his head. "I'm dog tired. I'll head back to the hotel and crash out. I can hardly keep my eyes open."

And they went their separate ways.

* * *

Tom lay in his bed, tossing and turning, trying to bury his head underneath the pillow. A thumping bass line penetrated his ears, even through the feathers. He peered at his watch. The luminous hands glowed at three-thirty. He couldn't believe that the Seventies disco in the hotel basement was still running. He hadn't been able to get any sleep at all. The hollow boom of the music reverberated up the walls and echoed dully inside his room.

And try as he might, he couldn't stop his brain from working. Each time a record started up, he would try to identify the song through the beat of the bass line. Tom had met the BeeGees on a couple of occasions, and he knew that they were real nice guys, but he wished that they had been less prolific with their musical output.

He couldn't get his mind to relax. Maybe it was Jim's fault, for latching on to that crazy notion about Phil being his cousin. He found himself getting to dislike Phil a little more each day. It had been one problem after another since he showed up. And Susan couldn't seem to leave him alone. She was always beside Phil, talking quietly, and smiling at him.

Tom tossed and turned some more, and groaned inwardly. Why was all this crap happening to him? Maybe it was down to that Creole girl that he had upset a few months back. She was a backing singer, doing some sessions with them while they were recording in a New Orleans studio. He had complained that she was singing flat, and she had got mightily pissed off. Maybe she had put a voodoo curse on him.

Tom suddenly realised that there had been silence for several minutes. He held his breath, and listened for the booming bass to start up again, but the silence persisted. He sighed with relief, and finally dropped off to sleep.

* * *

Tom was sitting in the hotel dining room on Wednesday morning, yawning over his third cup of coffee, when the others appeared.

"Trams woke you up again, huh?" Jim ventured, as he noticed Tom's haggard face.

"The disco in the basement kept me awake all night," Tom said, thickly, "And when that ended, the trams started up."

"It's really quiet at the back," Joe chipped in. "I didn't hear anything."

Tom scowled, and remained in a sulky silence whilst the others had breakfast. He began to absent-mindedly hum a tune that was looping through his head.

"I wish you'd stop humming that awful song," Susan complained.

"What song?"

"That's the way - uh huh - uh huh - I like it - uh huh - uh huh."

Tom yawned. "It was all part of my Seventies nightmare. When I eventually drifted off to sleep, I dreamed that I was in a Karaoke bar with Starsky and Hutch, and I was singing that song. But instead of a microphone, I had a lollipop in my hand." He shook his head to clear the bizarre dream from his mind.

"It could have been worse," Susan remarked. "At least you didn't dream that you were wearing flares."

"He used to wear a medallion," Jim told her. "I remember seeing it one Christmas, when he came round to my house. He walked into the lounge, and when he spotted the flashing lights on the tree, he started to dance wildly and sing, " Ah ah ah ah - staying alive - staying alive"."

"It wasn't a medallion," Tom argued. "I was my cousin Bobby-Joe's Olympic bronze medal. He was in the relay team."

"Really?" Joe gasped, with admiration. "It was nice of him to let you wear it."

"He owed me a favour," Tom explained. "When we were kids, we used to go stealing apples. If the farmer saw us, I always used to get caught, because I couldn't run as fast as Bobby-Joe. He always let me take the blame."

"It must be wonderful to participate in the Games," Joe murmured wistfully. "I loved that film, Chariots of Fire."

Susan sniggered and remarked, "There was great hilarity in France when that film was released."

"Why was that?" asked Joe.

"Chariot" is the French word for supermarket trolley."

* * *

"How much booze do we need to drink?" Jim asked hopefully, when they boarded the bus a couple of hours later.

Susan said tartly, "You don't need to drink any of it."

"We can't leave it on the bus," Jim insisted. "Janek has got to take it back to Prague neat and tidy."

"How will you get home from Prague?" Joe asked Janek.

Janek waved his thumb in the air as reply.

"So he can't take any booze home with him," Jim smugly informed Susan.

Pete chipped in, "I can sell the leftovers in Bucharest."

"It's more fun to drink it," Jim argued. "We'll be on the bus all day. It will help to pass the time."

"Get your thieving hands off my malt," Tom said tetchily, as Jim reached for the bottle.

"Oscar the Grouch on a bad day," Jim muttered quietly, as he abandoned his attempt to commandeer Tom's favourite whiskey. "Why don't you get some sleep. You'll feel much better for it."

"Good idea," Tom concurred, and he curled up in his seat, with the bottle wedged between himself and the side of the bus.

Pete was busy doing a stock-count. "We won't get through all this lot," he concluded. "We can either finish the beer or the spirits. If we try both, we probably won't be able to get off the bus in Bucharest. Let's drink the beer. We'll get more money for the spirits. How many salami do we have left, Phil?"

Phil had taken two salami out of the baggage hold ready for lunchtime, and he had quickly locked up again before Pete could do an inventory on the remaining sausage.

"There be a full box still down there," Phil informed him.

Pete nodded happily as he pressed the numbers on a calculator.

* * *

The road to Bucharest made its way alongside a river for half of the day, skirting the Carpathian foothills in an attempt to follow the gentler contours of the land on its journey southwards.

Tom slept soundly until two in the afternoon. "Can we stop for coffee?" he appealed, stretching his parched mouth when he woke up.

"There's nowhere to pull in," Susan told him. "We've been looking for a lay-by for the last half-hour."

Tom groaned, and used his bottle of malt to freshen his mouth. "How much further to Bucharest?"

"We're only half-way. Have a chunk of salami."

"Don't we have any bread?" Tom demanded.

"Phil just ate the last piece."

Tom muttered to himself in a mood of deep discontent, while the others continued their card game.

"Phil, you've put greasy fingerprints all over the Ace of Spades," Jim complained.

"Sorry 'bout that. It must be off the salami what I ate."

"Just so long as you weren't trying to mark the cards," Jim ended, with a slight slur. He had been making valiant efforts to reduce their supply of beer, and he was keen to let Phil know that the absorption of alcohol did not diminish his powers of observation.

Susan sat idly looking at the scenery, and contemplating how much money she would soon receive when Phil sold the contents of his box. She was feeling cheerful, and she quietly sang a little tune.

"Will you stop that awful gurgling noise," Jim snapped at her. "I can't hear myself think."

"You're just jealous, because I've got such a nice voice," Susan replied archly, and she sang louder.

Jim curled his lip at her. "You couldn't hit a note if you had a hammer and a ten-dollar bill."

"For your information, my voice has been trained."

"Trained for what?" Jim sneered. "Unarmed combat?"

As Susan gave Jim a malevolent glare, he continued, "Why don't you do something useful, like tidy up the bus."

Susan picked up an empty beer bottle, her eyes still fixed on Jim.

"We can get some money back on these," Pete muttered, as he wrested the bottle from Susan's grasp. "They're no good if they're broken."

Jim, blithely unaware of his close encounter with mild concussion, continued, "Women these days, they're all allergic to housework. My last wife was the world's worst housekeeper. I complained to her one day, "Just look at the state of this house - it looks like a tip!"

"And she replied, "Damn, the pixies must have missed us today.""

"What pixies?" I asked her.

"And she replied, "The pixies who come in to clean up, while I'm out at work all day. Maybe it's because I haven't paid the goblins their protection money for a while. That's probably why the pixies missed us out.""

Joe widened his eyes, and asked, "Was she drinking a little during this stage of your relationship?"

"Dunno," Jim tersely replied. "How quickly does bourbon evaporate? The bottle seemed to empty itself fairly rapidly."

"Maybe the goblins were taking it, in lieu of their protection money," Susan suggested, dryly.

Tom gave her a sideways look, then took a mouthful of whisky and went back to sleep.

* * *

When Tom woke at six p.m., the bus was lurching erratically through heavy traffic. Car horns sounded from all sides as Janek attempted to cross a busy junction.

"Which way now?" Janek demanded, as the bus became caught in the next clutch of traffic, moving spasmodically forwards.

Susan studied her street map. "Straight on for a while, then bear right, then left at the next square."

As they travelled further into the heaving centre of Bucharest, the street widened into a boulevard, with crowded buses and trams competing for road space. The vehicles ahead of them suddenly came to an abrupt stop, and Janek stood on the brakes fiercely. They sat in the traffic jam for ten minutes, then Janek muttered a few impatient words and turned right into an adjacent side-street.

"Where's he going?" Susan complained, desperately scouring the corner buildings for a street name. "We'll get lost in this labyrinth."

"He's taking the scenic route," Jim observed, with tipsy disinterest.

The big bus twisted its way through a maze of narrow streets, while Susan frantically tried to trace their route with her index finger on the map. They suddenly drew level with a towering building which cast its long shadow across the street. There was a police car parked nearby, with two uniformed officers leaning on the vehicle, studying the passers-by.

"This is the Inter-Continental," Tom remarked, as he saw the hotel name. "Are we staying here?"

"No," Susan answered, "But maybe we can get directions from the policemen."

The officers looked surprised to see the bus, and eyed Susan with interest as she approached. She held an animated conversation with them for several minutes, then the two policemen nodded their heads, and climbed into their car.

Susan boarded the bus.

"Follow them," she instructed Janek. "They'll take us to the place that we're looking for."

"How did you get them to agree to that?" Tom asked, with surprise.

"They think I'm ex-KGB," she said, sardonically.

"Can you prove that you're not?" Jim mumbled, under his breath.

The police car led them down a boulevard, then through another maze of narrow side-streets, until they reached the hotel that was listed on their itinerary.

The police car disappeared away down the street, and the bus halted.

"The end of the road," Tom murmured. "One more gig, then just count the cash."

"Amen to that," Jim agreed, as he swallowed the last mouthful from his bottle of beer.

CHAPTER 32

They walked through an archway, and were accosted by a babble of voices and background music. They were in a large courtyard which was crammed with tables, and heaving with people. The courtyard was enclosed by a three-storied wooden building, with balconies overlooking the inner square. Timbered staircases ran up to each level, with carved balustrades that were of Moorish design.

Susan glanced around. "Have we strayed on to the set of Seven Voyages of Sinbad?"

Joe's eyes widened in excitement, and he gasped, "It's a Caravanserai! How wonderful! Never in my wildest dreams did I imagine that I'd be staying in a genuine caravanserai."

"You'll have to keep dreaming about it," Tom told him, abruptly, "Because we ain't staying here."

Susan gave an exasperated sigh. "It took us ages to get here, and now you want to trek off again. Why are you being such a pain?"

"It's too noisy and too crowded here," he snapped. "I want some peace and quiet. We'll go to the Intercontinental."

"Let's take a vote," Jim chipped in, with a hiccup. "Hands up for staying at Sinbad's place?"

Everyone except Tom raised their hands, and Jim said smugly, "Tough luck, misery-guts. You're out-voted."

Tom glared at him and said angrily, "You'll go where I tell you, beer-breath!"

Jim squared up to Tom and balled his fists.

"Yeah? And how you gonna make me?"

Susan suddenly remembered that the first-aid cabinet on the bus was Luigi's hiding place, so she quickly stepped between the two men and said, "I can't stand the sight of blood. Let's sit down and have a drink instead." She pulled Tom over to an empty table.

Joe chewed at his thumbnail. "I'm sorry. I didn't mean to cause trouble. I really don't mind where we stay. I'll take some photos of this place, then we'll go wherever Tom wants. I'll go and fetch my camera off the bus." He scuttled away as the others sat down and tried to catch the attention of the waiter.

Joe dashed out of the courtyard, and stared up and down the street, looking for the bus. Janek had parked at the far end of the street, where it was wider, and Joe walked briskly along, concerned about photo quality in the fading evening light. As he passed the entrance to an alley-way, a movement caught the corner of his eye, and he glanced sideways. A man turned quickly, and limped back up the alley. The figure seemed vaguely familiar to Joe, and he paused briefly, scouring his memory. A squawking bird suddenly flew overhead, swooping in the gathering dusk, and Joe quickly directed his thoughts back to the lenses that he would need for low-light shots.

* * *

In the beer garden, the others were having no luck in obtaining drinks. The two waiters were dashing back and forth between tables, and they stoically ignored all the waving and gesticulation of the impatient customers.

"This is worse than being in a London pub," Susan grumbled.

Tom gave a grunt of agreement, and lamented, "I went into a London pub some years ago, and I couldn't get served for love nor money. It was an old-world place called the Flying Duck, and it was packed solid. I was crammed up at the front of the bar, waving my money in the air, but the barman ignored me totally. He served people each side of me, and people behind me, but he just didn't see me at all. I eventually gave up, and went back to my hotel. As I walked past the doorman, I said to him, "Can you see me?" And he replied, "Yes sir, of course."

"And I said, "That's a relief. I was beginning to think that I had turned into the Invisible Man. He chuckled and said, "I take it, sir, that you have been trying to get a drink in the Flying Duck?"

"I nodded, and he winked at me and said, "When you go into a pub, walk directly into the gent's toilet. Do your business, then when you come out, make as if to go straight back out of the pub. The barman will shout verbal abuse at you, and insist that you purchase a drink."

Joe sprinted up to their table, carrying his photographic equipment.

"Do you think they'll complain if I take photos?" he fretted. "I'd like to go up to the balcony, but I suppose that area is for guests only."

"We are guests," Susan reminded him. "They've got our reservation, so wander about wherever you want. If anyone challenges you, say that you'll check in when you've finished your photos."

Joe's face lit up with relief, and he dashed off to explore the historic inn.

"I went into a London pub once," Pete remarked. "Me and the wife sat there for twenty minutes, waiting for the waitress to serve us. I eventually fell in to the fact that you have to go up to the bar. You could die of thirst in that town, and nobody would care."

He continued, "Even then, we didn't get what we wanted. I asked for a dry martini for my wife, and she said that it tasted nothing like a martini. They were real stingy with the gin."

"In England, martini means vermouth," Susan explained.

"You mean, I paid that amount of money just for a teaspoon of vermouth?" Pete muttered, aghast. "Jeez. Just as well I didn't get the real thing."

"Do you think if we set fire to the table, that the waiter would notice and walk over here?" Jim debated, as he toyed with a box of matches.

"Maybe we should wait for Joe on the bus," Susan suggested, and she hurriedly got to her feet, simultaneously tugging Jim off his chair.

It was nearly dark, and as they edged their way out between the tables, Joe scurried down a timbered staircase and caught up with them.

"The rooms are enormous," he told the others. "Apparently, merchants from the East used to rest in them, with their entire caravans."

"I wonder how they got the camels up those steep wooden stairs?" Jim murmured, as they made their way back to the bus.

* * *

Janek found his way back to the Intercontinental, which was set alongside a small, grassy park.

"They might not let us have rooms," Susan speculated. "These big places are very sniffy if you don't have a reservation. I think Janek should come in with us, in case we need a translator."

They shuffled wearily into the hotel foyer, dragging their bags behind them.

"If they say that they're full, I simply won't believe it," Tom declared. "This place is the tallest building around here."

The band sank into deeply padded armchairs, while Susan and Janek approached the desk and held a protracted conversation with the clerk. The well-groomed receptionist was shaking her head gently, so as not to disturb her neat coiffure, whilst Susan was flourishing the tattered itinerary, trying to convince her that the band were VIPs.

Susan's loud persistence brought the front desk manager from the adjoining office. He studied her grimy list of hotels and venues, and looked unimpressed with the sheet, holding it by one corner with an expression of distaste on his face.

Susan continued to harangue the manager, and he eventually spoke a few words to the desk clerk before swiftly disappearing back into his sanctuary. Five minutes later Susan sauntered across to the band, clutching a handful of card-keys.

"We've got a suite on the sixth floor," she announced, proudly. "They didn't want to give us rooms, but I can be very persuasive when I want to be."

Joe nodded. "I expect the manager was swayed by your personal charisma."

Janek gave a short laugh. "She threaten break both his arms."

They entered a lift and glided silently up to the sixth floor.

"Why do they put carpet on elevator walls?" Jim pondered, as he squinted at the plush interior that he was leaning on. "It's a tad disconcerting if you've had a few drinks. You don't know if you've fallen over or not."

As the others prised Jim out of his resting place, Susan went ahead to open the door of the suite. She inserted the card-key, but the handle refused to turn. She withdrew the card, then shoved it back in more speedily. The door was still firmly locked. She tried again, this time pushing the card in more slowly. The door handle remained rigid.

"I hate these stupid cards!" Susan snapped. "I'd stand more chance of opening the door if I used the card to force the lock!"

Tom plucked the card from her hand and opened the door instantly, giving a nonchalant shrug to Susan.

* * *

An hour later, they were strolling along the boulevard away from the hotel, looking for a restaurant that met Joe's requirements.

"We have to find one with gypsy music," he insisted.

As they walked past each restaurant, they peered inquisitively through the window, then moved on up the street. The boulevard was fringed with numerous shops, cafes, and airline offices.

"I've never heard of half these airlines," Tom mused, as he gazed at the advertising display of a travel shop.

"There are hundreds of little airlines that you never hear about," Susan told him. "Some have very peculiar names. When I was working in a travel shop, I came across an invoice from a company called "Icarus Airways". What a totally unsuitable name for an airline."

"Remind us who "Icarus" was?" Tom said, with a puzzled frown.

"He was the bloke in Greek mythology who made himself a pair of wings. He attached them to his shoulders with straps made out of wax. But he flew too close to the sun, and the wax melted. His wings fell off, and he plummeted into the sea."

Tom raised his eyebrows. "Hmm. I see your point. Maybe it ain't the best of names for an airline."

"Maybe they only fly at night," suggested Jim.

Susan continued her train of thought. "Then I came across an invoice headed "Infinity Tours". What a spooky name for a travel company."

"Maybe they use Icarus Airways," muttered Pete.

"They could have some great advertising slogans," Jim conjectured. "Your next vacation destination will be Paradise," he quoted, in a sepulchral tone.

Joe chipped in, "Talking about vacations, I'm thinking about going to Disneyworld again."

Jim shook his head sagely. "No, think twice about it. It's a dangerous place. Me and my youngest daughter were strolling through the crowds at Epcot, one Sunday afternoon. She let go of my hand, and went off to look at the fountains. I was mooching along, slow and aimless, and when a little hand joined up with mine again, I just carried on walking. Suddenly, my daughter appeared in front of me, and said in a puzzled voice, "Daddy, what are you doing?"

"And I looked down and saw a little girl who was a complete stranger to me, holding on to my hand. She had obviously grasped the wrong hand in the crowd. She looked up at me and screamed, then she started to cry. Just then, an agitated woman dashed up to me, and shrieked, "What are you doing with my little girl?"

"It took me ten minutes to convince her that it was a genuine mistake. She was all for calling the police!"

"I went to the Magic Kingdom once," Pete informed them. "It was a terrible experience."

"Why, what happened?" Joe asked.

"We got on to a Disney bus, and the driver made us sing - "The wheels on the bus go round and round", and "If you're happy and you know it stamp your feet". It was awful. I should have complained to the management."

* * *

By the time they found a restaurant that contained a small gypsy band, it was very late. Three guitar players in lavish costumes strummed stridently, whilst a dark-eyed gypsy girl with flowing tresses of ebony hair danced lithely to the spirited music.

The music was too loud for any conversation, so they obtained a good supply of drinks from the waiter, and settled into a quiet torpor as they waited for their meal, and Susan disappeared into the ladies room, to splash cold water over her face as a tonic to drowsiness.

The men were mesmerised by the exotic swaying of the gypsy girl. As she twirled and flounced, the dazzling colours of her swirling skirts emphasised her narrow waist and slender thighs.

Jim nudged Tom and murmured, "She could make an old man very happy."

Tom nodded in agreement. "I could do her a favour or two."

"That's very generous of you. I'm sure she'd be very grateful," Susan commented in an acid tone, as she slid into her seat.

"What I meant," Tom hastily burbled, "Was that I could fetch her groceries, or paint her house."

"If you're in that sort of mood, you can come round to my house and dig the garden for me. And anyway, you should steer clear of gypsy girls. You can't afford the dental work."

Tom frowned. "What do you mean?"

"Her brothers will probably rearrange all your fillings."

Tom took a gulp of beer and slid down in his seat.

Jim gave Tom a derisive sideways look. "What's the point in being pussy-whipped if you ain't getting no pussy? Well, if you ain't up for the gypsy girl, I sure as hell am." And he smiled broadly at the vivacious dancer as she twirled her skirts.

* * *

Thursday dawned, bright and sunny. The band were to play their final concert that night, and they were busily organising themselves. After breakfast, they clambered back on to the bus and told Janek to return to the Eastern inn.

"We wait for Jim?" Janek asked.

"No, he's otherwise occupied," Tom replied, with a meaningful wink.

In the narrow streets of the old town, close to the inn, they found a thriving bazaar district, where shabbily-dressed characters displayed their diverse wares. When Janek found a suitable parking space, they heaved the boxes of unopened bottles off the bus, and ranged them along the kerb. Phil had removed the salami from the baggage hold before they left the hotel car park, but he was now lurking close to the side of the bus, keeping his eyes on the locked baggage compartments.

Pete arranged the merchandise to his satisfaction, and Susan was obliged to stand holding a carrier bag full of toilet rolls, with one clutched in her hand in an attempt to advertise the goods.

The street was thronged with enthusiastic shoppers, and the entire stock of bathroom tissue was quickly purchased by a middle-aged woman who spied the roll in Susan's hand, and promptly offered a handful of dollar bills after a swift inspection of the bag.

The alcohol was proving more difficult to peddle. The local shoppers seemed suspicious of the labels, and were trying to embark on a product-tasting exercise. Pete resolutely refused to open any of the bottles, and waved away the prospective customers with feigned anger.

"How come there's no vermouth in these boxes?" Tom asked, as he sorted through the bottles.

"I'm saving it for emergencies," Susan told him. She had planned to carry three bottles on to the plane to help her through the flight home.

Their sales picked up with the arrival of a group of young men who looked like students. They recognised the labels on the bottles of spirits, and quickly pulled handfuls of lei out of their pockets. Pete shook his head and said loudly, "American dollars".

The young men looked disappointed, and turned to walk away.

"Take their money," Susan hissed at Pete, "Or we'll be standing here all day!"

Pete grudgingly accepted the Romanian notes, and other passing shoppers immediately became interested in the bottles. Soon there was a little queue of eager customers, and the stock was disposed of by late morning.

"Have I got time to take some more photos of the inn?" Joe asked, hopefully.

"Me and Janek have got ter get to the hall," Phil quickly cut in.

"You two can take off," Tom agreed. "We'll get a cab back to the hotel. I want to look around here, see if I can find another doll to take home."

"I'll see you at the hotel, this afternoon," Susan whispered to Phil, as he boarded the bus. She anxiously watched the bus as it moved off down the street. Susan still remembered what the back-packers had said, about the town of Constanta being heaving with crooks, and she was worried about Luigi.

Tom noticed her fretful gaze. "A penny for your thoughts?"

Susan was momentarily taken aback, then she blurted, "It was a stroke of luck, checking into a hotel that's right opposite the venue. Janek can take Phil to Constanta this evening and get back in time to take us to the airport tomorrow morning."

"They could have left for Constanta now," Tom murmured. "I don't know why Phil wants to hang around for the sound check. The crew can manage very well without him."

They squeezed their way through the twisting, teeming streets, where numerous traders were selling an assortment of ethnic goods, from colourful pottery to hand-embroidered linens. As they struggled through the crush, Susan noticed a shop that had some gaily-painted marionettes on display in the widow.

"That would make a nice Christmas present for your niece," she suggested, pointing to a doll dressed in an opulent costume of red and mauve velvet.

Tom pushed through the crowds to the shop window. The doll had a wooden head, with a happy smile painted on it. She had bright blue eyes and rosy red cheeks, with blonde curls framing her pretty face. There were thin strings attached to her wooden wrists and ankles, and she glowed with craftsmanship.

"Oh, what a little darlin," Tom enthused. "Maybe the strings will be a little tricky to use, but I've never seen anything like this back home. She's mine!"

CHAPTER 33

They returned to the hotel at lunchtime, and as they entered the suite, the gypsy girl was on her way out. Jim was sprawled across a sofa, yawning widely.

"Did she finally get tired of you?" Tom asked.

"No, she has to go to work," Jim replied. "She may be at the show tonight, if she can get a friend to stand in for her at the restaurant." He eyed Tom's bundle with curiosity. "What have you got in the package?"

Pete smirked. "He bought another dolly."

"She's real cute," Tom asserted, and he undid the wrappings to show his marionette to Jim.

"Nice face, shame about the wooden legs," Jim observed, dryly.

Susan was counting up the money that they had made at the bazaar. "I'll take this lot down to the exchange office this afternoon. Give me the rest of your Romanian notes."

Pete frowned. "Did Janek give you his takings from the salami box?"

As Susan shook her head, Tom said, "Let him keep it. He can have it as payment for taking Phil to Constanta and back."

"How is Phil going to get back to Dubrovnik?" Joe pondered.

"I don't know, and quite frankly, I don't care," Tom replied, brusquely. "We've done enough for that guy, bringing his lamp stands half-way across Europe."

Joe persisted. "Couldn't Janek take him back to Dubrovnik?"

"Janek could take him as far as Timisoara," Susan cut in, "But then their routes diverge. I'm sure he'll be able to do the rest of the journey on his own."

Joe gave an anxious sigh. "I wonder if his car has been repaired? It's a bizarre coincidence. Hugh in Bristol had a violet Porsche, and Terry in Prague, and Phil in Dubrovnik. All with right-hand steering, too."

"Maybe it's just the one car," Jim ventured.

Joe widened his eyes. "I hadn't thought of that. But that means Terry and Phil have been driving a stolen car. Shouldn't we tell them? They might want to inform the police."

Jim gave a snort of derision. "Which planet are you on? Terry is obviously a hot wheels dealer. That's why he has a different car each time we see him."

"You've got an over-active imagination," Susan said. "He's just an ordinary used-car dealer. If he was a crook, he'd hardly be working for our sponsors, would he?"

Joe nodded. "I think Susan's right. Terry is such a nice guy. We could do with car dealers like him back home. I always get ripped off. Matter of fact, I was thinking of getting a new car when I get back home. I fancy one of those cars with an on-board computer. It tells you if the fuel is getting low, or if your speed is too high, or if your lights should be switched on."

"My wife does all that stuff," Pete scoffed. "I don't need another nagging voice in the car."

"I bet Janek could tell us about the hot car trade out here," Jim murmured. "He's a street-wise kinda guy. I wonder how they get the cars across the frontiers?"

"Most of Europe doesn't bother with check-points any more," Susan told him. "It slows the lorries down too much. It's only the British officials that insist on seeing a passport."

Jim gave a sardonic grin. "Is that to keep the immigrants out, or the British in?"

"It's to keep alive the traditional art of smuggling," she said, facetiously.

"That's not funny," Joe scolded her. "I feel sorry for these desperate people who swallow drugs to smuggle them across borders."

"Smuggling never used to be so depressing," Susan countered. "In the good old days, people used to smuggle glamorous things, like Swiss watches or diamonds."

Joe shook his head sternly. "Smuggling is a bad thing, regardless of what the contraband is."

"A Swiss watch never killed anyone," Susan retorted.

Jim chuckled. "It would probably kill you if you swallowed it."

"No, it wouldn't kill you," Pete said. "But it would keep your bowels as regular as clockwork. And if you swallowed a handful of diamonds as well, you could have a five-jewel movement."

Tom glanced at his watch. "Talking about time, it's about time that we went downstairs for lunch." He sighed. "Tomorrow lunchtime, I'll be on my way back to my Southern-fried mansion."

As Susan gave him a baffled look, he explained, "The air-conditioning don't work. I can't afford to get it fixed."

"It may be hot down South, but at least there's no smog," Jim commented. "That's the number two reason why I moved from California. People in the Sixties all used to think that they were getting high from smoking pot. Little did they know that it was toxins in the air pollution that was making them light-headed."

Susan was puzzled. "What was the number one reason why you moved?"

"Do the words San Andreas mean anything to you?"

She curled her lip at him. "No, but it's not my fault."

"I'll be glad to see the end of this tour," Tom grumbled. "It's been two months hard labour."

"It could have been worse," Susan remarked. "You could have been sentenced to three months summer season at Butlins, Barry Island."

"What the hell is that?"

"It's a holiday camp. Like the summer camps you have for kids in the US. You live in a dingy hut and it rains all the time. And the camp staff dress up in silly costumes and make you sing happy songs. At Butlins in Barry Island, they used to have a big fence running around the perimeter of the camp. You could make believe that you were in Colditz."

"Do British people pay to go and stay at this place?" Pete asked, with incredulity.

Susan frowned thoughtfully. "I think they pay when they want to leave."

Tom groaned. "I went to summer camp when I was a kid. They had people there playing guitars and singing "Kum-Ba-Ya" every damn evening."

"They can't do that in Europe," Susan told him. "It's against the Geneva Convention."

The door to the suite was flung open, and Janek strolled in.

"Phil tell me to come back to eat, so I leave him in hall. You go to dinner now?"

Jim nodded as he eased himself out of his seat. "Janek, maybe you could settle an argument for us. Is it easy to buy stolen cars out here?"

Janek shrugged. "Cars here always stolen. How else you get them?"

"How do you find the car you want? You can't exactly go into a showroom and look at stolen vehicles, can you?"

"You meet man, and he show you photos of many nice cars," Janek explained. "You pick car you want, they deliver to you, and you pay cash."

Susan's stomach went cold as she remembered the photos that she had delivered to Terry's friend in Debrecen. She followed the others out of the suite, chewing nervously at her lip as she thought of the package in her suitcase.

* * *

When the band went out to do the sound check that afternoon, Susan set off for the exchange office, to convert their Romanian currency back into dollars. Instead of walking down the boulevard, she decided to stroll through the small park that ran parallel to the street. After a few minutes, she passed the concert hall where the band was rehearsing. Susan could see the bus and the big rig parked at the back, and she suddenly realised that normal life would seem a bit dull after all this. She hoped that Phil would get a good price for Luigi when he got to Constanta. Her half-share, plus her nest-egg in the pair of socks, would give her the chance to take a long holiday somewhere exotic. She emerged from the park, and went into the exchange office.

Ten minutes later, Susan was cursing severely, and making her way back to the hotel. It had not occurred to her that the lei would not be convertible into dollars. The exchange office staff had resolutely refused to buy her Romanian currency, at any price. Pete would be livid, and he was sure to blame her. As Susan drew near to the hotel, a shifty-looking man suddenly appeared from behind some shrubbery. He approached swiftly, and hissed at her in broken English, "You want to change money? I give you good rate."

Susan paused, and asked hopefully, "Will you give me American dollars for lei?"

The man frowned, and hesitated before giving a reply. The sound of footsteps close by caught his attention, and he glanced sideways, then darted away, vanishing back into the bushes. Susan looked around and saw two policemen walking towards her. She recognised them as the officers who had guided them to the inn on the previous evening. She had a brief conversation with them, then they set off again on their patrol of the area.

Susan made her way into the hotel foyer, and as she walked across to the lift, a voice suddenly whispered behind her, "Why were you talking to those policemen?"

Susan was startled, and she spun around to see Terry slinking stealthily behind her, with Ahmed padding quietly along, a few steps away.

"What are you doing here?" she exclaimed, surprised by their unexpected appearance.

"Why were you talking to the policemen?" Terry repeated, impatiently.

"They told me not to have dealings with the black-market money changers," she replied, flustered by Terry's aggressive manner. "They said I could probably reconvert my lei at the airport, but I need receipts to do that, to prove that I changed dollars into lei in the first place. And I haven't got receipts, because we got most of this cash by selling some stuff at the market. But I didn't want to tell the policemen that, of course. They're nice blokes, though. They showed us the way to the inn, last night. But it was a waste of time really, because we didn't stay there."

As Susan paused for breath, Terry pushed her into the elevator and whispered urgently, "Why didn't you stay at the inn? I've been looking for you all day!"

"Tom didn't want to stay at the Inn," she explained, "So we came here. We haven't stayed at any of the hotels on our itinerary, for one reason or another."

"It's probably just as well," he murmured, exchanging a sideways look with Ahmed.

When they were inside the suite, Terry asked anxiously, "Do you still have that package I gave you?"

Susan nodded. "It's in my suitcase."

"I'll have it back, please," Terry demanded. "There's been a change of plan."

Susan frowned at him. "I want to know what's going on. It's something to do with those photos, isn't it"?

Terry stared at her, aghast.

"How do you know about the photos?"

"The box fell open when I gave it to the man in Debrecen. I didn't think anything of it, but Janek was just telling us about the stolen car trade out here. You've got me involved in your shady dealings, haven't you? I could have been arrested, carrying all this stuff around for you. How could you be so callous?"

Terry's lower lip trembled.

"Me and Ahmed are trying to get enough money to buy a bar in Sorrento. The stolen car trade is very lucrative, and safe as houses most of the time. But my sales rep, Serge, told me that a policeman had been asking questions about me. He advised me to hide my contacts book on the tour bus, in case I was stopped and searched. I thought he was just being a drama queen, but when you told me that a man in a cashmere coat had been looking for me, I decided to do what he suggested, until we could check things out. That's why I gave it to you to look after."

"Serge? Is he the man in Debrecen?" Susan cut in.

Terry nodded.

"The cashmere coat man was following us that week," Susan told him. "He appears in some of Joe's photos. He got into the hotel suite and cut up Tom's doll. I suppose he was looking for the black book."

Terry clicked his tongue in annoyance. "They must have been in it together from the start. When Ahmed checked around, he found out that the cashmere coat man is an informer, not a policeman. He sells his information to Interpol, or the Russian Mafia. Whoever pays the most. Ahmed said that we should be more careful, and that's why we used you as a go-between. But it didn't occur to me at all that Serge was trying to double-cross me."

Susan shook her head. "I thought it was a bit strange, when I saw them together in the park in Kecskemet."

Terry grimaced. "They were probably planning to relieve you of my cash. I would have been up shit creek without that money. I was being pressed for payment by my suppliers. They'd heard a rumour that I was about to do a runner, and they were threatening to rearrange my kneecaps."

"So how did you get wise to Serge?"

"Quite by chance. We were supposed to be in Dubrovnik this week, looking at cars, but the borders are too tight. They're on the lookout for some arms dealer. So we decided to visit the caravanserai and have a farewell drink with you and the band. When we got there, we saw Serge and the cashmere coat man deep in conversation. I knew then that I was being set up."

Susan frowned. "What were they going to do?"

"Those papers that I gave you contain a copy of my sales book. As I said, Serge was my sales rep. He takes the photos around and shows them to customers. They pay him for the car, he takes his commission, and sends the rest of the cash to me. I noticed that he'd been taking a bigger percentage lately, and when I challenged him about it he demanded to see my sales book, to prove that his numbers were correct And I was stupid enough to fall for it. The sales sheets are in my handwriting, and have the chassis numbers on them. They could trace all the stolen cars back to me from those sheets of paper."

Susan gasped. "I might have been arrested when I handed the papers over to them!"

Terry shook his head sagely. "No. They were probably going to blackmail me out of business, and set up for themselves. Still, it's all over now. You managed to stay in all the wrong hotels, so they couldn't find you. Your incompetence has been my salvation."

Susan spluttered with indignation. "You've got a nerve! If it hadn't been for me being your donkey, you wouldn't have got your cash from Szeged!"

"I think the word is mule, luv. Anyway, can I have my papers. We need to be somewhere else."

Susan opened up her Gucci shoe box. As she handed the contents to Terry, she said, "You haven't paid me for this mule trip. I think you owe me some cash."

Terry sighed heavily. "How much do you want?"

"I want all these Lei in dollars."

Susan gave him the Romanian currency. Terry counted up the notes quickly. He pulled a wad of dollar bills from his wallet, and speedily counted out the notes. Then he and Ahmed darted to the door, checked that the corridor was empty, and disappeared.

Susan counted up the notes, and calculated the amount that was due to Pete. There was a tidy sum left over for her, and Susan smiled happily as she pulled the rolled-up socks from the bottom of her overnight bag. As she withdrew the roll of notes, she noticed that the rubber band had become fluffy, entwined with blue threads from the socks. Susan paused, as she suddenly realized that Tom and the rest of his socks would be in a different continent by the following night. "Oh my god," she murmured to herself. "I've got used to having him around!"

* * *

Over at the venue, the guys were lounging about in the dressing room, waiting for the crew to finish miking up before they could start their rehearsal. Tom was looking despondent, and he sighed heavily. "It won't be the same without Susan around."

"I'll drink to that," Jim muttered.

"Why don't you try and make things up with her," Joe suggested.

"I'm sure Susan is still fond of you. She's probably forgiven you for your indiscretion with Sophie."

Jim sniffed. "That's about as likely as a Palermo judge getting life insurance."

"I don't know what you see in her," Pete added. "She's about as affable as a flock of dyspeptic geese."

Tom tilted his head sideways and gazed vacantly into space. "There's just something about her. I feel lost without her."

"You were obviously destined to be soul mates," Joe responded, in a romantic tone.

Jim gave a snort of derision. "Cell mates, more like. As in, padded cell."

Tom pressed his lips together thoughtfully. "I wonder if Susan would agree to be the manager on our next US tour?"

"No way!" cried Jim. "I was thinking of getting together a good collection of sexy videos that we could watch on the next tour. Keep us from getting bored."

"Yeah? Like the last one that you brought round to my house?" Tom reminded him, scornfully.

Pete leaned forwards. "I didn't hear about this?"

Jim gave a sheepish grin, and explained, "My kids were visiting me one weekend. I went into my son's bedroom and noticed a video cassette lying on the floor. As I picked it up, I saw that it had a hand-written label. Loin King. I decided that he was too young to be watching blue movies, he's only twelve, so I took the video away. Anyway, me and Tom settled down to watch it one evening, and it turns out to be The Lion King. It was obviously a pirate copy done by one of my son's dyslexic friends."

Lazlo appeared at the door, and called in a bored voice, "Ready now."

The band followed him on to the stage, shuffling wearily to their instruments.

As Jim approached his drums, he frowned. "Where's my high-hat?"

Phil magically appeared from the wings and studied the drum kit briefly. Then he announced sagely, "I think I probably knows where her is."

He sauntered across to Tom, and raised an eyebrow expectantly. Tom clenched his teeth, reached into his pocket for the customary bills, and thrust them ungraciously at Phil, who strode away, whistling cheerfully.

When Phil returned five minutes later, he was carefully wiping bits of grass off the shiny cymbal.

"Where was it?" Jim asked, crisply.

"Some kids had got hold of it, and they was using it as a Frisbee out in the park. I had ter pay them to get it back."

At the end of the sound check, the crew dispersed and the band made their way out of the hall. As they walked through the park, Joe commented, "It's lucky that we had Phil with us on this leg of the tour. He's been very helpful in retrieving all our lost equipment."

Jim gave a short laugh. "Has it not occurred to you that maybe Phil has been stealing our stuff, then selling it back to us?"

Tom stared at him. "Why didn't you mention this before? I've been paying to get all this goddam stuff back!"

Jim shrugged. "Phil's been getting rubbers for me since we got to Romania. He seems to know his way around the black market. I didn't want to piss him off."

Tom clenched his fists. "I can't believe this! He's been ripping me off, and all you care about is your sex-life!"

Jim raised one eyebrow. "And your point is?"

* * *

Phil reached the hotel just ahead of the band. Susan let him into the suite, then led him through to the privacy of her bedroom. It was nearly six in the evening.

"Are you all set to go?" she asked.

"Oh ar. Janek be waiting on the bus for me," Phil assured her. "We should get ter Constanta by eleven. I'll unload me lamp stands at the docks, then I'll send Janek off fer a drink, and I'll slip away to sell Luigi."

Susan nodded in approval. "Janek is picking us up at nine-thirty tomorrow morning, to take us to the airport. We'll be waiting in the lobby, with our luggage. Come in with him, and give me the cash in a paper bag. Pretend that it's a present of some sort, an embroidered handky, or something like that, so that the others don't get suspicious."

"Right-o."

Susan heard the band enter the suite, and she said hastily, "I must go and have a quick shower before dinner. We're having a lavish meal tonight, as it's the last show of the tour."

"I'll be seeing yer, then," Phil concluded, as he moved towards the door.

"Good luck," Susan called over her shoulder, as she disappeared into the bathroom.

Phil remained standing by the door until he heard the sound of a cascading shower.

Five minutes later, Tom came out of his room, walked across the lounge, and knocked on Susan's door. As he touched the wood, the door opened and Phil stepped out, with his hands thrust deep into his pockets.

"I was looking for Susan," Tom blurted, surprised by Phil's presence.

"She be in the shower," Phil told him, and he darted quickly out of the suite.

Tom stared after him, open-mouthed, just as Susan emerged from the bathroom in her dressing gown.

She smiled at him. "Hello Tom. Did you want something, or are you practising for the world gargling championship?"

"I was looking for that shoe box you once lent me," Tom burbled.

She pointed across the room. "It's in the bin."

"Oh, right," he mumbled, and he grabbed the shoe box out of the waste paper bin and beat an embarrassed retreat.

Susan unzipped her overnight bag to get some fresh underwear, and she immediately noticed that the contents of the holdall were in disarray.

"Typical," she sighed. "He rummaged all through my bag, when the shoe box was sticking out of the bin right in front of him. Men!"

* * *

After the show, late that Thursday night, Susan and the band staggered noisily into the hotel, and lurched across to the elevator. Jim had a buxom blonde clasped to his side, because the gypsy girl had failed to appear at the concert hall as promised. As they piled boisterously into the lift, no-one noticed a lone figure standing behind one of the potted palms in the foyer. The gypsy girl stood with her hands on her hips, frowning angrily, as she saw Jim and his female companion being whisked up to the sixth floor.

CHAPTER 34

Phil and Janek reached Constanta just after eleven that night. The roads of the town were quiet, and Phil directed Janek through a tangle of narrow backstreets that led to the harbour. The dockside was lined with dark warehouses and interspersed with looming, shadowy cranes. Small portacabins were scattered across the wharf, with bright lights shining within, revealing shipping clerks who were slumped behind desks which held untidy mounds of paperwork. The huge harbour complex was broken into segments by jutting piers, most of which were unoccupied. Phil pointed to a pier where a small freighter was anchored, and instructed Janek to park as close as possible.

They approached the jetty, which was harshly illuminated by overhead arc lights, and saw that the stevedores were busy loading cargo, using a huge net. The weighty net was swung between ship and quayside by a system of ropes and pulleys, which were operated by the hefty dockers. None of them paid any attention to the bus, and they carried on with their arduous work as it halted close by.

Phil went into the adjacent portacabin, and held a conversation with a clerk who was dexterously assembling and stapling sheaves of papers. Janek strolled along the dockside, and watched with fascination the lading of the boat. He had been to the Baltic coast once, but he had seen only containers being hoisted on to the ships. This contrivance of a heavy rope netting, swinging back and forth, was a novelty to him. Janek stood next to a swarthy man in a naval cap, who was issuing continual instructions, and studied the proceedings with interest.

When Phil emerged from the portacabin, he was clutching several sheets of paper. He ambled across to the man in the naval cap, took a roll of notes from his trouser pocket, and counted out a substantial number of bills. The skipper took the cash, checked it over, then shouted a sharp instruction to a couple of the men. Phil went across to the bus and

284

unlocked the luggage compartments, and two stevedores began unloading the wooden crates of lamp stands, piling them up beside the other cargo.

Phil boarded the bus, and emerged shortly afterwards carrying the small wooden box that held Luigi. He sauntered over to Janek, and said casually, "The Captain here is going ter take me out in a little rowing boat, so as I can scatter Luigi's ashes. Luigi always liked the sea. You might as well go off fer a drink, if you wants. They'll be a while loading this lot, and we can't leave until I've got me bill of lading off the clerk. He won't type it out until all the cargo be on board. There's a bar just beyond them warehouses," he ended, pointing into the dark distance of the harbour perimeter. "Wait there for me."

Janek nodded obediently, but he lingered on the pier, engrossed by the sight of the pendulous net, as it swung silently back to the wharf. There was a sudden splintering crash behind him, and Janek spun around to investigate the cause of the mishap. The stevedores had dropped one of Phil's crates, and the contents lay strewn on the quayside. Janek's eyes opened wide in astonishment, and he moved quickly towards the pile of crates that had been unloaded from the bus. As he did so, the empty cargo net suddenly swung rapidly through the air. The net made heavy contact with the back of his head, and Janek saw stars, then blackness.

* * *

When Janek woke up, he found himself on the bus, squashed into a seat, in the foetal position. He gingerly stretched his arms and legs. As he moved his head, a throbbing pain shot across his neck, and he carefully rubbed the place where the net had hit him. He realised that it was nearly daylight, and he glanced down at his watch to see that it was five in the morning. He staggered off the bus and on to the deserted wharf. The ship had sailed, and the stevedores had vanished. Inside the portacabin, the shipping clerk was still sorting and stapling sheets of paper. Janek went into the small office and held a short conversation with the clerk, then he boarded the bus and manoeuvered off the pier, commencing the long drive back to Bucharest.

* * *

At nine-fifteen on Friday morning, in the InterContinental, the band and Susan were fidgeting on armchairs in the foyer. They had all woken up early to have plenty of time for packing and breakfast. Tom had packed his marionette into the Gucci shoe box, and had taped the lid down securely. He was determined not to let the box out of his sight, and he was prepared to hand-carry it all the way home.

Susan was preoccupied with thoughts of Luigi. She felt sure that Phil would get a considerable sum for him. Susan suddenly remembered that Phil still owed her for the towing of his car in Dubrovnik. She would remind him of that when he got back.

Jim was out on the street, waving farewell to his blonde companion, after bustling her into a taxi. As he turned to go back into the hotel, he caught sight of some approaching pedestrians, and he sprinted into the foyer in an agitated manner. He frantically grabbed his bags and hissed urgently at the others, "I'm gonna get a cab to the airport. I'll see you later."

"What's up?" Tom demanded, astonished by Jim's frenzied behaviour.

"I've just seen the gypsy girl coming down the street with some guys. Three of the biggest, ugliest bastards I've ever seen in my entire life! I'm outta here!" And he hurtled outside in a flash.

Pete glanced nervously at Tom, and said fearfully, "If they don't find Jim, maybe they'll take us, as second best."

Tom leapt to his feet and grabbed his luggage, saying to Susan, "Wait here for Janek. Tell him thanks for everything. We'd better take off." And he dashed away with the shoe box tucked under one arm, and the suitcase rolling speedily beside him. Pete and Joe were two steps behind him, and Joe just about managed to call a polite "See you at the airport" over his shoulder to Susan, as they made their undignified departure.

Susan decided to make herself scarce, so she hurried across to a flourishing potted palm, and hid behind the luxuriant foliage. She peered cautiously through the fronds, and after several moments saw the gypsy girl stride into the lobby, escorted by three burly men. They approached the desk, and held an animated conversation with the receptionist. After the clerk had convinced them that Jim had checked out, they turned and marched out of the hotel, disappointed that their quarry had eluded them.

Susan remained behind the leafy shrub until she was certain that the vigilantes had disappeared, then she returned to an armchair to wait for Janek and Phil.

* * *

Susan glanced at her watch. It was nearly ten o'clock. It was not like Janek to be late. Maybe he was caught in a traffic jam. Still, it suited her to be there alone. It would be much easier for Phil to hand over the cash. The sound of rapid footsteps drew her attention, and she looked up to see Janek hurrying towards her. He gazed around anxiously and said abruptly, "Where are band? They not here!"

"They took a taxi to the airport. There was a bit of a panic." She peered beyond Janek, expecting to see Phil following into the foyer.

"Where's Phil? Is he on the bus?"

"I miss them!" Janek exclaimed, with disappointment. "I not get bonus!"

"Is he on the bus?" Susan persisted, impatiently.

"Who?"

"Phil!"

Janek shook his head dolefully. "Phil gone."

Susan frowned. "What do you mean, gone?"

"He go on boat, with his crates. Shipping clerk say boat sail midnight. I not see it go. I get hit on head, and everything go black. When I wake up, ship gone, everyone gone!"

"Maybe you misunderstood the shipping clerk," Susan suggested, hopefully. "Perhaps just the crates went on the boat. Phil might still be in Constanta."

"Clerk show me papers," Janek insisted. "Phil pay for cargo and passenger, then he pay captain big baksheesh."

"But Phil didn't have any money," Susan argued. "Did you stop anywhere before you got to the harbour? Did he take his little wooden box to someone's house?"

Janek shook his head then winced. His head was still fragile from the painful collision with the loading net.

"He take money from pocket," Janek told her. "Big roll of notes, with blue fluffy band. Then he pay captain, then go to bus for Luigi. He say he go to scatter ashes in sea. Then I have accident, and when I wake up, everyone gone."

A cold tremor ran through Susan as Janek mentioned the blue fluffy band. She quickly unzipped her overnight bag and frantically searched for the rolled-up socks. When she pulled them out of the bag, they felt soft to her touch. The firm centre was no longer there. She swiftly turned the socks inside-out, and shook them desperately. Her roll of money was gone. Susan stood stupefied for several seconds, then she deftly ransacked her bag, tossing the contents on to the floor in her frantic search. There was no cash anywhere in the overnight bag.

"The thieving bastard!" she shrieked. "He's taken my nest-egg!"

She kicked the bag ferociously, then re-packed her belongings, swearing quietly as she did so. Then she gathered together all her luggage, and said despondently, "Let's get to the airport. There's no point hanging around here."

Janek gave her a grimace of sympathy, then put his hand into his pocket and extracted a wad of lei notes.

"This salami money," he declared. "I forget to give it before. You take it."

"No, you keep it," Susan replied, morosely. "Tom said that you could have it. Lei notes are no good to me, anyway."

As they walked out of the hotel, Janek murmured, "We both short of money now, all because of Phil. If I had seen band before they leave, I maybe get good bonus."

"You've got the salami money," she retorted. "How much were you hoping for?"

"I need much money for college. My grandfather, he sick for many months. He not work."

"I can't imagine that your grandfather could earn enough to pay your college fees," Susan remarked, sceptically. "What are you studying, anyway?"

"Modern languages. I do one more year."

"What will you do after that?"

"If I finish course, I work for EC in Strasbourg," he replied. "If I not get money to finish course, I drive bus."

They reached the tour bus and climbed aboard. Susan instantly went to the first-aid cabinet, in the vain hope that Luigi might still be inside, but the unit was forlornly empty. Susan slumped into a seat and sighed heavily. Janek eased the bus away from the kerb, and they drove off to the airport in a depressed silence.

* * *

Meanwhile, at Otopeni airport, the band were sitting comfortably in the departure lounge. Tom looked at his watch, and saw that it was ten-thirty.

"Susan should be here by now," he mused. "It's only a half-hour drive."

288

"She probably stopped to do some shopping," muttered Pete. "You know what women are like."

"How come we're flying out on Malev Hungarian?" Jim grumbled, as he studied his boarding card. "It says we have to change planes at Budapest. I reckon we could have got a direct flight home on Delta."

"I think that Terry and Ahmed have friends who work for Malev," Joe told him. "Maybe we got a discounted fare."

"So much for the tour management," Jim scoffed. "Those two unloaded us quicker than a one-night stand." He took a hefty swig from his drink.

"Why did you get us two drinks each?" Pete asked, as he surveyed the tray full of tumblers on the small table in front of them.

"I didn't want to go up again," Jim explained. "The service at the bar is terrible. You have to stand in line for twenty minutes. They ought to have a cocktail here called "A Long Slow Queue Against The Wall"."

Tom gave a vague smile, and sat fidgeting with his Gucci shoe box. He had placed it on the seat beside him, and he was concerned that no-one should accidentally sit on it. He gazed around abstractedly, anxious as to why Susan had not yet arrived. Tom suddenly noticed a man, wearing a black raincoat and dark glasses, wandering about in an aimless manner. Tom smiled in amusement at the sunglasses. As the man turned in his direction he caught Tom's eye, and immediately stiffened with alertness. Tom quickly looked away. It wasn't a good idea to make eye-contact with odd-looking strangers in foreign airports. Tom turned his attention to the conversation at hand, and he didn't notice the man in the black raincoat moving stealthily up behind him.

Joe was chatting eagerly about the things he planned to do when he got back home.

"My wife says that we need to get an electrician to re-wire the attic, and a plumber to install a new downstairs shower. She didn't want to do it while I was away, because it's so difficult to find workmen who do a good job."

Pete gave a despondent grunt. "Are there any tradesman these days who won't try to rob you blind"?

Tom gave a low chuckle. "A piano tuner."

Joe frowned in disapproval. "That's a bit tasteless," then he broke off and stared past Tom.

Tom turned and saw the man in the black raincoat leaning over the seat beside him. The stranger quickly grabbed the shoe box, dropped an envelope on to Tom's lap, then darted swiftly away through the throngs of travellers.

"Hey! What the hell!" Tom cried in astonishment. He jumped up and started to sprint after the robber.

Jim immediately leapt to his feet and clutched Tom's arm. "Let him go! You won't catch up with him. If you go back through passport control, they might not let you board the flight!"

Tom gave a distraught wail. "But he took my marionette!"

"Forget her! She's just a painted doll!"

Pete and Joe sat open-mouthed, astonished by the bizarre spectacle.

"And I thought that New York had the world's most ruthless Christmas shoppers," Pete muttered, with a shake of his head.

"That shoe box seems to be particularly unlucky," Joe observed.

"What's in the packet?" Jim demanded, agog with curiosity.

Tom sighed heavily, then sat down and opened the bulky brown envelope. He pulled out a sheaf of bank notes, and stared with disbelief. He quickly counted up the money, and gasped, "There's five thousand dollars here!"

"This is all very odd," Joe murmured. "I think we should report it to security."

"They just called our flight to the gate," Jim said, firmly. "Do you want to spend the rest of the day in a small room with sweaty airport security men?"

"No, not really," Joe admitted. And they made their way out of the departure lounge.

As they waited at the gate, Tom was still fretting about Susan.

"What can have happened to her? I don't like to leave without her. Something may be wrong."

"Maybe she decided to spend some time with Phil," Jim suggested, pointedly.

Tom gave a reluctant grunt of resignation, then he said to Jim, "I think I'll stop over in Budapest and buy another doll. Y'all can go ahead home without me."

"Suit yourself," said Jim. "You can buy a whole shop-full of dollies with five grand!"

"I'm only gonna buy one more doll," Tom asserted. "Hopefully, it will be third time lucky."

* * *

Janek pulled up outside the airport terminal building, and waited in a queue of vehicles that were edging slowly forwards, moving into the spaces that were set aside for drop-off only. Susan glanced at her watch. It was just after ten-thirty, so she judged that the check-in desk would still be open for the midday flight. Janek was in a disconsolate mood, and had been uncommunicative during the journey. Susan sat staring gloomily out of the bus window, as they crawled along at a snail's pace. A sudden flurry of movement caught her eye, amongst the unhurried meanderings of travellers laden with heavy luggage.

A man in a black raincoat and dark glasses sprinted out of the terminal, and dashed across to a large, black car that was parked a short way ahead, in a tow-away zone. The man looked familiar to Susan, and as she peered more closely, she noticed that he was clutching something in his arms. The car door opened and a man climbed out of the vehicle. Susan gasped as she recognised the sinister man in the cashmere coat. As he stood beside his black BMW, the man in the raincoat approached him, and promptly handed over a shoe box. The man in the cashmere coat swiftly slit open the box, and examined the contents. Then he waved the box angrily in the air and let it fall carelessly to the ground as he grabbed the man in the black raincoat by the throat, and began to shake him vigorously.

The pretty marionette dropped on to the pavement and landed in an undignified pose, her legs dangling into the gutter, with the hapless shoe box lying close by, like an upturned doll's coffin.

Several men in dark suits suddenly materialised from nowhere, and they strode purposefully towards the black car. The cashmere man loosened his hold on the raincoat man as they drew near. At that point, Susan's scrutiny of events was interrupted by Janek saying, "We pull into parking bay in just a few moments. You ready to go?"

The parking space that Janek was advancing towards was just a few feet away from the black BMW and the cluster of strange men. Susan hastily announced, "I've changed my mind. I don't think I'll take the flight, after all. I've never liked flying, and today definitely seems to be an unlucky day. Keep moving until you find the exit road."

Janek shrugged his shoulders in exasperation, and followed Susan's instructions. As they drove past the huddle of men beside the black car, Susan flattened herself on the seat so that she was out of sight.

When they had left the environs of the airport, Janek asked her in a concerned tone, "How you get home?"

Susan pondered for a few moments. "I'll travel with you to Prague."

"Long journey," Janek commented. "Two days on bus."

291

Susan gave a grimace of resignation, then suggested, "Let's take the scenic route through Transylvania. We're bound to find some hitchhikers along the way. If we charge them for the ride, we could make a bit of money."

Janek nodded in agreement, and they drove northwards.

After a few miles, Susan sighed and said, "It's odd, the way that Phil went off like that. I don't understand it at all. Where was the boat going to, anyway?"

"Caucasia."

Susan frowned. "Where's that? Is it in Russia?"

Janek shook his head. "Azerbaijan, Armenia, Georgia. Not Russia any more."

"Why would he take his lamp stands there?" she murmured. "They're poor countries. I don't suppose they go in much for fancy floor lamps."

"He no take lamp stands. He take rifles," Janek said, tersely.

"Rifles?" Susan echoed, scornfully. "Don't be absurd. That knock on the head has confused you."

"They rifles!" Janek hotly insisted. "Crate get broken, and guns fall out. I see them."

"Are you sure?" Susan pressed, in a shocked whisper.

"I know rifle when I see rifle!" Janek retorted, indignantly.

Susan was stunned into silence, and she sat in a daze as they travelled the rough road back towards the mountains.

CHAPTER 35

The following afternoon they were travelling along the motorway just south of Prague. They had picked up the road at Bratislava, and at each motorway exit Janek would swing the bus off, negotiate the roundabout, then rejoin at the same junction, hoping to pick up passengers on the slip-road.

It had started to rain heavily when they entered Slovakia, so business was brisk. As the bus edged up this latest slip-road, two hikers were standing in the rain, holding soggy cardboard signs that read "Prague". Janek checked his mirror for police patrol cars, then eased the bus to a halt. As the hitchhikers approached, Susan leaned out of the bus door and told them, "It's five dollars for a ride, but you get to travel in comfort. We have onboard toilet facilities, and there are lots of interesting people to talk to."

The hikers exchanged doubtful glances, then nodded and climbed on to the crowded bus, digging their damp hands into their sodden clothing to extract the cash. As Susan collected their fares, she announced, "We have a card game running at the moment. Feel free to join at the next hand. The stakes are fairly low," she coaxed, with a persuasive smile.

As the new passengers made themselves comfortable, Susan whispered to Janek, "Those two boys from Hamburg keep pouring martini for me. They think that if they get me drunk, they might win some of their money back."

Janek gave a snort of derision, and pocketed the ten dollars that Susan handed him, while she returned to her Vingt-Et-Un table.

* * *

They were obliged to drive into the centre of Prague to drop their passengers at the bus station, then Janek drove out towards the airport. It

293

was nearly six in the evening and Susan was exhausted. They had spent the previous night on the bus, parked in a small lay-by somewhere on the Hungarian plain. Susan had slept fitfully, as the hitchhikers on board had produced a persistent chorus of snores.

As they wound their way out of Prague, Susan tidied up the bus, picking up empty beer cans and sweet wrappers. When the hikers had disembarked at the bus station, Susan almost found herself saying, "Thank you for travelling with us, and I hope you will use us again."

When they reached the airport, Janek parked in a bus stop bay, and counted up the fares that they had taken.

"Nearly three hundred dollars," he announced, happily.

"I made eighty on the card table," Susan gloated, as she handed him the notes.

"We split half each?" Janek suggested, as he shuffled the money into a tidy bundle.

Susan shook her head. "You can keep all of it. You need it more than I do."

Janek beamed with delight as he pocketed the cash, then he reached into his jacket pocket and pulled out the glitzy cigarette case. He presented it to Susan, and said, "You take this to New York, and sell to men who buy eggs. You get much money."

"That's very kind of you," Susan replied, with polite disinterest, "But you use this all the time. I wouldn't like to take it from you."

"I quit smoking now. Joe tell me it bad for health. Anyway, my grandfather make more, when he well," Janek informed her, with a wink. "You take this," he urged. "You get much money."

Susan capitulated, and accepted the gift, tucking it into her overnight bag. She thanked him profusely, giving an enthusiastic pretence of gratitude, as she did not want to hurt his feelings. After she had staggered off the bus with her luggage, Susan turned to wave goodbye to Janek, muttering to herself, "Sell to men who buy eggs? He's lost his marbles. It must have been that bump on the head."

Susan made her way into the terminal building, blew the dust off her credit card, and bought a plane ticket home.

* * *

Susan walked into her office on Monday morning, and noticed with irritation that Simon was sitting at her desk.

"You can move back to your own desk, now that I'm back," she tersely informed him.

Simon bit his lip nervously. "The trainee is sitting there. He started a couple of weeks ago. He's learning my job. We've had a bit of a reorganisation since you've been gone."

Susan's eyes narrowed. "Where exactly am I supposed to work, then?"

"I don't really know," Simon answered, vaguely. "But the boss said that he wanted to see you, on your return."

Twenty minutes later Susan strode out of the boss's office with clenched fists and gritted teeth. Reorganisation! That was just a polite word for redundant. He had talked in a condescending manner about how there might be a vague possibility of her obtaining another position within the company.

"I'll let you know if I find a window of opportunity," the boss had ended, fixing her with an insincere smile.

It was probably not wise for her to have snapped in reply, "If it's a second-floor window of opportunity, you can take a leap out of it!" But it was unlikely that he would have given her a good reference, anyway. She walked quickly along the corridor, her head down as she shoved the leaving papers into her bag. Moments later she collided with someone, and her bag fell to the floor.

"Why can't you look where you're going!" she exploded, glaring up at a man whose head was swathed in white gauze. "Hugh? Is that you under there? What ever happened to you?"

"Hello Susan. Sorry I knocked into you. The bandage keeps slipping over my eyes." He bent down to retrieve the contents of Susan's bag, and explained, "I had a bit of bad luck when I was on holiday in Florida. The wind got up nicely one day, and this chap I'd met in a bar took me out to the beach to show me how to surf. But I don't think he really knew what he was doing. I fell off the board and it came down on top of me and gave me an almighty smack on the head! Luckily, a lifeguard pulled me out of the sea. I remember him being quite abusive to me, just before I passed out. I don't know how they hope to encourage tourism, with that sort of attitude. Anyway, I was unconscious in hospital for a couple of weeks. Thank goodness for the medical insurance." His eyes widened as he picked up Susan's glitzy cigarette case. "This is nice. I had no idea you were a Faberge collector."

"Faberge?" she echoed.

"You only ever hear about the eggs, but they made heaps of other treasures. This is fabulous," he murmured, as he examined the case more closely. "Copy, of course. But they're not usually this good. I read somewhere that there are unscrupulous dealers in New York that try and pass them off as the real thing. Where did you get it?"

"A souvenir shop in Bucharest," she lied.

"This was probably made by some old Russian," he told her. "Most of the royal jewelers fled Moscow during the Revolution, but I suppose some of them have passed the skills down through their families. Anyway, nice to have you back. How was the East? Did you catch a glimpse of my violet Porsche on your travels?"

Susan stared at Hugh in alarm, then breathed again as he gave an ironic chuckle.

"Just joking. Was it hellish out there?"

"Oh, not too bad," she murmured. "It's very cheap. So, the police never found your car?"

Hugh shook his head. "The boss gave me the all clear to get a new one from the fleet people. Same colour and everything. Things seem to be on the up and up around here now."

Susan muttered under her breath, grabbed her bag from Hugh and marched determinedly away.

* * *

The flight to New York had come via Budapest, so it was almost full when Susan boarded. She took her seat next to a tall man who appeared to be asleep. Presently, the stewardess came along with menu cards and drinks for the new passengers.

"I'll have a dry martini please," Susan told her.

"Certainly. Do you think he wants a drink?" the stewardess asked, nodding at Susan's neighbour.

"I expect so," Susan answered. She nudged him sharply and shouted in his ear, "Do you want a drink?"

He opened his eyes and gave her a petulant look.

"I was asleep."

"No you weren't."

He was indignant. "How do you know I wasn't?"

"Because you weren't snoring."

"Men don't always snore."

Susan gave a snort of derision. "When they're dead, they don't!"

He smiled at the stewardess. "I'll have a scotch, please." He turned back to Susan and explained, "I always pretend to be asleep, so that I don't have to listen to people's boring conversations."

"Well, I'm glad that you're awake," Susan responded. "I want to tell you all about my varicose vein operation."

"I'd prefer it if you told me why you're flying to New York."

"Janek decided to give up smoking. Anyway, why are you on this plane? You should have been home days ago."

Tom gave a secret smile. "A little doll kept me in Budapest."

Susan elbowed him sharply in the ribs. "I don't want to hear about your conquests. I'm staying in New York for a few days. Can you help me find my way around?"

"What's it worth?"

"I could visit your agent and push her to get some bookings for you. I can be very forceful, sometimes."

"Yeah, I'd kinda noticed that. You don't take no prisoners, do you darlin?"

"Only if I want to torture them."

Tom stretched his legs into Susan's space, but she didn't complain.

Lightning Source UK Ltd.
Milton Keynes UK
UKHW020609120419
340936UK00005B/1041/P